METAL RAIN

Hans Baernhoft

If you enjoy this book, please add your review to Amazon. It makes a real difference.

If you have comments or if you would like advanced information about my next book, please write to me at hansbaernhoft@gmail.com.

Happy reading…

1.

As always, he planned to spend as little time as possible in the open. He squatted down and unzipped the leather holdall. From inside he extracted a black, padded nylon roll. He pulled open the Velcro seal, unscrolled it over the flat surface of the roof and shielded the exposed contents from the drizzle by pulling his leather jacket over his head.

The rifle inside was broken down into four components housed in parallel sleeves. There were also two magazines. He went through the familiar twists and clicks of assembly: the forestock to the buttstock, the scope onto the forestock and the bipod into the underside of the fluted barrel. It took twenty-one seconds. The magazines were simply to hold the ammunition. He rarely used automatic fire. Manual was more reliable, sure, but the contact with the bullet concentrated his mind.

He eased the bolt handle back and up, thumbed a bullet into the open chamber and closed it with a satisfying 'clunk'.

The longest official kill on record was just over one and a half miles - two thousand six hundred and fifty seven yards to be exact. It had made Corporal Rob Furlong of the Canadian Light Infantry a household name in some circles. Georgiy Zinic knew he had shot further - fortunately no one had been around to record it.

Like Furlong, Zinic used very-low-drag bullets that resembled large, sharp suppositories. He used to have them custom made but stopped after the Militsiya dug one out of a minor senator of the Duma and, in an unusual burst of professionalism, traced it back to him via the manufacturer. It had cost him two hundred thousand Roubles to buy it back and he never made the same mistake again. He had had his rifle modified to take the American-made .338 Match Hybrid BoreRider instead. They were marginally less effective but at only sixty dollars for a box of fifty, a whole lot cheaper.

The window wasn't visible to the naked eye. He knew it was somewhere over the chimneystacks to the southwest. At this distance the bullet would reach its target in around three seconds. He had calculated a drop due to gravity of a hundred and four yards. That is to say, the barrel would be pointing into the sky, one hundred a four yards above the target. The math had been done in advance and the scope was already zeroed for elevation. What he couldn't calculate exactly was the vacillating wind. For that, he relied on his intuition. It was the single quality that made him more than the sum of man, machine and ballistic projections. It was why he was paid more than any other marksman he knew. It was why he was here.

The cement wall surrounding the rooftop was a comfortable five feet high. He shouldered the butt and took a wide legged stance. He perched the bipod on the ledge, put his right eye to the scope and brought it into focus.

2.

To the great delight of his work colleagues, Tyler had been to the toilet five times that afternoon. They had stood on their chairs and cheered each return as if he were an athlete completing a lap. Confrontations always upset his stomach and he had been anticipating this one all day. Now he stood before Janine's door with a cheap bunch of flowers in one hand and a gift-wrapped parcel in the other mentally rehearsing his excuse. *I'm sorry Janine. I have to go to Yorkshire to see my dad this weekend, so I won't be able to take Rachel out.*

He was about to ring the bell when the thought occurred to him: he could call when he was on the road; pretend it was a last minute emergency. It was a kind of emergency after all. His father had never been very communicative but now he had disappeared altogether. He hadn't answered his phone for over a month. Surely he would have heard if there had been an accident, a heart attack or anything. In his more lucid moments Tyler admitted that he was 'there' for his father because he needed him to be 'there' for him. The fact that his father had little to say to him even when he was sober mattered less than if he had not been 'there' at all.

He was indecisively shifting from one foot to another when Janine whipped open the door.

"What are you doing here?" she hissed. "Thursday begins with a 'Th' and you don't come here until the day that begins with a 'Fuh'. Remember?"

Tyler felt suitably belittled. The doorstep gave Janine a couple of inches over him and he was easily intimidated. Janine's square face and angular jaw were at odds with her generous lips and large eyes. The contradiction extended to her character that vacillated between charm and fury. Having fallen for Tyler because he was handsome, educated and on PAYE, she soon figured out he didn't have the drive to give her the life to which she wanted to become accustomed. So she walked out, taking Rachel and leaving him the bills.

For two years he had supported them both, first voluntarily, then when money became tight, by court order. This left him, after rent and other necessaries, the sum of thirty-two pounds a week on which to live. The parcel and meager flowers he held in his hands was wrung from this pittance; precious offerings which were now soaked through. Janine looked up at the sky then back down at the bedraggled pup on her doorstep. She pinched in the corners of her fulsome lips and shook her head.

"It better be good" she said stepping back inside.

Tyler mumbled 'thanks' and followed her into the hall, shutting the door dutifully behind them.

"I've fiiiniiished" sang out a tiny voice.

Rachel came bowling out of a doorway pulling up the panties under her yellow check skirt.

"Daddy!"

Tyler squatted down and she launched herself into his arms. "Mummy said I had to wait until tomorrow." Then seeing the present and flowers, she stepped back, checked her first instinct and said "is that for Mummy?"

"Er yes." Tyler turned to Janine who accepted the bunch of moist roses without ceremony.

"Who's that for?" said Rachel jogging on the spot and pointing at the parcel.

"Have you wiped your bottom young lady?" said Janine. Rachel stopped jogging and threw a doleful look. "I thought to so. We'll discuss presents once you're in your pajamas."

Rachel appealed to Tyler who smiled obligingly but was of no practical help.

"Back to the bathroom young lady" said Janine. "If you're good Daddy'll read to you."

This needed no affirmation from the reader designate. Rachel yippee-ed and ran into the bathroom. Tyler smiled. For a second it seemed just like old times until Janine snapped round to him.

"But make it quick" she said. "Francis will be here soon. You know what he's like."

At the mention of his name Tyler experienced a tingling over his scalp similar to a sudden crisp frost.

"He doesn't live here does he?" he challenged angrily.

"That's none of your business Ty."

3.

Inspector Bob Grant was strangling his wife when the phone on his desk buzzed. He had come to work early especially to indulge in an undisturbed homicidal daydream. Who would have thought that having the car cleaned could be cause for an argument, but there it was. He had taken it to a valet service on the Morton Road when she had, apparently, intended to do it herself the following day. She was going to go to a self-clean garage in between her hair appointment and lunching with her mother at the Arndale Center. Now she would have nothing to do for that three quarters of an hour in an area where Grant knew - or should have known - full well that there was nothing else to do. Beside which he hadn't even checked if the car had been properly cleaned, and it hadn't.

The cleanliness of the car was neither here not there of course. Grant wasn't a detective for nothing. The real point, the unspoken complaint was that he didn't earn enough money. Never would, never could. Nanette's best friend was married to a TV producer who raked in two thousand pounds a day. They were forever chasing the sun around the world and the best Grant could offer was his parents' farm in Dorset. Never mind that he was the dike against the rising tide of violence and drugs and Melvin Hammerstein made the kind of daytime drivel you looped in a torture cell. Nanette scoffed at it herself - the hypocrisy of which made him dig his imaginary thumbs in even deeper.

He reluctantly put her down and picked up the phone.

"Just had a report of a man with a gun on a roof" said the desk sergeant.

Grant groaned audibly. Night in South London had started early. "Any shots?"

"Didn't say."

"Who phoned it in?"

"Didn't say."

"What the fuck did they say?" he snapped.

"Do you want to hear the playback?"

"Sorry Nigel." Grant rubbed his forehead. "No, just tell me."

"It was a woman. She didn't leave her name but she was well spoken. Said she had seen a man with a rifle on top of Totteridge House in the...

"...York Road Estate" Grant finished. Already he was suspicious. No name? Smart accent in one of the worst housing estates in London? Starring up at the roof? She would have had to be Superwoman to see anyone on top of a twenty five-story building.

"Did she phone from a helicopter?"

Nigel chuckled, as was his duty to the station commander. "Do you want to send an ARU?" the desk sergeant prompted.

"Who's on tonight?"

"MacMillan."

"Oh shit."

The Armed Response Units were not cat-stuck-in-tree guys and the ex-Marine sergeant was about as tough and unforgiving as they came. Still, the night was young and frankly, he couldn't take a chance. If this gun-toting prowler did turn out to exist and started taking pot-shots then someone would want to know why he hadn't taken it seriously.

"OK. But tell McMillan the truth. Let him know exactly what the call was. He'll understand." He hoped. He replaced the receiver and returned to his daydream. In his mind's eye the imagined sniper was aiming directly through Grant's kitchen window.

4.

Wandsworth prison was built in 1851 on the Panopticon principle: five wings radiating out from a central tower allowing all the inmates to be viewed at any time by a single observer. This suited Zinic just fine.

He scanned the spider-like brown stone building with the scope. Comparing it with his mental map, he identified C wing and found the room on the fifth floor at the end furthest from the tower. The light was on, but from this distance it was difficult to make out much of what lay behind the two windows other than a vague impression of dark furniture.

A change in the pattern of light indicated an unseen door had opened. A tall man with lank brown hair, a dark suit and lawyers' satchel entered. Zinic knew nothing about the target - not his name, not the reason for his dispatch, nor who had ordered it - but this was not him. The photo he had memorized was of a short man in his late fifties with a squashed face and distinctive tightly curled black hair round a balding pate. He understood he would be wearing a prison uniform and would appear at six o'clock. Zinic checked the position of the window again. It was the right window, the right time but the wrong man. He could wait. For thirty thousand dollars he could spare a few more minutes. He shuddered to think how much the initial contract was worth. The fee halved with each step as it came down through a series of intermediaries. There could be four or more. He rarely knew the employer. He calculated this hit must have cost upwards of quarter of a million. His share was the most he had ever been paid and indicated both the value of the target and the level of difficulty. If this was his best chance at hitting him, it must be the only one. He would wait.

The tall man crossed the room, passed both windows and disappeared from sight. The shadows on the walls stabilized again and Zinic imagined him sitting at a desk to one side. The two windows were approximately three feet wide by six feet high. From their position he guessed the room was around five hundred square feet of which he could see little more than a quarter.

The seconds dragged past and the drizzle thickened. Mentally, he made the minute adjustment he thought necessary to counteract the increase in precipitation but every moment's delay made the shot harder.

His thoughts turned back to Marta. He reached inside his jacket pocket and felt for the small, hand-painted icon he kept there. The Softener of Evil Hearts, as it was called, was a traditional depiction of the mother of Christ. The title itself should have been enough to recommend it to him but it was something else entirely that had caught his eye at the Udelniy flea market. The Madonna's doe-like eyes, tapering nose and moon-cup jaw were an uncanny likeness of the woman he loved. In the past, soldiers carried such icons before them into battle for courage. For him it was a form of absolution.

He had broken all his own rules by contacting her that afternoon but he couldn't wait to tell her his decision. This trip had made up his mind for him. He was used to being alone but he had never before been lonely. He hadn't been sure that at forty-eight he was ready to throw in the only life he knew and settle down on a farm with a shop girl from Nizhny Novgorod, but love changes everything. He had bought a pay-as-you-go phone and sent her a two word SMS: 'marry me'.

He wasn't to know she would never receive it.

He smiled to himself as he thought of the

welcome that awaited him. Her unguarded smile, her arms wrapped around his thick neck and the warm kisses she would rain on his beaten old face. He didn't regret his decision for an instant.

His attention was brought back to the present by a change of light in the room. His finger curled around the trigger. He focused on the second window from the door on the assumption that the target would cross the room too fast to hit it through the first. All he needed was an assured three seconds of stillness.

The door opened. To the left of the circle visible through the scope he could see two figures flit past the first window. As he had hoped, they came to rest just inside the second. The one he assumed was the target was shielded from him on the far side of a prison escort. The uniformed guard spoke in the direction of the unseen tall man then turned to the target. Zinic could see part of a head and all of a shoulder and waited for the guard to move. He departed abruptly for the door and the target walked forward in the other direction; out of sight before Zinic could even identify him.

Damn.

The patter of the rain on his jacket turned to a light drumming. For the first time in his career he really didn't want to be there. He felt distracted. In the hiatus, Marta's face and body floated back into view. He could smell the warmth of her bed and see her wheaten hair splayed out on the pillow. God, he missed her.

In the prison room, the unseen figures were on the move. He forced himself to refocus on the subtle variation of their shadows on the walls. How long was this going to take? The tension was getting to him. He pressed down his shoulders and stretched his neck to one side until it cracked. He had to relax. He assured himself this would be the last time.

Relax and concentrate.

He took a deep breath, let it out slowly through his nose and projected his attention so far into the night that the screech of car tires seventy yards below didn't even register.

5.

Janine closed the bathroom door behind her and Tyler was, once again, left in a state of regret. Regret seemed to be a permanent fixture where Janine was concerned. Every time he thought he was clawing back ground with her, he did or said something stupid that would be instantly slapped down. Sometimes he got the impression there was still some ember of affection there, that the right words could rekindle a tiny flame of passion. But the right words never seemed to come. He drifted into the sitting room-come-kitchen while the sound of running water and Rachel's excited chatter filled the apartment. Janine was a good mother, he thought, and this was a good home: tidy and clean. Of course she couldn't afford expensive furniture, and for that he blamed himself. He was far from being the world's greatest estate agent. If he had been, she may not have left him in the first place.

Man is a provider he mused, and I don't provide. He could barely provide for himself, let alone a wife and child.

He perched on the small sofa by the window and gazed round the room. There must have been upwards of a dozen photos of Rachel scattered on almost every wall and surface. They ranged from shots in nappies and prams to her favorite frog pajamas. He searched for a photo of himself, but there wasn't a single one. On the coffee table in front of him lay a photo album. He casually flicked through it looking for some evidence of his existence until he came across a shot of Rachel in the arms of Francis. The sight of them in such close proximity made the tiny hairs on his skin bristle like a cat. The photograph was too close to tell where it was taken, but by the angle of Francis's shoulder it seemed possible he was holding the camera. Tyler looked at his face: the small shrewd eyes, mean mouth, puffy jaw line and shaved head. He had attempted a smile and revealed two rows of small rat-like teeth with - yes - a glint of a gold filling. Just the sight of him set off a familiar feeling of panic. It happened often: a shortness of breath and a constriction in his rib cage. He battled against it until Rachel rushed into the room covered in printed frogs and hoped up onto the sofa beside him.

"Mummy said it's fooor meee" she said

pressing her tiny hands together and elongating the last word into a bubbling laugh.

"Why don't you take it into the bedroom" said Janine taping her watch significantly at Tyler "and Daddy can read to you while you open it."

"How about it squirrel?" said Tyler pushing himself up.

In gleeful silence Rachel slid down off the sofa and ran back out into the corridor. Tyler followed and at the door Janine grabbed him by the wrist.

"Five minutes. Then you owe me an explanation - OK?" She looked anxious. Tyler knew she was thinking of Francis. He furrowed his brow in quiet assent like a guilty child. There was a shrill cry of 'daaaaddy'. Tyler jogged down the short corridor and disappeared behind Rachel's door.

She shook her head. Had she done the right thing two years ago? Tyler was a good man after all: timid, but kind. At first she had hoped the separation might stimulate him, give him something to kick back at. She hadn't realized how badly his mother's cancer had weighed on him. Still did. He had done everything he could to make her last years happy but the end was sudden and devastating. She died within a month of their separation and he had never recovered. He had lost weight, looked as though he wasn't sleeping and started to forget things like going to work and (almost) Rachel's birthday. What Janine had assumed was clinical depression, a nurse friend had diagnosed as 'learned helplessness': a state where you expect things to go wrong because they always have. Tyler was a classic case. He failed to save his mother, failed at his marriage and failed at work. One thing led to another. He had fallen into debt and couldn't keep up with the child maintenance. She knew he lived from hand to mouth in a bedsit in Clapham and couldn't imagine how he would escape. It was a vicious spiral that got worse as it got worse. She had felt guilty at first but Francis, who was not exactly the Sage of South London, had hit the nail on the head. 'That's just the way he is' he had decreed. In other words, she was a symptom but not the cause. The proof was that he still hadn't recovered even after two years. He was incapable of it because (as the Sage had said) he was a 'fucking looser'. It had nothing to do with her.

Shame she thought, he's a good looking guy, then returned to the kitchen and hoped to God that Francis wouldn't turn up early.

Tyler sat on Rachel's bed and watched eagerly while her tiny hands pulled at the paper and tape round the parcel he had given her.

"Oh Daddy!" she exclaimed, "Longmane is my favorite."

She threw her arms round his neck. Tyler closed his eyes and breathed in that indefinable smell that was his daughter. He loved that smell more than anything and buried his nose in her neck, filling his lungs as if he could hold his breath and save it for later. She dropped back onto the bed and attacked the plastic and cardboard prison that held the dappled orange and black centaur.

"How did you know?"

"He told me. I was in the shop and he said 'hey, over here, I'm Rachel's favorite character'." She gazed uncertainly at the creature still trapped in its cellophane bubble wondering if it could in fact be true. While she studied it, Tyler noticed a black mark round her wrist. Dirt, he thought and licked his thumb to rub it off. When it wouldn't budge he thought it must be marker pen. He held her hand under the dim light of the bedside lamp and recognized the unmistakable signs of bruising.

"Ow" he gasped.

"What is it daddy?"

Tyler held his tongue out and rubbed the side with his finger. "I bit my tongue."

"Why did you do that, silly?" she giggled.

"I... I was thinking of something?"

Rachel returned to unwrapping. Tyler quietly fumed. His daughter, his own progeny, the one person in the world for whom he had a legitimate responsibility and whom he loved above all others was hurt. He made an immediate connection with the person whom he hated most in the whole world, the person who, in his eyes stood between him and any glimmer of happiness: Francis. He felt the deep well of bile surge to the brink - then swallowed it back down.

"What happened to you baby?"

Rachel looked uncertain for a moment as if trying to remember. Or trying to forget! Tyler thought.

"How did you get it?"

Rachel looked back at her toy and bent in close as though wishing to enter the bubble protecting her plastic friend.

Tyler tried another tack "Did you do it to yourself like I did to my tongue?"

Rachel continued to look stubbornly at Longmane until a noise from outside grabbed her attention. Tyler wasn't used to the particular sounds that anyone living in a house long enough comes to recognize. She had heard someone walking up the path. No knock was needed, no key sounded in the latch before it was opened and they heard the unmistakable rumble of a male voice.

Tyler watched Rachel's little face keenly, looking for signs of fear and anxiety or worse, affection. But he saw none of these. Instead he observed the tension of concentration around the mouth and eyebrows melted away. Her face seemed to relax. The gaze that had been so fixed on her new toy a moment ago now turned inwards and she put it down between them and sunk into her sheets.

She looked up at him. "Will you tell me a story Daddy?"

Tyler hesitated. Did he want to know about the bruising? Or was he afraid of the answer? He persuaded himself Rachel would be upset if he pressed too hard. He hesitated then scooped a book up off the floor.

"You want me to read this?"

"Tell me a story"

"I... I don't know any stories." His mind was stirred and he was sure he wouldn't be able to concentrate.

"Make one up"

"What about?" he stuttered.

"A squirrel."

"A squirrel?"

"Like me. I'm a squirrel. A squirrel who likes milk."

6.

The target had come back into view at last but wouldn't stop moving. The short man with the curly hair paced back and forth gesticulating wildly and erratically. In his evident rage, he would stalk half the length of the room then suddenly stop and spin round. He would by turn, clasp his hands to his face in frustration or throw them out wide in exasperation. Zinic only needed him to hold his ground for a predictable three seconds but the man seemed incapable of it. He jetted forward, flung himself back or even jumped up. Zinic felt like killing him just to keep him still. Finally, the tall man in the suit came into view and put his hand on his shoulder. He said something that appeared to calm him down and carried on speaking until a measure of control was established.

The tall man turned towards the window and pointed to something on the ground outside.

The Burris Black Diamond rifle scope gave Zinic a thirty two times magnification so that even over two thousand and nine yards he could tell the lawyer looked nervous. The short man joined him at the window and he adjusted his angle a fraction of a second. The lighted reticle formed a bright red cross in the center of the scope that showed up against the silhouette. On the vertical hair below the cross were a series of short horizontal lines. These were to visually compensate for bullet drop in the event the target was further away than the specified range of the scope. But since Zinic had already minutely prepared his range three days before using a laser range finder, no holdover was necessary and the cross hovered over the center of the target's chest.

Zinic's gentle contraction of his trigger finger stopped when the man impatiently moved on again. He took a long calming breath. Once more, the lawyer pointed outside and insisted the other take a look. The target approached the window, squinted, cupped his hands round his face and pressed up against the metal-grilled glass. The tall man flicked his eyes up in Zinic's direction then backed off behind the wall.

So that was how it was.

Zinic pushed his breath all the way out, intending to fire at the bottom. It never arrived.

The slamming of car doors far below scratched at his attention. He could have ignored it but his antennae told him something was wrong. He pulled up from the target and snatched a brief look over the edge. Leaning forward he could see the top of a silver white BMW with fluorescent orange and yellow bands on the back and sides. If that wasn't clear enough they were accompanied by POLICE in big blue capitals. The car was stopped near the entrance to the building. The doors were wide open and three policemen in fluorescent yellow jackets were looking straight up at him.

Behind them other men in uniform were fanning out around the circumference of the building. As curious civilians emerged from the night the police ushered them out of the way and into covered areas. From the way they were placed it was clear the police thought he was armed. He pushed aside the question of how they had seen him and concentrated on what would happen next. It wouldn't be long before they would send in a storm team. He had no more than a few minutes to spare.

One of the reasons he had chosen this roof when he had scouted it three nights before was its solitary entrance. In the center of the roof was a rectangular block with one metal door. Nothing else but a thousand square yards of rusty needles, fag ends and used condoms. The sides of the building were sheer drops. He could try to charge down the steps and hide out in the building but knew he wouldn't get far.

The rain swept suddenly away to the west taking the rain with it. He closed his eyes and forced himself to think. He did not want to go to prison. He knew that even in famously tolerant England everything had changed since 9/11. New terrorist laws meant he could be locked away almost indefinitely. He thought of Marta. She would never look at him again once she knew the truth. He tried to contain his frustration and annoyance. But the time he opened his eyes he had decided what he was going to do. There was really only one option.

7.

Francis did his best to look casual, but he wasn't happy. He sat at the kitchen bar popping peanuts, sucking on a bottle of Grolsh and flicking through October's Muscle Cars magazine. But his mind was on other things. Even an article on gold plated spoilers couldn't stop him brooding over Tyler's unwanted presence. When Janine had told him Tyler was in the house he had merely shrugged and pulled up a stool but she could almost hear the skin tightening over his swelling anger. She rattled away with saucepans and food in a forlorn hope that noise could dispel it, but Francis's ability to concentrate on customized cars had never been surer.

"I'm making pasta. Is that alright for you?" Janine ventured.

Francis grunted something that sounded like 'wanagoaa'. Janine frowned as she attempted to penetrate the meaning and tentatively repeated, "do I want to go out?"

"I fancy a curry"

"You know I have to book a babysitter in advance Francis. Don't let's go through this again."

Francis slowly raised his eyes to her while his brain attempted to formulate a telling response that would included Tyler's presence and dubious manhood, but he couldn't quite grasp it. Instead he returned his gaze to a calf-skin covered '65 Ford Mustang and yawned.

"Yea. I forgot".

Janine drew a large tolerant breath and released it quietly. She knew Francis's moods and this was not going to be an easy one. She emptied a tin of peeled tomatoes into the blender and flipped the switch. Francis didn't bat a muscle of his eyelids, and continued pouring over the auto-porn until he heard Rachel's door open and softly close. By the time Tyler entered the room he had found a fascinating article on how to gull-wing a Cortina.

Tyler didn't see any need to rouse the beast so contented himself with "thanks Janine. I'll call tomorrow."

She wiped her hands and stopped him at the door. "You promised me an explanation Ty."

His reply caught in his throat and instead of the well-practiced excuse, he croaked. This was followed by a sustained dry cough that gave Francis the reason he needed to break his marathon read and gaze at Tyler with a look normally reserved for canine excrement on his shoe.

"I'm sorry" Tyler eventually gasped, thumping his chest, "I'll call you tomorrow"

Francis interposed: "She asked you a question."

"OK" Janine cut in. "But if it's about this weekend, you better call me in the morning".

"Hold on" said Francis dismounting the bar stool. "He breaks the conditions of the court order without explanation and you think that's OK."

"It's not OK, but it can wait until tomorrow."

"And what about me..." Francis started.

"What's it got to do with you?" Tyler retorted angrily.

Francis's voice lowered a pitch and took on the solid, level tone of someone squaring for a fight.

"Suppose we have plans?"

Tyler had no such capacity for self-restraint. His hitherto contained fury now piped out like steam from a kettle and his voice took on the same shrill tone.

"I don't want you anywhere near my daughter".

"How's that?"

"I've seen the marks..."

"What?"

"You know what I..."

"Are you accusing me..."

"He's not accusing you of anything." Janine broke in abruptly, physically placing herself between them. "Are you Ty?"

"She's my daughter," he continued with his eyes focused on a patch of floor a few inches in front of his feet "and I have a right to protect her."

Francis coughed contemptuously.

"What... what in God's name are you going on about?" stuttered Janine, genuinely surprised. She had never ever heard Tyler raise her voice, let alone threaten someone.

"She's got bruises."

"Where?"

"On her wrist."

"And you think I..." Francis started.

"Shut up Francis." Janine said turning to him with real fire in her eyes. He backed up against the bar and Janine swiveled angrily back round to Tyler.

"Do you think... do you really think Tyler that I would let anyone - anyone - harm Rachel?" It was the kind of rhetorical question Janine excelled at. Tyler could do little more than open his mouth before she continued.

"Do you think I would let anyone near her unless I fully trusted them? She's my daughter too you know..."

She was cut off in full flow by Francis who,

in attempting to remount the bar stool in a confined space, missed his footing and sent it crashing to the floor. In the process, his legs became tangled in those of the stool and he flopped heavily on top of it. His chest hit the padded seat edge and he let out an 'ooof'. Winded by the fall he tumbled off the fallen stool and rolled limply over onto his back, grazing Janine's calf as he did so.

Janine jumped forward. "What the...!" she screamed furiously. "What are you fucking doing?"

She limped over to the sofa, sat down and rubbed her leg. Tyler was the only person left standing. He looked down at Francis, prostrate at his feet and gasping for air like a landed fish. The sight of that ugly shaved head lolling helplessly pleased immensely. He watched as his large mouth opened and closed mechanically and his eyes bulged as if they were about to pop. He had a strong urge to ram the tip of his shoe deep into his left temple. That would put an end to all his misery. His life could return to normal. Rachel would be safe, Janine would come back to him and his self-esteem would be recovered all with one small muscular effort.

His ham twitched involuntarily as if preparing for the simple swing of the leg that would restore order to his universe.

"Get out Tyler!"

He looked round at the still furious Janine.

"Leave. Now. Call me tomorrow".

Tyler hesitated and looked back down at the beached whale. Francis managed to haul in an almighty breath and life came shuddering back into his body. He heaved himself up onto an elbow and Tyler's moment was lost.

"Go Tyler, please."

Tyler sensed the fear in her voice. Her terrible fury was giving way to a pitiful anxiety. The wind of power was shifting quarter again. Tyler had ridden it for a moment with his own febrile anger, then Janine, but now it was back where it belonged.

"For God's sake get out" insisted Janine, rising from the sofa.

The ham muscle that had, a moment ago, been so eager to flick Tyler's foot forward now inched it back. He left the room and headed down the short corridor.

Behind him he could hear Francis rise to his feet and snort angrily. Tyler hurriedly opened the front door, and rushed out into the night. The last thing he heard Janine say before he pulled the door behind him was

"It's not his fault."

8.

MacMillan had seen the suspect immediately. He could not tell if he was armed or not, but he wasn't about to wait around for proof. He left one man back to liaise with the second car and instructed Mat, the driver, to find the best way up on the roof. All Armed Response Units carry the reliable Glock 17 automatic pistol on their hip and he now supplemented these with two Heckler & Koch MP5s from the boot. Mat took the proffered sub-machine gun and led them to the base of the stairwell that corkscrewed up the center of the building giving access to all floors before visibly piercing the skyline.

MacMillan left the third man guarding the lift entrance and hit the concrete steps running. Mat followed. MacMillan knew from experience that the next few minutes would be crucial. If it was just some kid with an air rifle, the shock arrival of heavily armed police would be enough to make him spray his pants. If it went on longer and the crowd started to egg him it could easily turn nasty. MacMillan was possibly the fittest and strongest man in the force, a regular pentathlete and the current holder of the Met's middleweight boxing title. His forces background was also fairly well known and he had a reputation for bringing his battlefield tactics to the blighted streets South London. He led the way as he always did, two steps at a time.

Twenty-five stories up, Zinic opened the door and listened to the sounds of the police scaling the stairwell. He judged he had about three minutes. One hundred and eighty seconds in which every movement was already mapped out in his mind. With stern determination he put them into action.

9.

As Tyler bowled down McDermott Close the shouting continued after him.

"I'll fucking kill him."

"Shut up, you'll wake Rachel."

"The little shit."

"He never touched you."

It faded as he approached Ingrave Street but he wasn't sure if that was because of the distance or something more sinister. He hated himself for not having the courage to stop and turn round but persuaded himself that Janine would handle it better alone.

Like the swirling wind around him, Tyler's impression of what had just happened in Janine's front room was misty and confused. For a brief shining moment he had felt in control of events. Not when Francis was prostrate on the floor but before, when his anger had erupted with vehemence he had never before experienced. It was frightening, but he liked it. As he trotted along at a rate of an Olympic walker he had a vision of himself returning to the house where Francis was still exploding like a firework display.

'You're disturbing my daughter', he says coolly.

Francis blusters and threatens. Tyler ignores it.

'If you touch a hair on her head I'll cut off your balls and stuff them down your throat!'

'Oh yea, I'd like to see you try' Francis leers, at which point Tyler jerks a knee up into his groin and his nemesis doubles up in pain. This is followed by an upper cut busting open his nose and sending him sprawling back into the hallway just as Janine appears.

'Oh Tyler?' she swoons.

'If this scumbag gives you any more trouble I want to hear about it.'

Janine nods meekly.

'The next time I'll cut him up and feed him to the fishes.'

He like the sound of 'feed him to the fishes'. There weren't many man-eating fish (or even fishes) in Wandsworth but it had a kind of Mafia twang to it and he smirked at the turn of phrase.

He heard a noise behind him that could have been a window opening, or a front door. He turned his collar up against the wind and rain and hurried on without daring to look back. Rachel used the same principle - he knew, by covering her eyes she thought she was hiding. Ingrave Street was quiet but well lit. At the bottom, to his left, it gave out onto Falcon Road. In the angle between the two, the blocks of flats of the York Road Estate rose high above the trees and streetlights into the dusk. He thought he could make out blue flashing lights coming from somewhere inside the Estate. It wasn't unusual to see police round here.

His dirty white Fiat Uno was parked on the far side between a battered yellow Vauxhall and a black Mondeo. It wasn't much of a car, but he didn't own anything else of substance and was paranoid about it being stolen. In truth it was probably the last car in the road anyone would want to steal, even if they could get it started.

As he stepped off the pavement to cross the road he heard the tap tap tap of running feet behind him.

Don't look back. He said to himself. Don't turn round. Ignore it. It's got nothing to do with you. Get to your car, get in and go home.

The phrase 'feed him to the fishes' came back to his mind, but now it was him that was being fed, and the fishes had baseball bats. The steps got louder and closer. Despite himself, Tyler could not bear it any longer and swung round just as Francis arrived and shunted him in the chest with both hands.

10.

Zinic broke down the rifle in a practiced thirty-two seconds and slipped it into the pockets of the roll up that he closed and sealed tightly with the Velcro. The two minutes or so that he thought remained had to be revised when he listened carefully to the sound the boots were making on the stairs. They seemed much closer than he had anticipated and instead of slowing down, they were speeding up. He grabbed the wrap and the holdall, ran over to the stairwell, opened the door and peered down. The angle only allowed him a view over half the floors but he could see dark helmeted shapes already. He had a possible sixty seconds. No more. He stripped off his leather jacket, laid it on the damp roof placed the gun package crossways at one end and rolled it up inside. He hesitated when he realized that in his urgency he had left his phone and icon inside the jacket.

He briefly considered unrolling the jacket and taking them out but the crescendo of stomping feet forced him to abandon it. They seemed no more than a few floors down. Another ten to fifteen seconds and it would be too late. He stuffed the rolled jacket into the holdall and zipped it up.

Unbelievably, the police were already at the door. He sprinted to the far side of the entrance block out of their immediate sight. He had no time to find a good landing spot. The best he could do was to choose the side of the building furthest from the police. Griping the holdall by the handles he spun round like a hammer thrower.

He released the bag after the second turn and as it lifted into the night the stairwell door crashed open.

11.

Tyler's feet had no chance to catch up with his body. He landed hard on his backside and the momentum sent him rolling heels overhead until he was sprawled flat on his face in the middle of the road. Along the way he hit the back of his head that made him feel groggy. Francis shouted something at him but a persistent buzzing like a thousand angry bees in his skull blocked out the sound. Tyler moaned and turned on to his side. When he opened his eyes, he could see Francis' ornate black brogues inches from his face. He had surprisingly small feet. Even in his semi-comatose state he recognized the irony. Only minutes ago it was Francis who lay gasping on the floor as Tyler toyed with the idea of kicking him. There was no chance of Francis 'toying' with such an idea. He wasn't governed by the same moral straightjacket as his middle class inferior. Francis would as soon kick him when he was down as squash a bug.

He clawed his arms up over his head and face and balled his body into as close a resemblance of a woodlouse as he could manage. The incessant bees filled his inner world and he lay there, muscles contracted, tight as a barrel, ready to take the battering. The strain of holding the position was exhausting and after a while he relaxed enough to peer out through a gap in his arms. The shoes were still there and he snapped shut again.

Francis shook his head in disgust. This 'thing' that crawled and cried wasn't a man in any sense of the word he understood. He was a disgrace to the word. He despised people who had the best possible opening in life: money, accent, education, and failed do anything with them. Francis would have loved to have put the boot into the pathetic creature. He wouldn't have hesitated normally but he had a grander, more vicious plan in mind. He placed the sole of his shoe on Tyler's leg and pushed.

"Get up you twat."

Tyler shrunk under the pressure of the foot and, if it were possible, curled up even tighter.

"You're fucking pathetic" growled Francis, grabbing him by the hair and angrily yanking him to his feet. "Look at me."

Tyler cowered and got his ear slapped.

"Hey dickface. I'm here. Look at me." He slapped him again. "I'll stop hitting you if you look at me. You listening or what?"

Tyler raised his flinching eyes to the beast expecting to see a fist or forehead come crashing in.

"You are fucking pathetic. Let me hear you say it."

Tyler cringed.

"Go on" Francis reiterated, "say it."

"What?"

"You are fucking pathetic."

"I am pathetic" Tyler mouthed listlessly.

Francis pulled him back by the hair until he was stretched backwards over the side of a car.

"I am FUCKING pathetic, moron"

"I am fucking pathetic."

Despite his complete mastery and Tyler's absolute subjugation, Francis felt cheated. Giving up without a fight was almost like winning. Soft-skinned wankers like Tyler never fought for anything and somehow floated through life on a cloud of superiority. Francis grafted hard for every penny he earned; not all of it legal, and most of it certainly immoral, but he fought all the way.

"I'm going to tell you this only once Tinker Tyler" he said. "I don't ever want to see you here again. You don't belong here and Janine ain't nothing to you."

"Rachel" Tyler managed to splutter.

A sinister grin cut across Francis's face.

"Where's last month's cheque eh? How

d'you suppose Janine can look after your little brat if you don't cough up?" He crushed Tyler's head onto the car roof. "Eh?"

"Aaa!"

"No money, no time."

"You can't... stop me seeing my daughter."

"A judge can. You break a court ordered child maintenance and that's it."

"Janine would never..."

"We'll see about that."

Tyler pushed into the larger man's chest and struggled to get upright.

"We clear then? You don't pay you don't see your daughter."

"Keep your hands off her."

Francis shoved his face against Tyler's so that his stubble scratched along his cheek.

"I don't like what your implying Tyler" he whispered in his ear. "Rachel's just a kid. She gotta learn just like anyone else. That's what fathers are for. And if you ain't around then she'll have to learn it from me."

Tyler screamed and flailed with his arms and legs that broke impotently over the solid bulk. Francis brought his knee up suddenly and Tyler felt a searing pain in his groin. He coughed violently and clutched at his testicles. The pain was momentarily unbearable and he felt on the verge of fainting. He slid down the side of the car to his knees groaning in agony.

12.

Zinic sat on the concrete wall with his hands clearly in sight and watched the two men in baseball caps and body armor spring out onto the roof. Because he had positioned himself on the blind side of the central block, they didn't immediately see him. Had this been back in, say, Afghanistan or Chechnya those empty seconds would have made all the difference and, Zinic reflected, at least one of them would already be dead. The other, either by luck or design, kept the wall to his back until his muzzle swung round the corner and found its target.

MacMillan kept the Heckler & Koch leveled straight at Zinic's chest and shouted "Mat. Over here."

After he was satisfied the rest of the roof was clear Mat circled around the other side of the stairwell and approached the trapped man at an angle of ninety degrees to his commanding officer.

"Get off the wall" shouted the ex-sergeant. "Keep your hands where I can see them."

Zinic knew the drill. He lifted up his arms and slid unhurriedly to his feet.

"Lie down" MacMillan continued in a parade-ground bark.

Keeping his arms high in the air, Zinic placed first one knee then the other on the damp concrete.

"On your front. Keep your hands away from your body."

Zinic reached forward placed his palms in front of him and lowered his body flat.

MacMillan took two steps forward with his machine gun poised down at the prostrate man like a bayonet and ordered Mat to check and cuff him. Mat approached from the far side so as not to block his commanding officer's line of fire. This would have been his second death the Russian decided. Instead of giving Zinic the handcuffs, he knelt down and clicked them into place himself. It would have been relative simple to roll into him and snatch his pistol. The young officer's body would have given him cover and it would have all been over in a second. The stupidity of it disappointed him but there was no point taking on the whole British police force. Once his hands were securely fastened behind his back, Mat patted him down from shoulders to shoes.

Nothing.

"Check the roof for weapons." instructed MacMillan without taking his eyes off the captive.

While Mat probed the gutters and corners with a torch beam, MacMillan spoke into an unseen microphone.

"Suspect secure." Then, after a pause, "nothing yet. We're taking a look."

Mat returned. "All clear."

MacMillan nodded then nudged Zinic's leg with his toecap. "Get up."

Zinic rolled to one side, rose slowly to one knee and onto his feet. MacMillan stepped right up to him. "Where's the gun?" he growled.

"I don't know what you're talking about?" Zinic replied in his perfect English.

MacMillan looked him squarely in the face and instinctively knew something was amiss. He was twenty years younger than the Russian and, at five foot ten, about the same height. Zinic was stocky with heavy shoulders and a broad chest. Though Macmillan gave the same impression of bulk, it was mostly body armour. Both had taught feral skin but the Russian's face was swarthier by nature and deeply lined.

MacMillan stepped closer and abrasively repeated the question a decibel louder. His reply was an easy stare that might have been taken for arrogance had it not been accompanied by an almost imperceptible change in body posture. MacMillan was reminded of his Jujitsu instructor at Lympston. A man he had never seen bested in hand-to-hand, even against two or three well-trained man. One thing he had never taught, but MacMillan had noticed, was the way he relaxed just before an attack. Whatever his posture, his knees would bend almost imperceptibly and his shoulders would drop a fraction of an inch more. He had tried to copy it himself with limited success. To 'be like water' - in the words of Bruce Lee - it was something you were born with, not something you could learn.

He recognized the same fluid stance in the man before him now. It was understood rather than known. There was an aura of dangerous energy that perhaps only another professional could really appreciate.

"What gun?" Zinic asked with as much of an air of innocence as he could fake. MacMillan wasn't taken in. He had a bad feeling about this strange man on the roof without a coat in the rain. His self-possession in the face of two heavily armed and armored police officers told him he was either completely nuts or a pro.

"What are you doing here?"

"Taking a walk?"

"On the roof?"

"I'm looking at the stars."

MacMillan glanced at the cloud covered sky.

"I'm an optimist." Zinic shrugged. He shifted from one foot to the other and MacMillan had an overwhelming sense of impending danger. He took three steps back and a voice crackled in his earpiece.

"I don't like it" he replied into the microphone. Then after another pause he added "no weapon, but there's more to this than meets the eye. Make a thorough search of the building and the perimeter. I don't like the look of this bastard. I don't like it at all."

13.

I t was a full minute before Tyler realized Francis had disappeared. He rolled over onto his back with his legs splayed apart and his eyes fluttering in pain. He could have stayed like that in the middle of the road indefinitely had it not been for a loud thud somewhere in the direction of his car. He craned his neck round but there was no further movement or sound. In fact, apart from the distant traffic and flashes of blue police lights everything was eerily quiet.

He let out a deeply felt groan, shook the fog out of his head and rose to his feet. He staggered, disorientated, placed a hand on a nearby car for support and vomited over the bonnet. It was surprising how profoundly effective such a blow could be. The shock gradually subsided leaving an intense residual pain in his groin. It felt as though his balls had dropped a full foot and bounced between his knees as he walked.

He groped his way along the line of cars towards his old Fiat, carefully rummaged in his trouser pockets for his keys, unlocked and opened the door. With the utmost care he turned his back towards the driver's seat, loosened his trousers, placed one hand on the door, another on the frame and slowly lowered himself backwards into the car. As he touched the seat, sharp pangs shot through his testicles. When they had subsided he cupped both hands under his left knee, lifted it up and into the car then repeated the operation with the right. Once in position, he arched his back against the seat raising his buttocks up and pulled down the waist and crutch of his trousers again as far as he could before finally relaxing.

Oh - my - God...

He had never considered before how every movement of his body involved the muscles of the lower abdomen. They, in turn, tugged on his sack and throttled his battered orbs. But even the pain was nothing compared to his feeling of helplessness and self-loathing. Francis may despise him, but it was certainly less than he despised himself. Tears welled in his eyes. Only the thought of a renewed wave of pain stopped him from giving in completely to his grief.

After a few minutes he was ready to drive. He slid the key into the ignition, turned it and gently - ever so gently - pressed his foot on the gas. To his surprise the engine turned over first time.

My first bit of luck all night.

He started the windscreen wipers, eased down the clutch, delicately disengaged the handbrake and shifted into reverse. There were a good four feet between him and the car behind but after only half that distance the car bumped to a halt. The engine gave a choke and cut out.

"Shit."

He angrily punched the steering wheel and immediately regretted it. Pain shot up into his throat and made him cough. He wiped his eyes and restarted the car. Once more, the engine miraculously spun into life. He maneuvered forward then reversed again taking care to keep clear of the pavement that he was sure he must have hit the first time. But it wasn't to be. After two feet, the same bump and the same gut wrenching jerk.

"Shitshitshit."

This was too much. He cursed his car; he cursed Francis and everyone who had ever lived and contributed to his misery. He especially cursed God whom he hoped would send a thunderbolt to finish his sorry life. There was nothing for it but to get out and take a look.

He found that an even pressure applied to the front of his crotch stopped it swinging and he ambled like a sailor to the rear of the car. In the shade he could make out a dark lump behind the nearside wheel. A bin bag? He took a wide stance and reached down but instead of gripping on plastic his fingers slipped off thick leather.

"What the..?"

He pushed it with his foot and spotted a grip. It was a bag, like a gym or kit bag, and was wedged under the tire. With his left hand pressed firmly into his groin he made a final effort and snatched it up onto the boot.

As soon as it was out in the open under the light he became conscious of the countless windows staring down at him. It hadn't been there when he had parked he decided. What was it? A drug drop? A dead baby? He was not naturally courageous but anger made him light-headed. He unzipped the bag there and then in full view of anyone who cared to look. Inside he found more leather - some kind of coat or jacket rolled up. He grabbed an edge and pulled at it but it was wedged in hard. It was either very large or wrapped around something else inside - probably more clothes.

Before he had a chance to consider it further a policeman turning the corner into his road caught his attention. Tyler was not in a position to pass up little gifts from providence. Maybe the night hadn't been a complete loss after all. The jacket and bag alone would probably sell for a hundred pounds or more on eBay. He zipped it back up, popped his trunk, slung the bag inside, and shut the lid. He hobbled back to the front and lowered himself back inside. The unexpected find had taken his mind off the pain and he felt substantially better. As he turned the ignition a light skimmed across the windscreen. The wipers cleared the rain. There it was again, sweeping across a car a hundred yards down the road. After a moment he caught sight of another policeman walking down the far side of the road. He was carrying a torch which he shone under and round the cars parked on the far side. He seemed to Tyler to be looking for something.

The policeman on his pavement was going through the same procedure. Surely they weren't looking for the gym bag. It wasn't possible. On the other hand, it would be just his hard bloody luck.

14.

When Ikea opened in a new Mega Mall on the outskirts of Nizhny Novgorod they hardly needed to place job ads in the local Birzha, Nizhegorodskie Novosti and Prospekt newspapers. The shopping mall was the biggest news since building of the Gorky Nuclear District Heating Plant had been abandoned after ten years and one billion dollars. The outcry of pain from a city still reeling from the conversion to capitalism was almost audible. The plant had attracted tens of thousands of migrants who were now without a Rouble or a scruple to their names.

Marta Rozhdestvensky had already sent five letters about a job in the Mega by the time the ads came out. She had even written to Lennart Dahlgren, the general director of Ikea Russia. She was thirty-two years old and apart from two years as an unpaid clerk in her ex-husband's food processing factory she had no experience outside her parents' household farm. There would be over one hundred and fifty shops in the mall: the kind of boutiques and coffee shops where they employed glamour girls from the city. She had high hopes of something in cleaning or general maintenance. When she received the letter for an interview she danced non-stop for three hours. When she was offered a post as a cashier in the Ikea store itself she passed out on the kitchen floor. They said she perfectly fitted their brief for people who were 'motivated, organized and welcoming'.

Three years on and she earned (with overtime) the dizzy sum of four and a half thousand Roubles a month before tax. This was twice as much as the farm took in cash. Though she contributed handsomely to the household accounts, her father proudly refused her offer of rent. So she did her best to improve their shared space with a new washing machine, a microwave her mother refused to use, a dishwasher she adored and even a computer. The last time Georgiy had visited, she had raised the idea of fulfilling her lifetime ambition and taking them all on a trip to Paris. It was the first time she had been angry with him. For some reason he refused to discuss it. He had suggested a hundred other things to spend her money on until she had shouted at him and he had reluctantly told her the truth. She earned in a year what the poorest in France earn in a month. Four and a half thousand Roubles would hardly pay for one hotel room for one night and the airfares alone would be more than all her savings.

Hanna broke into her dismal recollection.

"I think you've got an admirer" she sung out quietly.

Marta shook the argument with Georgiy out of her mind and looked round.

"Don't look!"

A blond young man with protruding ears and a wispy moustache and beard was the only other person in the coffee bar at that time of night and seemed to be taking no interest in them at all.

"You've got men on the brain." said Marta.

"I promise. He's been looking at you ever since we got here."

Marta smiled vaguely and raised the tartan-patterned cup to her lips. Hanna was her best friend from work. Her father had been a skilled engineer at the Gorky plant and died of alcohol poisoning after five years as a street cleaner leaving her as the sole provider for her mother and handicapped brother. They always took a cup a chocolate together in the Chappo (Spirito dell'Italia) after the late shift on Thursday.

"I'm sure I've seen him before somewhere."

"He probably works here."

"Do you want to hear about my date?"

Marta didn't really. Hanna had subscribed to a dating site a year ago and had been on a succession of one night stands ever since. Men, their discovery and conquest, were her singular interest now. There seemed to be a new one every week but it never got more serious than an occasional trip to the clinic. She told her story, as usual, and, as usual it sounded very much like the one from the week before.

"You should try it."

Marta pulled a face.

"It's just that you're not the same."

This was news to Marta. "What do you mean?"

"I don't know. Since your mysterious boyfriend was here you've been... I don't know, different."

Marta shrugged.

"You know I saw him."

"No. When?"

"I saw you going into a restaurant together last Friday. The Minin and Pozharsky. It's very expensive. Is he married?"

"Hanna!"

"I was just asking. He's quite old."

"He is not."

"How do you know he's not married? He comes and goes when he pleases. You don't even know what he does."

"He's in business."

"What sort of business?" Hanna scoffed.

"I don't ask. He travels a lot; so it must be a good business."

Why would a rich unmarried businessman be interested in a plump, middle-aged shop girl from Fedyakova? was the question on Hanna's mind. But she didn't ask it. They were friends after all.

Marta knotted her headscarf under her chin as they waited at the bus stop in the car park.

"That's new" said Hanna, smoothing over the silk twill and admiring the deep orange color with its motif of gold keys and purple tassels. She picked at the label. "Hermes. You didn't buy that in the Mega mall."

Marta smiled.

"No need to explain" Hanna continued, shaking her head. "The most I ever got was a pair of crotch-less panties."

She kissed Marta goodbye on the steps of the 272 for Kstovo and waved until the thick fog swallowed up the bus. She looked at her watch. It was still only eight twenty. She didn't fancy going home. Maybe she'd try a movie. As she was walking back to her car she saw the boy from the bar emerge from the gloom and hurry across the near empty car park. Maybe she could forget the movie. By altering her course she managed to intercept him in the most casual manner.

"You haven't seen a blue Astra anywhere

have you?"

The boy stopped and looked at her blankly.

"I can't see anything in this fog and the car park is so large."

"No." The boy looked down and was about to continue on when she stopped him again.

"Hey, aren't you the young man who was looking at my friend in the coffee bar?"

He looked startled.

"That's OK. She's gone home anyway. I think I've seen you before. I know. Don't you live somewhere round the Prioksky District? I have a friend who lives there. I'm sure I've seen you."

The young man glanced nervously at his Daewoo as if searching for an answer.

"Don't be shy." Hanna continued. "Lots of young men go for older women nowadays. It's very fashionable. Why don't we go for a drink?"

The young man looked her straight in the face for the first time. He seemed undecided at first but slowly nodded and said, "OK. My car's over there. I know a place nearby."

He indicating for her to lead the way then fell into step quietly beside her.

"You're very serious. I'll have to show you how to laugh."

The young man grunted and opened the passenger door. As soon as Hanna sunk into the seat and the door was closed she turned to see another slightly older man with cropped hair sitting behind her.

"Oh." She giggled uneasily. "Two of you?"

The cropped hair man smiled warmly offered his hand. "My young friend is a little nervous. He's never done this kind of thing before." He winked and Hanna gave a nervous laugh. Two men were more than she had bargained for but, what the hell, you only live once. The young man slipped into the driver's seat, started the car and pulled away.

The older man leaned forward and said, "don't forget your seat belt. Here, let me help you." He pulled it down with his right hand and slipped his left around her body to catch the buckle. Hanna squirmed but didn't resist. Once it was attached his hand brushed up the outside of her coat, found the lapel and slipped inside. His cold hand on her warm breast sent a shudder right through her and she whimpered. It then continued on up, caressing her naked throat, chin and lips while his other hand extracted a thin-bladed Korshun hunting knife from his belt.

The car didn't even slow down. As it skirted one of the ditches surrounding the complex, the passenger door swung open and Hanna's body tumbled out. They left the car park by the southeast corner and eased out onto the M7 in the wake of the 272 to Kstovo.

15.

The engine spluttered into life for the third time in as many minutes. Tyler worked the accelerator until he got a constant hum, slipped into reverse and carefully inched back. This time there was no bump. He slipped into first, pulled the wheel round and just made it out past the bumper of the Vauxhall in front. Five yards further on and he was in second and about the pass the policeman on the far side of the road. He seemed too busy to bother him and Tyler realized he was about to get away with it. It wasn't a huge victory in his life, but it was something. The surge of euphoria rising in his throat, however, was choked down when the policeman abruptly stepped out into the road and flagged him down. Tyler was so surprised he stabbed down on the break without using the clutch and the car kangarooed to a halt. The engine gave a gasp and cut out.

The policeman approached the side, lowered his level palm and Tyler obediently rolled down the window. He was dressed in rain gear with a long black plastic poncho and a tight plastic cover over his helmet that resembled something from a sex education video.

"Good evening sir" he said. His eyes searched Tyler's anxious face. "Are you the owner of this vehicle?"

"Yes."

"Can I see your registration documents and driving license please?"

Tyler reached over the glove compartment and rummaged through the miscellaneous junk (food wrappers, bills, Tupperware top, a pen knife) for the papers which he were sure were buried somewhere within.

The policeman observed the grime on the back of his suit jacket. "Had a fall sir?" he said.

Tyler located the slim plastic A4 document wallet containing the papers and handed it over.

"Yes. I... I slipped."

Keeping the wallet and contents inside the car and out of the rain, the policeman carefully extracted the driving license and shone his torch on it. "Visiting friends here sir?"

"My wife. We're not divorced" he added confusingly. "Just separated. And my daughter."

The policeman took his time looking over

the license then replaced the documents in the wallet and handed it back. He scanned the torch beam along the back seat and into the foot well and then the front passenger seat.

Tyler was beginning to feel unwell. Try as he may he couldn't stop shaking. He could feel his body temperature dropping - or was it rising? Anyway, he felt cold.

The policeman stepped back and dropped the line of his torch. The young man didn't look like a hardened criminal; he couldn't smell alcohol or drugs and his pupils looked normal. Still, they had very specific instructions to check everything and it was more than his job was worth to let him go because he looked ill.

"You look a bit peaky if I may say so sir." Then almost as an afterthought "Could you open the boot for me please?"

Tyler was stunned. "What?"

"Open your boot please sir."

The boot. With the bag. Tyler could feel a fever coming on like a racehorse.

"Won't take a moment sir. Would you step out of the vehicle."

Tyler fought back the dizziness, and opened the door.

I just found it. Stuck behind my wheel. It's not mine.

In his panic Tyler had forgotten about the pain from below, but as he got out, the physical, mental and emotional pressure all crowded in together and he leaned against the side of the car in a faint.

"You alright sir?"

"I..." He rubbed his head and shivered involuntarily.

"Looks like you've caught something nasty."

The irony of the remark struck him as he opened the boot and there slung on top of the flat spare tire, the remains of a MacDonald's Happy Meal, an old T shirt and a collection of house flyers was the leather holdall.

"Tut tut" said the policeman in a practiced tone of reproof. "What do we have here?"

16.

Even after the third glass, Julius Kriegmann was still shaking. He closed his
eyes, settled deeper into the hot water
and balanced the crystal tumbler on his forehead. A single shot of Talisker '81 while he
took a bath was a regular treat after a stress-
ful day and he had prepared it that morning
knowing he would need it. He had no idea how
much. After fifteen minutes, the bath salts had
failed in their promise to 'calm and relax' and
he had topped up with more boiling water. But
it couldn't begin to sooth the inner turmoil
that milled at his soul and sent periodic shock-
waves through his pusillanimous frame.

However did he get into this mess? He tried
to convince himself that he was a lawyer and
not a gangster but the truth, as he knew full
well, was not so neat. As O'Hagan's legal fac-
totum for seven years he was as guilty of hiding his numerous frauds as his employer was of

committing them. It had served him well. He had a large house in Holland Park and at least nine million dollars stashed away in offshore accounts in Panama and the Caymans. But it was his private beach in the Bahamas that was his particular joy. That was where he planned to retire. It was from there that he launched regular trips to Cuba to indulge in his taste for young, dark meat. Girls or boys, it didn't matter which. They were pretty much alike at that age.

He could have packed up and disappeared there already if it wasn't for those damned Russians. He had met the twins when O'Hagan had started handling some of Alexandr Olevsky's assets. The Olevsky's were huge clients and as O'Hagan worked his charm he found he was drawn more and more into their business. The first was finalizing the contract for an extensive land deal in Middlesex. The worst was personally travelling to some godforsaken wilderness in Ukraine and handing over secret bank codes to a sadistic mob of bandits who called themselves freedom fighters. It had taken him two weeks in the Bahamas to decontaminate but the effects still lingered.

A month ago he had received a CD ROM through the post with a video of him in flagrante delicto with a brother and sister team from Santa Clara whose combined ages didn't amount to more than the twenty five dollars he had paid their father. The package with the CD had been posted anonymously to his Portland Place office and opened by his secretary. The thought that she could have watched it still brought a wave of nausea to his throat and for three weeks after, he had suffered a torment equal to his assigned place on the seventh terrace of Purgatory.

He was thinking of Dante's fiery punishment for the unnaturally lustful when there was a thunderous crash on the outside of the bathroom door as though something heavy had been thrown against it. He jolted and the cut glass tumbler slid off his forehead and shattered against the marble sending lethal shards into the water. Julius jumped up just as a second impact splintered the frame and sent the door arcing round with a violence that smashed one of the handmade ceramic tiles lining the walls. In the opening stood a large man in a black bomber jacket. The right side of his face was disfigured with burn scar tissue and he hid his shaved head under a grey-and-white-flecked flat cap. Julius was so shocked he didn't think to cover himself but stood there naked with the water lapping against his meager calves and his rolls of flesh glowing a finely boiled lobster-pink. The man's eyes immediately dropped to the peeled prawn peeking out from beneath Julius' stomach. He smiled gleefully and stepped back.

Bruno pushed past him and bowed his head under the lintel to enter. It was a spacious bathroom but Bruno was so large and ungainly that he made any room look like a cupboard. Unlike his trim and well-tailored twin, Bruno had always reminded Julius of a character from a German Expressionist movie. He was six foot five, angular and scary. His face was almost triangular. He had a broad forehead and pointed cheekbones which dropped to a sharp, though not prominent, chin. His narrow mouth was tight and mean and the lack of lines on his face indicated a man unbothered by introspection, doubt or humor. Julius knew little about the ethnic makeup of Russia but Bruno's height, fair skin and thick joints made him think of the Viking 'Rus' who had founded St Petersburg and given their redhead moniker to the name of the country. And though his pupils were ice blue, the eyes themselves were pinched and slanted, almost Asian. His lank, light-brown hair was swept back from where it started high above his forehead and dropped straight down to just above his shoulders. It clung to the edges of his bulbous cranium and swung from side to side as he stalked briskly forward.

Bruno was not one for formalities.

"What the fuck happened?" he snarled. The accent was so thick that even the words sounded Russian.

Julius felt a warm stream of urine trickle

69

down between his thighs and Bruno sniffed the acrid air like a dog.

"Don't fuck with me!"

Julius gasped in a lungful of air "I don't know" he squeaked in his curious cartoon voice.

Bruno approached the edge of the bath. Julius was a tall man, but despite standing on a higher level he was still several inches smaller.

"I did everything as you said" Julius piped. "But nothing. I couldn't keep him any longer. They don't allow it. I waited as long as I could."

"The police caught him on the roof."

"What?"

"He was arrested."

Julius was already in the grip of a tornado of fear and panic that was way beyond his control. "Oh my God" he exhaled. As if under-age rape and billion-dollar fraud weren't bad enough, it now looked as though a hired assassin could finger him in a murder conspiracy. He shook his head slowly, trying desperately to find some solid ground of sense. "You said he was a professional. The best."

"Exactly."

"Then how in God's name..."

"He must have been set up."

"What do you mean?"

"Someone told the police."

"Told the police. That's just great! How many people were in on this?"

"Just you and me" Bruno insinuated with the subtlety of a knife between the ribs.

"Then who the hell...?"

"You tell me you fucking pervert."

That was a bit rich coming from Bruno but Julius decided this wasn't the time to challenge him on it. "What... what did he say?"

"Do I look like a policeman?"

"We need to know."

"That's right."

"Well?"

"He'll need a lawyer."

Julius's mouth dropped open at the thought. "No. For God's sake. No! I'm not that kind of lawyer."

"You're the best kind Julius. You'll do whatever it takes to get him out."

"What if he's already told them about O'Hagan... about me, for Christ's sake?"

"He won't."

Julius decided he had to get a grip on this conversation before it spun out of control. The first step was something to wear and he moved to one end of the bath to get out. As he did so, he stepped onto the jagged rump of the shattered whisky glass, screamed in pain and flopped over the edge onto the floor. The underside of his foot was lacerated. Blood quickly welled out of the deep gash, flowed down his long narrow sole and pooled on the carpet. Julius howled and after a couple of attempts to touch the injured part resigned himself to clutching desperately at the ankle and writhing on his back.

Bruno quickly lost patience with this display, picked up the bottle of whisky standing open by the bath and poured the contents on the open wound. Julius let out a long stringing shriek that caused Bruno's face to pinch at the nose and mouth in his semblance of a smile. He then knelt down and slapped the distraught lawyer across one of his fleshy jowls.

"You betrayed me."

Despite the pain, the danger of the accusation got through to the lawyer. "No no" he cried out.

"No one knew about the hit except you and me."

"I swear it. I didn't tell anyone."

"If it happens again I won't be so nice."

"It's too late! Too late!" Julius screamed. "The trial's on Monday morning."

"That gives you the whole weekend."

"I can't..."

Bruno slapped him so hard on his exposed waist it left a bright red handprint.

"I can't get in. It's not allowed. They won't let me. It's the weekend." The words came tumbling out now in near hysteria.

Bruno's large hand found an unguarded patch on his victim's stomach and left another glowing welt.

"Stop! Please! Stop!" Julius was crying now. Tears streamed down his cheeks and he rolled over onto his stomach to protect himself. Bruno's hand immediately slapped down pitilessly on the flabby buttocks with a loud crack: once, twice three times. Each one provoked a noise like a whip that echoed round the tiled bathroom. When he stopped Julius was a quivering mound and from his mouth, which was buried in the carpet, came a deep childlike sobbing.

"Find a way" said Bruno, "Before the trial. Understand."

Julius had not even heard. Bruno stood up and crossed the room to where the flat-capped man was standing in the doorway, still grinning and overtly rubbing an erection in his jeans. Bruno walked past him.

"Make sure he understands," he said.

17.

Zinic zipped up, flushed, rinsed his hands and returned to the bench. He had never been in an English holding cell before and was pleasantly surprised. Russian police cells fell into two categories, cages and dungeons and you didn't want to be in either. At about ten by fifteen feet with a toilet, a sink and a foam mattress, this one was better than many Moscow apartments. The walls were white and the cement floor was painted the color of... cement. It was warm, dry and so spotlessly clean that the odor of sweaty feet seemed bizarrely out of place. On arrival, the custody officer had taken his watch, shoes, belt, fingerprints and personal details. After a brief and efficient medical examination, he was pronounced in good heath, and every thirty minutes a guard passed to check he was living up to it. He had been given a dry T-shirt, a bottle of water and even offered food, which he had refused. He stretched out on the mattress with his hands behind his head.

If we had been treated as well as this in the army, he reflected, there would never have been a revolution.

He noticed the CCTV camera in the corner above the door and wondered what was happening the other end. The Armed Response Unit had delivered him to the station over three hours ago (reckoned by the regular half hourly walk-bys). By now they would have found the gun, checked his prints and started a background search.

Where had he gone wrong? Who had seen him on the roof? He went over the events again, starting with the walk from the hotel to the estate. London had more surveillance cameras per square yard than any other city in the world. He had downloaded a CCTV map from the Internet and deliberately plotted a course to avoid them. This was not one hundred percent possible, but it could take years before they found the right cameras and it didn't really answer the question anyway.

He had carefully scouted the rooftop two nights before to ensure his position was not overlooked, and he was convinced he had not been seen entering the stairwell. Once there, the wide parapet had hidden him and his rifle from below and yet, within minutes, there was a heavily armed response unit charging up the stairs. And the policeman's first question still stung: 'Where's the gun?'

How did they know?

Was it possible that an insider had tipped them off? Every contract went down through a hierarchy of contacts. Each link in the middle had two contacts but little or no idea where the chains led. There was no connection at all between the two ends. The contract killers lived a life wildly apart from those who employed them. Most were ex-soldiers like himself who picked up work through old contacts or former superiors. Whoever had shelled out for this job would have done everything necessary to ensure it was watertight.

Quite apart from that there were the simple logistics. Zinic had been contracted in St Petersburg where he lived. Even if the police had got wind of it, there was no co-operative agreement between Russia and Britain - quite the opposite. Furthermore, the planning of the operation had been his and his alone. Nothing had been booked in advance. The trains he had taken across Europe had been paid for at the ticket offices and in cash. And though he had searched in advance for possible hotels in London he had only registered on arrival. He was a meticulous planner and no one else had been involved. No one knew where he was - not even Marta.

No, the only possible conclusion was that

somehow he had been spotted. It wasn't easy to accept one was getting old and careless, but he supposed he wasn't the first nor would he be the last. He wondered how many years in jail he would get for possessing a firearm and wondered how long Marta would wait for him, if at all, once she knew the truth.

18.

The Phoenix document normally sapped Grant's will to live. Even when he had finished the ten-page form of depressing tick-boxes and a hand written description of the arrest, it still had to be retyped into the Police National Computer along with photographs, fingerprints and a DNA swab. That didn't even include the interview report.

They didn't teach us this at Hendon he reflected sourly. I should have gone to Pitman's.

It was all a far cry from the car chases and mockney banter of The Sweeny that had inspired him to enlist as a teenager. He had excelled at his first posting in Essex where he even met John Thaw, the star of the TV series. It was while he was hobnobbing with the technicians on a second unit shoot that he had met Nanette, a pretty young assistant with the most spectacular breasts he had ever seen. She had been attracted by... what, exactly? He had never been quite sure. He wasn't good looking, even then. His nose was the shape of a blunt chisel and his eyes were slightly too close together. He had too much hair which even when cut short resembled something that collects on the underside of a boat. He had always been in good physical shape, but his total disregard for his appearance made even the sharpest suits look like they should be returned to Oxfam. As it happened, it was those very qualities that had turned her on. As she explained it, the world in which she worked was a fantasy and Grant was the real deal. As opposed to her friends and colleagues who made it all up, Grant did actually spend his day 'collaring villains'. It even brought her a kind of kudos when she married outside the business.

All that soon faded when they had their first child, the hard grind of life kicked in and she started to cast envious glances back at the world of make-believe. He wished he could hate her for it, but the truth was he understood completely. He himself would rather be John Thaw than Bob Grant. At least he could get to the end of each episode with a satisfying sense of completion. There was nothing more disheartening than knowing your mission could never, ever be accomplished. And as if the tidal wave of drug induced terror wasn't enough, there were now real terrorists ready to blow themselves and everything else to hell - for what? It baffled him.

Grant turned his attention back to the Phoenix forms. For the first time he could remember they actually made interesting reading. The subject was five foot ten... stocky... muscular... dark thinning hair... heavy eyebrows... close-set brown eyes... The list of body scars was impressive. It ran to several pages and was finally explained by the faded tattoo on his left pectoral (over the heart, he had noted). It showed a dagger pointing downwards overlaid by an open parachute across which was written a single word in Cyrillic: ВЫIМПЕл. Even the National Police Database couldn't help with that one. It had taken a lot of guesswork and Googling before he had discovered it was the insignia of the Yympel, a Russian Special Forces unit.

Information on this group that may or may not have been disbanded in 1993 was scarce. Wikipedia described them as a 'dedicated OSNAZ unit specialized in deep penetration, sabotage, universal direct and covert action, embassy protection and espionage cell activation.'

Quite a CV. The helpful hyperlink explained that 'Osnaz' was the name originally given to Special Forces within the KGB, now referred to as Spetsnaz. Even Grant had heard of Spetsnaz, that catch all-word for various branches of the Russian military elite rumored to be behind everything from the war in Chechnya to civilian massacres in central Moscow.

An article in the Wall Street Journal was even more specific.

"Vympel was originally established to handle special tasks outside our country," its former chief, Gen. Vladimir Pronichev, told Russian media earlier this year. "Until the early 1990s, Vympel trained its specialists first in foreign languages to insure that they would not be uncovered by a wrong accent or pronunciation. They were taught the history of a specific region, its national traditions and mentality and the details of everyday life," he said, to create a "universal soldier." "[This] special-purpose group -- professionals of the highest caliber -- simply did not know the word 'impossible.'"

Grant reflected dolefully on that last point. He wondered how a Vympel agent would view his job.

The desk sergeant knocked at the door. "Ready for you in room two" he said cheerily. Nigel had helped him with some of the research and was equally impressed by the subject's pedigree. "Rambo's in room one with a straight jacket and an intercom" he added with a smirk.

Zinic stood up when Grant entered (not something he could ever remember happening before). He indicated gruffly for him to sit back down, asked the constable to close the door and instinctively confirmed the time for the recorder. It was an old and unnecessary habit since all interviews nowadays were videoed and time coded. He sat down and placed the dark red Russian passport with its gold, embossed double headed eagle on the interview table between them. It had been recovered from the hotel desk. It seemed in order and their consulate in Moscow had verified the visa inside.

"What are you doing in London Mr. Zinic?"

"I'm visiting" he replied in flawless English. "On holiday."

He saw no point in acting the clown. They had photographed his tattoo and were sure to have worked out what it meant even though no one actually working undercover would be stupid enough to print their regimental colors on their chest. It was Yeltsin's fault. After the new president had reorganized the regiments and fucked everything up, he and seventy percent of his colleagues and officers had refused reassignment and resigned their commissions. A gang of them had spent an angry drunken fortnight in Anapa on the Black Sea during the course of which (he couldn't remember exactly when) they had all had themselves tattooed. He had often thought of having it removed, but the Russian brand of nostalgia was stronger than vodka: 100% proof.

"How long have you been here?"

"Four days?"

"You are a Russian, from..." he opened the passport "Utissisy"

"Uztzisky."

"What is your profession?"

"I am a farmer: some cows, some fields, you know."

"Is this your first time in the UK?"

"Yes." It was the truth.

"Enjoying your stay?"

"Very much."

"And you've been here...?"

"I arrived on Monday."

"From?"

"Holland."

"Which flight?"

"I took the ferry."

Grant absorbed this. The route between Harwich and the Hook of Holland was a rat run. Half the cannabis in the country came in on those ferries. Security was fairly poor at both ends.

"May I ask why?"

"I'm on a tour of Europe" Zinic said with a smile and a shrug. "Germany, Holland, England and I'll return through France and possibly Spain or Italy. I haven't decided."

"Farming must be good business."

Zinic laughed agreeably. "No no. My uncle

died and left me a large forest a few years ago that I just sold. I live alone, I speak English and German and French but I never had the chance to travel before so..." He spread his large hands out in the air like an eagle about to take flight.

"Your English is remarkable."

"Thank you. I'm sure you know I was trained in a special military branch before the revolution, but they never sent us anywhere further west than Belgrade."

"According to the doctor's report, it must have been dangerous."

Zinic made a face. "Inspector, I left the army sixteen years ago. I'm a civilian now."

"With some very fresh scars."

"Farming is dangerous too."

While Grant sat back and thought about this, Zinic decided to take the initiative. "Look Inspector, I know why I'm here."

Grant raised his eyebrows.

"I was seen on the roof" he continued. "Someone reported it and when you got there you found an ex-soldier with a foreign passport."

"That's an understatement."

"I understand, but as I said, it was a long time ago. I'm a middle-aged farmer now."

"What were you doing up there?"

Zinic threw out his large hands again, this time palms up. "I was just looking at the stars, the rooftops, London. That's all, I swear it."

"It's a restricted area. You read English. You could see the signs."

"Really Inspector, is that it? Are you going to charge me for walking on the roof?"

"There was a report of a gun."

Zinic felt a wave of joy at the thought they hadn't found it after all this time. "That's ridiculous" he said. "Who told you that?"

"Did you have a gun?"

"Of course not."

Grant wasn't convinced. He had wanted to draft a few more officers to continue the search, but there just wasn't anyone free. Nonetheless, there were two men still on the spot and they would keep going for a while yet. Furthermore, MacMillan had been more than clear. 'This man's a pro' still echoed in his ears. If anyone should know, it was the ex-Marine Sergeant.

Grant pursed his lips and leaned forward again, fixing Zinic with his grey/blue eyes. He still wasn't sure exactly what he had here. "Under section 23 of the 2006 Terrorism Act we can detain you for up to twenty eight days without charge."

"Terrorist...?"

"You have the right to a lawyer."

"I don't need a lawyer."

"After we've contacted the authorities in the Russian Federation you may change your mind."

"But Inspector, you have no idea the problems that will cause."

"Problems?"

"Russia is a very bureaucratic country. Getting a Visa is very difficult. If they can create a form for it, they will. They'll want to know everything - in triplicate. Who? Where? Why? Once it starts, it never stops."

"Are you trying to influence my decision Mr. Zinic?" said Grant with more than a hint of irritation.

"Of course not."

"I don't believe your stupid story." He suddenly had the bit between his teeth. "We're going to check every inch of that estate until we find out exactly what you were up to and why? And I'm going to keep you here as long as it takes."

19.

Tyler was dreaming of a woman. She was at least eight or nine feet tall and stark naked with bright golden skin and long golden hair. She was chasing him through a wood and whenever he tried to hide behind a tree she was able to look over the top and find him as though she were even taller still. Eventually he found a rabbit hole, and against all reality he was able to crawl down into it and escape. But the woman's golden hand reached down into the hole behind him, groped around and eventually caught him by the leg. Tyler struggled against the hand, trying to kick it away, but the grip was too tight. Soon, the woman was, impossibly, down in the rabbit warren with him. She had now let him go and they were in a dark chamber of indescribable size. Tyler was aware that watching him somewhere in the chamber was his father. He wanted to find him, but it was too dark.

The golden woman was now his confidant. She whispered something in his ear but he could not hear it. He asked her again and she whispered again, but a noise of pouring water filled the chamber and he still couldn't hear. He asked her a third time and when she opened her mouth she seemed to be some kind of robot or android and emitted a shrill ringing tone. Out of nowhere, Tyler's father said *you must answer her*, but when Tyler tried, she had disappeared and all that was left was the shrill ringing that persisted until he woke up.

Tyler struggled with the lapping tide of consciousness until it dawned on him that the ringing came from his mobile phone. He snatched it up from the floor beside his bed and sunk back down into his stupor.

"Yea?"

"You don't sound so good."

"---?"

"Where are you?"

"Who's 'is?" he mumbled weakly.

The girl on the other end laughed. "After two years of staring at my tits you don't recognize my voice."

The thought of Yolanda's breasts buoyed him slowly to the surface. Yolanda was a statuesque black beauty that dominated their office and no one had the courage to ask out, or so he imagined.

"You need to get round here. Thatcher isn't

looking too happy."

"Ok" he replied, even though nothing she said had quite registered. The noise of the rushing water from the cave was still in his head, and the thought of Yolanda brought back a sensual vision of the golden woman that he was not quite ready to leave behind.

"I told him you were meeting that couple this morning for the house on Aldeny Street. OK?"

"That was yesterday" he said groggily.

"He doesn't know that. OK? I told him it was this morning, so get your story straight."

Tyler was coming round slowly, but the rushing water and the intermingled thoughts of Yolanda and the golden woman were giving him an erection and he found it hard to con-centrate.

"Hello" Yolanda called into the phone. "Earth calling Tyler: are you receiving me?"

Tyler's hand had found his uncomfortably rigid prick and in doing so he discovered he was still wearing his clothes from last night.

"Yea. I got you. Aldeny Street."

"That's where you are right now. With Mr. and Mrs. Coleman-Banks. Don't let me down Tyler. OK?"

"No."

"No what?"

"I won't let you down."

"Oh and Tyler..."

"Yea?"

"Stop playing with yourself."

Tyler snapped his hand out of his pants. The phone went dead and he closed his eyes again. A delicious wave of oblivion rose up to meet him, his hand snaked back inside his pants and he imagined was looking up between the legs of the tall golden woman; only now she was a tall black woman. Her thighs curved skyward like mahogany trunks and at the top he could make out the form of a rich dark fruit playing peek-a-boo amongst the upper foliage. He reached up and gently touched it with the tips of his fingers. His legs were tightly clasped around the trunk and as he shinned up... the phone rang again.

"Tyl..."

"Are you still playing with yourself?"

"No" he cried indignantly.

He could hear her smile in the pause before she said, "are you dressed yet?"

"Yes."

"Then get undressed and have a shower you smelly git. And hurry up!"

She hung up again and, just as she had intended, he supposed, the moment was lost. Try as he may, the fruit tasted sour now he had been discovered, and he flipped himself out of bed; or rather off the bed, since he hadn't actually been covered. He shook his head in self-disgust as he realized he was still dressed from the night before. His jacket was lying on the floor; his shirt resembled a discarded chip wrapper and smelt like one too. He squeezed his hollow eyes with his fingers and counted to ten. Little by little, the fog was rising, but the rushing sound still refused to go away. What had Yolanda said? 'Aldeny Street'. 'Colman-Something'... no, after that... 'wanker'?... 'shower!'

When he stood up, his balls ached. What had he done last night? As he stripped off his trousers he noticed a savaged pack of aspirin on the kitchen surface. He had been feverish. That much he knew for certain. Little by little the other memories returned to roost. Francis had attacked him, kneed him in the balls. That explained why they felt bruised. He remembered being stopped by the police for a flat spare tire. There was something else. Rachel? No, something else: a bag. He had found a bag that was still in his boot. That's right, he remembered now. He was going to sell it.

He was finding it difficult to concentrate because it seemed he was still half asleep. The noise of the water from his dream was still with him. No, he was wide-awake. The noise was coming from the bathroom. Tyler crossed the full-consciousness barrier with bang. He hopped out of his pants, took the two steps to the bathroom door and tugged it open. The shower was running full blast and the room was filled with steam. He lunged in and turned it off.

"Oh for Christ's sake. It's been running all night. That's going to cost a fortune. You stupid bastard. How are you going to pay for that?"

He flopped back on the bed and covered his face with his hands. His life, he decided, was one disaster after another. It was at moments like this he thought of his mother's overdose. Had she felt the same sense of injustice? Was she afraid to leave it behind even though it had become intolerable?

When does the moment come when you know it's time to just give it all up? he thought. No one will care if I disappear. Even Rachel would be better off without me.

"What' the point?" he said out loud.

He wasn't even sure there was a 'point', but there was usually a reason to keep going, and this morning it was Yolanda. He persuaded himself he had a responsibility to her since she had lied to cover for him. The least he could do was try to go with her plan even though, in his current mood, he thought he was bound to fail in this as in everything else.

He rose wearily from the bed and lifted up the mattress until it was resting against the wall. With a damp sponge from the kitchen he did his best with the dried in dirt on his jacket then neatly folded it and his trousers and laid them out on a piece of Styrofoam placed on the bed base specifically for that purpose. He carefully lowered the mattress back down and returned to the shower. The plastic cubicle that passed for a shower was so humid he could have had a sauna if he had had the time. The thought of protecting Yolanda was taking on noble proportions in his imagination and he showered and shaved with the ritual diligence of a knight.

20.

The electric lock buzzed mechanically. Zinic pulled open the front door and trotted down the stone staircase that curved down from the first floor to the pavement around one corner of the building. It was the neatest police station he had ever seen. He took in the newly pointed red brick facade, the blue police lantern and cast iron railings. It reminded him of the Sherlock Holmes and Agatha Christie books he had been assigned as part of his English culture immersion all those years ago.

The rain had stopped but the road and pavements were still silver from the night's downpour. High, dull grey clouds blanketed the sky in all directions and the low sun threw up splashes of indigo and red from somewhere behind the block of flats opposite. His polo shirt had dried in the cell overnight but it was all he had and his skin goose-pimpled in the fresh breeze dropping in from the north.

At least he was free. No explanation, no excuses and no reprimand. The detective who had threatened to keep him locked up for 'as long as it takes' wasn't even around to sign the release forms. Maybe it wasn't so mysterious. Without the gun they had no evidence. Maybe he did actually convince them he wasn't a terrorist after all.

It's a good thing I don't wear a turban, he mused.

Despite his good fortune he had an uncomfortable foreboding. This was not over. He had not finished the job he had been paid for and he had lost his rifle. There would be ramifications. He wasn't sure yet what they would be, but he had no doubt they would be serious. He needed to think. He would go back to his hotel to shower and change. His stomach gurgled loudly reminding him he had not eaten since lunch the day before. First he should get some breakfast. He thought of the return slip the desk sergeant had made him sign and the four fifty pound notes that nestled again in his back pocket. He doubted he would ever get used to English eccentricity.

A plaque on the station wall told him he was standing in Battersea Bridge Road. He brought to mind his map of London. The police station was on a crossroads and the tree-lined road stretched crossed the Thames at the eponymous bridge somewhere out of sight to his left. On the two opposing corners to his right were a squat bunker marked 'London City Mission' and the blue and white painted Union Arms. Both were closed; no salvation and no drink.

He looked at his watch. Eight o'clock. There was a steady flow of cars and busses along the road in both directions. He stretched his arms up with his palms to the sky pulling the tendons and muscles, then down like wings until his vertebrae cracked. He waggled his head from side to side, loosening his neck and upper spine. As he did so he noticed a dark blue Ford parked in the cul-de-sac directly opposite. It was the only parked car he could see. The main road and even this tiny side road were bordered with red lines indicating a no-parking zone. From where he stood it looked like a top-of-the-range affair with blue tinted windows, a high back and flat tailgate like a Kuga or possibly a Galaxy. The car was facing his way and the sunlight fell in such a way that he could see the silhouette of a man in the front seat. He knew it was a man because he could make out the shape of a flat cap. A double-decker 345 to Peckham crossed his line of site. When it had passed, the silhouette was gone.

He walked over the Victorian bridge and stopped to watch the silver blue river flow underneath. He estimated it to be over two hundred yards wide. The tide was high and the waves gently lapped against the grey granite embankments to either side. He looked up to see a red ambulance helicopter coming out of the blurred sun to the east, following the course of the river. It flew over the fairy-tale Albert Bridge, over his head and passed the tower blocks of the World's End Estate. After a minute it started to bank to the left opposite a tall sharp pointed tower on the north bank. He frowned when he realized he didn't recognize it, and then shook his head. His mental map of London was over twenty-five years old. Things change.

Once he hit the north bank he walked along the Embankment, and turned left at Albert Bridge. He marched straight up Oakley Street with its white Georgian terraces until he hit the King's Road. He dawdled to see if he could catch sight of the blue Ford from behind shrubs or reflected in car windows but there was too much traffic. Instead of continuing straight on up Church Street, the way he had come from his hotel the night before, he turned right onto the Kings Road. He stopped at a newsstand and bought the Times and the London Info, one of three Russian language newspapers on offer. He looked around for a place to eat and alighted on the wood and glass fronted 'Restaurante Picasso'. On the pavement terrace beneath its brightly striped awning, a group of hard-core smokers had collected with cold cappuccinos and grim determination.

The interior was surprising spacious. He chose a booth well inside where he could discreetly examine customers coming and going. A pretty Italian girl approached him and he ordered a large black Arabic coffee, two rounds of toast and jam followed by what looked like the largest breakfast on the menu: bacon, two eggs, baked beans, sausages, mushrooms and more toast. The coffee was excellent and he found the English brand of grilled bread strangely beguiling. While he waited for the main event, he spread the newspaper on the table and scanned through it.

The front page of Info led with yet another 'Oligarch' story. He had heard something about the forthcoming trial, but felt a sense of patriotic shame that it was front-page news. The article kicked off with a publicity still of the Olevsky twins wearing sober suits and standing in their mahogany lined Mayfair office. Older, he thought, but easily recognizable from the days when they were the youthful faces of Gorbachov's 'perestroika'.

Alexandr and Bruno were both tall with thinning hair but any similarities ended right there. Alexandr, with his broad smile, strong jaw and neatly trimmed hair was a cutout for any board of directors. There was no making that mistake with Bruno. Zinic had never met them but he could see the photo had been re-touched to hide Bruno's missing left earlobe. He was deemed to have lost it in some long forgotten rumble and given his reputation as the twin's enforcer, it was a story he encouraged. The truth was less romantic. Word was that it had been bitten off by a Georgian boy he had tried to rape. The boy, they said, was rewarded with a concrete apartment deep in the foundations of a Moscow tower block and the terrified workers could hear his screams for a week as they slowly built overhead.

The article outlined the so-called facts of their heady rise to billionaire-dom. Some of them Zinic already knew; others he knew were untrue and yet more, he knew, were unprintable. The twins had been born in the unremarkable town of Komarovo in the heart of the Sverdlovsk Oblast on the Asian side of the Urals. Their success had its origins in the money they had raised for the restoration of their local church after the fall of communism in 1989. This proved to be so lucrative that after the church was completed they found they had a surplus. They took their unexpected windfall seriously and started making short term, secured loans to local shops and businesses. It was almost philanthropic and very soon they were not only wealthy but the go-to men to solve any of the endless internecine disputes. After an ugly confrontation with the Church who claimed (with some justification) that the money and profits belonged to them, the brothers fled to Moscow where they arrived in time for the biggest property boom since the retreat of Napoleon.

Zinic read with interest how connections within the government had lead to lucrative contracts, though not how Bruno cultivated those connections by procuring young boys for the industry minister. After making their first billion, the twins fell foul of a Kremlin regime change and fled to London in 2001. Here they hooked up with an Irish entrepreneur/banker named Desmond O'Hagan. O'Hagan wrapped them into his own international portfolio and the projects piled up. In the UK alone they included a Coventry industrial center, a government housing project for inner city Glasgow, a string of golf courses, two hotel chains, shopping malls etc. etc. Along the way O'Hagan had persuaded Alexandr to allow him to manage his personal investments and other diverse interests. The mucky stuff hit the fan when O'Hagan came under investigation by the Serious Fraud Office. His investment fund had been one of the first to collapse in the financial crisis sparked off by the subprime debacle. Along with Bernie Madoff and Sir Allen Stanford the collapse of the markets had revealed dubious practices and over a billion in unsecured debt. His trial at the Old

Bailey would start Monday morning. Though this was ostensibly about investment fraud, O'Hagan had hinted at much more interesting revelations in which the Russian government was also now taking a strong interest.

Zinic looked at the picture of O'Hagan taken standing next to his beloved Derby winner Minstrel's Choice. He had thick curly black hair, a heavy scowl and a broad smile which, when acting together, threatened to squash his wafer-thin nose. He looked like a malevolent pixie. Not a face easily forgotten or mistaken - even over a distance of two thousand and nine yards.

The pretty Italian waitress returned with a loaded breakfast plate. Zinic was so involved in his thoughts and the newspaper written in his own language that he forgot where he was.

"Spasibo" he mumbled absent-mindedly as he cleared a place.

She put the plate down and said "you're Russian?"

He frowned. "Guilty as charged."

"I always ask people where they are from." She announced triumphantly. "Then I add a few words in their language and they give a tip."

Zinic smiled at her insouciant charm. He had no doubt it worked every time. He picked up his knife and fork. "What words?" he asked.

"Da."

"It's a good start."

"Spaseebo balshoye."

"Ah. Vy gavariteh par rusky?" he replied and off her blank look added "I asked if you speak Russian."

She mock-grimaced and made a slow shrug.

"So you must say 'Net. Ya ne gavariu na ruskom.' No I don't speak Russian."

"Net. That means 'no'. Ya ne gava..."

"...gavariu na ruskom."

She repeated it to herself as she weaved her way back through the tables. He idly watched her buttocks piston under her tight black dress and realized he wasn't the least bit interested. She didn't remind him of Marta and, besides, he had other more pressing thoughts.

Zinic had never met the Olevskys, but he had worked for the Tambov and Orekhovskaya crime syndicates in St Petersburg so his recommendation was not a surprise. In fact he couldn't think of anyone else better qualified than himself.

The linguistic waitress returned with another plate of toast.

"Spasibo" he said teasingly.

"Nezachto" she replied in a flash. Then with a light curtsy she added fluently "ya ne gavariu na ruskom."

Zinic nodded his sincere appreciation of her sharp wit and sharper business sense.

She must make a fortune he thought, and all

with her clothes on.

As she left the table he flicked his eyes around the room to see if anyone else had noticed their all-to-conspicuous exchange. There was a group of what looked like 'regulars' chatting animatedly at the three tables near the door. From their ages, and way they were dressed, they seemed to have nothing in common except perhaps this morning coffee. In the booth in front of him an old woman was quietly working her way through a boiled egg. The tables in the center were unoccupied except for a Sikh in a tweed jacket and distinctive turban sipping tea and otherwise wholly absorbed in a paperback. On the far side of him a group of six Italians or maybe Greeks were engaged in an intense but quiet discussion with a lot of hand gestures. Behind them, a man whose face and body was entirely hidden behind a copy of the Daily Telegraph. Turning to the booths directly behind him, Zinic took in a black couple whose sour expressions seemed a sure prelude to divorce and a white couple force-feeding toast and marmalade to their bewildered baby. No one was in the least bit interested in the scruffy man chatting up the waitress.

He returned to his breakfast and finished an exquisitely greasy sausage with a piece of buttered toast. It didn't take a genius to see that O'Hagan had been set up by one or both of the Olevsky brothers. It had been his job to make sure that he never stood trial and he had messed up. They were not going to be happy and he decided his best option was to leave the country as quickly and quietly as possible. He would take a train and ferry to Northern Ireland, get as far away from the epicenter as possible, then either lie low until he could see which way the trial was going or fly straight back home. Not home of course, they would be waiting for him there - to Marta.

Zinic caught the waitress's attention as she passed and asked for the bill. She promised to bring it and continued on to a table further in. Now that he knew what he had to do a myriad of other problems popped into his head? What happened when the police found the rifle? What should he do with the Olevsky's money? Would he have to go into hiding? Change his identity? How would he explain that to Marta?

Through all this he could hear the waitress working her charm on another customer in her lilting Italian accent.

"Da" she chirped, then in response to a some-thing unheard "net. Ya ne gavariu na ruskom."

Zinic pinned his ears back like a cat. He tried to block out the other sounds: the rumbling traffic, the Greeks arguing in hoarse whispers, the mewling baby, but heard nothing more. As he tried to recall what he had noticed about the man behind the newspaper the waitress wafted by his table, smiled at him said, "won't be a moment" then headed towards the cash desk.

He reached into his back pocket for the money and wondered how much he should tip her.

Whatever it is, he thought, she's worth every penny.

21.

"**S**o how's things with the ex then Ty?"

Tyler wasn't irritated by Thatcher's shortening of his name per se; it was more the free and easy use of it. He felt it lacked respect, as if the diminutive of his name was a diminution of his character. Though he would be the first to acknowledge he did not deserve much more consideration, the carefree contempt upset him more than he showed.

The manager's office had a floor to ceiling glass front that theoretically allowed him to survey the main foyer where the agents had their desks. In practice, however his depth of vision stopped at the sales sheets and this morning the whole agency's focus of attention was directed the other way, towards Tyler's back. The spacious office was decked out like an IKEA version of a gentlemen's club. A heavy rosewood desk squatted in the center with four matching chairs clustered around and a small meeting table to one side. Behind the desk hung a painting of what looked like a Highland landscape with deer grazing serenely in the sunset while a Highlander galloped across on a foaming horse from left to right apparently clutching a scroll in his hand. Whatever was written on the scroll would remain a mystery forever, but by the look of urgency in the horse's eye it must have been very important. The rest of the taupe-colored wall was bare except for two brass up-lighters that would not have looked out of place in a country pub. On the other two walls hung a selection of arty black and white photos of inner city buildings none of which, to the best of Tyler's knowledge, had ever been represented by the company of Morton & Brown. All the walls lacked to complete the fantasy, were a couple of sepia portraits of Messers Brown and Morton - names invented at an investor's meeting some fifteen years ago. In one corner stood a filing cabinet disguised as an antique drinks cabinet. In the other corner a real drinks cabinet disguised as a remarkably good model of the Empire State Building.

Thatcher dressed the part. He wore a sober double-breasted dark cotton suit and white shirt with a bright mauve and pastel-blue diagonally striped tie with some kind of insignia. His neatly trimmed salt and pepper hair was swept sharply back from his forehead as though he lived in a wind tunnel. Tyler sat facing the power desk in one of the red upholstered meeting chairs while Thatcher reclined in his padded leather swivel with half his attention still on his lap top giving the impression of a James Bond villain nonchalantly scanning a background check.

"We're not actually divorced" Tyler answered.

"Do you see much of each other?" Thatcher continued blandly.

"Last night actually." Tyler didn't want this conversation, but Thatcher had taken a proprietorial claim over his private life that was difficult to dismiss.

"That's good. Things any better."

"Er. Yes. You know. There's a good chance we'll get back together."

"That's good news. And your daughter, er... is she er..."

"Rachel. Yea. She's good."

"You have regular contact?"

"Oh yea. No problem now. Much better."

Thatcher seemed genuinely pleased by this fantasy news flash. Over time, Tyler had observed that he would rather accept an up-beat lie than any dull reality. It was meat and drink to him. He seemed to live his professional life buoyed up by magnificently presented half-truths and copper-bottom deceptions. People who came to him with problems and complaints were confronted with a reaction ranging from confused to resentful. They were also very quickly shown the door. It was much much better to lie with a smile and change your story later.

"So back to some real work at last then Ty."

"Yes sir!"

The slightly flippant tone seemed to penetrate Thatcher's buoyant mood and he continued almost without a break "because you know, there are people asking me why I've kept you on for so long."

Tyler's spirit snapped like a hamstring: "oh - I can imagine" he stuttered.

"Can you? You see they know - everyone knows I was at school with your father. That's nothing to be ashamed of - it was a very good school. How is your father, by the way?"

"Oh he's doing really well."

"Did I read they were planning a TV series?"

Tyler had no idea. "Yes. I think so. They're offering ludicrous amounts of money for the rights."

Thatcher brightened again. "That's good news."

"He sends you his best. I'll see him this weekend."

"Likewise. We must meet up one day. I've been saying it for years, but once you're back on track we must do it."

"I'll tell him."

Thatcher rose from his chair and Tyler followed suit.

"No. Sit down." Thatcher closed his laptop thoughtfully, took two paces toward the Empire State building then turned and settled in front of the Scottish sunset. Tyler could feel the eyes of his co-workers on his back like laser beams. They were waiting for a show and Thatcher was about to give it.

"I'm not a hard man, Ty, you know that, but I have to be firm. Firm and fair: fair to your colleagues, fair to the firm, and fair to you. It would be wrong of me to string everyone along, including you, on the strength of an old school tie."

Tyler was about to interrupt but Thatcher showed him a palm and continued.

"When you first came here, I saw a bright, bright future for you. You were sharp, intelligent and most important of all self-assured. People liked you. The clients liked you and trusted you. Trust is very important in our business; trust and integrity. That's what it's all about: inspiring confidence; confidence and trust. Everything about our business hinges on the confidence we inspire. Look around the sales floor, what do you see?"

It took a moment for Tyler to realize this was more than a rhetorical invitation. Thatcher swept his hand out and across to indicate his domain beyond the glass wall and Tyler turned round. It seemed the same as always. Most of the dozen agents were at their desks or chatting with clients with no obvious interest in what was happening on this side of the glass divide. He had never noticed before how soundproofed Thatcher's office was. The constant salesroom clamor that often gave him a headache by the end of the day was here reduced to something like the murmuring of a distant stream. It was another world: Olympian.

"Nothing about our business is left to chance. The position and shape of the desks, the colors on the walls, the cut of our suits and the smiles on our faces are all designed to create one single overwhelming impression."

He paused again and Tyler turned back round.

"Do you know what that is Ty?"

"Confidence" Tyler replied dutifully.

"Exactly. Confidence" The mandatory rote pleased Thatcher enormously and like the rider in the painting behind him he was now fully in his stride, bearing an equally mysterious yet urgent message.

"And how do we do that? How do we inspire confidence in our clients?"

He paused, allowing Tyler to finish the mantra.

"By having confidence in ourselves."

"That's right! Self-confidence is the foundation of our business. You can't buy it, you can't sell it and you can't fake it, but without it we are nothing. Our clients expect it of us. They look to us to squeeze every penny out of their properties. We are soldiers on the front line and when we go to war we fight to the death. We offer no mercy and expect no quarter. We fight to win and our clients put absolute trust in us."

"I understand."

"Do you Ty? I wonder. Over two years I've seen your slide into a pit until you're almost ready for the last rites. Now, I know you're not happy with that. I know you can't afford to live on what you earn in commission here..."

"I'm back on track. As I said..."

"I know you have child maintenance payments" he steamrolled on "and no one, no one, can say I haven't been indulgent. But there comes a time when you have to stare reality in the face."

He paused, sat back down unexpectedly, fixed Tyler in the eyes and stopped talking. It had the intended unsettling effect and Tyler found himself wondering how he was supposed to react. Were they going to continue in that position like rutting stags until one of them backed down? Should he back down and demonstrate that he had been beaten into line? Should he show some backbone and attempt to outstare him? The first option felt too feeble and the second too challenging. He could have pretended he hadn't noticed, but it was already too late for that. He was trapped, rabbit like, in the mesmerizing glare. After only a few seconds, it felt silly. Tyler was sure Thatcher would crack up, but he didn't. This was serious. His eyes began to water and he feared that if it went on much longer he may start to cry. He wondered how the mighty Yolanda would have handled such a situation. As the regular winner of the agency's highest monthly commission it would, of course, never have arisen. She was often in and out of this office for champagne celebrations, which did not, as far as Tyler was aware, end up as staring matches. Then for the second time that morning, she came to his aide. She despised Thatcher's management platitudes and her particular favorite was the one that sprung to Tyler's lips now.

"Failure is not an option" said Tyler in a steady even tone that made it seem as though the long pause was simply a way of savoring the magic phrase.

Thatcher's face broke into a broad and open smile then a profound laugh as if he had heard it for the very first time and it touched something deep within him.

"Good boy" he nodded and rocked forward. "That's the spirit. I always knew you'd bounce

back. Let's get this whole stupid episode behind us and get out there and make some real
dosh. The girls love a bit of ready and once
you start splashing it about again I've no doubt
that wife of yours will be pounding on your
door at all hours."

He stood up abruptly and this time allowed
Tyler to follow. He strode to the door and before opening it, grabbed Tyler at the top of
both arms as if he were about to kiss him and
said, "great to have you back on the team Ty.
Let's kick some arse!"

The door opened with an airlock-like
whoosh! and the change of pressure sucked
him back onto the sales floor. Before he knew
it, the rarefied atmosphere of Olympus had
given way to the everyday hubbub of his normal surroundings and, wandering back to his
desk, he knew he felt no different and next
week would prove to be as disastrous as the
last.

22.

Zinic hailed a taxi on the Kings Road and had himself deposited in the center of Hyde Park. He walked around the Serpentine Gallery and headed northwest along one of the many paths that cobwebbed the grass. If there had been anyone following him they would have had to abandon their car and follow on foot. After ten minutes he stopped to look around. The park was flat and relatively empty. It would have taken a magician to avoid being seen and Zinic was convinced he was alone. He continued on to the Bayswater Road and caught another taxi back to the New Chelsea Cloisters Hotel a mere ten minute walk from where he had breakfasted. He jogged up the three steps and straight to reception.

"I'd like to settle my bill" he said to the very young-looking man at the desk with Brilliantined hair, a tattoo on his earlobe and a badge marked Martin Coughlan.

"Room sir?"

"One two two."

Martin checked the screen. "There's a message for you sir." If he had heard about the police checking Zinic's room the night before and confiscating his passport, he gave no sign of it. He disappeared through a narrow doorway behind the desk and returned with an envelope marked with the hotel's name.

"You had a phone call. I'm afraid I didn't understand a word" he admitted with candor "but I wrote down what I thought he said and took the number from the hotel switchboard. It sounded urgent."

Zinic nodded his thanks and took the envelope.

"I left my key at the desk last night."

Martin returned to the hidden room and when he re-emerged gave him the keycard printed with the hotel's name and crest. "I'll prepare your account sir."

Zinic crossed the lobby to the open elevator and walked straight in behind a small, dumpy, elderly woman in a red track suit.

Who the hell knows where I'm staying? he thought. Only the police and they speak English.

"What floor?" the woman said in a vigorous American accent.

Zinic told her. She stabbed the buttons and the doors closed. He extracted a compliments card from the envelope and read the message written in block capitals on the back.

Then carefully reread it.

'7.34am.　　6　　Oct.　　Rose　　Defki. 007.421.893.678.'

The doors slid open with a ping. After a few moments, the woman looked across at man beside her. "This is your floor sir."

Zinic looked at her blankly.

"Are you alright?" she asked with real concern in her voice. "You don't look so good." After this failed to illicit a response she added, "should I call someone?"

Zinic heard her voice and saw her face as though looking through the wrong end of a telescope. As he regained his composure he recognized in himself the unmistakable signs of shock. His heart was pumping wildly and his breathing was shallow and rapid. His mouth felt dry and his skin was cold and clammy as the blood rushed inward to bolster the vital organs. The lift doors started to close and he shot his arm out between them. They bounced back open again and he staggered into the hall. At his door he inserted the card, slammed the door shut behind him, crawled his way along the walls, sat down heavily on the edge of the bed and read the note again. It was easy to see how the receptionist had made the mistake. Rozhdestvensky wasn't easy to spell - even for a Russian. But how could they have this number? How would they even know what country he was in? There was only one way to find out.

He reached for the phone on the bedside table and slowly started to dial the number off the message, even though he knew it by heart, hoping he would find a mistake. He didn't. The various exchanges clicked and whirred and finished in an echoing engaged tone. He tried again, making absolutely sure of the number with one stabbed digit after another. Engaged.

He walked over to the window, aimlessly drew back the net curtain and recognized the same Ford as he had seen that morning, parked directly across the road. Was it the same? On reflection he wasn't entirely sure what model he had seen earlier, let alone if this was exactly the same car. With the more oblique angle of the sun on the tinted windows it was impossible to tell if there was anyone inside. By chance another car of exactly the same make and color drove passed it. Zinic blinked deliberately and shook his head. He was getting paranoid; old, careless and paranoid. There was probably a perfectly reasonable explanation for them having his phone number. He was panicking over nothing. He picked up the phone and this time punched redial. There was the briefest of ring tones before it was anxiously snatched up.

"Hello?"

"Maksim. It's Georgiy."

"Gosha!" Marta's father choked out the familiar diminutive of his name as though it had been stuck in his throat.

"Maksim. How did you get my number?"

"Help us Gosha, help us." he wailed.

Zinic froze. "What is it?"

"She's gone."

"Maksim!" Zinic cut in loudly. "What are you talking about? Who's gone?"

The wailing howl from the speaker forced Zinic to hold it away from his ear. It faded and there was a clunk at the other end as though the receiver had been dropped. He could visualize the scene. The telephone was on a small shelf in the narrow entrance hall just opposite the door to the kitchen that was always open. There was no other furniture in the hall except for a hat rack and Zinic guessed the receiver must have knocked against the wall. He could hear heated exchanges in the distance and could guess exactly what was happening. Maksim had answered the phone because that was his role as a man and as the father of the house but Raisa would not be far behind. Maksim was a strong, honest, hardworking man. No one could best him in that. But if his routine was disrupted, or if he encountered problems of an abstract nature he crumbled. Raisa on the other hand was made of sterner stuff. If Maksim was an oak, she was the bedrock on which it stood. Zinic heard the phone taken up.

"Georgiy, its Raya" she said steadily, almost formally.

Zinic could barely hear her for the thumping of his blood in his ears. He checked a torrent of questions and simply said, "what's happened?"

"Marta has disappeared."

Zinic felt an icy hand grip his heart. "What do you mean?"

"She didn't come back after work last night."

"Marta?"

"Did you... did you check with her friends?"

"Hanna, her friend... is dead."

"What?"

"Her best friend..." Raisa stopped for a moment as she held down a sob then continued strongly "...Hannah. The police identified her this morning."

Zinic felt the icy hand tighten. "What happened?"

"She... they cut her... cut her throat and left her in a ditch."

Zinic took a deep shuddering breath. "And Marta?"

Raisa's voice was faltering but she did her best to be clear and precise. "She took the bus as usual and the driver says she got off in the same place as always. But she never came home."

"Was Hanna with her?

"No no. That was back at Ikea."

"And Marta went missing between the bus stop and the house."

"Yes."

"What do the police say?"

"Last night they said they couldn't do anything. We drove round looking for her 'til morning. They didn't take it seriously until they found Hanna."

"And now?"

"They don't know." She burst into tears and Zinic could hear Maksim's accompanying wail in the background followed by a banging of what sounded like saucepans. "What happened to her Gosha? Who would do such a thing?"

Zinic wished he wasn't able to answer that question. "Have you tried her phone?"

"There's no answer. We leave messages but she doesn't reply.

"How did you get my number?"

"It showed in the phone?"

"What did?"

"Your number. Marta bought us one of these new ones where you can see who called. You phoned when we were out looking for her."

Zinic's brain was sparking with the implications this threw up. "How did you know it was me?"

"Who else would call from another country?"

Zinic knew full well he hadn't called anyone from the hotel last night, let alone Marta's house. But someone had. Why?

"It was this number? The hotel number was in your phone?" It was a stupid question and he knew it but he was losing his sense of control.

"Of course. How else..."

"Yes I'm sorry" he covered quickly. "I'm just shocked - like you."

He now realized why Marta had never replied to his SMS. His proposal was either locked away in her phone or frozen in some data center waiting to be called in. He was trying to grasp at the possibility of tracing her phone when Raisa cut back into his thoughts.

"We need you Gosha. Maksim is falling apart. He can't take it. She's our only child and he never forgave himself for letting her first husband... you know. The police. They don't do anything for people like us. I'm not stupid, I know what goes on. There are very bad people. I hope to God... It tears me inside when I think what might be happening to her. We need your help Gosha. You have money. You can talk to the police. You know how. You have connections." She started to cry again and the words came out haltingly like the last drops squeezed from a rag already wrung dry. "Please Gosha, help Marta, we can't live without her. She's all we have. We love her so much."

Raisa fractured voice collapsed into huge wracking sobs. Tears welled in Zinic's eyes and he gnawed the inside of his lips.

"I'll try" he said. "I'll do whatever I can. I promise. You'll get her back."

But she didn't hear him. The line had been cut and replaced by a lifeless monotone.

23.

Roman's eyelids started to droop again and this time he fell asleep. His foot remained wedged against the gas pedal and the car slowly veered across the road into the oncoming lane. He awoke with a start at the sound of an angry claxon and opened his eyes to see a long distance truck coming straight towards him. It saved his life. The car was on a collision course with one of the cement pylons that had lined the road for most of the night. Before he had time to reflect on either danger, he stabbed down on the break. The truck swerved around him with a ship-sized honk and Roman rolled to a mercifully controlled halt on the grass verge at far side of the road.

He turned off the engine. His heart was pounding. He placed his palms over his face then drew them down over his furry cheeks until his eyes were pulled wide open. Even so, he couldn't shake the vision of the huge grill of the truck bearing down on him. They had been a whisper from oblivion. He looked round at Ilya still slumped on the back seat with the tiny bottle held to his chest. His injuries looked far worse in the daylight. The flesh around his left eye had swollen overnight into the size and color of a plum. Through the cake of dried blood he could just make out the pattern of deep scratches round his eyes and nose. He didn't believe the eye itself could ever recover. He had only had time for the briefest of examinations in the dim cabin light of the car before they had left, but it had looked bad. Through the blood and fluid he had thought the cornea looked concave, as if one of her nails had punctured it. Where his pupil should have been was a red and milk colored blob. More than that he couldn't tell. Ilya had been screaming so loudly he hadn't dared hang around.

They had been supposed to take the driving in turns. It hadn't worked out that way and all he had to guide him were Ilya's scrawled markings on a road map. Once he had regained the M7 he had headed north again. He had felt a certain chill driving passed the Mega mall and seeing the ditch where he knew the first girl's body lay and had been relieved not to see any police. It was almost ten by the time he had passed through Ksotvo with the Volga looming dark on his right. He carried on through the industrial eastern suburbs and hilly Upper City of Nizhny Novgorod. By eleven thirty he was crossing the decrepit Molitovsky Bridge over the Okra. He continued on through the Lower City that he knew so well and a little after midnight crossed over the double storied Volga Bridge. It seemed absurd for someone who had lived all his life in the city but he had never made the journey just a quarter of a mile north over the river. The change was immediate. The skyscrapers of the business district and the golden cupolas of the churches were replaced by low marsh and scattered peasant smallholdings.

Civilization had started again when the P-159 hit the outskirts of Nekyludovo. It had come and gone with other towns as the road continued north east. At three o'clock in the morning he reached Shakunya and decided to stop. He consulted the map again by the bright light of a garage forecourt. He had reckoned he was a little over halfway to their destination but he was dog-tired. He had parked in the entrance to a field on the far side of the town, inclined his seat back and fallen asleep immediately.

Four hours later and the blackness of the sky and forest had turned into a miserable twilight. Still yawning he had pulled back onto the main road. It was just before Orlov and the turning south that he fell asleep at the wheel and almost ended up under a truck.

He was sure the Chloral Hydrate wafting through the car was to blame. Ilya had kept it in a vice-like grip even after it had knocked him out and he had had no chance to use it on the girl. He'd had all night to curse Ilya for his stupidity. The first girl had got his blood up in more ways than one. It had made him aroused and over-confident. Instead of surprising the second as planned and getting it over and done with he had tried to play with her. God knows what he had been thinking but it hadn't worked. She had attacked him like a wildcat, her claws tearing into his flesh and searching out his eyes with deliberation. It had been all Roman could manage to pull her off and finish the job himself.

God he was tired. It was now eight thirty and in half an hour they would be late for the rendezvous. Not that he had any idea what to do once he got there now that the brains of the outfit was comatose on the backseat.

He opened the door, stretched out his stiffness, ambled round to the back of the car, put his ear to the lid of boot and listened. Nothing. Maybe she was dead. He imagined it could happen. She'd been in there all night. She could have suffocated or died of cold or just plain fright. He sincerely hoped not. Keeping her alive was very much part of the contract.

There was little traffic about but he made a cursory check then popped the lid.

Marta was bound at the wrists and ankles with silver grey duct tape, another ribbon of which was taped across her mouth. He brushed back her hair. Her eyes were closed and the left side of her face showed a black and green contusion from where he had punched her. He unconsciously rubbed his bruised knuckles as he remembered the blow that had knocked her senseless and saved Ilya's other eye. Was it normal she was so still after all this time? He placed his hand on her neck and was relived to discover it was still warm although he detected an insistent shiver. Leaning in, he could hear her breathing was labored and irregular. He reached into the outside pocket of his camouflage jacket and took out a flick knife. It sprung open and he carefully pierced a slit in the tape over her mouth between where he judged her lips to be. There was an immediate intake of breath which sucked in the frayed edges of the tape then blew them back out again as her entire body inflated gratefully, then relaxed. He waited a couple of minutes to see if there would be any further change but there wasn't. Marta's eyes stayed firmly shut and her body barely moved except for the continued trembling. He wondered if she was feverish or just cold. He put the flick knife in his trouser pocket, took off his jacket and laid it over her body. It wasn't as if he cared for her personally. He didn't. It was simply that they had very clear instructions to keep her alive. If he wanted to gain a reputation for himself and progress in his chosen career - not to mention get paid and stay alive himself - he intended to do the job properly.

Fifteen minutes down the road he pulled into a service station for gas and coffee. He filled up the car and paid by cash at the desk. There were a few cars and trucks parked near the entrance to the metal-walled restaurant so he drove round and parked on the far edge looking into the unbroken forest. The idea of a solitary black coffee went by the wayside when he entered the bar restaurant and saw the full 'Zavtrak' menu. He settled himself in a corner booth of the mock dacha interior with a view over Ilya's silver grey Daewoo. The coffee arrived in a mug the size of a sledgehammer and was accompanied by a plate-sized omelet made with morsels of potato and sausages. He reminded himself that a good Russian needs a good breakfast to support a good day's work and tucked in heartily. He didn't think an extra fifteen minutes would make much difference under the circumstances. Besides, there was the very real possibility he would fall asleep at the wheel again if he didn't get something inside him.

He was on his second coffee when a white

van pulled up next to the Daewoo. The cup stopped halfway to his mouth. Two men in work clothes alighted. One went round to the front to piss while the other lingered by the car. From where he was sitting Roman could see his attention was drawn by a noise from the boot. He watched the man cock his head, listen attentively then frown. His friend returned and they listened together. Roman could tell they were uncertain as to what they may or may not have heard. They discussed it and shrugged their shoulders. That might have been the end of it had they not decided to peek through the back window. Ilya's bloody corpse lying comatose of the back seat changed their minds. They looked around the car park and down the siding towards the forest then, after further discussion, decided to head into the cafe.

The workmen looked around suspiciously as they entered. They were both big men with dungarees, broad rounded shoulders and large hands. The older one with the greying beard and an Amco baseball cap went straight to the bar and asked if the serving girl knew who the silver Daewoo belonged to. She did. It so happened she had noticed it belonged the man sitting in the booth by the window. But when they looked round, he had gone.

"Hey, he hasn't paid" said the girl.

24.

The meeting was necessarily brief since the Commander was due in court at any second. He had been in charge of an investigation into a betting and prostitution racket organized by Turkish immigrants and this was his big day on the stand. He should have been preparing himself, but here he was pacing the corridor of Southwark Crown Court because he couldn't refuse an old school friend. The truth was Julius Kriegmann was never much of a friend even at Westminster. While the future Commander in the Met was a straight-talking, straight-dealing rugby and sport fanatic, Kriegmann was one of those curiously circumspect boys one suspected of de-winging butterflies and drilling holes in the toilet walls. Since then, however, he had become extremely wealthy and well connected. He was, for instance, a very good friend of Assistant Commissioner Anderson to whom he was directly responsible and dependent upon for his next promotion.

So it was with an air of forced conviviality that he smiled and extended his hand to the tall flabby lawyer as he passed through the security grill. Kriegmann wiped his brow with an already moist handkerchief and tucked it back in his trouser pocket. It wasn't his habit to run after anyone, but he had to catch Commander Buckhurst before he got tied up in court for the day. It was the unusual burst of energy, as much as the thought of Bruno's reprisals if he failed, that caused him to transpire.

"Thanks for seeing me Peter" he gasped. "I wouldn't bother you if it weren't important."

The Commander guided him along the corridor and their heels tapped in time on the polished oak floorboards. "As I said last night, I don't think there's much more I can do."

"My client is very anxious and... how can I put this... very influential."

Buckhurst didn't like his tone and let him know it. "I thought you only had one client nowadays Julius and his influence was limited by the prison guards" he snapped back.

"Ah. Dirty business that. Entirely political. Nothing of substance in it at all" he lied fluently. "In any event this is quite a different matter."

"Still seems pretty dirty to me. I spoke to

the duty officer first thing this morning and he gave me the full run down. Russian national, ex-special forces caught prowling on the roof - with a gun."

"A gun?"

"Allegedly."

"Allegedly?"

"Someone reported it."

"But...?"

"They didn't find it."

Kriegmann digested the first good news in weeks. "Perhaps because it doesn't exist?"

The Commander pursed his lips thoughtfully and watched a court usher make his way towards them. "This'll be for me" he announced with relief. "Is there anything else?"

"How long will they hold him?"

The Commander frowned. "You should speak to your clients more regularly Julius. He was released this morning."

"Oh..."

"That's what you wanted wasn't it?"

"Oh yes. Thank you. Thank you very much."

Buckhurst held out his hand. "Give my regards to Assistant Commissioner Anderson when you see him." Julius shook his muscular hand and the Commander turned on his heel and followed the usher.

"Oh, one last thing" said Kriegmann trotting alongside. "Do you happen to know who's the investigating officer?"

"Grant" he said after a moment's thought. "Inspector Robert Grant. But I don't see..."

"Just in case there are, you know, any loose ends. May I use your name?"

The usher held open the plain modern courtroom door and Buckhurst paused momentarily. He didn't like this way of doing business but didn't have time to get into it further.

"If you must" he said.

25.

The shower hissed forcefully into life. Zinic twisted his head this way and that allowing the scalding jets to massage the tension round his neck and shoulders. His love of very hot showers came from half a lifetime of enforced cold ones. The water liked him too and clung tightly to his stocky frame before swirling down and off his solid ankles or shooting off the end of his thick, dark penis.

He reached for the plastic wrapped soap on the side of the bath and picked at the hotel label that held it all together. The lavender scent filled him and brought a vision of Marta so clear she could have been standing before him. He discarded the wrapper and ran the slippery lozenge over his skin with its numerous scars. He had never given them any thought until Marta had discovered them. He remembered her examining them, kissing and caressing every one in turn. The image of her kneeling over him naked, counting and naming his scars came flooding back. She had declared it was good for a man to have his history written on his body. Even though he had refused to answer many of her questions she said it meant he had 'lived'.

Mystery she had said is only a truth we don't understand.

He pondered the mystery of her disappearance. How was it connected to him? Why had someone called her house from his hotel? He had an extraordinary memory for numbers. He never wrote anything down and could recall it on command. It had been a part of his training he had never had to sweat over. The ten-digit number to that telephone in the Rozhdestvensky hallway was locked firmly in his head. Yet someone else had taken the trouble to find it out and then call it from his hotel in London. A hotel, furthermore, that he had not reserved or even contacted in advance. He had chosen it by hazard from a free guidebook he had picked up at Harwich.

He concluded that someone had followed him to the hotel. Although how they found him in the first place was still a mystery. They had then called Marta's house from somewhere in the hotel. What would have happened if they had answered? Who would have spoken? What would they have said? The connection to Marta's abduction was not yet clear in his mind but he had no doubt it existed. He was also sure that he was to blame. Marta was completely ignorant of what he did for a living. But anyone determined enough to get to him, may not know that.

Half an hour ago he had felt completely helpless. The woman he loved was somewhere unknown over a continent away. Her friend had been murdered and there was no reason to suppose the same fate hadn't already befallen her. The connection to him at the hotel suggested a powerful and professional network and the police would be of no use. Tens of thousands of people disappeared in Russia every year, most of whom were never found again. Whether she was dead or alive, whether this was some kind of revenge or attack he wasn't going to wait around to find out. He had had thought through every clue and discovered an advantage. It may not be much but it was something. The anger built inside him as he thought of what he was going to do. He didn't yet know who, but someone was going to pay.

He pushed the handle of the mixer tap over to the far left and an ice-cold spray slapped the broiled flesh on his upper chest like a whip. For thirty seconds his breath came in fitful gasps. It was a full minute before he had wholly contained the initial shock. He breathed easier and turned his back to the jet receiving a second, even less welcome blast to the sympathetic ganglion nerves, literally a chill down the spine. Another thirty seconds and he arched forward allowing the freezing water to pummel the tender kidney area. By now the adrenaline had kicked in sending increased oxygen and glucose into his blood system and brain. His heart rate had notably increased as had, he assumed, the stroke volume. After four minutes the shower no longer felt cold and he recognized the familiar inner warmth spread into his muscles and bones. He turned off the shower, stepped out of the bath again and examined his pupils in the mirror. They were fully dilated.

He dried himself down with methodical diligence and returned to the bedroom. The feeling of power after an ice cold shower was always extraordinary. He had a deep seated glow of energy and the impression that his muscles were exploding under his taught skin. He felt almost superhuman. His change of clothes was already laid out on the bed but he walked straight passed them to the window.

Sloane Avenue didn't seem to be particularly busy even at the tail end of rush hour. Like so many London streets it was lined on both sides with mature plane trees. He could hear children's voices from the school on the far side to his right. From his window three stories up he could see them playing in the yard. The building directly opposite was dressed in scaffold with a delivery van double-parked outside. His eye found the parking space at the far end of the scaffolding where he had seen the Ford parked earlier. It was empty and he had a hollow feeling of disappointment. A few pedestrians walked through the tunnel of metal poles ignoring the art gallery and the estate agent inside. He watched the deliveryman slam his back doors shut and climb into his cab. He waited for a gap in the traffic then pulled away revealing a dark blue Ford Galaxy with tinted windows. Zinic withdrew from the window. The hollow feeling had disappeared.

26.

Tyler wasn't the only one in the office to have perfected the art of looking busy but he practiced it with the most conviction and skill. There was, for instance, no end to the number of times he could call an empty house. He was also particularly good at engaging passing customers in conversation on any subject under the sun so long as it had nothing to do with buying and selling houses. It has to be said, they liked him for it. His low-pressure approach meant they felt more comfortable with him than say, Piers, who cut to the chase faster than a foxhound.

Today's empty house belonged to his father. He had been trying to contact him for months on and off, but with no success. As far as he was aware, his father didn't possess a mobile phone or if he did, had never given him the number. The unhelpful person at his publishing house had refused to give out any further details such as an email address and so he was down to a single telephone line that was never answered.

"I'm off" said Yolanda as she breezed past his desk.

Tyler hung up. "Already?"

"Got a client wants to take me to... tea" she teased out the last word in cheeky aristo lilt. "See you later Crocodile."

"Oh..."

"Ty-ler" she warned in a low voice.

"My father. I said I would go to see him."

"In Yorkshire?"

"Yes."

"Tonight?"

"Maybe."

"Is that who hasn't answered your calls all day?"

"It's arranged."

"When Tyler? When did you arrange this?"

Tyler didn't answer.

"Tyler when are you going to learn? It's over. He's done his job. He isn't interested any more. You're out there. You're on your own. You have to live with it."

"It's not like that."

"Oh no."

"He needs me."

She shook her head despairingly. "Whatever. It's Friday night honey. You know what that means, right? I'll see you later. Right?"

Tyler reluctantly nodded his assent. Yolanda smiled triumphantly and flamingoed out of the door. He knew, alas, that she wasn't the least bit interested in him personally, but she liked to win and he didn't like to disappoint. He sighed audibly, picked up the phone and hit redial.

27.

"Your account sir" said Martin as Zinic walked past the reception desk. He noticed the Russian had showered and changed into a light polo shirt despite the chill but was not carrying any luggage.

"I've changed my mind." He put the room key on the desk, as was his habit when he went out. "I'd like to stay a few more days."

Martin nodded efficiently and tapped away at his computer.

"I made a call last night" Zinic continued. "I'm not sure if I connected or not. Can you check?"

Martin said he would try. The Ford was parked directly opposite the entrance and Zinic fixed it firmly in his sights through the glass doors. He was sure he could make out someone, maybe two people in the front. The back windows were too dark to see through.

"I can't see any calls at all sir."

Suddenly the Ford backed up three feet and stopped. The front wheels pivoted and it started to pull out.

When Zinic didn't respond to what he had said, Martin looked up. "No problem with the room sir. You can keep..."

But Zinic never heard how long he could keep the room. As soon as he saw the car move he knew they were onto him. He pelted forward, pulled open the glass doors and leaped over the three marble steps onto the pavement. The Ford was facing into the traffic and had been held up trying to cross the road. When the driver saw Zinic shoot through the cars parked outside the hotel he put his foot down. Zinic launched himself across the street just as the Ford sped away. A speeding BMW skidded to a halt that, were it not for the ABS, would surely have crushed him. Zinic flew on regardless and flung himself at a tinted rear window. He bounced off, and as the car picked up speed he tumbled into the empty parking space behind.

"Shit man! What you doing?" The owner of the BMW threw open his door in the middle of the road and was standing over Zinic before he had time to recover. He was a large, black man with an Armani suit and waistcoat but no shirt.

"You almost trashed my car you fucking maniac."

Zinic rose groggily to his feet. He had hit his right temple on the trailing edge of the Ford and stood for a moment with his hands braced against his bended knees waiting for the giddiness to pass.

"Good job you're still alive 'cause I'm going to bloody kill you" said the waistcoat, bouncing from one Gucci-soled foot to the other like a boxer.

Several seconds and deep breaths later Zinic stood straight, stepped out into the road and look grimly at the back of the disappearing Ford. It was already a good hundred yards away but through the traffic he could just make out the brake lights glow red up as it joined the queue at the Fulham Road intersection.

The waistcoat gripped Zinic's shoulder with a massive hand. "Hey I'm taking to you." Before he knew it, the smaller man in the polo shirt had swiveled round, grabbed his wrist in one hand and had the palm of the other pressed against his extended fingers pressing them back into his forearm. The pain was abrupt and excruciating. With a twist of his elbow, and a kick in the seat of his pants he found himself propelled head first back through the open door of his BMW where he crash landed across the front seats.

Zinic dropped his head and sprinted down the center of the road ignoring the klaxons of the cars passing on both sides. After fifteen seconds of explosive energy he was at the junction with Ixworth Place: halfway there. On the Fulham Road the lights turned green and the small line of traffic shunted forward. Zinic didn't stop. He lengthened his stride in an attempt to close the widening the gap. The Ford made it through the lights on the first attempt and surged over the intersection, heading north. The chase was already lost but Zinic continued to pound forward as though the car was only an arm's reach away. He hit the busy Fulham Road some twenty seconds after the Ford and weaved between the cars like a heat seeking missile.

Pelham Street was a narrower road and the traffic was heavier and slower. More cars but fewer pedestrians. Zinic took the pavement on the left. He could see the Ford rolling forward a hundred yards ahead. It wasn't doing any more than twenty miles an hour but still too fast for anyone but an Olympic sprinter to keep pace with, let alone catch up. Zinic carried on regardless. He sidestepped a young woman pushing a pram on the pavement by stepping into the road where he almost collided with a cyclist who swore at him in German. The long row of mid Victorian terraced houses was broken halfway up by a turning into Pelham Place. By the time he reached it the Ford had joined the queue at the South Kensington junction and had indicated to turn left. This was his last chance. Once it was out of sight, he knew he would lose it for good. He was tiring fast but now that the car was stationary the gap was mercifully closing. He had made no more than ten yards however when the lights turned green, the line of cars crawled forward and the Ford turned left into Onslow Square.

The anaerobic rush that had flooded his body for the first explosive one and a half minutes was subsiding. His muscles were now sucking in oxygen faster than his blood system could supply it. Fatigue was taking root and painful cramps would soon follow. There was still over a hundred yards to the turning. In peak condition, the fastest man in the world might cover in ten seconds, but a puffed out middle-aged man who had already run a quarter of a mile would be lucky to make it at all. As he slowed, his mind turned over the possibilities. He knew that the street he was on formed one side of a triangle with Onslow Square and he was near the apex. If he could somehow cut across he could still catch up. He doubled back to the small road he had passed a few seconds earlier. Pelham Place started promisingly but quickly turned left and dog-legged back the way he had come. He cursed and ran back out into the traffic scanning the terrace of houses for any point of access. He found it next to number 2. Where the terrace of Pelham Street met that of Pelham Place was a small gate with 'Park House' painted on the gatepost. The gate was open and led into a narrow alley. He ran in.

The alley was overhung with ivy on the walls and trees from the neighboring gardens. After twenty yards it ended in a solid iron gate eight feet high. He threw himself at it, and scrabbled up and over, snagging the front of his polo shirt on the fleur de lys spikes. On the far side was a massive house set in its own small grounds and surrounded by trees isolated from the sights and sounds of the traffic outside. Were it not for the security cameras he might have dropped into a Jane Austen novel. He sprinted across the front of the house towards the wall he had spotted on the far side. With the help of an adjacent Lime tree he scaled the wall and dropped down into a cobbled mews. It ran behind the terrace of house bordering Onslow Square and directly in front of him was an alley giving out onto the road itself.

He could hardly believe he had had made it. But had he made it in time? He sprinted along the alley and burst onto the pavement just as a 345 bus opened its doors at a bus stop and let the passengers off. The Ford, stuck behind the bus, saw him first. Caught by surprise it swerved suddenly away and cut across the oncoming traffic.

Alerted by the angry honk of a car horn,

Zinic spotted it just as it disappeared into a street directly opposite. He dodged round the back end of the bus and followed in the Ford's wake. It had entered the northern side of Onslow Square, clearly marked 'no entry'. With cars parked solidly along both sides it was only wide enough for one line of traffic and the Ford was heading the wrong way. After twenty yards it came head to head with a red MG.

By now Zinic's legs were buckling like a drunk. He couldn't see why the Ford had stopped but he didn't question his luck. He dropped his head and pounded on for what would have to be the final assault. His quadriceps and hamstrings were searing hot and the tendons at the base of his calves felt as though they were ripping loose. The sweat poured from his forehead and stung his eyes. His lungs stung with every breath and the lack of oxygen to his brain caused his vision to swim and tiny pale grey spots to twinkle in the periphery of his vision.

As he approached the rear of the car he could hear the Ford's klaxon. The driver stuck his cropped head out of the window and swore in Russian at a vehicle ahead. He turned when he felt Zinic thump against his tailgate and rapidly closed the window again. The young driver of the MG watched the spectacle in front of him with an open mouth. Zinic clawed his way round to the side of the car and grasped the handle to the back door. Locked. He swallowed dry and hard, leaned his back against the rear door and swung his right elbow against the driver's window: once, twice. Not a crack.

The MG driver was broken out of a near hypnotic trance by the Ford shunting forward into his bumper. He resisted the urge to jump out of the car and slammed it into reverse. It disappeared so suddenly that it left the driver of the Ford was unprepared. He plunged down too hard on the accelerator and Zinic felt the car lurch forward and cut out. One last last-chance. In the two seconds it took to turn the ignition, Zinic propelled himself away from the car, spun back round and aimed the crown of his head at the tinted rear window like a dying bull. Focusing every ounce of his remaining energy into the balls of feet, he pushed down hard and charged.

The window cobwebbed.

Inside the car, the two occupants of the back seat watched in stunned silence as Zinic's head burst through up to his shoulders. To this point they had been mere observers in the drama outside and now it seemed like a TV character had punched out through the screen. His left arm struggled to find a grip in the door crevice while his right punched through the remnants of the window and clasped the lapel of the man sitting closest.

The driver found first gear at last. The car

gave a roar and coursed forward. Zinic was trapped and his shoes scrapped along the road shuddering his bruised leg muscles. Everything was a chaotic blur. Already exhausted by the run, the impact with the window had pushed him to the edge of unconsciousness. He gained a fleeting, confused impression of the interior. Next to the driver was a man with a scarred face and a flat cap shouting violently in Russian and brandishing something in his hand. The person whose lapel he was anchored to was too close for him to have any impression except that he had grabbed his wrist. Beyond him, on the far side of the back seat, pressed against the door was a face he recognized immediately. Perhaps the person he had least expected to see. So improbable that even before the sharp crack on the back of his head that caused him to black out, Zinic thought he must have already been dreaming.

28.

For half an hour after Roman pulled off the motorway the roads steadily degraded. The smooth asphalt soon gave way to uneven gravel then increasingly weed-ridden dirt tracks. Signposts became rare, rarer still, and finally extinct. The map open on the seat next to him was almost useless. He stopped continually to check it, looking for any landmarks that could confirm where he was but they were few and far between. The forest around him was broken only intermittently by agricultural land and the occasional farm building. None of the roads seemed to correspond. Most of them were not marked at all, and those that were seemed to be in the wrong place. Ilya would have known them by heart of course, but he was still drifting painfully in and out of Nirvana. The girl had obviously awoken. He could hear her kicking and screeching every time he hit a bump. It was a long and anxious journey, not least because he wasn't sure if he'd ever find his way back. So when he crossed an ancient wooden bridge over an unnamed tributary to the Volga his heart soared. He was able to place it on the map within an inch of where his partner had marked his dacha.

From what little Ilya had told him, the family holiday home had been a gift to his grandfather during the time of Stalin. He had, apparently, been a stalwart of the Remlev County Communist Party and, as was common in those days, was rewarded with a farm that had been abandoned during Collectivisation. Roman knew virtually nothing of history, but as he drove carefully down what remained of the approach drive he reflected that Stalin couldn't have liked the man very much.

The place was a rotting backwater. He parked behind the traditional two-story house with whole timbers crossed at the corners. Facing it was a smaller narrower building of the same height and character, but raised up on stilts like a grain store. Further away to his right, through the birch trees he could see a long low clinker-sided building he guessed served as a woodshed and toilet. All of them were black with neglect. Various seeds had taken root on the roof over time that was now green with grass and the occasional small bush. He cut the engine, took a deep breath and blew out his cheeks. He wondered why in hell's name they had to travel all this way and hoped whatever Ilya had planned wouldn't take long. He stretched round to look at the proud owner.

"We're here."

Ilya made not the slightest response.

"Come on for fuck's sake. Wake up. What do we do now?"

From the boot, came the noise of the girl kicking at the inside again. The tap-tapping and moaning seemed to penetrate Ilya's stupefied mind and he began to stir. He hovered a hand over his face, afraid to touch it and groaned horribly. Roman got out of the car and opened the back door. Placing his hands under the injured man's shoulders he helped him to a sitting position and surveyed his battered visage. It was bad. The left half had now to the size of an orange that extended from his eyebrow to halfway down his cheek. The slit in the middle behind which his damaged eye was buried oozed a grey green puss. Though the right side of his face was barely touched it too was bruised and puffy and he had difficulty opening his right eye.

"Where's the key?" asked Roman.

Ilya grunted and pointed to a rucksack at his feet. Roman pulled it out taking care not to go anywhere near his face. In an outside pocket he found an iron key ring the size of a horseshoe on which were hung two keys of corresponding grandeur. He took the bag with him and rounded the side of the main house. The front overlooked a drop down to a peat bog and the banks of the river.

For most of the journey they had travelled through mixed forest of pine and birch but here, the silver stemmed trees in their autumn colors were omnipresent. The remnants of stumps indicated that someone, once upon a time, had tried to thin out the wooden army, but it must have been long ago. The space surrounding the building was filled with saplings and trees up to ten years old.

The door was set into an annex that projected from the side of the building. He chose a key and slipped it into the old iron lock. It turned stiffly and the door opened into a small vestibule. Directly in front of him was a staircase leading to the upper floor. To his left was a large room with a stove, cupboards and a sturdy table. Judging by the mouse droppings that carpeted the floor, they had been the only inhabitants in years. He crunched his way across the floor and deposited the bag on the dusty table. All the windows had shutters and all the shutters were closed, but the light from the door was enough to tell it was a spacious room with doors leading off on both sides. Through one of them he discovered a living room with a fire place, stove, table, chairs and even tapestries on the timber walls. Two further doors led into two ground floor bedrooms each just large enough for a slatted wooden bed frame and a small stove.

Upstairs he found a long bedroom with two more empty bed frames and, slung over a trellis hanging from the ceiling, out of the reach of rodents, the mattresses, blankets and other linen. At least they wouldn't freeze to death. He pulled opened a window to give the room an airing and was in the process of extracting the plank that secured the shutters when he heard a strange noise from outside. It sounded like something being hit. There it was again, this time accompanied by a muffled scream. He threw the plank on the floor and thumped open the shutters. The car was stationed almost directly below him and he could see Ilya standing behind it wielding a broken piece of branch. As Roman watched, he swung it heavily down on the squirming body trapped in the boot.

"Ilya!" he screamed. "Stop!"

Ilya ignored him. If anything it galvanized him. Roman sped down the stairs, out of the front door, round the building and threw his shoulder into Ilya's waist, knocking them both to the damp forest floor. The older man was incensed. He flailed at Roman's back with the improvised club but because he was frail and half blind he was soon overwhelmed.

"You fucking idiot!" Roman pinned Ilya's arms with his knees until he was subdued then shot up and returned to the car. He saw at once from the impact marks around the rim of the boot and the inside of the lid that not all of them had found their target. Marta looked up at him with terrified wide eyes and shrunk into herself as he leaned in to examine her. She was still covered in his padded combat jacket and, from what he could make out, there was nothing broken.

"Alive!" He snarled at his prostrate partner. "She's supposed to be alive, shit-for-brains. You can do what you like with her when we're done, but until then you don't touch her." Roman approached and dug the toe of his boot into Ilya's ribs. "Understand? Understand!?"

Ilya grunted his assent. It was a fair compromise. He knew he wouldn't have long to wait.

29.

Tyler hated Friday nights even more than Monday mornings. At the setting of the sun, packs of diverse office and shop workers emerged from the Clapham savannah and descended on the watering hole known as Joe's bar in the Northcott Road. Drink was the excuse, but the primal impulse was to bind, bond and stratify. After five long days of work, Friday night was dedicated to recounting the adventures and adjusting the hierarchy according to success. Success was the key. Success in the hunt placed even the most loathsome in a position of power and, above all, respect. Not to come was tantamount to ostracizing yourself from the group and resulted in a lonely, lingering death during the week. Equally, to show any sign of weakness was to invite even your own kind to turn on you with savage ferocity.

As a result, no one sat at Joe's on a Friday

night. There were tables, but no one thought to use them, or if they did, like Tyler, would never have admitted it. The banter was loud, demonstrative and always conducted standing. Colleagues who barely shook hands during the week and were safely separated by desks and 'personal space' were here crammed together and inhabitually tactile. Weekday arms and hands, normally crossed and clamped firmly in pockets, now clasped, thumped and caressed anyone within reach. With good reason: the clammy atmosphere of music, talk and laughter was so thick it was impossible to communicate in any other way. And at the watering hole, at the gathering of the tribes, Yolanda was the queen.

At five foot eleven, she towered over most of the men. Not one to play down an advantage, she routinely wore three inch heels or higher if she had an important meeting. She was always impeccably dressed and today wore a Requiem suit consisting of a pastel-mauve knee length brushed-silk skirt and matching jacket with sleeves that stopped in a white ruff just below the elbow. Her flawless deep brown ebony limbs were unadorned except for a diamond and emerald 'wedding' ring, which she freely admitted, wasn't much of defense with many of her richer clients. Her neckline plunged no lower than the uppermost curves of her medium sized breasts and with no sign of a shirt or bra, Tyler found himself wondering if she was not in fact entirely naked underneath.

He was pressed uncomfortably close to her while three of the biggest and most boisterous of the group foraged at the bar for the first round of drinks. As the highest grossing agent of the week it was Yolanda's privilege to pay for the first round and she had laughingly waved a fifty pound note in Mark Armstrong's face and asked him to bark for it - which he had done with the enthusiasm of a puppy at feeding time. Piers Faulton was now holding forth to the remaining group of seven huddled near the center of the room about how he managed to trick a young couple into paying thirty thousand pounds more for a riverside apartment when he had discovered the size of their existing mortgage. Yolanda laughed outrageously at this and Tyler felt a tinge of disappointment. He found her course and often cruel side quite at odds with his lofty fantasy of her. She was easily a match for any of the men when it came to foul language or bawdy stories and was more than their equal when it came to the inhuman job of skinning, bleeding and hanging punters out to dry.

Tyler didn't usually have much to say at these events for the simple reason that he had nothing to boast about. Ever since Janine had left him, his confidence had been on a bumpy downward slide and his sales results had come bouncing after. In all honesty, he was never that keen on the job to begin with. He had had aspirations as a journalist, had published a few articles after college and found a part-time job as a sub-editor on the South London Gazette. When Janine surprised him by getting pregnant and producing Rachel he suddenly found he had unexpected financial commitments he could not hope to meet. It was Janine who suggested being an estate agent.

"You're smart, you speak like a toff and you look as though you're rich" she had said.

With these qualifications alone he had applied to various companies until Thatcher had recognized his unusual family name - Primovelli - as someone he had been to school with. For him, this was an unqualified sign of reliability even if Tyler himself had only gone grammar. His father had no recollection of Thatcher at all but wisely summarized that he was probably impressed by the name of even a middle-ranking writer. This had proven to be the case, and Thatcher never missed an opportunity to introduce him as the son of a famous novelist as if he were a fairground attraction.

For the first six months, Tyler had enjoyed the challenge. He quickly picked up how the game was played and fell in with the various scams of overpricing and underselling. He clearly remembered his first sale, a fairly standard terrace house in Wimbledon that broke the price record for that road. He was elated and so was Janine. That night she fucked him like he was the king of the jungle and gave him an unspeakably intense orgasm the like of which he hadn't experienced before or since. Other sales followed, but they remained as mundane as the prices - and the sex. He was intelligent enough to play the game it seemed, but not tough enough to win it.

"So when can I have your desk?" Mark Armstrong jeered, shoving a cold pint of lager into his hand.

Mark was tall, blond and overweight both in physique and character. He reminded Tyler of a playground bully called Nigel Deer from his prep school. Deer was also large and had remorselessly pushed, punched and pinched the other, smaller boys. One day he shoved Tyler to the ground during a gym class and Tyler had snapped. He turned on Deer before anyone could stop him, grabbed him round the neck and dragged him to the ground with the ferocity of a young lion. Deer had cowered and turned on his stomach while Tyler sat on his back pounding the nape of his skull with his little fists until Mr. Graham had picked him off still flailing and screaming. The week of detention was worth every minute. Deer never bothered him again and for a short time after Tyler bathed in the warm admiration of his classmates. It didn't last long. It was the last time he had been in a fight and the last time he had felt such a glow of self-achievement.

"Why do you want my desk?" Tyler replied, genuinely confused. The others laughed at his presumed wit.

"Cause when I stretch out I want to put my feet up" Mark rejoined briskly. "Cheers" he added and drank off half a double vodka martini.

"What did he say Tyler?" Yolanda pressed. "Come on, spill it."

"Who? Thatcher?" he asked, pretending not to catch the point.

"No, the Pope you numbskull" spat Mark.

"Shut up fatty" said Yolanda.

There was a general "oooo"

"Frigid bitch" said Mark.

Yolanda ignored him and turned back to Tyler. "You can't keep it a secret you know."

"Nothing" said Tyler. "Not very much anyway. You know how he goes on."

"'Failure is not an option?'" she mimicked.

"No. I said that."

"Good boy! So he didn't fire you."

"Oh no."

"He should do" Mark butted in.

"Oh come on Mark, that's a bit unfair" said Piers.

"You keep out of it you fagot"

Yolanda laughed in her cruel way again.

"Mark is pissed because his new client caught him wanking over a pair of knickers in her bathroom."

This caused general laughter. Mark shrugged: "her daughter was wearing them at the time."

More laughter and the conversation spun on. Someone had found a shopping basket full soiled underwear, another had visited a repossessed house where the walls and floor where covered in blood and shit. The tales got more and more lurid and outlandish and, as the drinks flowed, the laughter grew more raucous and cruel.

At least they've stopped talking about me Tyler thought.

His mobile phone rang. He picked it out of his inside jacket pocket, looked at the screen and groaned. This was not a call he wanted to take and he let it ring.

"You out?" prodded Piers.

"It's my wife."

"That'll be for me then" Mark chipped in. "I can be round in an hour."

Tyler smiled sourly and indicated he'd have to take the call somewhere quieter. As he wandered towards the toilet Yolanda finished a story about a female client who insisted on following her up the stairs while visiting a house.

"Then I caught her looking up my skirt, the dirty bitch."

Mark could barely contain himself at the thought and snorted like a pig. "Did she buy?"

"What do you think? I slipped off my knickers and showed her the attic."

In the laughter that followed, Piers added something Tyler didn't catch and it was followed by even more laughter.

"Hurry back Mr Luvver-luvver" called Mark scornfully.

By the time he had made it to the gents, the phone had mercifully stopped ringing but he felt strangely light-headed. The four urinals were all taken so he opened one of the two cubicle doors. It was filthy. He unspun a length of toilet paper, gingerly lifted up the seat with it, threw the paper into the bowl, unzipped and let fly. While he was in full flow, his phone beeped indicating a message had been left. He was on the point of dialing his server when the cubicle door slammed into his back. Tyler was knocked forward.

"Bloody hell!" he shouted spraying his hands and trousers.

"Oh sorry mate" said the voice before backing out and trying the neighboring door.

He cast and angry glance at the adjacent cubicle wall but thought better of swearing at the man now emptying himself next door. It was his fault after all for leaving the door open.

He put his phone back and angrily pulled out half the roll of toilet paper. First he wiped his hands then dabbed at his trousers that were soaked almost to his knees. He undid his belt, let them down, dried his legs and wiped the inside of the trousers. When he pulled them back up again there was a large stain the shape of Australia right across the front. He had wet himself. Right there in the pub, with his pitiless pack of work colleagues right outside. He was about to bury his face in his hands when he realized they stunk of sour urine. So he dropped them by his side and just stood there, like a cow in a stall.

Yolanda didn't miss much. She noticed Tyler sheepishly open the toilet door, weave behind the crowd as far away from their group as possible then almost run out of the entrance.

Once outside, he crossed the short terrace and as he stepped off onto the pavement missed his footing and sat heavily on the ground.

"Have another drink!" giggled a couple of passing girls.

He felt dizzy and the road started turning as if he were drunk. A combination, he supposed, of the stuffy interior, the noise and the anxiety. A group arrived and pulled open the bar doors. The sound of cheerful chatter and music momentarily filled the street then cut out as the doors closed. Tyler grabbed a hold of the railings next to where he was sitting and pulled himself to his feet. He staggered again and the pavement shifted beneath his feet like a conveyer belt. He couldn't be that drunk, not after only three pints of lager.

"Hey Tyler, wait up."

Yolanda came striding towards him in her purposeful catwalk fashion.

"How are you feeling?" she said.

"Oh, OK I think. I'm going home. I'm tired."

"You look terrible. Let me get you a cab."

"No no. I'll walk" he said, thinking of the money.

"I don't think you'll make it to the end of the road honey."

"Oh I'm fine. Honest."

Yolanda sniffed the air. "What a stink."

She looked around with a puzzled expression then followed the smell back to Tyler.

"Is that piss?" She turned him in the light, saw Australia and loosed her unforgiving laugh.

"What did you do? Piss yourself?" Yolanda peeled with cruel pleasure. "I don't believe it Tyler. How did you do that?"

He opened his mouth to explain but decided it wasn't worth the breath. She would go straight back in and tell the others anyway. They would laugh themselves stupid and come Monday morning he would find his desk covered with helpful little presents like stain remover, nappies and a potty. The story would then be filed with all the others and rolled out remorselessly every Friday evening. His self-esteem would take another pummeling and Thatcher misplaced loyalty to Tyler's father would finally wear out.

It was the last straw.

"Bye" he said and turned his back.

The Northcott Road at this time on a Friday night was buzzing. Every alternate shop front was a bar or a restaurant; hundreds of people shuttling too and fro or spilled out onto the pavement idly drinking and chatting. No one however paid any attention to Tyler weaving from side to side until a taxi pulled up outside the Ho Hum Chinese Restaurant and Takeaway. Yolanda stuck her head out of the window.

"Come on hon. I'll give you a lift."

Tyler pinched in the corners of his mouth. He didn't want to get in the taxi with his pin-up while he smelt like a toilet mop. On the other hand what did it matter? He had already decided he wasn't going back to work. He'd never see her again.

She opened the door and Tyler climbed in. She pulled down a collapsible seat.

"You sit over there" she said and tucked herself away in the furthest corner. She roped her long naked legs around each other and opened the window.

"Where do you live?"

He told her. She leaned forward to instruct

the driver then sat back down and looked intently at her fellow traveller.

"How do you feel?"

"Stop asking me that" Tyler said irritably.

Yolanda shrugged.

"Fucking awful" he added.

"They spiked your drinks."

"They..." Tyler frowned as he absorbed this latest insult. "Oh Jesus." He closed his eyes and let his head drop back against the glass separation.

"I thought you might want to know."

Tyler looked at her uncomprehendingly. "Why would I want to know that Yolanda?" he said bitterly. "Why would I want to know that my work colleagues gang up to make fun of me like it's a playground? And you're the worst of the lot."

This seemed to stir her. Her visage flickered and she looked as if she was about to reply. Instead, she lifted her face back to the open window and allowed the fingers of air to caress and comb her hair. In her own good time she turned back and settled her languid gaze on him.

"Do you know what kind of men ask me out?" she asked.

Tyler gave a puzzled look and opened his palms. "All kinds."

"You're wrong there honey. Only one type of man ever asks me out."

"Go on then."

"Guess."

He raised his eyes to the ceiling. "Rich?"

"I wish" she chuckled.

"Tall?"

She thought about that. "Sometimes."

"Black?"

Yolanda howled with laughter. Not the evil cackle of earlier, but a deep steamy gurgle that drew Tyler in, made him smile and momentarily forget he was feeble little boy smelling of urine.

"Well are you going to tell me or what?"

"You're not trying."

"I really don't know Yolanda. Not someone like me that's for sure."

"That's the point honey. Do you know how many times Thatcher has hit on me?"

"But he's married."

Yolanda laughed again. "Don't' make it sound like a disease. Or Mark?"

"Oh yea. I can see Mark. He practically dribbles when you ask him the time of day." Then a thought struck him. "You didn't... I mean you haven't... Not with Mark."

"No honey. Not with either of them; though it's not for want of trying on their part."

Tyler felt relieved. The taxi pulled to a halt and Tyler was disappointed to discover they were parked outside his shabby apartment block. Yolanda peered through the window, clearly unimpressed.

"Someone has to live there" said Tyler.

"Shame it has to be you."

Tyler reached into his pocket for some money.

Yolanda tut-tutted with unfamiliar warmth. "Keep it for Rachel."

Tyler didn't remember the last time, if at all, they had discussed his daughter. Thatcher's 'no problems' attitude was all-pervasive at the agency and no one spoke about difficult personal issues. He mumbled his thanks and opened the door.

"Hey hon."

Tyler already had one foot on the road and froze in the doorway. "Yes?"

"Aren't you going to ask me up for coffee?"

Tyler raised his head so abruptly it hit the doorframe with an audible crack.

"Ow ow ow." He clutched the top of his skull, rubbed it briskly then turned to her with a hopeful grimace.

"Do you want to?"

He regretted it as soon as the words had passed his lips. Who did he think he was? Tyler Nobody, standing outside the cheapest apartment block in South London, smelling like a bog brush and inviting the Naomi Campbell of estate agents to share a chipped mug of Nescafé. He held up his hand before she had a chance to reply.

"I see" he said shaking his head in mournful comprehension. "I thought it was a bit strange you offering me a lift. Well you can tell them it didn't work. Or you can lie and tell them what a prat I am to hit on you. I really don't give a fuck."

He slammed the door angrily and turned round without even checking the expression on her face. The taxi pulled away and he kicked open the gate to his lousy, filthy apartment block. Once inside the stinking hallway with its piles of unwanted circulars, free newspapers and unforwarded letters he felt for the light switch. It was broken as usual and he fumbled his way forward to the steps in the vague streetlight thrown though the frosted-glass door-panel. He hauled himself up to the fifth floor, past the sounds of blaring TV sets and musical violence until he was face to face with his own sad front door. He thought of the emptiness waiting for him on the other side and it took him a moment to find the courage to enter.

He flicked on the light and the first thing he saw was the black hold-all he had brought home the night before. He had forgotten all about it and there it was waiting patiently for him next to the sofa. He took off his jacket and up-ended the bag onto the bed. Out tumbled a rolled-up leather jacket.

"Wow."

He unrolled it and some kind of thick black nylon roll tumbled out. He picked up the jacket by the lapels and held it up to the light. It was still slightly damp but looked fantastic. He slipped his arms inside the Bordeaux silk lining. It was a trifle large round the shoulders but by pushing them back and straightening his back he found it was an almost perfect fit. He went to the bathroom and examined himself in the mirror. The leather was mat black with that expensive distressed look. He zipped up the front and turned up the collar. He hardly recognized himself. Not only did he look different, he felt it. Goodbye Tyler the nerd. Hello and welcome Tyler the film star, Tyler the tough guy, Tyler the gangster. He ran some water over his hair, brushed it back and pointed to his reflection with a scowl.

"You lookin' at me?"

It was his mobile phone that answered. Its beep reminding him he had a message. He returned to the main room, dug the phone out of his work jacket and dialed his service.

"You have one new message. Message received at eight thirty five p.m."

When I was in the bar being poisoned.

It was Janine of course. She was hesitant at first.

"Hi, Tyler, it's me." She stopped abruptly and Tyler swore he could hear a man's voice in the background.

"Look I know you're not coming tomorrow, which is a shame, because I would like to have had this out with you face to face..." Another hesitation accompanied by what sounded like rustling and tapping.

"The child maintenance was refused by your bank today" she continued with renewed energy. "I waited for you to call, but you didn't - as usual. Why am I surprised? I should have seen it coming with that lame excuse about visiting your dad. It's not good enough Tyler. You're always late and you always have an excuse. This is the last time. You know that under the terms of the agreement, if you don't pay, you can't see Rachel. That's it. OK? I've already called my lawyer and she said you're not to come round. Not tonight. Not this weekend. Not ever. And Francis will be here anyway so don't try it. It's not fair on me and..."

She sounded as if she were about to burst into tears "...and it's not fair on Rachel. If you come anywhere near the house or Rachel or me in the meantime I'll file for a restraining order and that'll be the end of it."

The message ended abruptly and he turned off the phone. He sat down on the bed, too stunned to think or feel anything. His heart was as hollow as the silence that echoed through the room.

No Rachel.

No money.

No job.

No friends.

No family to speak of.

He looked down at the black roll-up that had fallen out of the jacket and idly picked at the Velcro seal.

30.

Zinic's eyes flickered open. They took in the hanging table, then closed again in disbelief. He told himself he was dreaming. The vision of a kitchen table wrapped in chains and suspended upside down like a torture victim was too surreal to be true. Yet as his mind slowly regained consciousness the hallucination taunted him and when he reopened his eyes it was still there. Still upside down.

There was a dull ache all along his spine and since his internal gyroscope refused to confirm which way up he was he examined the table, trying to figure it out for himself. Attached to one of the frail wooden legs was a corroded iron chain. It stretched away in a straight line and his eyes followed it to a butcher's hook embedded in a high, paneled ceiling. His eyes scanned across to a sculpted cornice then down to an elegant, white paneled wall. There were four of them. From the size of the ceiling he guessed he was lying in the center of a large room. A very large room. It was a fleeting impression. He closed his eyes again. He had the notion he was falling back into a deep dark hole but lost any sense of just how deep, long before he reached the bottom.

The same scenario played out several times before his body felt the need to be active. He would open his eyes, stare at the table and the ceiling then close them and drop back down the hole. Finally they stayed open. He had no idea who or where he was. The first notion that entered his head was of Marta. He had an uneasy sense of menace but couldn't remember why. He frowned and pinched his eyebrows between his thumb and first finger trying to squeeze out the pips of his memory. They wouldn't come. He brushed his hand up his forehead and over the top of his scalp and winced with pain when he touched his crown.

His hair was sticky and on retracting his hand, he found it covered in deep red clots. He had seen enough blood in his life to recognize it even in his current state but exactly how it had happened was a mystery. His mind was swimming. There was something else nagging at him. Something he had to do. It concerned Marta. Disconnected images flitted before his inner eye like paper cuttings dropping from a scrapbook. A car with tinted windows...

Marta's father crying on the phone...

He became aware he was lying flat out on a grey leather sofa. When he tried to twist his head an electric twinge shot down his back. He gritted his teeth and breathed in sharply. As the pain subsided, the snippets of memory started falling in to place. A call from Marta's parents... chasing a car... his head smashing through a window... that was the last thing he remembered. No, there was still something else: a face in the car. Someone he recognized.

Gingerly, he tried his neck again. It was stiff but workable. He turned it to his left then his right, fractions of an inch at first, then gradually further and further. It was the blow against the car window, he decided, that had caused it. He had to be careful. Any sudden movement and he might never walk again.

The increased movement allowed him to take in more of the room. Spaced around the high white walls were half a dozen large modern paintings. The one directly in front of him was in the style of a thirties Russian poster in Communist red, black and grey. At first glance it seemed to depict a typical worker looking skywards in a proud Leninist stance against a backdrop of chimneys and factory roofs. On closer inspection, however, he recognized the silhouette of the Eiffel Tower in the horizon line, then Big Ben and the (now destroyed) Twin Towers. Looking again at the heroic worker, he could see he was wearing a business suit. His hand, which was thrust upwards and would normally be brandishing some symbolic tool of the proletariat, flaunted a VISA card.

Tortured tables, twisted propaganda? *Where the hell am I?*

He tipped onto his right elbow, reached up to grip the back of the sofa with his left hand and carefully pulled himself up. He cautiously rotated his buttocks on the smooth seat and descended his feet to the parquet floor. When they made safe contact he sat back and released a heavy groan.

He was now facing a suite of three other grey sofas exactly the same as his that together formed a spacious square around the silently suffering pendant table. The effect was decidedly unsettling - and mad. A brief look round the brightly lit room however confirmed that the insanity was far from over.

He pushed down on the sofa with his hands, gently rocked forward until the weight was all on his feet then unfurled into a standing position. He could feel his vertebrae had been compacted but it seemed there was not as much damage as he might have expected. Given time and rest he would recover. He wondered how much of either he would get. Using his head, shoulders and arms he gently pulled and stretched his tendons until he had some semblance of mobility.

The room was the size of a dance hall. In daylight it would have been lit by eight tall bay windows spaced along a single wall. He walked towards them and looked outside. Stretching away into the night was an extensive landscaped gracefully illuminated by concealed lighting. There were low stone walled terraces to either side of a massive lawn with a lake and gazebo in the distance. Apart from the helipad surrounded by a circle of low lights twenty yards from the house, it looked like the grounds of an English stately home.

Looking back into the room his impression was confirmed. Though he seriously wondered if the current owners were either English or stately. As well as the CCTV cameras in every corner the room was full of bizarre objects. There must have been a dozen or more, spaced out like displays in a gallery. They weren't sculptures, so to speak, at least not in his understanding of the word. They were 'things' - like the hanging table. Right next to him, for instance, was an unhappy life-sized bull seated on its hindquarters. Unhappy, because a rope attached to a ring through its nose disappeared up its rectum and was so short that he was twisted almost into a ball. As if this wasn't torment enough, its skin was a patchwork of badly stitched scraps of leather. Zinic blinked in amazement. It looked like a refugee from

Frankenstein's zoo.

Beyond it was a waxwork of naked woman standing in a bathtub, transpierced by metal rods emanating from a showerhead. Next to that, a six-foot reptilian fetus in a giant preserving jar. It was one startling installation after another. He walked through a tunnel of transparent plastic boxes full of dismembered human body parts. On the far side he discovered two dozen black bin-liners set in pools of red paint that were fashioned to resemble Muslim women kneeling in blood... and so on and so on, each piece attempting to outdo all the others in eccentricity and bile. It reminded him of a battlefield with its innumerable agonies of death. He couldn't conceive why anyone would want to bring that sensation into their home. It took a huge color photo of a woman to remind him why he was there. She was naked from the waist down and holding an aerosol can. Presumably she had just used it, because her vagina and pubic area was sprayed in vivid red paint that trickled down inside her bare thighs. Zinic stood there incredulous. He had known many men who would have appreciated such a picture. Thankfully most of them were either dead or locked up. At the clatter of a key in a lock, he turned to see the door at the far end of the room swing open.

Not only was Bruno Olevsky taller in person than Zinic had imagined but everything else about him seemed equally disproportionate. He fixed Zinic and walked straight towards him. As he bore down the open passage between the windows and the exhibition space, Zinic had time to study his angular limbs and long loping stride and ice-blue slanted eyes. Mongol blood, Zinic decided disdainfully. An impression compounded by Bruno's guttural Russian and odd phrasing that brought to mind his obscure origins on the far side of the Urals.

"You owe me a new suit Georgiy Zinic" the tall man called out aggressively before he had half crossed the room.

Zinic looked at the left lapel on his light grey suit that was torn at the seam and flapped open like a fish mouth as he walked. So this was the man he had grabbed in the car. He wondered where the other one was. The one he had recognized - the lawyer.

Bruno stopped abruptly with a good yard away to spare as if acknowledging that the shorter man was, after all, a professional killer.

"You let me down," he pronounced.

Behind him another man wearing a flat leather cap had follow him into the room and shut the door. Even from this distance Zinic could see the distinctive web-like remains of a burn scar across half his face. He had a flashback to the man who had ridden in the front seat of the car and knocked him out.

Zinic took a deep breath, inflating and un-knotting his vertebrae then allowing them to settle back into place as he exhaled. He was still afraid that any sudden movement might paralyze him for good. Nonetheless, he reasoned, they hadn't brought him all the way to this chamber of horrors to kill him. It was just as well because he was in no state to defend himself.

Bruno sized him up. Although he was aware of his reputation, it was the first time he had seen the assassin. When he had made the first tentative enquiries for an impossible shot, Georgiy Zinic's was the only name that counted. It was backed up by a solid gold reputation. Even amongst special-forces soldiers, ex-Vympel officers were held in particular awe. Zinic had been one of the originals recruited by Evald Kozlov in 1979 and had taken part in the storming of the Darul Aman Palace in Kabul. Their skills were legendary. They were world-class athletes, masters of foreign languages, explosive experts, engineers, pilots and, of course, ruthless killers. For over ten years the Vympel were the hidden fist of the KGB both inside and outside of the Soviet Union. The revolution changed all. It was both their crowning moment and their undoing. It also provided them with an emotional legacy that set them apart from any of the other ex-Spetznaz Bruno had encountered over the years. This much he knew: in the complicated political climate of the early 90's Vympel threw in its lot with the popular candidate Boris Yeltsin. Even when, as President, Yeltsin had dissolved the Soviet Union and brought the economy to its knees Vympel stayed loyal to its oath of allegiance. Bruno clearly remembered the televised storming of the government White House that saved Yeltsin's Presidency by force. The Vympel had been instrumental in this and yet, within a year, Yeltsin had reorganized the Spetznaz forces and the once proud elite-of-the-elite was put under the control of the Ministry of Internal Affairs: the police. One hundred and ten of the one hundred and eighty serving officers resigned in disgust and the man standing before him was one of them.

Bruno had been a starving teenager at the time and Moscow had seemed like a world away. Zinic deserved all his respect and more, but Bruno was as perverse as he was sadistic. After an uncomfortably long silence he said "here's what you're going to do."

Zinic smarted at the tone of his voice. Bruno noticed his body and face tighten almost imperceptivity and made his lupine imitation of a smile.

"...if you want to see her again, that is."

Any possible reply was cut short by a loud chopping sound from outside the windows.

They both looked up into the sky as the lights of a helicopter appeared from behind a dark copse of high trees to the right and started its descent.

Bruno's face clouded over.

"Mother of fuckers" he spat and followed the helicopter with a black expression as it hovered then descended onto the landing circle in the middle of the lawn. Bruno made an uncharacteristic show of cracking his knuckles and chewing his lip, clearly uncertain what to make of this unexpected arrival. He exchanged an unfathomable look with Flatcap then after a few faltering moments turned back to Zinic.

"Stay here" he growled then charged back across the room and disappeared through the door. Flatcap closed it firmly behind him and extracted a packet of Kent cigarettes and a Zippo lighter from the pockets of his black bomber jacket. Then he lit one and settled against the doorframe.

Zinic walked to a window and watched the helicopter touch down. It had been a while since he had flown in one but he recognized it immediately as one of the Sikorsky S-76 series, probably the new S-76D. With a cruising speed of 180 miles per hour and a range of 500 miles, it could have left anywhere from Copenhagen, Zurich or Biarritz within the last three hours without refueling.

Bruno waited outside by the house until the helicopter blades stopped rotating and the steps unpeeled onto the grass. A tall blond woman in a trouser suit emerged from another part of the house's extensive Georgian facade and walked over to meet him. His brother rarely took flight attendants with him so he was the first out of the cabin. The blond woman took his briefcase and indicated Bruno's presence. Alexandr briefly glanced over at his skulking brother. His expression, if there was one, was unreadable over twenty yards of dim light. Two more men in suits emerged from helicopter and he introduced them to his personal assistant who led them back in the direction from which she had emerged. Once they were safely on their way, Alexandr headed over towards his brother but stopped when he saw a strange man staring out of one of the windows in the Long Gallery.

Bruno walked forward to meet him.

"Who the hell is that?" Alexandr snapped angrily.

Though the two twins were much of the same height and build no one would mistake them for monozygote. Alexandr was a strikingly handsome man and often compared to Charlton Heston. His thinning blond hair was swept back like his brother's but kept short, emphasizing his forceful brow and regular nose. He had the same high cheekbones but whereas Bruno's chin dropped to a dull point, Alexandr had a firm, almost overlarge, jaw and prominent masseters. His eyes were crystal blue like his brother's. Whereas Bruno brandished his violence like a mace, Alexandr's was concentrated into his lazer-like gaze. It had been the deciding factor in many an eleventh hour negotiation. He wore his habitual dark blue suit and autumn colored tie.

"That's the shooter," Bruno answered frankly.

Alexandr turned to face him. "You brought him here?" he said in disbelief.

"I didn't have a choice. He attacked my car in the middle of the road."

"What the hell are you talking about?"

Had it been anyone else Bruno would have lashed out unhesitatingly but his brother's dominance had been built up over many years. He shrugged and said "he spotted our car outside his hotel."

Alexandr absorbed this and shook his head sadly. "So the police released him then."

"I organized it" Bruno said proudly.

Alexandr looked at him in astonishment. "And suppose the police now trace him back to you?"

They can't" said Bruno defiantly. "I used Kriegmann."

Alexandr simmered. Kriegmann was not to be trusted at the best of times. "For Christ's sake Bruno. You don't have much of a job as it is. I run the business, you clean up the shit. That's the deal. Do I have to spell out what happens if O'Hagan gets into that courtroom?"

"It's not my fault OK. He fucked up."

"Have you spoken to Kriegmann?"

"He was in the car."

Alexandr rolled his eyes. "Better and better" he said bitterly. "Anything else I should know?"

Bruno pulled a sour face. "It's OK" he said. "I'll deal with it. Don't worry. Kriegmann's OK for Sunday at one."

"I want to speak to him" said Alexandr.

"He's gone home."

"Not Kriegmann. Him." Alexandr nodded in the direction of Zinic.

"Why?"

"Because it's my fucking life on the line. I want to make sure he understands what's at stake."

"I said I'll take care of it..." Bruno snapped angrily.

"You don't want me to talk to him?"

"It's not that..." stammered Bruno.

Alexandr placed a large hand on Bruno shoulder and shot him a lizard smile. "I know you think you could run things on your own Bruno but believe it, without me all you'd be running are a few whores in the Kitai-Gorod." He looked at his watch. "I have five minutes before two of Germany's most influential bankers get bored with staring at Tara's legs."

He walked towards the house and turned when Bruno didn't move. "You coming?"

"I have to make a call" he replied pulling out a phone.

Zinic watched the exchange between the twin giants carefully. Twenty years ago he could lip-read fluently, in three languages no less. He doubted he could do so now even if the light had been better. On the other hand he didn't have to be a mind reader to see the mutual animosity. Nor did he miss the acid look on Bruno's face as Alexandr left. While Alexandr made his way through the house to the Long Gallery, Zinic watched Bruno dial his phone. There was a long pause followed by a brief conversation followed by an explosion of anger. Even through the windows, Zinic could hear him swear and threaten all sorts of painful outcomes if the thing he wanted was not achieved within one minute.

Alexandr entered through the same door as Bruno. He had the same imposing presence and the sense of menace was even greater for its studied control. The difference was most noticeable in Flatcap who rectified his habitually thuggish slouch into something more attentive and wary.

Alexandr sized Zinic up immediately. He had an instinct for people that had never failed him. He called it the 'first second' theory. In the very first second he saw the assassin, he judged him to be honest, reliable and extremely dangerous. In short, not a man to be bullied.

"Do you know who I am?" he asked plainly.

Zinic noted the family trait of no-nonsense Q&A and nodded.

"Do you know why you were hired?"

"I don't need to" Zinic replied.

"You're right" he mused. "But I'll tell you anyway so there's no mistake." He turned to watch Bruno on the lawn shouting angrily into his phone. "The man you're assigned to kill is an Irish banker named O'Hagan." This much he already knew. "If he goes to trial next week I'm as good as dead." He turned back to Zinic. "Do you understand?"

"I understand. But it doesn't make any difference."

"So what happened?"

"You don't know?"

"Tell me."

"I was set up."

Alexandr's eyes narrowed. "What do you mean?"

"Someone informed the police."

This was news. Bruno had simply told him he had been caught. "Who?"

"How would I know? They gave them my exact location and told them I had a gun."

"Maybe you were careless."

"That's what I thought..." he hesitated.

"Go on..?"

"Until my girlfriend disappeared."

"Disappeared?"

"Kidnapped. Last night in Nizhny Novgorod, on her way home."

Alexandr frowned. "I don't see the connection."

"Whoever took her knew where I was staying in London. They followed me to my hotel and sent the telephone number back to her parents. It is meant to frighten me."

Alexandr turned back round to the window and rested his gaze on Bruno who seemed to have calmed down and was now looking at the screen of his phone.

"That's not so mysterious. You fucked up. This is to make sure you don't do so again."

Zinic paused, weighing his words carefully. He was treading on dangerous ground but if he wanted to see Marta again he had no choice. Alexandr's gaze was drawn back to the vacuum created by the assassin's silence. Zinic considered what he was about to say.

"There's a three hour time difference between London and Nizhny Novgorod" he said eventually. "Marta was taken while I was still in my shower. Before I even left the hotel. Whoever did it, knew I was going to fail."

Alexandr crossed his arms thoughtfully and turned back to the window. Bruno had disappeared. He turned the idea of his brother's betrayal over in his mind. Bruno was mad, certainly, but was he that mad? Alexandr ran the business like a lion and was the public face that Bruno never could be. On the other hand he could never have done it without Bruno's war machine rumbling along behind. He had a network of thugs and informers all over Russia and now Europe that owed their livelihoods directly to him even if it was Alexandr that ultimately paid the wages. Bruno couldn't hope to run the business without him. No business, no money. No money, no power.

The door swung open violently and Bruno stalked back into the room still holding his phone. Alexandr caught him suspiciously by the eye but Bruno ignored it and handed the phone to his brother.

"Trust, brother. It's all about trust." he said triumphantly.

Alexandr looked at the screen and digested what he saw. Zinic watched his pensive expression carefully but could read nothing in it. After a few moments, he nodded to Bruno then walked over to Zinic and handed him the phone.

"Is that her?" he asked.

Zinic cradled the iPhone in his hand and felt a shock like a hammer blow to the chest. He staggered with the phone over to the nearest sofa and fell into it. Buried inside the smooth lines of the ultra modern phone was a live feed to the Dark Ages. The picture was murky and obscure enough to make the blurred edges of the image blended into the black frame of the phone like a pinhole camera. In the center, Marta lay on her back, naked and spread-eagled inside a slatted wooden frame with her arms and legs tied to the corner posts with grey tape. The camera was placed at the foot of the bed distorting her proportions so that her legs and darkly thatched mons pubis were preternaturally enlarged and her upper body shrunk by the acute perspective. Even so, he could see her head rolling from side to side intermittently revealing the bluish swelling on the right side of her face. Had there been audio on the tape Zinic was sure he would have heard her moaning as her mouth opened and shut repeatedly.

Suddenly she stopped, raised her head and stared straight at the camera. Zinic swore she could see him and his heart stopped. Her face was frozen into a tragic mask of loss as if she had accepted she would die here and hoped with all her heart it would happen fast. Then she opened her mouth wide and screamed so loud that the veins and tendons on her neck stretched to breaking point. A scream so heart-felt he thought he could hear it despite the thousands of miles that separated them. It cut him to the heart. He tried to imagine where she might be; in an apartment or a house, in

Nizhny Novgorod or Moscow. She could even be in St Petersburg by now or in any of the tens of thousands of square miles of forests and backwater villages in between. Was she above ground or below? Was it hot or cold? Damp or dry? Who could tell? All he knew for certain was the terror he had seen on her face. He had never felt so helpless. This blurry image and the gossamer connection that stretched half way round the world was her only lifeline.

Bruno wasn't interested in Zinic's reaction. He focused all his attention on his brother.

"That should concentrate his mind" he sneered.

Alexandr looked back thoughtfully. Violence had been a part of their life for so long this newest horror barely scratched the surface of his conscience.

"He tells me she was taken before the police arrived." he said without inflection.

A flicker of hesitation twitched across Bruno's ugly face. "So?"

Alexandr paused then said "that's good thinking. Every business needs insurance." He looked at his watch again. "I must go. Send him back to his hotel. Give him thirty six hours to sleep and prepare himself properly." He walked over to where Zinic was still sitting on the sofa with the phone in his hands.

"Tomorrow you should relax, visit the sights of London, take in a movie. Sunday, my brother will pick you up - personally - at the Battersea heliport at one o'clock." He looked over at Bruno for any signs of dissent then continued.

"Pay your bills and pack your bags because you won't be going back. Bruno will take you to the hit himself and make sure there are no more mistakes."

"And Marta?" said Zinic without taking his eyes off her.

Alexandr looked over at his silently fuming brother.

"She'll be released of course. That's the deal."

Zinic looked up for the first time, searching for something more than a 'deal'.

"I give you my word" said Alexandr.

Zinic got to his feet and extended his right hand in a gesture of conciliation. Alexandr took it and the two men locked eyes.

"And I give you my word: if she is returned unharmed," Zinic said, "I'll let you live."

Bruno snorted like a horse but the other two ignored him. Alexandr didn't share his brother's contempt for people who worked under or with him. He too remembered the siege of the White House and the role the Vympel and this man, as a young officer, must have played in it. It had been an important step towards the devolution of the Soviet Union of which he was a whole-hearted supporter. It was his one weakness and the reason he was in this mess today. Zinic had already earned his respect though not for any reason Bruno would understand.

"I give you no such promise for your brother." Zinic kept his attention focused on Alexandr. "Now that's a deal."

Alexandr gave him a cold stare, released his grip and turned on his heel. He walked towards the door, passed a bug-eyed Bruno and said "I'll send Tara round with a car."

31.

The mobile phone on the bedside table shrieked like a bottled bee. Kriegmann sat up with a gasp. It had taken half a liter of his best scotch to wipe out the image of the assassin's head smashing through the car window and it was the first thing that returned to him now. For an hour after he had slumped into bed he had relived every nerve-wracking second of the chase through the traffic. The longest five minutes of his life. He had never seen anyone so determined.

The whisky hadn't done its job at all and he had feverishly twisted, turned and sweated until his pajamas were so sopping wet he had to toss them on the floor. He didn't have the strength to change the soaking sheets so after changing sides instead he finally dropped into a restless slumber in which he was pursued in turn by a rhino, a cannon ball and a colossal penis. It seemed he had only just fallen asleep when the phone rang.

He threw himself across the damp and rumpled sheets and hit the button on his digital alarm: one fifty.

Christ!

Half drunk and half asleep he fumbled forward until he found his phone and without thinking to check the caller ID, answered it.

"Yea" he said breathlessly.

"I want the gun." said the heavily accented voice the other end.

"Oh God" groaned Kriegmann exasperated. When is this nightmare going to end? "What gun?" he said groggily.

"The gun. You know what fucking gun! The gun."

"Bruno. It's two o'clock in the morning."

"Find it" Bruno said brusquely.

"What?"

"Find his fucking rifle."

"When the police arrested him..."

"I don't give a damn shit."

Kriegmann attempted to continue. "But they must have searched..."

"He's not a fucking magician!" Bruno bellowed. Kriegmann held the phone away from his ear. "It must be somewhere. The police must know something."

"Why?"

"What?"

"Why do you want the rifle?"

There was a shocked pause before Bruno said "Mind your own shitting business you baby-fucker. Get me the gun before Zinic does or I'll roast your shrimp sized dick in a toaster and feed it to your mother."

There was a click and burr as the line went dead.

Kriegmann lay unmoving with his eyes open. Thankfully his mother had passed away. But he knew Bruno wasn't given to metaphors and felt a prescient pain between his legs. How long would it take him to pack his bags and leave for the Bahamas? No, that wouldn't do. In his heart, he knew there was nowhere on earth Bruno wouldn't find him. The thought of being surprised in his tropical bed or pursued down the beach made him feel ill. In fact the feeling of nausea was rising fast. Bruno's call had been so furious he hadn't had time to register the shock but it was coming on fast now.

He turned suddenly and vomited on the empty side of the bed. He managed five hurried breaths then wretched again. He hadn't eaten since lunch and the substance he ejected was thin, sticky and smelled of whisky. He flopped back onto his pillow. As he attempted to resist the swell rising up in his stomach he tried to remember the name of the man in charge of the arrest. Buckhurst had given it to him. It was in the tip of his tongue.

Grant. Robert Grant.

32.

Tyler sat propped up in bed with the fully assembled rifle across his lap. The stock was gripped firmly in his left hand and with his right he worked the bolt action thoughtfully back and forth. Click-click-clunk... click- click-clunk... click- click-clunk...

It was still dark, or what passed for dark since the sodium glow of the street lamps kept his room in a luminary limbo. The rain tapped on the windowpanes and he watched the insect-like shadows it made on the walls and ceiling. Despite it being almost dawn, he was still dressed in his white shirt, black suit trousers and the newfound leather jacket. Beside him on the bed lay the mobile phone and the painted icon he had found in the inside pockets of the jacket.

The phone, a Nokia, was new: a more expensive version of his own. It had fifty hours of free calls and was seemingly unused. He had called his own mobile to check that it worked and then turned it off again. The other object was more of a mystery. He had immediately recognized the six by four inch painted wooden board as a Russian icon. It depicted the head and shoulders of a woman draped in red cloth and praying. What intrigued him however, were seven tiny swords or slim cruciform daggers balanced on her shoulders all pointing inwards to the center of her chest.

Connecting these disparate items was a puzzle he had long since abandoned. Instead he had spent the night turning over and over the situation of his life. The rifle had helped. He had found the very fact of holding a powerful gun in his hands somehow crystallized his emotions. If he was honest with himself, for instance, he had known the child maintenance payment would not pass. It was an issue he should have confronted immediately. Maybe Janine was right and he had manufactured a crisis with his father in order to avoid a showdown. He thought back to his parents and the way they avoided conflict. His mother never challenged her husband about his lack of communication and he, in turn, avoided the reality of her cancer by drinking heavily.

Avoiding confrontation was what he had been doing all his life in one way or another. It was nowhere more true than with Francis. With good reason. Francis was practically a gangster and he was physically afraid of the man. But sitting there now in the half-light with a weapon in his hands gave his thoughts and feelings an altogether grimmer edge.

He raised the gun and spotted one of the rain-shadow bugs. He traced it down with the optical sight until it reached the skirting board then fired. There was a metallic clunk as the hammer fell on the empty chamber and the bug disappeared into the gloom behind the sofa. He raised his sights again and spotted another. As it descended he attempted to keep the crosshairs within the center of the bug and maintain them there through the jolt made by the firing pin.

He had been fantasizing about killing Francis for hours. With him out of the way his life could return to normal. Janine could be wooed back and with her would come Rachel. He decided he was not the man he had been when Janine had booted him out two years ago. It was true that on the surface he had changed for the worst, but given a chance to start again he would do a better job. With his family restored to him his self-esteem would surely follow and with it his courage and reason to succeed. Francis was the key and he allowed himself the harmless fantasy of eradicating him.

He had murdered him in his car and in the street outside Janine's. He had even followed him back to his house (a place he could only imagine) and shot him in front of his family and friends whom it had then been necessary to massacre. He had shot him in the head, the heart and in the balls. He had shot him down while protecting Rachel and (this was crucial) Janine was always on the spot or found out afterwards. In his mind it had become an act of heroism for which he was rewarded. When he was deep within his thoughts, these scenarios seemed terrifyingly plausible and he would map them out with meticulous cunning. But as the dawn arrived in the form of a less grey sky and the city birds trilled out their hopeful chorus, these darker mediations faded like the night. After all, he was still the same Tyler. Only the jacket was new.

The streetlights cut off abruptly. The rain continued to drum on the windows but the shadow play was gone and the dull light that now infused the room was infinitely less interesting than the artificial one.

Was his taciturn father really the right man to turn to in his hour of need? They had barely spoken in over two years and even then only when Tyler called. Now he didn't answer the phone at all. If he drove all the way up there today, what could it possibly achieve? Money? Advice? He had a feeling he wouldn't get either. On the other hand he knew for certain that all his problems began and ended there. Maybe there would be a psychological resolution; a kind of catharsis.

"What have you got to lose?" he said out loud.

Nothing.

That was the truth. He really had nothing to lose. The realization was both liberating and energizing and he felt a sudden urge be active. He left the rifle on the bed, undressed and walked straight into the shower. He had only slept fleetingly but he felt strangely exhilarated at the thought of having nothing left to lose. It reminded him of a song, a snatch of which came to his lips as he took his shower.

"Freedom's just another word for nothin' left to loose /And nothin' aint worth nothin' but its free,"

He vigorously washed his hair and scrubbed himself from head to foot with a nailbrush. It smarted, but that felt good too. When he had finished washing, he impulsively did something he had never done before: he turned off the hot water and turned up the cold.

It was freezing.

He held his breath and stayed with it for as long as he could. His hand hovered over the tap ready to turn it off, but the longer he stayed with it the easier it became. He dropped his hand and turned around, allowing the shower to evenly freeze him front and back. Eventually he barely noticed the cold at all and reluctantly shut the water off.

"Wow!"

Now he was awake.

He toweled and shaved - something he never normally did on the weekend. He found some old hair gel out of the bottom of his cupboard, liberally massaged it in to his thick mousey hair and combed it straight back. He returned, naked, into the bed-sitting room where he checked the pockets of his crumpled work suit, rolled it up and pushed it into a plastic carrier bag that he dug out of the kitchen bin. Then he shook his duvet and pillows and remade his bed while trying to remember the last time he had made the effort.

He was feeling high. It was a heady mixture of lack of sleep, the freezing shower and the irrepressible energy of freedom. He had to keep active. He turned to the kitchen. It was a mess as always. He cleared every surface that then experienced a damp cloth for the first time in months. Mold covered plates were recovered from under his bed, washed, dried and stacked away. He emptied the putrid waste that had collected at the bottom of the bin then rinsed it thoroughly in the shower.

He banged the seat of his small sofa until a cloud of dust forced him to open the window. Still naked, he slipped out into the hallway to a communal cupboard on the landing. Among the mops and brushes he found a vacuum cleaner. It looked as though it was held together with sticky tape and string but as soon as the head touched his carpet the metal tube clattered as though he was Hoovering a beach. The creases at the back and sides of the sofa yielded so much small change, cutlery and other hard objects he had visions of a new science of Soft-Furnishings Archaeology.

He disassembled the rifle lying on the bed and carefully fitted every part back into its tailored sleeve. He rolled the ensemble up, resealed it with the Velcro and placed it in the black holdall along with the phone and the icon. He would ask his father's opinion on what he should do with it all.

Then he made the bed.

When he had finished, he returned the vacuum cleaner and rinsed off in the shower. He chose his best weekend clothes: a dark blue shirt, black Dockers and a pair of dark grey trainers and topped it all off with his new jacket. He recombed his hair and took a long look in the bathroom mirror. He didn't recognize himself. It was as if there was a stranger in the room. Nor was it just a question of how he looked. He had a strange out-of-body sensation as if he really was looking at a different person.

All that remained was to put together his things for the day. He had twenty-two pounds thirty pence in cash. Since his Visa card was maxed out he didn't even have enough for the petrol out of London, let alone to Yorkshire and back. There was nothing else for it. He opened the drawer in his bedside dresser and rummaged round in his pants and socks until he found an unopened envelope from American Express. The replacement card had arrived three months ago and he had hidden it away swearing never to use. He tore it open, tossed the sheaf of publicity papers into the bin and tucked it into his back pocket.

He picked up the holdall and opened the front door. Standing on the threshold he surveyed his tidy room with a sense of achievement and pride. And in that positive frame of mind he snatched up the plastic bag containing his suit. He would drop it off at the dry cleaner. It was another thing he couldn't afford but - to hell with it - he may as well be hung for a sheep as for a lamb.

33.

D.I.V.O.R.C.E. was not a word that had ever been uttered in the Grant household. That was, not until last night. Bob Grant blamed himself. At forty-nine years old he was stuck at Inspector and being leap-frogged by younger men with half his ability. Only last week he had been refused a transfer to the CID. It wouldn't even have been step up, merely a shuffle sideways. His head hurt from banging against a career ceiling. Commander Buckhurst's interference had been the tipping point. He had returned home in a foul mood and poured out his frustration to Nanette.

She had had some news of her own.

She had been offered a job as a co-ordination assistant (whatever that was) on a TV series. Needless to say it was one of Hammerstein's sorry shows. Grant had caught ten minutes of Ka-Ma-Yu one night and it seemed to consist of people being given ridiculous tasks and then running around like headless chickens. It was pure pap but had two redeeming features: they were all under twenty-five and all half naked. It was shot somewhere in the Indian Ocean and since Nanette complained she hadn't had a decent tan since they were married she was understandably eager to go. Grant protested that he had a job and didn't have the time to take care of Nanette's two King Charles Spaniels let alone Billy who was supposed to be studying for his A levels. As for Marion, at fifteen going on thirty she needed the kind of attention that came with a watchtower and Alsatians.

It was at this point the D word made its appearance.

For once, Grant was glad to be back at work. He sat down at his desk with a mug of hot black coffee. He stirred in the four spoons of sugar and went through his messages. There were four: one from the Rotary society confirming his attendance at a charity ball next week (he couldn't see Nanette going for that) and one from DCI Williamson reminding him to update a credit card fraud enquiry report (more paperwork) and another from an old colleague giving the name of the restaurant where they were having lunch at one o'clock. The last was from a lawyer named Kriegmann who had said he would call back. It wasn't a name he could place, but he didn't have long to wait.

Before his seat was warm and his coffee cool, the lawyer had called again.

"What does he want?" Grant drearily asked the desk sergeant.

"He's says he's been referred to you by Commander Buckhurst."

Grant almost gagged. Kriegmann was put through and though Grant wasn't particularly disposed to meet him, his interest was piqued when he discovered it concerned the Russian on the roof.

And so it was that the lugubrious lawyer greeted him at the Brasserie on the top floor of Peter Jones at twelve fifteen precisely. Grant wasn't wearing his uniform, but Kriegmann picked him out immediately and led him to table over looking Sloane Square. There was an open bottle of champagne and two glasses on the table.

"Celebrating?" said Grant taking his place and sizing up his opponent. The lawyer, he decided was a strong candidate for a heart attack. Though his expensive suite covered up most of the damage he was clearly overweight. His complexion was waxy, and his hair lank. His shirt collar was already marked with a sweat ring and he was wheezing so much Grant wondered if he would last the meeting.

Kriegmann poured a glass for Grant and said "just a little pick-me-up."

Grant left his glass resolutely on the table. "I

suppose I have you to thank for letting our bird fly the coop."

Kriegmann gave him a puzzled look before catching on. "Oh No. Not at all. That had nothing to do with me. Well in a way I suppose. Binky... Commander Buckhurst" he corrected himself deliberately "took it on himself. From what I hear you had nothing to charge him on."

Grant sat back with his arms crossed. "Then what are we doing here?"

This brought a wry and appreciative smile to Kriegmann's face. He finished his glass and said "touché Chief Inspector."

Grant was sure he knew he was only an Inspector, but didn't rise to the bait. "What is it you want exactly Mr. Kriegmann? Are you representing this Russian?"

"No... not as such."

"Look, I'm not having a good day OK? And this affair is not making it any easier. Why don't you spit it out and we can both be on our way."

"It's delicate" he said, pouring himself another glass.

"...which is why you felt it necessary to call on Commander Buckhurst."

Kriegmann wagged his head. "In a way."

"Then let me be as clear as day. Georgiy Zinic was found on the roof of a high rise in the York Road Estate after we received an anonymous tip-off of a man wielding a gun. When the

Armed Response Unit arrived they found Zinic but no gun. End of story."

"But you kept him overnight."

"The man's a professional killer" Grant snapped angrily. "Ex-special services for Christ's sake. God knows what he was up to on the roof but I had every right to hold him until we found out the truth."

"And did you?" Kriegmann asked coolly.

Grant had allowed his temper to get the better of him again. He sat back. "The Commander effectively closed the file when he ordered his release. We're understaffed as it is. I don't see the point in solving cases that aren't even open."

Kriegmann took all this in with a silent nod of his head. "And the gun?"

"What gun? I told you it was never found."

"So you're convinced he had one."

Grant opened his mouth to answer then snapped it shut. Was he that transparent?

"What if it came to light?" Kriegmann continued.

What if it came to light? Grant mulled that over. It would be one in the eye for Buckhurst that's for sure. He would have uncovered a serious threat to public safety and even if this Zinic fellow was long since gone it would be a handsome feather in his cap - possibly even a pip on his shoulder. On the other hand, the case was very definitely closed. "If you know where it is" said firmly "you have a duty to tell me."

Kriegmann held up the palm of his hand. "No no. I don't, but my client would like to know."

"And who is your client exactly?"

He hesitated fractionally before saying "Desmond O'Hagan."

Grant blinked slowly. "O'Hagan?"

Kriegmann reached into his top pocket and pulled out a business card to emphasis his credentials. "I have a private practice in Portland Place. O'Hagan is my only client."

Grant knew no more about O'Hagan than he read in the newspapers but that was quite a substantial amount and none of it flattering. Lowly inspectors didn't get to tackle that kind of crime.

"Isn't he in prison?"

"In custody" Kriegmann corrected, "pending trial."

Grant nodded his head. All of a sudden this conversation had moved up into an entirely different dimension. Big money and important people equaled high profile cases and promotion. He unconsciously toyed with his champagne glass.

Kriegmann knew he had taken the bait and bided his time. "Cheers" he said lifting his glass.

"So why is your client so interested in this?" the policeman asked eventually, unable to restrain himself any longer.

Kriegmann placed his glass on the table and stared at it for a moment as if considering how much he should say. "This must be off the record." He raised his eyes but Grant remained non-committal. "My client is a victim of a political purge. I won't tell you that he is whiter than white, but he's not as black as he's painted either." Kriegmann had lowered his voice almost to a whisper obliging Grant to lean forward. "In his capacity as chairman of an investment bank my client had dealings with several Russian businessmen who for one reason or another fell foul of their own government. You know how it is" he confided, "one moment you're in favor the next you're out. No reason given."

Grant nodded gravely perhaps thinking more of his wife than machinations with the Kremlin.

"But along the way, without going into details, he accumulated details on these businessmen that they would rather were not aired in an open court. And yet..." Kriegmann placed his two hands on the table top and splayed his pudgy fingers "to defend himself against the charges, they must be aired."

Kriegmann sat back again and allowed the insinuations to circulate in silence. It was far better if Grant pieced the puzzle together himself.

"And so O'Hagan..." he stopped and then

started again. "Where is he being held?"

"Wandsworth Prison."

Now Grant sat back. The fog was clearing.

"You think this Zinic was there to..." he leaned forward again "assassinate your client."

Kriegmann raised his eyebrows and pulled a face of positive possibility.

"But it must be..." he stopped to calculate the distance "...over a quarter of a mile between the estate and the prison.

"Is that a long way?" asked Kriegmann genuinely intrigued. He had no idea how far someone could shoot and was poor at calculating distances and spaces in general.

"Our sharpshooters do one thousand yards, top. It's twice as far."

"Apparently this Zinic has a reputation."

"You know of him?"

"Not personally you understand and there's nothing you could prove."

That was true. Grant had viewed the negative results from Interpol with dismay. "Unless you had the gun" Grant added with a piratical smirk.

"Exactly."

"But what can I do? You said yourself there's nothing on him. Even if he's still in the country, which I doubt, I couldn't reopen the case without pissing off your friend the Commander which wouldn't exactly be a good move, career-wise."

"I wouldn't say 'friend'. We were at school together. No more" Kriegmann said with a sour expression. "He thought he was doing me a favor because of my friendship with Liam Anderson."

"Assistant Commissioner Anderson?" said Grant unguardedly. This was getting better and better.

Kriegmann nodded.

"As I say," Grant continued with a note of resignation, "my hands are tied."

"But you had your suspicions. If the case had stayed open you would have found the gun."

"We had a small lead. Nothing substantial. Probably nothing at all."

"Needless to say, any line of enquiry that could lead to my client's life being saved would be extremely appreciated."

Grant pondered the significance of that phrase. 'Appreciation' from billionaire - even one in jail - could be very handy in dealing with Nanette's holiday requirements. Not to mention the direct line to the Assistant Commissioner's office.

"There was a car" he said. "When Zinic was arrested, the head of the ARU suspected he may have thrown the rifle off the roof. He's very sharp and had men searching the grounds within minutes. One of them stopped a car with a young man in it. He was very nervous."

"Did they search the car?"

Grant nodded. "Nothing."

"Except?" Kriegmann said. His heart was pounding so loud he was sure the policeman could hear it.

"There was a bag in the boot. Not long enough to take a rifle. At least, not unless it was broken down. As I say, it's probably nothing."

"Did they get the number plate?"

"Better than that, he checked his license."

"So you have his name?"

Grant smiled. So that was the crux of the matter. The name. It was an unusual name. Easy to remember. He thought of his lunch appointment. He was late but it could wait. He looked into Kriegmann's face and his small off-colored eyes that reminded him of a smoked mackerel. He wasn't a man to be trusted, of that Grant was sure. Had the lawyer offered him a bribe? Fiscal 'appreciation' to the police would be a modus operandi for a man like O'Hagan. He could do with being 'appreciated'. And quite apart from the money, that career ceiling was suddenly feeling a lot more fragile.

Grant leaned forward and cupped the champagne glass between his two hands. "What exactly do you mean by 'appreciated'?" he said at last.

34.

Z inic picked up the receiver. He was not looking forward to the call but it was the least he could do. They would be sitting down to lunch at this time. Slowly, painfully he dialed the numbers. He'd been awake for hours but had put it off as long as he could. The truth was he was still a little dazed. Eight hours of sleep had helped as had the Paracetamol and a hot shower but nothing could salve his stricken conscience.

The phone was snatched up almost immediately.

"Hello?"

It was Raisa. She sounded less panicked than yesterday.

"It's Georgiy" said Zinic unconsciously rubbing the raw patch on the top of his skull.

He could hear Maksim call out behind her, asking who it was.

"Georgiy!" she repeated. "It's Gosha" she

cried out to her husband. "Oh Gosha."

"Tell him the news" the older man cried out.

"I will. I'm telling him."

"What news?" said Zinic almost believing for a moment that by some miracle Marta was not stretched out naked on a wooden bench and had been found safe and sound.

"They've seen her!" Raisa screamed with joy.

"What?"

"In a car. Not seen her. They heard her."

Zinic's chest was suddenly thumping. "I don't understand."

"Let me tell him woman" said Maksim advancing on the phone. "He'll never understand a thing with you crying like that."

Maksim took the phone from his wife who, now that she had some good news had dropped all pretense of Stoicism and Zinic could hear her wailing as she receded into the kitchen.

"Maksim. What's going on? Who found her?"

"The police. Hanna's sister is married to a policeman in Prioksky."

"Hanna?"

"The girl that was killed." Maksim silently crossed himself.

"So they're helping."

"It's a manhunt. You can't believe it. God help the bastards when they catch up with them."

"So they know where she is?"

"Not yet. It's hundreds of miles from here, I

don't even remember the name, but someone reported a car. There was an injured man on the back seat and someone in the boot."

"How do they know it was her?"

"The car. Don't you see? They have cameras in the garage in case people drive off without paying. They have the number plate of the car."

"I still don't see..."

"It's the same. The same as in the Mega car park. They have cameras everywhere!" he announced with a jubilant whoop.

Zinic didn't feel quite so confident. Just because they spotted a car, even if it was the right car, didn't mean they had the killers. It was an unexpected bonus to have the police on their side, but Russia was a very very big place and they could be anywhere.

"And the car. What do they know about the car?" he asked assuming it was stolen.

"They traced the owner. His name is Ilya Gregorvitch. They're looking for him."

"What makes them think it's him?"

"They're sure of it." Maksim declaimed with absolute assurance. "They found a knife he dropped on the path where Marta was taken. They're convinced they'll find it's got his fingerprints."

That sounded just like the Russian police, Zinic thought.

"Besides he's not at home and he is a criminal."

Zinic was not very convinced but at least the trail wasn't completely cold.

"That's good news" he said. The feeling of guilt was starting to catch up with him. What would they say if they knew he was the one responsible for all this? "How is Raisa holding up?"

"Oh you know Raya. She hides her feelings."

It didn't sound as if she were hiding them at that moment since Zinic could hear her crying and calling out to her husband to get off the phone in case the police called. Zinic wondered about the way the balance of authority seemed to shift back and forth between them.

"Give her my love" Zinic said. "I'm praying for you all. Especially Marta of course."

"Thank you Gosha. Thank you" said the old man wearily. "When are you coming back?"

"Soon. As soon as I can. I promise."

Maksim put the phone down without saying goodbye, as was his habit, as if he were simply turning his back. Zinic held the receiver in his hand, listening to the blank tone. He had a feeling he wouldn't be returning any time soon. He had seen the truth and it wasn't pretty. Marta's life depended on him alone right now. It depended on him shooting a man he didn't know with a gun he didn't have.

35.

He had decided to think positively. Assuming the trip would go well, his first stop was the dry cleaners. They assured him his suit would be spic and span for eight o'clock Monday morning. The price for a single day turn-around (they were closed Sunday) was a bit of a knock so early in the day but he decided he had no choice.

By ten o'clock Tyler was sitting behind the wheel of his Fiat listening to Capital Gold and heading west on the South Circular. He bypassed a Texaco station and drove into a Tesco he knew. The second knock came when he saw how much a full tank cost. He rarely filled his tank up and the price seemed to have doubled since the last time. He started to count how much the day had cost him so far. Almost a hundred pounds and he'd only gone five miles. At this rate he'd have to strike oil in his father's garden.

As he approached the pay cabin he caught his reflection in the glass. With his swept-back hair and new jacket he decided he was looking pretty cool. He liked the new Tyler. Once this weekend was over he'd try it out on Janine. She was sure to be impressed. He walked up to the cash desk and snapped down his brand new Amex with carefree assurance.

The fat Indian woman behind the counter asked him to wait a moment while she changed a roll of paper. As she did this, his attention was caught by a book wall to his left where he had unconsciously registered his father's name. He walked over and located it on the spine of a book. 'Mansion of Stone' by Marc Primovelli wasn't a title he recognized and when he pulled it out he discovered it was brand new. The front cover showed a grim photo of a five bar gate looking onto an open moor with a small stone croft in the distance. He turned it over and looked at the back. It was another in the DCI Sandler (retired) series: the 'much loved, hill-walking, ex-detective and his faithful Labrador Lolly...' it said. At the bottom was a photo of the author wearing a bulky white polo neck sweater and seated on a stile with Merry, his own Labrador (for many years Tyler's only friend). The caption underneath said Primovelli had written over twenty novels and lived with his dog in the Yorkshire Dales. A casual observer would have formed the impression of a rugged, pet-loving out-doors type perfectly in keeping with his 'much loved' breadwinner.

It's not the man I know he mused. They may as well have used a picture of George Clooney.

"Sir" called the woman behind the counter. "Your card."

"Excuse me," he said slipping back in front of a pretty young brunette who had just entered. She pushed up her obsolete sunglasses and they exchanged a warm smile.

The cashier pushed the card across the counter towards him. "It isn't signed" she said.

Tyler's bubble burst with astonishing speed. His mouth dropped open and he mumbled "but I don't have another card on me. And I don't have any cash." It looked as though his journey was over before it began. He would have to abandon his car and walk back home. The embarrassment was making him hot, and sweat started to form on his forehead.

"You just have to sign it," she said.

It took him a second to process the information. "Oh, right. Then it'll be OK?"

"Honestly it doesn't make any difference to me but in case you lose it or anything - you know - it should be signed. D'you want that as well?"

She pointed to the book in his hand.

"Oh" he said uncertainly. He wasn't even aware he was still holding it. He didn't really want to buy it and was sure his father would have a copy and said, "It's my dad."

"What?"

That wasn't what he had meant to say at all, and now he had to explain. The presence of the girl six inches behind him was bringing a hot flush to his face. "It's my dad. That's all." He showed her the name on the book. "Primovelli. Like on my card. See."

She looked at the card with an indulgent air and said, "so do you want it?"

"OK. Yes."

She lazered the bar code, swiped his card through the machine and handed him a pen.

"Thanks" he said gathering up his things. He smiled again at the girl as he passed but this time she moved swiftly forward and avoided his eyes.

When he crossed the river at Vauxhall Bridge it was still only half past ten. He headed north and joined the A302, one of the main arteries out of London, near Westminster Cathedral. From the street level he could just make out the top of the red and white striped brick tower rising above the concrete office blocks like a chimneystack. Immediately beyond drab Victoria was the plush Georgian quarter of Belgravia. The road skirted round Buckingham Palace Gardens and Hyde Park before plunging into the endless conurbation of St. John's Wood, Maida Vale, Cricklewood and on and on. It was rare that he drove through this side of London. The traffic was depressingly slow. Everyone seemed to be out shopping and there were lights every two hundred yards. He reckoned he was doing an average of fifteen miles an hour. The uniform terraces that lined the road on both sides, divided off into innumerable tributaries like a giant laboratory maze.

No wonder it's called a rat race he thought.

By the time he reached the North Circular and, with a sigh of relief, joined the M1 it was already five to twelve. Fifteen minutes later and the last of the concrete tentacles dwindled into green fields and tidy woods. He cross the M25 at Leavesden and finally felt free; as though he had escaped the clutches of a giant spider.

The motorway wound on through the open countryside. Everywhere, rolls of hay dotted the fields and, due to the unusually wet late summer, a new green carpet was showing through with the occasional crop of wild flowers. He observed and named ox-eye daisies, purple vetch and even a few brave buttercups huddled against stone walls or in the field corners.

After twenty minutes the suburban outskirts of Luton briefly engulfed him then fell away again. Somewhere past Northampton the rain started in sheets and Tyler noticed he was hungry. The sign to the Watford Gap Services Station appeared out of the gloom but he had eaten there once before and had sworn never to do so again. That had been just shy of two years ago on the way back from his mother's funeral (not the best time to become a food critic). An inglorious end to a ghastly day.

She had insisted on being buried in Ilkley cemetery near to a beloved brother who had died suddenly from a brain hemorrhage in his teens. Tyler remembered being perversely disappointed by the beautiful setting. The cemetery was an immaculate rectangular lawn in a crook of the River Wharfe dotted with ancient trees and rows of headstones. To her exact wishes her grave faced North. The town of Ilkley, where she had been born and raised was behind her and she had a view across the river up over Middleton Woods and onto the moors that she had loved so much. In fact, had she been able to turn her head she would have seen them rise up along the length of Wharfedale on both sides. She had likened them to the wings of a protecting angel. She had begged her husband to bring her back when she was first diagnosed and it was true that even though she grew increasingly ill after the move she was, in a sense, happy. Or if not exactly happy, then content to die in the place she called home. It's a good place to die she had often told her weeping son. He had never found it comforting.

He was so deep in his thoughts that he didn't notice the Leicester Forest East Services until he was under the built up walkway. In any event, the memory of his mother's suffering had stolen his appetite. Furthermore, every mile brought him closer to his father and that thought filled the empty space with an unwelcome anxiety. If he added it up, the time they had spent in conversation of any kind since that perfect spring day round the grave probably amounted to no more than fifteen minutes, and most of that was on the phone. He could divide that by three if he subtracted the awkward silences. The amount of time his father had spent with his mouth open could be measured in seconds.

The motorway snaked on through the Midland towns with their evocative medieval names: Nottingham, South Normanton, Clay Cross. When he passed a signpost for the village of Wales it led him quite naturally to think of his own upbringing in Cardiff and his father's origins. Though his father shared many of the Welsh characteristics, volubility was not one of them. Tyler's own schooldays had been unremarkable. His father was the son of an Italian sailor who had settled in Tiger Bay after the war; a time when attitudes were almost certainly harsher. Whatever had happened back then had clearly marked him because when Marc Primovelli wasn't drunk he was angry and selfish. Just why that was, Tyler had never got close enough to find out. His father communicated with the world through his books and that seemed to be enough for him.

So why exactly was he going to see him? It seemed to be such a hopeless quest and so unlikely to be a success that it was hardly worth the effort. "I've no choice" he said out loud. "What else can I do? It's not as if he'll turn me away. I'm his flesh and blood. That counts for something doesn't it?"

The answer was a sharp toot on a horn from a lorry closing fast in his rear-view. Tyler's first thought was that the driver was mad. Then he noticed everyone else overtaking him and his speedometer clocking little more than forty. He pressed down hard and decided not to think about if for the rest of the journey.

He exchanged the M1 for the M621 south of Leeds and circled North before taking the A660 to Otley, Burley-in-Warfdale and Ilkley. Free from the grimy suburbs the road weaved through lowland dales lined with dry stone walls and studded with sheep, cattle and yet more sheep. At the junction with the A65 he turned left towards the village of Burley and followed the signposts to the rail station. As a student he had travelled up by train as often as he could afford during his mother's illness and the house was only a fifteen-minute walk away. Since her death, he had driven up only once: for the funeral. He would know his way from the station.

By foot he would have hiked to Garth House across the fields that surrounded it on all sides. Today he took the long driveway past the cracked and moss-covered tennis court that had come with the house. When they had first arrived, the eastern side had been visible from the main road but over the years the untended trees had grown back their wild form and now it didn't come into view until you were practically upon it.

For all the pain he had endured here, this drab and lonely millstone farmhouse was still 'home'. The sight provoked an emotional heave of the chest and feeling of return. It was here that he had turned the page from child to teenager. It was down this driveway that he had biked to school each morning come snow or rain. It was through the back door that he had stolen out at night to meet Jeremy, Dickie and Big Mog in the village center. It was behind a stone wall he could see from his bedroom window that Anne Wrightsmith from the class below had touched his penis with her mouth one Sunday afternoon and made him come. All those first forays into adult life were launched from here and he was convinced it would also hold the secrets of their failure.

He knew the house and grounds so well that he could tell almost immediately something was wrong. He stopped the car on the gravel forecourt, turned off the engine and listened. The sound he craned to hear and the one he feared most was his father's voice: 'What the hell are you doing here?' 'Why didn't you phone first?' 'Don't you know I'm busy?' All he heard however was the rain drumming on the metal roof.

God knows what car his father drove now but it wasn't parked outside. That in itself didn't mean much. He had taken to parking in the converted barn after researching acid rain for 'Blasted Heath', the second Sandler book. Tyler opened the door, stepped out and looked up at the swollen rain clouds. Here and there were patches of blue but directly overhead was a slate-grey mass delivering its load. He zipped up his jacket and ran across the forecourt to the barn. The wide wooden doors were securely locked. There was a small window to one side and by standing on tiptoe he could just see through. The glass was filthy but he could tell the garage was empty. In fact it looked as though it had been given a much needed clean out. He carried on round the barn and approached the back of the house through what was known as the 'front garden', an appellation from pre-motorcar days when the modern front with the forecourt had been the working part of the farm. From the garden, the ground curved gently up and away through a patchwork of green fields before scaling over six hundred feet through a spectrum of oranges and reds to Rombalds Ridge. Sunlight and shadows played tag over the vast open expanse and at the very top he could make out the nick in the skyline that was the Thimble Stones, some three miles away. The moor had always been a mesh of contradictions. He loved it passionately. It was his playground, his place of dreams and even of private worship. But it was also terrible and dangerous. Some mornings in spring it would send a fog rolling down the slope like an avalanche that would engulf the house, white out his bedroom window and freeze the early flowers. It protected and suffocated at one and the same time and you never knew which to expect or when. Coming face to face with it again gave him a visceral thrill.

His father had allowed the garden to go to weed. His mother had been fastidious about it. She had spent almost as much time out as in, weeding and planting, planning and replanting. Once she was bedridden, he had engaged a gardener to keep it going but clearly that hadn't long outlasted her. The flowerbeds were overgrown and weeds and moss of all sorts had invaded the slate paving that flowed between them.

The first chill in his heart came when he

realized what was wrong with the house: there were no curtains. It stopped him dead. The back door was locked and he peered through the glass into the dimly lit corridor that ran through the center of the house to the front door on the far side. Normally it contained a narrow table between the kitchen and front room, a hat and coat stand, a telephone, some pictures, a couple of chairs and a long Persian style rug. The sun made a sudden appearance from behind a cloud and shone in over his shoulder. It revealed nothing more than a dusty tiled floor and a telephone, unplugged, wrapped in its own cord and left on the side.

It had never even rung.

The kitchen window told the same story of emptiness and neglect. He walked back a few paces and looked at the upper windows that once contained his parents' bedroom and his father's study. There were no faces in the windows and no shadows on the walls. His heart sunk. When was the last time he had actually got through on the phone here? Six months? Nine? Maybe more.

The rain increased. He pulled the turned up collar of his jacket around his throat and hurried on round to the car. By the entrance to the driveway he noticed a placard on a thin wooden pole laying face down in the grass. He caught the edge with his foot and turned over a 'for sale' sign. It took him a moment to digest the implication. His father had moved, emptied the furniture, restarted his life somewhere else and never even told him. He was stunned. He felt as empty as the house and it stared back at him with the same ghastly expression of bewilderment and loss.

Then another idea struck him: he was dead. His father hadn't abandoned him at all, he had died. It must have happened suddenly. Possibly as result of an accident or a heart attack (he was never in good shape). No one had contacted him because no one knew where he lived. Even his father had never bothered to ask.

Perversely, this second scenario seemed more comforting than the first. He tried to persuade himself that he shouldn't wish for his father's death but he couldn't help it. The alternative was far worse. Furthermore, if he was dead, he would surely have inherited the house - maybe more. He told himself he shouldn't be thinking of money, but he couldn't help that either. A sudden windfall would resolve all his current straits. He thought of his bank account, his unpaid bills and impossible rent. He thought of work, of Rachel and Janine, even Francis. He thought of the cloud under which he had lived since his mother's death. He thought of the way he had been tortured by his father's reticence. Whatever the problem, it was solved by his sudden and unexpected demise.

He had to find his solicitor. But how? He would most likely be local. He returned to the 'for sale' sign. The rain had washed the mud off and he read 'For Sale. Hawley Properties. Ilkley. Tel: 01943 821 142.' He unzipped his jacket and pulled out the phone.

"Damn." It was dead.

It had cut out after Janine's message and with all that had happened he had forgotten to recharge it. There was only one thing to do. He opened the boot of the car, took shelter under the lid and unzipped the black hold-all. The phone sat on top of the rolled up rifle bag undisturbed by the drive as though it had and just been placed there. He felt a twinge of hesitation before picking it up. Turning it on was a sure way of connecting him directly to the owner but he quickly shrugged the doubt away. After all, what could they do? They couldn't trace him and he was miles away from anywhere. He turned it on and waited for a signal. The small triangle of green bars filled up and almost immediately the phone bleeped.

There had been two missed calls. He didn't recognize the number of course and the caller had not left a message. He looked at the times of the calls. Twelve fifteen and two thirty two - an hour and a half ago. Doubtless they would try again, he thought. He didn't have long to wait. It suddenly burst into life with crisp old-fashioned bell-ring tone. Tyler took a sharp in-take of breath and his heart thumped in his chest. The phone in his hand felt electrified. The number on the screen was the same as the first two calls. He held it as far from him as possible as though expecting someone to jump out of it with a knife. It seemed like an eternity before it finally stopped. Even then he stared at it for half a minute before he plucked up the courage to use it himself. He was still hunkered under the boot lid but the rain was soaking the back of his legs. He closed it and ran back over to the signpost. He quickly tapped in the numbers and jumped inside the car with a shiver.

"Thank you for calling Hawley Properties" announced a man in a rich Northern accent. "We're open nine thirty to one and two to five Tuesday to Saturday. Please leave a message after the beep or call into our office during normal business hours." Tyler looked at his watch: four o'clock. The recorder started to kick in and he cut the line. Why weren't they open? There was still another hour to go. It occurred to him that since it was late on Saturday afternoon in the off-season they had probably packed up and gone home. They wouldn't open again until Monday morning. He could always go back home and try again then, but he was impatient. Besides he was on the spot and he wanted to meet with someone who could tell him what was going on. He called the number again.

"My name is Tyler Primovelli." He said into the answer phone. "I'm calling about the sale of Garth House in Burely. Can you please call me back on this number as soon as possible. I'm nearby and I'm trying to trace the owner, my father. Thanks. Call me, please."

As soon as he cut the line, the phone rang. He checked his first impulse to answer it and looked at the number on the screen. It was that number again. He felt easier in his mind about not answering it this time, waited for it to stop and slipped it back into his pocket.

Hawley Properties was probably in Ilkley. It wouldn't take long to find. And who knows what he may discover there. One thing was for sure, there was no point in going back home. Ilkley was only three miles further along the valley. But since Garth House was so high up he took the road that skirted along the edge of the moor and dropped into the town from the south.

The hand written sign in the window of Hawley Properties said 'closed for wedding.' The rain had momentarily lifted. Tyler pressed his face against the damp glass and found Garth House among the chequer board of advertisements. It was strange to see a potted history of his life in square feet and cryptic abbreviations. Just inside the window on the wall he could make out what looked like a short biography of Mr Hawley himself complete with a photo of a smiling, balding man with red cheeks and matching spectacles. So far so good. He knew what he looked like, where he was and, at that very moment, as if to guide him, the church bells started pealing.

36.

Christchurch Ilkley Methodist United Reformed Church, was only three minutes away on foot. He left his car and followed the joyous sound. Tyler knew the church well. All his mother's family were proud Olicanians (the name the locals derived from the Roman fort on which Ilkley now stood) and deep rooted Congregationalists. His grandmother never recovered from the merger of the Congregational and Presbyterian Churches in 1972 but grudgingly dragged Tyler along to the ungodly hybrid whenever his father was too drunk to stop her. The spire of this paean to mid-Victorian non-conformism jutted skyward on the corner of The Grove and Riddings Road. Adjoined to it at right angles were four sharp gable ends, three on one side and one on the other so that the whole structure resembled a clenched fist with the index finger pointing straight to Heaven.

By the time Tyler arrived, the wedding party had already started to filter out from the church. It was a respectable gathering of four or five dozen. Despite the shifting weather they were dressed optimistically. The ladies wore bright market-stall colors and the men, grey and blue work suits. Between the church and the main road was a small raised grass area where a photographer was already installed lining up the principal actors in the patches of late sun. Tyler stood on the far side of the road opposite the entrance looking for Mr. Hawley in the faces emerging from the service.

All the while the photographer called out 'family'... 'children only'... 'happy couple'... 'bride, groom and immediate family' while running to and fro from the camera like a sheepdog assembling the different groups and returning to capture them for posterity. It was a happy and intimate crowd. Tyler could tell by the way they circulated this was a group that knew each other well and, considering their average age, had probably done so for some time. Tyler spotted his man standing in a group of five smokers beneath the finger to God. He caught him just as he was coughing and crushing a cigarette out underfoot.

"Mr Hawley?"

Tyler noticed that he wore what looked suspiciously like his dark blue work suit, tarted up with a red waistcoat and silver bow tie. Hawley in turn scanned Tyler's expensive leather jacket and slick-backed hair with instinctive dislike. "That's me son. What can I do fer ye?"

"I left a message on your answerphone" he said.

"When was that?"

"About twenty minutes ago."

Hawley frowned. "I was in church lad."

"Yes I see that now." He looked at his feet. He wasn't quite sure how to start a conversation that would end with the words 'he's dead'. "It's about a house. You're selling a house."

"Aye. That's generally what we do." He coughed. "Any one in particular?" he said unenthusiastically.

"Garth House."

"Oh aye. Well if you stop by Tuesday morning..."

"Actually I'm not buying." This confirmed Hawley's first suspicion and he waggled his nose like a rat sniffing a bad smell. Tyler continued "I just wanted to know..." but what he wanted to know was interrupted by the photographer calling for a large group photo.

Given a perfect excuse Hawley said "'Scuse me son", turned his back and followed the excited troupe over to the side of the church where they clustered around the happy couple. Tyler decided to bide his time. Once Hawley knew who he was he'd be more co-operative. As the guests all scrabbled for position, Tyler wandered over to the far side of the main road where a group of passerbys had stopped to watch.

The photographer herded them all into position, made some final adjustment to the center and stepped back to his camera. The groom was an upright middle-aged man with a ready smile behind his neatly trimmed beard. He looked very elegant in his full battle dress: black-tail coat, grey striped trousers, pastel grey waistcoat, wing collar etc. all topped off with a white rosebud button-hole. If anything he was slightly over-dressed for the occasion. He cradled his brushed-grey top hat on his hip with his right arm through which the bride's gloved hand was resolutely looped even as she fidgeted with her dress and smoothed the front over her full bosom. There was something familiar about her. Tyler examined her cheerful round face and lazy blond bob poking out of a dusty pink bonnet. The photographer said something and two teenagers emerged from the throng and took their place beside the couple. Tyler recognized them immediately. They were Paul and Agnes and now he realized the woman was none other than Auntie Pru.

The heavens suddenly opened and out of an apparently blue patch of sky dropped a prodigious amount of water. There was a few seconds of groaning and confusion in which women tried to protect their hats with their hands and the children took shelter under grown legs. As if by magic, a panoply of umbrellas popped up over the group and covered them like a black rainbow. Tyler was amazed. He hadn't noticed anyone carrying an umbrella. He turned up his collar and backed under a shop awning on the far side of the road. The company that grouped back together for the portrait seemed even closer knit by the crisis. The swift and resourceful operation brought out barrels of laughter, none heartier than from Tyler's erstwhile aunt.

Pru wasn't really an aunt, but an old friend of his mother's who had cared for her unflaggingly during the worst of her illness. She had driven up to Garth House almost daily with bowls of soup and shopping that his scowling father couldn't or wouldn't do. She had cleaned the house and looked out for Tyler when his father was drunk. Paul and Agnes often came with her and stayed in the house watching TV or played in the garden. He had never wondered if she had been married. Paul and Agnes were so much younger than him that he never thought to ask them about their father. Here they now stood on either side of the happy couple smiling for the camera with the same broad toothy grin as their mother. Paul was a good four inches taller than the groom and at one point grasped him round the shoulders like a younger brother. He was a big, extrovert boy, easy to like with an infectious smile. He whispered something in the older man's ear which made him laugh. Anyone could see there was an easy and natural complicity between them. Pru leaned over to share the joke and very soon all four of them were wiping the tears of laugher out of their eyes.

"Thank you everybody" shouted the photographer.

There was an enthusiastic cheer and the formally arranged crowd unraveled onto the lawn between the church and the street still clutching their umbrellas and hiding the married couple from Tyler's view. It occurred to him that Autie Pru would know what had happened to his father. If he could catch her before she left he could avoid the condescending estate agent. Parked outside the church was an ostentatious grey Bentley with white ribbon bunting. As Tyler crossed the road towards it, the driver got out and walked round to open the back door. At the same moment, the crowd parted and formed an alley down which the newlyweds appeared in a shower of damp confetti. As they reached the pavement the crowd swarmed into the road and round the car preventing Tyler from getting any closer. Before he had a chance to struggle through, Pru blew a kiss then disappeared inside. The grinning groom braved the rain and mounted the running board.

"See you all at the hall" he said with a little wave. The crowd cheered.

"If we're a little - ahem - held up on the way" he drawled theatrically to the crowd's evident amusement "leave us a table in the corner." The crowd clapped and catcalled.

Tyler went rigid.

The Welsh accent was unmistakable, though deeper than he remembered it and more self-possessed. Tyler stepped into the road to get a closer look. The man in the morning suit was so unlike the man he had known as his father, he hadn't even recognized him. It was true that the beard was a novelty that hid half his face. It was evident that he had lost a lot of weight and gained a healthy tan. Certainly the suit was a change from the kind of shapeless sweaters and cardigans he had worn - even to his first wife's funeral. But what shocked him most was the smile, the laughter and general bonhomie. Tyler couldn't ever remember seeing his father smile and the only laughter that rung through the house was scornful and ironic. It was such a change that Tyler wondered if he wasn't imagining it.

Marc Primovelli surveyed his friends from his elevated position with a final salute. He swiveled round acknowledging their smiles until his gaze came to rest on the young man in the leather jacket standing stock still in the middle of the road. Their eyes locked. The father blinked in astonishment and the color and assurance dropped suddenly from his face. The wave of shock that passed through Tyler's soul laid flat all his well-rehearsed greetings, not that they would have been heard through the excited clamor. He was rooted to the spot. He found he was unable to smile, wave or communicate anything other than stunned bewilderment. In his father's eyes, however, he sensed he saw much more. The startled expression was mingled with a heavy layer of guilt. As it should have been! He had abandoned his son as soon as his mother had died, remarried and adopted a new family without even telling his own son. The shame may have been genuine but it was no more than a thin veneer. Below it, in sharp relief lay a thick grain of resentment - possibly anger. The message was clear: this is my new life and you are not welcome.

After a few seconds, the groom's hair was sopping wet and the water formed rivulets down his face and beard. It was then that Tyler saw yet something else. Fear. He was afraid. Afraid that Tyler would return. Afraid he would take those few steps forward and dash the happiness that he was clutching to his chest. Someone put their hand on his shoulder and he sunk into the car. In the blink of an eye he was gone. The driver closed the door and ran round to the front. If Tyler was expecting his father to suddenly pop back out and beg for forgiveness, he was wrong. The car started, nudged its way through the throng and motored slowly down the road. The excited crowd begun to scatter, some walking in the direction the Bentley had taken and others heading for their own cars. No one had the least inkling of the silent drama that had just taken place. The Bentley was still visible between the gaps in the crowd and Tyler stood there in the downpour with his eyes fixed on the receding back window. He still expected something to happen. Any reaction would be better than the void left by the wake of the car. He couldn't believe his father would simply disappear without a word or a sign. A hundred yards up the road the Bentley slowed to a stop and Tyler blinked the water from his eyes. It idled patiently and Tyler knew he had been right. It couldn't end like that. It wasn't correct. It wasn't just. The doors stayed firmly shut and he walked towards it. He was just picking up speed when a football rolled from in front of the car onto the pavement. A young boy picked it up and waved his thanks to the driver. The car moved forward again and Tyler watched until the curve of the road carried it out of sight.

The crowd dispersed gradually and he was left standing in the middle of the road like a soul in limbo. He looked back at the church and down the streets he had known so well as a child but they held no connection to him now. He was surrounded by shops, children, cars and all the signs of normal life but none if it made any sense. It was as if he had been dropped into a foreign country or onto another planet. The pattern and purpose of their existence was alien and quite beyond him.

He was woken from his trance by a car horn and drifted to the pavement. As he retraced the path back to his car the sense of detachment increased. He slumped into the front seat and stared out of the windscreen. The rain-streaked glass formed a wavering curtain into another dimension. The world outside he had once known was distorted and abstracted. Everyday objects were blurred into shifting colored shadows and he felt sure he was just as unreal to them. He had a vision of staying put and growing old without anyone ever noticing. The seasons would turn, snow would fall, his beard and hair would grow out and grey and he would finally rot away and disappear without trace. No one would see him in the car. No one would call him at home. His desk at work would be requisitioned without a second thought. He would vanish like ash in the wind.

He put the key in the ignition and the engine turned over. It was an automotive response to sitting in the car for too long. He really had no idea what would happen next. Where would he go? What we he do? He put the car into gear and swerved into the road without thinking. If he was a stranger to the world, he had the creeping sensation he was also becoming a stranger to himself. These were his hands on the wheel but he did not control them. They steered the car and changed gear as if guided by a will of their own. The road signs were in an unknown language and the road itself was a river in which he was carried by the current.

He left Ilkley through an arboreal northern suburb. The large houses stopped abruptly at the edge of the moor and the single-track road continued up the steep ascent to Rombalds Ridge. For ten minutes it ran parallel to a shallow watershed before winding round an ancient millstone quarry and breaking into the open moor. At a lonely crossing he passed one of the many outcrops of stone that rose dramatically from the incline like sentinels guarding the valley below. During the summer months they provided rallying points for hikers and picnic parties but today the impromptu parking area contained nothing but mud. He continued on up the slope until the tarmac gave way to an earth track that funneled the water pouring onto the moor. His wheels lost traction in the mud and he pulled over onto a patch of heather.

It was late in the afternoon. Above him a blanket of thin grey mist engulfed the top of the moor and all but hid the two tall radio masts at Whetstone Gate. He got out, circled the car and glanced briefly at the panorama spread out below him. The ridge, up which he had driven, plunged back down to Wharfedale where Ilkey town was cradled. It then rose again on the far side of the Wharfe through Middleton Woods up to the russet plateau of Middleton Moor also heavy with rain-cloud. Below him to his left the river meandered past the outskirts of Addingham and on for five miles through the patchwork pastures of Beamsley Vale before catching a shard of sunlight and curving out of sight near Bolton Bridge. To his right, the valley swung round more sharply and he could see only as far as Ben Rhydding. The sky was blackest over there and the high plains of Western and Asquith Moors on the far side were no more than a memory.

He hadn't passed one car since he had left the town and felt little danger that he would encounter anyone on the moor in this weather. He pushed his dripping wet hair out of eyes. Inside the jacket he was warm and dry but he couldn't stop the water collecting in his neck. He ran his hand round the inside of his collar and wiped the worst of it away. He tossed the car keys onto the front seat and closed the door. He opened the boot, took out the black holdall and closed it again. Already there was mud sticking to the underside of his shoes weighing him down. He knocked them against the tires to get the worst of it off then checked the soles. He had a long walk ahead of him.

37.

"It's my mother, you know." Roman said. "She hit her head on a tree branch and her face is swollen up like a balloon. She refuses to see a doctor. You know what old women are like, but I'm afraid it's infected. It smells funny and there's yellow puss."

The pharmacologist watched the strange man hop from foot to foot. There was no doubting his urgency. "She must see a doctor" he said.

"I told you she won't" Roman snapped back.

The pharmacologist was surprised at the violence of the reaction.

"I will take her" said Roman calming himself down. "I will force her to go. I just need something to stop the infection until then."

This wouldn't be the first young man to try to talk him into giving out prescription drugs he thought. It was why he had had a steel cage built round the medical cabinet two years ago. If the cage was opened without him hitting a hidden switch first it sent a silent alarm straight to the police station. Thankfully Pyortnan was a small town and the police were only three doors down.

"She needs antibiotics" he said. "You need a doctor to prescribe them."

Roman compressed his lips until they were white. The pharmacologist noted a look of panic in his eyes. Maybe he was worried for his mother. Maybe not. You just couldn't tell nowadays. Kids would kill you for a Rouble. Just because the drugs were locked up didn't mean someone wouldn't try it on.

"I'll give you something" he said soothingly. He turned and took two packets from the shelves behind him. "This is Betadine. Use it to wipe the infected area and any open wounds. It will help clean and sanitize it. She should take the Panadol everyday"

"Is that all?" Roman retorted.

"It's the strongest you can get without a prescription. But she must see a doctor. There's a cabinet in Deasveya Street." He looked at his watch. "It should still be open. If you like I can call"

"No no. I'll manage. How much do you want for this shit?"

Roman was glad to leave the pharmacy. The old man was looking at him suspiciously; even if he had no reason to. He was two hundreds of miles from where the girl had been murdered. The other one was stashed safely away in the woods with Ilya where no one would ever find them. The car was a problem of course. He was almost positive those two workmen had not taken the number at the service station but he wasn't taking any chances. He had walked to a bus stop Ilya had indicated on the map and ridden into town. No one could trace him even if they were looking, which they were not of course. Not out here anyway.

On the corner across the street was a single story concrete building with red shutters and a painted wooden sign swinging in the wind that said 'Jailbreak Club. Vodka. Beer. Pool. Dancing.' The first two at least were just what he needed. He waited for a gap in the cars and jogged over. The front door was set back in an alcove behind an iron grill that retracted into the ceiling. More to keep the jailbirds out that in, he reflected. Inside was a smallish room with cheap wooden tables and chairs. The bar ran down one the length of one side with the pool table almost against the wall at the far end. To his left as he entered he noticed a patch of black plastic vinyl in the corner no more than a yard square that he supposed was the dancing area. The two dozen or so men scattered about the room didn't look as though they would be using it any time soon.

To Roman's eyes they were a motley collection of backwoods drunks. The talk was loud and boisterous and the air hung thick with cigarette smoke. He felt instantly at home. He scuffed over to the near side of the bar and settled onto a stool facing the TV at the far end. An attractive blond woman in a sleeveless dress was giving the regional weather but the sound was too low to hear anything above the general din.

The barman was a scrawny whey-faced boy. He looked no more than fifteen but had rings under his eyes like an aging crack whore. Roman ordered the local vodka and a beer and looked at the weather girl's breasts. They were nice and she was very slim, unlike the fat cow tied to the bed back in Ilya's dacha. Hers were nice as well but she was too big and too old for his taste.

The vodka warmed his throat and lit a fire in his chest. For some perverse reason Ilya had not brought anything to drink. No alcohol at least. He had decided it was unprofessional. Ilya's idea of what was and was not professional was unpredictable to say the least. In fact the whole set up was more than a little troubling. What could have been a fairly straightforward job had turned decidedly ugly as a result of his partner's stupidity.

He thought back to the call he had received the night before. The man who had shouted at him down the phone had frightened him half to death. Luckily he knew enough about phones to film the girl and send an MMS before he blew his top completely. He had hoped to use this job to advance in the world and he was now thinking he was lucky that no one knew who he was. His current ambition was simply to get paid. For that he had to keep Ilya alive. He downed his beer, ordered another vodka and looked for a door that might be a toilet.

When he returned the fresh drink was waiting for him at the bar. He settled back down. He was in no hurry. There were busses every hour and a half until eight o'clock. The weather girl had been replaced by a dull looking local news reader and he wondered if he could hustle into a game of pool. There were four fat men gathered round the table who seemed to be more interested in arguing than potting balls. He'd wait bit. If he wasn't too drunk he'd challenge them to a game when they'd finished. He prided himself on his skill at pool and thought about winning a bit of cash. He turned his attention back to the local newscaster. His face was replaced by a picture of a girl that looked vaguely familiar. He wondered where he had seen her before and strained to hear what was being said. She couldn't be a celebrity like a TV or pop star because she was plump and middle aged and the photo looked like a passport shot. Before he had a chance to work it out, the picture was replaced by one that he did recognize:

Ilya.

The shock hit him like a thousand volts. His eyes flared open, his ears pulled back and his neck and shoulders stiffened. Ilya's photo disappeared as fast as it had arrived and Roman continued to stare at the screen until the newscaster's face was replaced by video of an army veteran's parade. He looked about him to see who in the bar had noticed. Nothing had changed. No one was looking at either him or the screen. There was a clack of a pool ball dropping into a pocket and the ambient noise returned to focus. Roman was left wondering if he really had seen what he had seen. He reached forward with a trembling hand and raised the vodka to his lips. He sipped it uncertainly and half of it dribbled down his chin. He finished the glass, put it back down, wiped his chin with his palm and then wiped his palm over his face.

The evaporating alcohol on his skin went someway to restoring his senses. He rubbed his temples and tried to piece together what had just happened. The girl on the TV was the one they had kidnapped. He was sure of that now. The photo of Ilya meant they knew who he was and that he was connected to the disappearance. If they knew that much they must also know about the murder. Showing it on TV meant they were looking for him. That much was self-evident but showing it on a local channel meant they were looking for him round here and not in Nizhny Novgorod where it had taken place.

Why were they looking round here? The car! The workers at the service station had taken the number after all and traced it back to him. How could Ilya be so fucking stupid as to use his own car? Thank God he had left it back at the dacha. Now it occurred to him that the dacha belonged to Ilya's family. How long would it take the police to put two and two together and come knocking at the door? If they did that, Roman knew his prints were all over the house and car. Ilya wouldn't hold his tongue and with the girl as an eyewitness, his picture would soon be up there on the TV replacing that of his over-sexed partner. There was no way he was going down for that idiot's bungling. He was suddenly furious that he would end up in prison or on a most wanted list for the rest life because Ilya couldn't keep his dick in his pants.

He ordered another vodka.

"How much do I owe you?"

The barman poured the drink and frowned as if he'd never been asked such a question before. "With this, nine Roubles fifty" he said as he placed the drink down.

Roman idly rotated the glass in his fingers as he turned the options over and over in his head. Whichever way he looked at it there was only one viable solution. He had to destroy all the evidence that could lead back to him. That meant the dacha, the car, Ilya and the girl. He would kill them both and burn everything. Luckily it was in the middle of the forest. It could be days before anyone would notice the smoke by which time he would be long gone. But the police were closing in. He had to move fast. He looked at his watch. There was a bus leaving from the market place in five minutes. He could make it if he ran. He knocked back the vodka, slapped a twenty Rouble note on the bar and hurried out.

38.

The path wound through thick scrub of crowberry and bilberry bushes at the top of a watershed. It was muddy but not bogged down as it would have been further up the moor. After fifteen minutes, the dwarf shrubs thinned out into a blanket mire of short coarse grass. The peaty soil was damp and its homely smell of warm, sweet decay rose to meet him. The path followed the edge of a gentle terrace that ran parallel to the valley. For a short while it hooked down and round a natural bump in the terrain before rising again and heading straight to the Badger Stone. At three feet high and nine feet wide, this isolated lump of worn millstone rose from the flat moorland like a miniature Ayers Rock. As he approached he could make out the familiar pattern of swirling prehistoric carvings that covered it like a tattoo. Tyler knew the rock well from his days rambling over the moors. From Badger

Stone there were clear sight lines to the Neb Stone and other carved rocks at Weary Hill and Will Hall's Wood. If you knew where to look, the whole area was studded with prehistoric motifs and standing stones whose functions were long since lost and forgotten. Round the stone's base were pools of muddy water so he climbed up, placed the bag beside him and sat down. He had intended to go further on to the Cow and Calf rocks in the hope of seeing Garth House but with the black weather coming in from the East he doubted it would be possible. The view over Ilkley itself, however, was still relatively clear and he could see the square patch of green in the crook of the river that housed his mother's grave. It was comforting to know that she was facing in the opposite direction. He unzipped the holdall, took out the rifle sack placed it beside him on the rock and unrolled it.

As he pulled the butt stock out of its sleeve the reality of what he was about to do began to hit home.

"Fucking hell" he muttered to himself. "Why are you doing this?" He wiped the raindrops and tears off the varnished walnut and continued to swear at himself and the world in general. He extracted the fore stock and screwed the two parts together as he had practiced in his bedroom the night before. "I suppose you're not even going to do this," he said to himself. "I suppose you're going to fuck this up like everything else."

His mind and mouth were working on two different planes. As he cursed and prodded himself into action his thoughts were formulating excuses and strategies. He told himself that the illness of his mother had been the root of his problems. But he didn't have the heart to blame the person whom he had most loved in the entire world and whom had shown him the greatest love in return. Instead his anger swung to his father whom he held responsible for her illness. He was the one to blame. It was his selfish egoism that had driven her to her death. He hated him with a passion that burned his soul. Yet even at this late hour he craved for his presence and reassurance. Only he had the power to save him now. If only he were there.

"All you had to do was say something" he said to him. "You didn't even have to explain. Just a sign would have done. A smile. Any kind of recognition. Anything." Tears were streaming thick and fast now and his face was flushed despite the cold rain. "You fucking bastard!" he shouted across the heath.

"I hate you! This is your fault! I fucking hate you." He pressed the moisture out of his eyes with the back of his hand then opened one of the magazine pockets in the roll-up. He hadn't dared fit it before but it didn't look too hard.

There was an oblong hole just in front of the trigger guard and he jammed the magazine inside. There was a simple click and it was in position. "Don't think about it" he said to himself. "Just fucking do it." He turned the safety off and looked down into the barrel. It was too long for him to reach the trigger even when it was placed against his forehead. He dropped the butt between his legs that gave him an extra inch and opened his mouth. With the hard end of the barrel pressed against his soft palate he found he could reach the trigger with his right thumb. He had decided not to think about it anymore. After all, once it was done there could be no more regrets. A shaft of sunlight suddenly lit up the cemetery far below. It was a sign. The moment was perfect. He pressed his thumb forward against the trigger and fired.

39.

Ilya decided to wait at least ten minutes after Roman left but in the event fell back to sleep. When he awoke it was dark outside. Roman could be back at any minute. There was no time to lose. He was going to do it and to hell with the consequences. His face throbbed like the devil and his vision was limited to one eye squashed into a slit. He was certain the bitch had destroyed the other and he would be at least half blind for the rest of his life - however long that might be. The thought alone incensed him.

He kicked the woolen blanket off and swung his legs to the floor. When he stood up he wobbled and had to steady himself with one hand on the couch. It was the after effect of the Chloral Hydrate, he reasoned. It wouldn't last. He hadn't taken any all day just so he could keep a clear head. There was a lighted paraffin lamp on the table by the door. The fire was still burning in the stove and despite the cold outside, the living room was warm. He staggered across the room and opened the door to the kitchen. In here there was no fire and it was colder. On the far side of the room were two bedroom doors. Both were closed. The one on the left was where he had seen Roman take Marta when they had arrived.

A wave of pain suddenly swept across his face. He howled and collapsed against the doorframe. The agony was worse than anything he had ever known before. It had been supportable while he was lying still but the movement seemed to inflame it. His hands hovered over his face but he dared not touch it. Even so the swelling was so large that he accidentally brushed against the top launching an agonizing wave of needle-like stabbing. He dropped to his knees, placed his hands on the floor and panted like a wounded dog.

When the worst had passed he pushed himself back up. The kitchen was little more than a blur. He grabbed the paraffin lamp and used it to light his way to the cooking area. The tiled surface was covered in the empty tins of preserved meat and vegetables and the dirty saucepans Roman had used to warm them up the night before. He placed the lamp down, found the drawer he wanted and took out an old carving knife. It had a bone handle and was long and thin from decades of sharpening. He had known it as a boy and it felt familiar in his grasp. He walked back round the table and crossed the room to Marta's door.

Marta had spent the whole day controlling her fear. Ever since she had been released from the cold coffin of the car boot she had regretted not freezing to death there. As soon as the lid was open, Ilya had attempted to beat her to death. Then Roman had brutally stripped her, tied her to the bed and even filmed it with his phone cam. The only mark of humanity he had shown was to throw a blanket over her. It was a small mercy. The slats of the bed cut into the soft flesh along her back, buttocks and thighs. The room was cold and, when he had closed the door, as black as a tomb. She had shivered and trembled and cried until she was exhausted. She had drifted in and out of sleep. It seemed that every time she found a blessed relief in unconsciousness some sound would penetrate the door and bring her suddenly awake. She would analyze what she had heard, try to fathom it was and listen for another. She was terrified they would walk in at any second and even more fearful that they never would. Of the two of them, the young man was intense and bloodless. He had ordered her to disrobe and then tied her down as he might pluck a chicken and truss it for the oven. The older man, however, had attempted to rape her. She didn't regret having fought back, but she bitterly regretted having not escaped. His screaming had been terrible to hear. His injuries were horrific and were certainly the reason he had attempted to kill her. When she saw him silhouetted in the doorway all her nightmares coalesced. She raised her head and shoulders as far as she could and cried out with a piteous fear that rose from deep with her.

Ilya surveyed the small room that had last been used by his aunt. The shutters were still closed and a dull light penetrated from the lamp in the kitchen behind him. He noted with admiration the way she had been secured to the bed. Roman hadn't lit the stove but he had found an old padded quilt and thrown it over Marta's body. He sniffed the air and recognized the acrid smell of urine. He waited until Marta had exhausted herself then walked towards something he had seen on the floor near the head of the bed. Her eyes scanned his black and bloated face. It was horrible and she knew she was responsible. In his right hand she saw a long blade that reminded her of a butcher's filleting knife. Her heart leapt and her stomach contracted with fear and panic. He stooped down towards the floor until the profile of his ghastly visage was only inches away from her. He prodded the shadowy object with the knife. When he realized it was a pile of Marta's clothing his mouth twitched into an awkward smile. He picked out a bra with the blade and raised it up so she could see. He turned it with the knife admiring the size of the cups. Marta watched helplessly. She was already faint with hunger and cold but the feeling of dread brought her back round.

Ilya folded back the quilt to expose her breasts. They were every bit as large as the bra promised but in her spread-eagle position they hung down into her armpits. He cupped the one nearest to him with his free hand and lifted it up onto her chest with a guttural noise like a hungry man at a feast. He rolled the nipple almost tenderly between his thumb and first finger then released it again. He bent back down and allowed the bra to slip off onto the floor. Next he spotted a pair of large beige cotton knickers. He turned them with the point of the blade examining them in the half-light then threaded the knife through the gusset. Marta strained her neck round but his hands were below the level of the bed and with his back to the door his face was in shadow. He looked across at her with his weeping half eye, raised the garment to his nose and closed his pinhole eye in mock ecstasy.

He let knickers fall back to the floor then leaned over the bed. He reached across with the knife, slipped the thin blade under the tape round her left wrist then severed it. Marta gasped when she found her arm was free. She flexed her hand several times and circulated the wrist until the pins and needles subsided somewhat. Ilya left the room and she could hear him cross the kitchen back to the living room. This was her chance. Her heart pounded ferociously and she reached over to her secured wrist and started to pick at the tape. It was infuriatingly tough and she hadn't even started to tear it when Ilya reappeared in the doorway with a fresh roll of tape.

He sat on the edge of the bed and placed the knife on the floor. Marta swung her hand at his face but he was ready for her. He grabbed her wrist and forced it over until it was pressed against the other. In one swift movement he wound the tape around both her forearms so that she was once again immobile though now her upper body was twisted onto her right side. Then he picked up the knife, cut the tape and threw the roll on the floor. Marta looked up fearfully into his face. What new horror did he have in mind?

"Be a good girl" he leered "and you won't get hurt."

Marta didn't believe him for a second and bucked franticly up and down but it was no good. She was attached solidly. Ilya shifted his sitting position to the bottom of the bed and pulled the quilt down to below her knees.

Marta screamed full force for the first time since he had come in. She twisted and bucked, flexed and strained every muscle in her body but to no avail. Ilya watched and waited until she had spent herself out and collapsed her head back onto the wooden slats with renewed sobbing. When he touched the inside of her thigh she tensed again and screamed but her energy was gone. She was too exhausted to fight anymore. He ran his hand up to her sex and when he made contact her body trembled and she released a stream of wet piss on his fingers. He smiled. When she was finished he wiped it between her legs and over her thick pubic hair and stomach. His erection was painful but it wasn't his plan to fuck her there on the bed. It was too awkward and he was afraid for his face.

He picked up the knife again and cut her right leg loose so that she was attached across the diagonal of the bed. Marta responded by shouting and kicking at him. He moved out of the way until she had simmered down then leaned over and grabbed her left nipple as he had done earlier. But this time he squeezed hard and pulled it away from her body so that her entire breast stretched into a cone. Marta screamed in pain and stared helplessly at the distended red thimble of flesh. When he had her full attention he placed the blade of the knife against the teat where it met the areola. Marta gagged in horror.

"Any more trouble" he slobbered with his lame lips "and I cut you up bit by bit. You understand."

Marta was speechless.

"Understand!"

Marta whinnied meekly and nodded. Ilya released his grip and returned to the foot of the bed. He cut free the other ankle then the other wrist. She was now completely liberated except for her two forearms that were bound together. Ilya prodded her to her feet. The quilt dropped to the floor and he marched her out into the kitchen.

40.

The downpour stopped abruptly. The black clouds to the East had rained themselves out and all that remained was a patchwork of white fluff that threw shifting shadows along the valley sides.

Tyler blinked.

He felt the warm sun on his back and blinked again.

The trigger had clicked, the hammer had fallen but he was still there. There had been no bullet in the chamber and all he had managed to do was bruise his soft palate against the muzzle. He had failed at shooting himself as he had in everything else.

He was unconsciously rubbing his tongue against it when the phone in his pocket sounded. His first thought on recovering his senses was that it could be his father. Hawley could have picked up the message and passed it onto him at the reception. He hurriedly put the rifle aside and plucked out the phone. When he saw the familiar number on the screen, his heart fell and he let it ring out.

The shaking started in his shoulders. He couldn't control it and very soon it had infected his arms and head. It quickly grew to a violent, seismic trembling. The more he tried to stop it the more the amplitude increased. He slid down off the rock to his feet and it spread all the way down so that he could hardly stand. He raised his fists to his head and pressed them to his temples but it didn't help. He was now a quivering mass like a flag whipping in the wind. He found a patch of grass and lay down shivering and jerking spasmodically. He knew it was the shock and he knew it would pass but the knowledge did nothing to help it pass quicker. Minutes went by until exhaustion finally overcame him and he relaxed. He balled into a fetal position and watched a Merlin hovering over a patch of scrub three hundred yards below. Its wings fluttered as it held its position. The wind tried to dislodge it but the bird flowed with the invisible current and effortlessly returned to the spot. Finally it drop out of the sky like a stone, grabbed in its talons a tiny squirming ball Tyler took to be a mouse and powered back up. Tyler followed it as it banked to the right and out of sight behind him. It was an everyday act of nature he had witnessed often in the past. This time, however, he found himself admiring the beauty of the bird and being totally indifferent to the fate of its prey.

The fierce internal tremors gave way to an almost soporific feeling of calm. He was as warm and content as waking up in his own bed on a Sunday morning.

41.

The late afternoon sun behind Tot-teridge House threw a giant shadow across Ingrave Street, across the cars and trees there, across the low-rise council housing opposite and the pavement on the far side where Zinic stood. He stared up at the tall building with its alternate horizontal bands of grey cement and dirty glass. It was a long way to the top and he figured his bag could have landed anywhere up to thirty yards away but not less than twenty within an arc of about forty five degrees from the corner where he threw it; a curved band which started at the base of another high rise and encompassed a strip of grass and several trees before crossing the road and ending in the low-walled front gardens of the ground floor apartments at number twenty. It was all accessible. He made a cursory search in the gardens, up the trees and on top of a white van advertising loft conversions. Nothing. The police would certainly have found it if it were there but it wasn't there and someone had definitely found it. He knew that for a fact because the phone had been turned on.

He had bought another pay-as-you-go that morning from a telecom shop directly opposite his hotel. He had called twice from his room and received a message that the number was not available. 'Not available' could have meant a number of things. The SIM card could have been stripped out, the phone could be in a zone with no signal, turned off or smashed to bits. He had almost given up hope until he had tried again around one o'clock and it had rung. There had been no answer that time, nor all afternoon but it meant that the phone had come to life. It meant movement. Someone had it in their hand and that someone, he reckoned, was probably near to where he was standing right now.

The single collective door to 20 Ingrave Street, was firmly shut and locked with a numbered key pad. Their front gardens however were shallow and the windows to the apartments were no more than three yards from the pavement. Despite the roar of the traffic from Falcon Road he was sure that if a phone were to ring inside he would hear it. He pulled his mobile from his jacket pocket and pressed redial. He kept it to his ear until he heard it ring then dropped it to his hip and turned his head to listen for the answering call. At that moment two cars passed by in quick succession. He squinted, as if this would help him hear better and craned his head over the wall.

"Hello?" called a voice close by.

Zinic looked around self-consciously. Apart from an elderly Asian looking woman crossing the road with two large shopping bags he could see no one. He scanned the building.

"Hell-o-ow?" the voice sang out. It was distinct but strangely distant. The noise of the cars faded as they turned off the street.

"I'm hanging up then."

Oh my God! "Yes," shouted Zinic even before the phone reached his face. "Who's this?"

Tyler clucked. "I hate that."

"What?"

"You called me. I hate it when people phone and say 'who's this.'"

"It's my phone" Zinic cut in indignantly then immediately regretted his haste.

"Is it?"

Tyler returned to the Badger Stone and placed his hand on the rifle. The man on the other end seemed to have a rather bland Home Counties accent. He could hear a gentle background roar like waves on a beach.

"Where are you? I can hear..."

But what Tyler thought he could hear was lost in a burst of static. Zinic thought he said 'sea'."

"I can hardly hear you." Zinic shouted urgently as he jogged along the pavement out of the shadow of the high rise. "Don't hang up. We need to talk."

In between crackles, Tyler thought he could hear Zinic running.

"What are you doing?" he asked once the line had cleared.

"Looking for my f-- phone!"

Tyler paused. "I can help you there."

"That's good." He dropped into a brisk walk. This was not the conversation Zinic had expected. The man on the other end sounded rather flippant - even simple.

"But I need your help in return" Tyler said.

This was more promising. "I'm listening." Zinic replied cautiously.

"I've managed to fit the magazine into the bottom of the rifle but I can't work out how to get the bullet up into the chamber."

Zinic stopped moving. His heart pounded loudly in his chest.

"I know I could put a bullet in the top," Tyler continued, "but I've already loaded the magazine, and I was just wondering how it worked."

Firecrackers went off in Zinic's head. "What... what are you talking about?" he groped hesitantly.

"It's not your gun then?"

Zinic took another deep breath. If it was a

trap, he was already caught. "How did you get it?"

"You left it under my car. You ... be more..."

Zinic looked at his signal in a panic. He'd stopped right under another block of flats. The whole road was lined with them. He had to get out of their shadow. Tyler looked at his own signal. Surprisingly strong for the middle of nowhere, he thought.

There was a cymbal crash of static and the phone cut dead. Tyler shrugged. He wasn't going anywhere. He looked back down at the rifle. He knew where he had gone wrong. He picked it up and levered the bolt handle up and back then back down and forwards. There was a clunk from somewhere inside.

The chamber was charged.

Zinic turned right into Woltencroft Close heading away from the estate but when he got to the bottom he found it was a dead end. It was far enough however. The signal bars filled up again and he redialled. When Tyler answered, Zinic launched straight in.

"That's not your bag" he boomed in a deliberately low octave. "It was mislaid and you've stolen it..."

The line went dead.

Zinic stared blankly at his phone. "Zasranec!" he swore under his breath. "Nu vse, tebe pizda."

He dialed again but it rang six times and

ended in a blank tone. "I don't believe it." He tried again; afraid the phone might have been turned off altogether and after the fourth ring it was answered.

"Did you cut the line?" he said sharply.

"Be nice" Tyler answered calmly.

"You don't know what trouble you're in. I can find you..."

Tyler cut the line again. Zinic was shocked at his own stupidity. He looked at the sky and turned in a slow circle repeating 'fuck fuck fuck'. What was he doing? Had he already forgotten three hundred hours of psychology training? He had been carried away with his own desperation and was sure he had lost him for good. The vision of Marta tied to the bed screaming came back to his mind. He stopped turning and took a deep breath. He dialed again and, to his relief, it was answered immediately.

Silence.

"I'm sorry." Zinic said eventually.

"The next time I don't pick up. OK?"

Zinic sat down heavily on the wall of a raised flowerbed at the end of the close. "OK."

It was a rare feeling to be so completely humbled. Even when being threatened by the Olevskys he had retained an element of advantage. They needed him to do a job and despite all his bluster he knew Bruno was afraid of him. This situation was totally different. He held no winning cards and was completely at the mercy of the nutcase on the other end. His shoulders started to slump then he righted himself and sat up straight as if defying his own prognosis. He wasn't defeated yet. There was always a weakness; he just had to find it.

"What do you want?" Zinic asked firmly.

"Oh it's OK" replied Tyler airily. "I worked it out in the end."

"What?"

"How to load the bullet."

The silent alarm bells started ringing again. "It's not a toy." Zinic said cautiously. "You could hurt yourself."

The irony of the remark choked Tyler into a spontaneous giggle. "That was the idea."

Zinic's mouth went dry. "What do you mean?"

"Do I have to spell it out?"

"You're kidding. It's a joke. Yes?"

"Want to hear the punch line" Tyler muttered ruefully.

Zinic felt the blood drain from his face. "Wait. No. Hold on." The thought of the police crawling over a dead body with his gun brought a feeling of panic that was becoming horribly familiar. "You can't. Not with that rifle."

"Why not?"

"Because... because it wouldn't do the job. Not up close. A rifle is never good. You'll just cripple yourself or end up paralyzed but still alive. It's not that easy. Believe me. I've seen it happen. Professionals even. It's not what you want to do."

"Bullshit."

Zinic thought back to friends and soldiers he had known who had tried it, some with pistols, some with rifles or even machine guns. Often their misery had only just begun; they survived but blew off their jaw or half their skull. Life was astonishingly resilient. "Look at the gun" he insisted. "It's a customized sniper rifle you have there. A precision instrument designed to drop a man up to two miles away. It's not a shotgun."

Tyler was intrigued. He turned the weapon over in his hands examining it in a new light. He raised it to eye level with his free hand and looked along the barrel. Two miles? He wondered how far Ilkley town was as the crow flies. He reckoned about a mile, half the effective range, but he couldn't even see anyone down there. Tyler pulled the optical sight out of the sleeve and scrutinized it.

"How do you fit the telescope thing on?" he asked.

Zinic held his breath. The next worst thing to suicide was taking pot shots at passers-by. He clenched his fist and silently pounded it against his forehead as he searched for a reply that wouldn't result in a dial tone.

"You still there?" said Tyler.

"Yup."

"Well?"

"Look" he started softly, "I don't know who you are or..."

"Tyler."

"Tyler. OK..."

"And you?"

Zinic hesitated. He was so completely thrown by the exchange he momentarily forgot his own name. "Greg" he said finally. "Or where you are..."

"Ilkley Moor." Tyler clenched the phone between his chin and shoulder and attempted to fit the optical sight onto the top of the forestock.

Zinic's head buzzed. It had been a long time since he had been force-fed the maps and culture of the British Isles but a drawer in his mind unexpectedly popped open. "Yorkshire? What's that noise."

"Oh I've done it. It's a lot easier than it looks."

"Fuck! What are you doing?" It was the first time he had cause to regret having a quick mount system for his scope.

"Two miles is an awful long way."

"What are you going to do?"

"Just have a look."

"Tyler, please. Listen to me. You're not going to shoot anyone?"

Tyler flipped open the protective caps at either end of the scope and lifted the rifle again. He pointed it in the direction of the town and looked into the eyepiece. He could see a thin red cross but everything else was out of focus. He tried looking for his mother's grave but it was just a green smudge. He was disappointed, but when he raised it up to Middleton Woods on the far side, tree trunks that weren't even visible to the naked eye jumped sharply into relief. He was impressed.

"How do you focus it?" he asked into the phone that was still clamped under his chin.

Zinic had a feeling of rising panic. If Tyler shot anyone and was caught that would be the end of it. No rifle. No contract. Marta dead. Tyler seemed to be impervious to threats. By his own account he had loaded the magazine and was now scanning for targets.

Tyler dropped the rifle to waist height and studied the scope more closely. It was essentially a mat black tube three quarters the length of the barrel of the rifle that projected back over the bolt. The tube was divided into three sections of different diameters, the two outermost tapering into the center like an elongated hour glass. The eyepiece closest to the shooter was roughly twice the size of the center and the objective lens at the far end was twice that size again. In the middle were two knobs; one on top and one at the side ringed with small white numbers. Between the eyepiece and the central tube was an adjust-able ring. He brought the rifle back up to his shoulder and turned it. As he suspected, this changed the focus.

"Ah, I've got it" he declared.

Zinic rallied his thoughts. He had to get through to this madman before he did some-thing... mad.

"I'll buy it off you." He said. He hadn't ex-pected to reach this point in the negotiation so soon but murder was a trump card.

"Keep your money Greg."

"A thousand pounds. Cash." Zinic didn't have more than a few travellers checks but details like that didn't seem immediately important.

"Hold on a mo" Tyler said. He leaned his front against an inclined side of Badger Stone and placed the phone down. Ignoring Zinic's protests, he dragged the holdall over and rested the rifle on top. It was just the right height for a perfect firing position. He was fa-cing East along the ridge and adjusted the scope to focus on a rocky outcrop on the hori-zon line. He judged the distance to be about five times the length of a football pitch. He laid the crosshairs over a protruding stone and, just as he had seen in a hundred films, gently squeezed the trigger. There was a powerful crack! and the rifle recoiled. The optic hit him hard on his right eyebrow and he cried out.

Zinic heard the unmistakable sound and his

heart leaped into his mouth. He was certain it signaled his worst scenario. He pictured a young man lying dead or wounded in the middle of an empty moor. Night was coming on. He would be dead by morning, if he wasn't already. Then someone would find him and report it to the police. He was shattered.

He shouted into the phone until he was hoarse. "Tyler! Tyler!" But there was no reply and he cursed himself for not offering more money.

Tyler rubbed the bony ridge of his eyebrow with the base of his palm. Despite a spot of blood indicating a cut it was the shock rather than the impact that had hurt. When he had fully recovered he picked up the screeching phone.

"Alright alright. I'm here."

Zinic threw his head back in relief and slid down the wall until he was sitting on the pavement.

"It hit me," Tyler continued sourly.

Zinic didn't have the strength to be angry. "For God's sake" he gasped. "What happened?"

"You heard didn't you" Tyler snapped, feeling the beginnings of bruise.

Zinic jumped back onto his feet in a flash of rage. "I've no fucking idea what you're doing and neither have you."

"OK. Keep your shirt on."

"What the hell are you shooting at?"

"A rock. That's all. Just a rock."

"You can't do that. Someone will see you and..."

"There's no one for miles" he lied. At least it felt like miles.

"It's not a fucking toy."

"If you were more co-operative..."

"What do you mean 'co-operative'?"

"You could show me how to..."

"Tyler I'm not going to teach you how to use my gun."

"It's my gun now Greg. Finders keepers."

Zinic opened his mouth to argue, but the tone of finality in Tyler's voice made him clamp it shut again. There was a long pause in which neither man spoke. The Russian knew he was cornered. Quarrelling was futile and would end with dead line and no rifle. He would never find Tyler by tomorrow morning, if at all. He had one last throw of the dice.

"Five thousand pounds" he said.

Tyler was about to say that the money wasn't important but the truth was that the urge to kill himself had receded. At some stage in the future money would be important. Five thousand would be enough to clear his debt, pay the child maintenance, allow him to buy Christmas presents for Rachel and set him up again, at least for a month or two. But once he thought it through further he came to the depressing conclusion that the New Year would see him recommence at zero. On past form the only possible direction from there was down. Greg had offered him a thousand pounds to begin with then quintupled it in as many minutes. Maybe he would do so again. Ten, twenty, twenty five thousand or more would be worth living for. Tyler had no idea how much a gun like this was worth, but knowing he had five thousand in the bank for starters made him feel surer of himself. All that, however, was in some hazy future. Right now, he was fascinated by the rifle he had in his hands. This was real. The solid walnut and metal frame, the satisfying clunk of the machinery, the astonishing range of the optical sight and the knowledge that he could sink a metal slug into anything within a two mile radius was immensely empowering. Furthermore there was a sense of self-assurance that came with just possessing the weapon. It made him feel different. Not in the same out-of-body way he had had earlier. Quite the contrary, he felt more like himself than he could ever remember and it was not a sensation he was eager to let go of.

His thoughts returned to the breathing he could hear at the other end of the phone. "Let's talk about that later," he said firmly. "Show me how to use the rifle."

Zinic was disappointed but sensed the tide had turned. 'Talk about it later' meant he was willing to bargain which meant he could get the rifle back, meet Bruno tomorrow and save Marta. Tyler had been on the brink of suicide. He didn't know the reason of course but he was shrewd enough to know the crisis was over. He also understood people's fascination with guns. Tyler wouldn't be the first person to externalizing his angst by shooting things. Provided he didn't get caught, this could work out well for them both. It was the first time he had thought of Tyler as a something other than an obstruction.

"Alright" he said. "But you must do as I say. It's a dangerous weapon and I want you to survive long enough to hand it back to me." After that you can do what you like, he thought. Zinic made him check and double check there was absolutely no one in sight. Tyler scanned the moor thoroughly with the scope, including all the paths he knew but didn't see one single person. This wasn't a surprise. It had been raining almost all day and the sun was now no more than a hand's breadth above the horizon. It was also getting cold and they had maybe twenty minutes of good light left.

"What did you shoot at earlier?" asked Zinic

Tyler told him and explained it was roughly five hundred yards.

"You missed it by about sixty feet" said Zinic.

"But I was aiming straight at it" Tyler protested

289

"The scope is zeroed at two thousand and nine yards. At five hundred yards your bullet would have flown over the top by the height of a five story building."

"I don't get it."

"Put it this way, if you had been aiming at the front door you would have hit roof."

"But why?"

"Because the moment the bullet leaves the gun gravity pushes it down."

"Then why did it fly over the top?"

Zinic decided to sidestep the ballistics lecture. "Imagine you throw a stick for your dog. If you want to throw it a long way you throw it up in the air, right? It's the same with a bullet."

"A bullet goes a little faster than a stick."

Zinic ignored the tone. "The muzzle velocity of that rifle is about two thousand miles an hour, almost three times the speed of sound. It's fast. But gravity is faster. Over a long distance you have to lob the bullet up into the air. The scope you are using is adjusted to a target a mile and a quarter away. While the scope looks directly at the target, the rifle barrel is pointing in the air. They're not parallel. In fact they cross. The bullet rises to a height of over a hundred feet before falling back down and hitting the target at the point the scope is focused. In this case, two thousand and nine yards."

Tyler had never given much consideration to the finer details of bullet trajectory but if anyone had asked he would have said they flew in a straight line.

"So that means I have to readjust the tel... the scope" he said.

Zinic sighed. "Yes, but for that you need a laser."

"Yea yea."

"Seriously. It's a little gadget you stick in the muzzle and it lights up the target. You then adjust the reticle - the crosshairs in the sight - until they are over the laser spot. It's the only way."

"So what did they do before lasers?"

Zinic had to admit it was a good question. Maybe Tyler was brighter than he appeared. "They did it the old fashioned way" he said with a sigh.

"Which is?"

"More complicated."

"Try me."

Zinic could see that Tyler was not going to be put off that easily. He took a deep breath and instructed him to empty the chamber, un-clip the magazine and put it somewhere dry. Tyler slid the ejected bullet back into the magazine and put it in his pocket.

"Now take out the bolt. It's the same as if you're loading the chamber" he said patiently. "Lift up the bolt handle and pull it back. Now, you feel the point where it resists. Push the handle further over to your left and pull back again."

Tyler did as he was told and, much to his surprise a slim, well-greased metal tube slid back out of the barrel.

"Pull it all the way out and put it somewhere where it won't get dirty."

Tyler brushed off the holdall and laid it carefully on top.

"Now you need to find a stable place where you can lay the rifle down; preferably a few feet off the ground. At the same time you should find a target about a hundred yards away to point at."

On the far side of the Badger Stone was a slatted wooden bench for weary picnickers who wanted to keep their bottoms dry. Tyler tried to rest the forestock between two slats with the butt hanging over the edge but it wouldn't hold. After a few fail attempts he decided to brave the cold and take off the leather jacket. This made an impromptu rest that, after a bit of molding, seemed to do the job.

"Now look through the hole left by the bolt and find your target."

To his surprise, Tyler could see right the way down the barrel and out the other end. He adjusted the position of the rifle until he managed to get the center of the black tunnel lined up with a fist sized stone he had chosen lying on its own in a patch of open peat.

"Now you're going to zero the scope to that

distance. That means that once you've done it, you should hit whatever you aim at."

"But only at a hundred yards."

"More or less" said Zinic without wanting to be drawn on more details. "Look at the scope. You have a knob on the top in the center. That adjusts the angle of elevation. You're going to need to turn that quite a lot."

"What's the one on the side?"

"That's for windage - the horizontal adjustment for wind. Is there any?"

Tyler looked up. The onset of evening had brought with it a Biblical serenity. The remaining clouds had lifted and were turning light pastel shades of yellow and gold. The high blue sky stretched right across the dome and filtered down to a hazy mauve on the eastern horizon. In the valleys, the stone walls, trees, farm buildings and even sheep cast long shadows across the twilight colored fields. There was no wind but he knew it would pick up as the sun dropped and the difference in air temperature provoked a rush of air from the sunny uplands to the shaded valley.

He resisted the urge to share the beauty of the scene with his instructor and simply told him no.

"Look through the scope and keep turning the elevation knob clockwise until it's on target. Be careful not to move the rifle, but if you do, just resight along the bore, get the target back in the middle and continue. If you need to adjust the scope to the left or right turn the windage knob. Got it?"

Tyler put the phone on the bench and started. He found the scope was pointing down at the ground some twenty feet in front of him and several times he had to adjust the focus as well to see where he was. Little by little, however, he got closer and closer until he had the stone bang in the center of the barrel and the cross hairs at the same time.

"Now fit the chamber back in the barrel and you're done. You've successfully bore-sighted a sniper rifle." Zinic had been standing in the shadows of a high-rise building for some time and knew it would soon be sunset. Even earlier further north. "Now let's talk about the money" he said hopefully.

"You can talk about it if you like" said Tyler. "I'm going to try this out."

"It's getting rather late?"

Tyler looked around again. It was astonishing how fast the sun dropped at the very end of the day. Even the blades of grass now threw long shadows over their neighbors. But he guessed what Zinic was angling for and he was not to be put off.

"Maybe you're right" Tyler said casually.

Zinic's mind snapped to attention.

"Maybe we should start again tomorrow."

"No!" Zinic said urgently. "We settle this tonight. If not tonight then never. I'll play your game, whatever it is, but it finishes tonight. Tomorrow is too late."

Tyler noticed the change of tone in his voice. He wasn't hectoring like at the beginning; he was almost pleading. He hadn't got as far as to thinking what he would do tonight but he could probably drive back home. Why not? He took the magazine out of his pocket and clicked it back into the underside of the stock. Remembering his former mistake, he charged the chamber using the bolt action.

"Do I have to fire from the same place?" he asked.

Zinic reluctantly replied that he did not and Tyler returned to the Badger Stone. The increase in height was more comfortable and allowed him a better view on his target. He put the phone on loudspeaker and placed it on the stone. Then he rested the rifle on the holdall and took aim at the fist-sized rock.

"Make sure the rifle is tight into your shoulder." Zinic said. "It kicks."

"I know. I almost lost an eye."

"You don't need to be so close to the scope. You can be six inches back, so long as you can see the crosshairs and the target. If it's too dark the reticle will automatically light up. Now take a breath and release it slowly, keeping the target steady in the cross hairs. Do this three times."

The first time the target moved as Tyler hit the bottom of his breath. He took another. The second time he managed to control it better and the third time it was almost perfect.

"Do it again and fire at the bottom of the third breath. Gently squeeze the trigger." He felt like a fairground instructor. Tyler concentrated, did exactly as he was told and fired.

This time he was ready for the recoil. When it bucked into his shoulder his face was well back from the scope and he succeeded in keeping his eye on the target stone even after the shot was fired. It didn't budge.

"What happened?" asked Zinic.

"Missed."

"Did you see where it landed?"

"Over to the right I think, about a foot."

Zinic made the calculation in his head and said "turn the windage three clicks anticlockwise."

Tyler did as he was told, lined up the stone again and fired. This time it jumped into the air in a violent spinning motion that sent chips flying in all direction. Tyler whooped enthusiastically.

Even though Zinic was itching to discuss the exchange he couldn't help but smile to himself at Tyler's loud woops of joy. He called and hollered and congratulated himself like a man who, against all logic, had found a pot of gold at the end of the rainbow.

"What about that!" Tyler said when he finally picked up the phone.

"Congratulations" said Zinic grudgingly. For a person who had never touched a rifle before, to bore sight it and hit the target on the second attempt was, he admitted, quite exceptional - and he said so.

Tyler was touched by the unexpected praise. "Thanks Greg" Zinic acknowledged the change in tone and what it signified.

"So what about the money Tyler?" he said eventually.

Tyler had forgotten all about it. He didn't want to discuss it. Not now. He wanted to shoot something else. Zinic had no choice but to agree and Tyler replaced the phone on top of the stone while he scanned for another target.

The sun was clipping the western horizon and half of Warfedale and Ilkley town was now in the shadow of Rombalds Ridge. The moor was virtually featureless and all the major outcrops of stone were too far away. He would like to have tried for them but he knew he would have to boresight the rifle again and he didn't have time. Finally he spotted an empty white milk carton trapped in a clump of heather further down the slope. He moved round the Badger Stone, lined it up carefully and fired. When it didn't move he felt slightly annoyed.

"Is there any wind?" Zinic asked.

There was a very slight breeze but it was

going down hill in the direction of fire and Zinic didn't think that would account for it.

"It could be the humidity. It's getting late and the damp pulls the bullet down. You need to adjust the angle of elevation. How far did it miss?"

"It's too dark to see."

"Then you have to stop."

"Take a guess."

There was no point in arguing. The light would stop him in a few minutes anyway. "You're on a moor" Zinic said, "shooting close to ground level so the humidity might be quite high. Without measuring it, it's only a guess. You can try a couple of clicks clockwise."

Tyler adjusted, aimed quickly and fired again. This time the carton gave a little jolt as the bullet pierced it and disappeared into the heather behind. Tyler cried out again joyfully. He stood up to survey the scene from higher up. He couldn't even see the carton in this light at a hundred yards. Only a finger of the sun remained now and he decided he had time for one more shot.

"That's enough Tyler" Zinic tried to insist. "Let's talk about the money. If you can't see the target..."

Tyler cut the line. He was just getting the hang of it and he didn't want this man spoiling his fun. Just to make sure, he turned the phone off. He knew he couldn't keep the rifle but he wanted to think things out for himself and not be bullied. Besides, it wouldn't do Greg any harm to sweat a little. It was a negotiating tactic he had seen Yolanda use time and again. Maybe he'd up the price. He judged he had a minute of half-light remaining and searched round for something, anything to shoot. The heather where he had spotted the milk carton had disappeared into the dusk. Only the higher reaches of the ridge to the east caught the scraps of remaining light. He spotted the flash of something white on the moor above him and circled the Badger Stone again so that he was facing uphill. Through the scope he could make out a colony of rabbits quietly tucking into their first meal of the night.

Zinic used up every swear word he had ever learned in Russian, English, French and German and even a few in Ukrainian. He impulsively raised the phone high over his heard with the urge to smash it on the pavement but stopped himself at the last moment. A woman walking towards him pushing a pram crossed over the road to avoid him. He kicked the wall, slapped it with his open hand and finished by lightly tapping his forehead against it in despair.

"Five thousand" he screamed at himself scornfully in Russian "You idiot. Why didn't you offer more? You don't have it anyway so what's the difference? Fifty thousand. A million. You fucking moron."

He tried the phone again but instantly fell on the answer phone. He was tempted to leave a message begging him to name his price but cut the line. Despite everything he sensed that Tyler was just working out the last of his personal problems. He would probably call back after the light failed. He hoped.

Tyler chose a rabbit in the middle of the group. He figured that if the bullet flew off course for any reason (humidity, wind and whatever else), he may hit one of the others around it. His heart was beating so fast he had to deliberately try to slow it. Night was dropping fast now and he could feel the cold and damp seeping up through his thin cotton shirt. His toes were freezing.

He concentrated so hard on the rabbit that when it unexpectedly looked up, he thought it must have seen him. Tyler watched its nose twitch as if it could smell him and lay the center of the crosshairs straight between his eyes. It was a sure shot; more so than before because the colony were only about half the distance of the other targets. Tyler felt the metal trigger against the middle crease of his index finger and breathed in and out, three times, calming his heart and steadying his aim. But at the bottom of the third breath he relaxed his grip and allowed the rabbit to hop to one side. It wasn't him. He wasn't a rabbit killer. It had been fun, but there was a limit.

He stood up and slipped his jacket back on while he thought of his next move. He would call Greg and arrange to sell the gun back. But how and where? What was Greg anyway? A gangster? A hunter? A killer? A shiver shot down his spine as he imagined meeting him face to face. It would have to be somewhere public with lots of people. He looked at his watch. It was almost six o'clock. Greg had said it had to be done tonight or never. He could be back in London by midnight but where could they meet that would be safe? He decided to think about it in the car. Then he thought of Janine. He had to speak to her and persuade her not to go through with the injunction. He would tell her about the money but he had to see her face to face - without Francis. She had to understand that he had changed.

Had he changed? The idea struck him as strange. On the surface if there had been a change it was for the worse. He was now an orphan. The truth however was that he felt stronger and surer of himself. He wanted to impress that on her more than anything else. Tonight was his only chance. Francis always went out alone on Saturday night. It was a sacred ritual to spend it with his mates in the Railway Tavern and Janine was normally at home with Rachel.

It was decided. He stretched his arms up to the sky as though awakening from a deep sleep

and breathed in the night air. The entire panorama was in bathed in darkness. The lights of
Ilkley and the other towns strung out along
the valley glowed like beads of dew on a gossamer web. He looked over to where he had
parked the car. It too was engulfed in blackness
but the path lead the way back with an eerie
glow. He jutted his chin out in a silent gesture
of determination and started to disassemble
the rifle.

42.

Marta felt the blade of the knife press against the side of her neck. Part of her training for Ikea had included an emergency medical course (in which she had earned one hundred percent). She had learned things that she had thought she would never need to know - up until now. The carotid artery for instance, ran along the side of the neck and supplied oxygen to the brain. It was one of the major arteries of the body and she knew that if she moved a fraction of an inch and the knife cut it she would bleed to death in minutes. She didn't want to die. She had a lot to live for: parents who depended on her, a job she adored and a man she loved. She wanted desperately to see them all again so she spread her legs and allowed her left cheek to be pressed onto the kitchen table.

Ilya pressed the knife against her neck with his right hand and forced his left between her buttocks. With his swollen eyes and the fading light he could make out little more than the vague outline of her white skin. Her thighs were moist with urine and her buttocks clenched. He ran his finger over her labia and fumbled for her clitoris. But when he couldn't find anything he recognized he poked the place he judged to be the center. Marta squealed and the sound aroused him. His prick swelled to burst. He moved his hand to his flies to liberate it but got tangled in his underpants. He undid his belt and trousers, let them drop to the floor, unhooked his pants, pushed them down and thrust his penis blindly between her legs.

Marta squeaked again, more from humiliation than pain. But the last thing she wanted to do was to give him any excuse to use the knife. She feared that more than anything. When he had threatened to cut off her nipple she had felt a rancid sickness she wanted to avoid again at any cost. She also knew that her moment would come. When it did, she had to be ready. As he groped and prodded behind her she played out the scenario in her head, rehearsing her movements slowly and surely. Fear churned her stomach at the thought of what would happen if she failed but she had no choice.

Ilya raised his left hand to his mouth, worked up a ball of spit and licked it onto his palm and fingers. He lowered it between

Marta's legs and rubbed it against her mound. This time his finger found her hole. Marta tensed involuntarily and her legs snapped together. Ilya re-applied the pressure on the knife and kicked her legs apart. When she complied, he started to imagine she was enjoying it. He pulled his finger out, ran it up her crease and tried to force it in her other hole. She clenched her buttocks again. He chuckled to himself at the size of her cheeks and slapped them hard.

He found her cunt again and pushed his penis inside. Marta screamed, lifted both feet off the floor and clamped her legs shut. Her vagina tightened and Ilya felt a wave of pleasure course through his body. He pulled one cheek apart with his free hand and thrust deeper. He groaned with satisfaction when it reached as far as it would go then started to fuck.

Marta suffered his manic pounding as quietly as she could. With his free hand he alternately slapped her painfully on the left buttock, grabbed at it or attempted to find her arse hole with his thumb. Occasionally he would run his hand forward along her side to grasp her breast. She tried to arch her back so as to stop him pinching her skin against the wood. All the while he kept his right hand pressed firmly on her shoulder with the blade resting against her neck.

Very shortly, Ilya could contain himself no

longer. He had planned a long series of sexual tortures but they would have to wait. He could feel his sperm rising. He increased his rhythm. The slapping of his stomach against her cheeks grew faster and louder. His penis was hardly even inside her anymore. It snagged on her outer lips and hair increasing his sensation. He dropped his head back and roared.

Marta felt the pressure of the knife decrease slightly as he prepared to come. The timing would be crucial. She felt his penis swell and listened carefully to his breathing. Then, as his stroke lengthened and slowed for the final thrust, she turned. Her arms, still bound together at the wrists and stretched out above her head, swept round, pushing away the knife. She had a fleeting advantage. Continuing the movement, she swung her clenched fists up and hit Ilya on his bloated eye.

He howled, dropped the knife and stumbled away clutching his face. His penis spasmodically spurted in the air as he went. He fell onto his back in the center of the room screaming like a devil. He kicked madly with his feet, pushing himself along the floor into a far corner.

The kitchen was black except for the indirect red glow from the stove in the living room. It was enough for Marta who had been in darkness for most of the last twenty-four hours. So far everything she had planned in her head had worked out. He had even left her the knife that she now picked up. Holding it in her hands, she pointed it back at her body and attempted to saw the tape that bound her forearms. It was no good. Her wrists were pressed together and she didn't have enough mobility in her hands to create any leverage.

Ilya's puss filled abscess had burst under the impact of Marta's blow leaving his face and body splattered with blood and fluid. His hands clawed at his skin trying to root out the source of the pain and in doing so cleared his good eye. Partially relieved of the swelling, he could now see Marta standing naked at the far end of the room trying to cut her bond. Even in his extreme pain, the site of her plump body and pendulous breasts aroused him. But not as they had before; not sexually. It was the slavering of a wolf observing a lamb. He wanted to carve her up and feast on her. Anger pushed him to his feet. He roared and rushed forward at her with his fingers poised to grasp her by the throat and rip it open with his nails. Marta saw him coming at the last moment and tried to turn the knife in her hands.

In the fear, noise and confusion neither was sure what happened. Ilya's hands found their target, but the pressure was weak. Marta was still holding the knife in both hands but found she couldn't move it. They were pressed together in a mortal embrace both trembling and screaming. Ilya's cry turned to a gurgle. He grimaced and padded at her face with the insides of his fingers. Marta was terrified. She wanted to break away but not without the knife. She struggled and finally pulled to one side. As she did so, the knife, which had been embedded in Ilya's stomach, sliced across it releasing a mass of hot intestines onto her body and the floor.

The smell was vile and she gagged. Ilya sunk to his knees. When he realized what had happened he attempted to gather up his innards and push them back inside. Very soon, however, he lost consciousness and fell face forward onto the slimy floor twitching and kicking. Marta's adrenalin was still high. She suppressed the reflexive nausea by gulping down air and focused on the next few minutes. She had no idea where Roman was and why he hadn't come when he heard the noise but she was certain he could walk through any door at any moment. Her first priority was to cut her wrists free. Making an effort not to look at Ilya, she speared the knife into the tabletop then sawed her binding up and down the blade. When she was free she ran back to her detention room and grabbed her clothes and shoes. The thought of being trapped again by Roman drove her mad with fear. Instead of dressing, she ran straight out of the room, through the kitchen and out of the house.

The half moon hidden behind thin and shifting clouds gave the forest the shallow relief of a stage set. The out-house was only three breaths from the front door. She ran round to the protecting shadow on the far side and took stock of her position. To her right, parked at the rear of the house, was the car. Its presence increased her suspicion that Roman must be somewhere nearby. Not in the house of course. Not even in the immediate vicinity but perhaps down at the stream, the noise of which must have covered the screaming. She couldn't think of any other reason why he would have left the car and not heard anything. The car keys were probably somewhere in the house. She cursed herself for never having learned to drive. Even so, now she was free she was terrified to return inside. As the shock subsided, she began to feel the cold. It was exacerbated by the sweat and slime on her breasts and stomach that she attempted to wipe away with her hands. The smell as it dried on her skin rose up to greet her nose giving her a vivid recall of Ilya's stomach bursting open. She clamped her lips and fought back the tears. From the bundle of clothes in her hands she pulled out her thin IKEA uniform and used it to clean off. The nylon cotton mix didn't absorb anything. She had the impression she was simply smearing the fluid over her and the stinking vapor caused her stomach to heave. But, once again, she refused to give in to it. She scraped off the worst, wiped her hands and dropped the dress to one side.

Her attention was caught by the noisy crack of a branch from the direction of the stream. She froze, eyes wide, ears pulled back and listened intently. She had been right, Roman was down there. The rushing of the stream formed a sonic backdrop against which she tried to pick out and analyze a myriad of smaller sounds. Her attention was broken by a piercing moan from the house, as if Ilya had finally found the strength to greet his maker. When his rasping call subsided the forest hush returned. Marta held her breath.

The buildings were built on a rise with a steep escarpment behind the outhouse and down towards the stream. From somewhere in that direction came another noise she was convinced was a footfall.

She felt for her soft, sensible brown work shoes with her feet and slipped them on. She ignored her underclothes and Georgiy's Hermes scarf and picked up her padded down jacket. She had just got one arm in when she heard another heavy crack from below the level of the ridge, but closer. Roman was working his way round. She retreated as quietly as she could and after ten steps fell backwards into a void. She tumbled head over heels down the incline and came to rest at the bottom.

When she picked herself up, she saw Roman's silhouette emerge from the trees. She turned suddenly, stumbled, found her equilibrium and ran through the trees attempting to catch the arm of her coat flapping uselessly behind her.

The forest here was not thick but the ground was irregular and littered with fallen branches. She was thankful for her shoes but it was hard going. The coarse grass, bushes, sticks and other traps of the hidden undergrowth scratched and battered her legs all the way up to her bare thighs. She didn't dare look round to see how close Roman was. Instead she crashed on and on for several minutes until she reached a short manmade embankment. She scrambled up and onto an overgrown road. The moon was so positioned that it lit the bottom of the parallel earthen tracks that stretched away in each direction before being swallowed up by the ubiquitous forest. She fancied she could make out a yellowish gleam in the sky over the treetops to her left. Assuming it could indicate a town or main road she set off in that direction without pausing for breath.

43.

Roman put the phone back in his pocket. At least he knew who he was working for now. Once he had explained the situation he was surprised how well Bruno Olevsky had taken it and how ruthless his response had been. There was no question now of disappearing. He knew Olevsky's reputation and had no intention of being buried in concrete or fed feet-first into a meat grinder. On the other hand the stakes were certainly higher. A successful conclusion to the affair would bring him closer to the kind of man he wanted to work for - a man of power. The word that came to his mind was 'khozyain' which might refer to a businessman, elected official or head of industry. He thought of it in the original sense a village strongman whose absolute authority was to be feared but also respected because he brought law and order. He was fed up with kowtowing to the mediocre Ilyas of this world. He wanted to escape the provincial drudgery of Nizhny Novgorod and had a vision of himself as an enforcer for a major gang in Moscow or St Petersburg. This job was his stepping-stone and he would prove he could be every bit as cold blooded as the professional killers he heard about in the news.

He was lost in these fantasies when he heard sounds of running on the road ahead. Out of the darkness a figure was coming pell-mell towards him. He thought to hide to one side of the road but the person saw the beam of the flashlight he had bought in Portnyan and called out.

"Help. Please!"

It was a woman's voice. He had a good idea who it might be.

Marta was convinced Roman was behind her and focused all her hopes on the silhouette ahead. She was so exhausted and frightened she would not have recognized her young captor in broad daylight. As she approached she slowed to a lumbering trot. Her breath grated sharply at the back of her throat and when she coughed she was sure she tasted blood. Finally she tumbled into his arms. Roman silently observed her beaten and stained face in the gauze of moonlight. Her hair was matted to her face and the hot smell of blood, sweat and fear rose up through the collar of her jacket. He could almost guess what had happened and mentally cursed Ilya for an amateur. He would deal with him as Olevsky had instructed.

"Please" she gasped, "they're going to kill me."

Her absolute helplessness nourished his growing sense of self-importance.

"Not yet my lovely" he said grimly. "Not yet."

Marta looked up. Roman's familiar granite blue eyes took her breath away. How did he get in front of her? It wasn't possible. The last vestige of her rebellious power drained away. Her eyelids fluttered, her knees dissolved and she fainted into his arms.

44.

Tyler saw the ambulance immediately. He could hardly miss it. The blue light turned slowly, illuminating the small crowd that had gathered outside Janine's flat. Down the short path, Tyler could see her door was wide open and the lights were on inside. He pulled to a halt where the ambulance blocked the road and stared at the scene in shock.

The crowd held back a respectful distance and he walked straight past them into the hallway. It was as silent and empty as an open grave. He looked through the door to the front room and saw nothing unusual except an upturned plastic bottle and some of Rachel's sweets on the carpet. Noise and movement further inside the house caught his attention and he continued down the corridor to Rachel's bedroom. The door was wide open and inside he could see the backs of three paramedics dressed in day-glow fatigues clustered around Rachel's bed. Tyler's skin goose-pimpled. There was no talking in the room but the sense of urgency was more acute for the hush. When he reached the doorway he saw Janine standing at the head of the bed staring down with her fists clenched tightly together under her chin.

She must have been crying for some time because tears had streaked mascara down her chalk-white cheeks. She made no effort to wipe it away. Instead, the black gullies flowed freely round the cut of her large jaw and onto her skin-tight knuckles. Her eyes were wide and raw and full to the brim with pain.

Tyler pushed between two of the paramedics and saw Rachel lying flat out on the bed in her pajamas. There was an acrid smell of old vomit and Tyler noticed trails on the pillow, sheets and pajamas. Her face was even whiter than her mother's. Her tiny forehead was moist from sweat and her long straight hair was spread out on the pillow like a halo. She was dead. Or at least he thought so until he saw the rapid movement behind her thin, blue-veined eyelids and noticed her tiny hands frenetically clenching and unclenching.

When he tried to speak Tyler found his throat was sealed dry. The tide of events moved swiftly around him. To his right, one of the paramedics had finished preparing a gurney.

"OK. Let's move her" he said.

"What's happened?" Tyler croaked.

Before anyone could answer, Rachel suddenly jerked as though she had been prodded with an electric baton. Her body arched momentarily and shook. She collapsed back down moaning and shivering and someone covered her with a silver foil blanket. Tyler pushed past Janine and knelt on the bed next to his daughter's face. He reached out to touch her but one of the medics guided him away and grasped the sheet under Rachel's head. Another did the same for her feet while the third hooked up an IV bag.

"One. Two. Three." On the third count the medics swung the sheet up and onto the gurney and Tyler watched in horror as they injected a needle into her forearm and attached a transparent plastic tube from the hanging sack. Janine choked loudly and threw her arms around Tyler's neck. She buried her face in his neck and her hot tears ran down his skin.

"I'm sorry. I'm sorry," she intoned.

The medics flowed towards the doorway taking Rachel with them.

"What's happening?" Tyler demanded again of no one in particular. "I'm her father for Christ's sake."

He shook Janine off and grabbed the arm of the last man to exit the room.

"Overdose" the medic said contemptuously. "Looks like ecstasy to me mate. What do you think?"

Before Tyler had time to swallow the implication of his phrasing Janine threw herself back around his neck and hung there sobbing. Rachel was wheeled briskly down the hallway and Tyler staggered after them with Janine in tow. He put his arm around her waist and took her weight. Through her sobbing she repeated her apologetic mantra.

"I'm sorry. I'm so sorry."

Why? What had she done? He couldn't make sense of it. Ecstasy? As they passed the living room door, the multicolored 'sweets' scattered on the floor took on a new meaning. While the medics pushed through the crowd outside and hurried towards the waiting ambulance, Tyler diverted Janine into the empty room.

"Janine. Janine! Look at me" he shouted.

She buried her face in her hands then fell to the floor and curled up into a ball. He could understand she was distraught but he had never known her to be so... feeble. It was as if she had been waiting for Tyler's arrival and could now cede him the responsibility.

Tyler had never seen ecstasy before. He dropped to one knee and scooped up a handful of the pastel pills. They came in various shapes (lozenge, round, triangular) and colors (blue, green, pink) all about the size of a finger nail. Most had a simple design or word pressed into the surface: a smiley face, a Volkswagen symbol, 'love', a tao and many more. He could see how Rachel had mistaken them for sweets. What he couldn't understand was how they got here.

He asked Janine but she maintained her fetal defense. He angrily unrolled her and shouted "Janine! Look at me. Where did these come from?"

When she refused to answer he gritted his teeth and angrily pulled her hands away from her face.

"Answer me for God's sake. Are they yours?"

Then it came to him in a flash. "Francis" he whispered.

Janine screamed. He reacted without thinking and slapped her hard across the cheek.

Janine cowered. "I didn't know Ty. I promise. He left the bottle under the sink. I didn't know..."

She was cut off by the sounds of car horns and shouting from outside. Tyler pulled her up.

"Come on" he said. "We've got to go."

Before they reached the hall a man entered the house. "Your car man" he said. "It's in the way."

They sprinted out and Janine climbed up into the back of the ambulance where Rachel was already being treated.

"I'll meet you at the hospital" Tyler said.

"I'm so sorry Ty," she said plaintively. A medic gripped her by the arm, guided her forcefully inside and slammed the door.

"Where are you taking her?" Tyler asked the driver.

"St Stephens. King's Road."

Tyler's car was parked right in front and already someone had climbed inside and seemed to be looking for the keys. A mixed race boy in a white tracksuit was going through the glove compartment, clearly looking for more than his keys.

"Get out" he shouted, grabbing him by the collar and trying to yank him out.

The boy turned and slapped his hand away "Get the fuck off me you freak".

Tyler's fury boiled over. His fist crashed into the boy's cheek and he fell back into the car. Tyler grabbed him by the hair and flung him onto the pavement. The boy was soon up on his feet. He may have been young, but he was a good two inches taller than Tyler and ready to jump him.

Tyler stepped right up to him. "Get out of my face or I'll put a bullet right between your fucking eyes."

The boy looked at him. There was no mistaking his fury but the veracity of his threat was something else. The ambulance sounded its siren. The boy shrugged meekly and backed down.

"Only trying to help," he said as a parting shot.

The ambulance was nose to nose with his Fiat and Tyler was forced to back up into the first available parking space. Once free, the siren came on and it surged past in a blur of noise and color. The road was too narrow to turn round, so Tyler pulled out and headed in the opposite direction. He turned left and left again following a route he imagined was parallel to the ambulance. When he lost it, he rolled down the window and listened out for the siren. The traffic was heavy as always at this time on a Saturday night. People moved from restaurants to pubs and clubs or back again. He stopped at traffic lights and listened as the siren faded out into the distance. The ambulance wouldn't have to stop as he did. And he wondered how long it would take them to push through the endless stream of cars. No more than five ten minutes to the hospital he thought. What time was it now?

He looked at the clock on his dashboard: 11.53. It stuck him that his rendezvous with Greg was in seven minutes. So many things were turning round in his head at the same time he found it difficult to concentrate on any one of them. He tried to concentrate on Rachel but Francis' hateful face kept floating into his mind. When he saw it, his jaw clenched, his hairs spiked and the blood seemed to drain from his skin. It was a purely visceral reaction. He wanted to tear at him with his nails, to eviscerate and crucify him. He had to shake his head to banish the nightmarish fantasies. Then there was Greg. 'Tonight or never' he had said. Something he had repeated when they had fixed the rendezvous and the price. Ten thousand pounds they had agreed on. It was the kind of money that could change his life completely. He could pay the outstanding child maintenance and protect Rachel from Francis. He could get a good lawyer. He could start to win Janine round, if that were possible.

The traffic light before him turned red and he gratefully slowed to a halt. Francis, Greg, Janine, Rachel, the money and the gun swirled around in a perpetually evolving matrix of cause and effect. Where did it all begin? Where should he start? At which of these points should he reach in and break the circle?

45.

The light drizzle seemed to lubricate rather than dampen the spirits of the midnight revelers. As Zinic weaved between them he bitterly regretted his leather jacket. In the fifteen minutes he had been padding back and forth outside Joe's Bar his woolen blazer had soaked up the moisture like a kitchen cloth. He shifted from foot to foot and took in his surroundings. In the space of a hundred yards he counted four Indian restaurants and five wine bars. Groups of smokers congregated outside each one with drinks in their hands and the collars turned up. The road was buzzing. There were hundreds if not thousands of people in various stages of sobriety milling along the pavements on both sides. The traffic flowed slowly but surely down the middle in both directions.

He chose well thought Zinic.

It was crowded enough for Tyler to feel safe,

but not so choked he couldn't get lost and escape. Joe's bar hadn't been difficult to spot. It was the largest and most raucous of all the bars in what, by daylight would pass for an ordinary suburban road. A blue 'handwritten' neon sign proclaiming the name of the establishment hung inside each of the two large windows. It vaguely reminded him of an American TV series he must have seen but had long since forgotten.

By quarter past midnight he was starting to feel anxious. He had been monitoring everyone entering the bar for the last half hour but had seen no one carrying his bag or wearing his jacket as agreed. Now he wondered if there was another entrance or if Tyler had got there before him. He decided he could just as well watch the door from somewhere warm and dry. Inside, the bar was heaving and as new people piled in all the time, it gave no sign of letting up. Zinic found himself a space close to the door where his line of sight wouldn't be blocked. He felt conspicuous standing alone in a wet jacket without a drink but people were either too drunk or polite to pay him any attention. He extracted the sealed beige A3 envelope with the Chelsea Cloisters crest on the back. The damp had made it slightly transparent and he could just make out the writing on the torn pages of newspaper inside. It was obvious to anyone who was looking for it but he hoped Tyler would be too nervous to notice. He didn't care much anyway once he had his hand on the bag he defied anyone to take it back.

Tyler walked towards the rendezvous with a heavy heart. He had been obliged to park his car some ten minutes away and even then in a place so illegal he would probably be deported. On the drive over he had had the bright idea to take the SIM card out of his old phone and place it into the new one. This meant that Greg could no longer call him but Janine could. He had an inkling that mobile phones didn't work in hospitals but she had called immediately. Rachel had gone into emergency care but seemed to be doing well. He was reassured and apologised for getting stuck in traffic. He felt guilty about not going straight there, but reasoned there was nothing he could do anyway except hold hands. Not something he was inclined to in his present mood.

If all went well, he could exchange the bag for the money, be half an hour late and ten thousand pounds richer. Bennerly Road gave onto the Northcott Road about halfway up. He turned left and joined the throng. Joe's Bar was a thirty yards away on the far side. He kept his head low and his eyes wide. As he walked he deliberately brushed all the possible problems out of his mind. He didn't want to dwell on them. If it all went wrong, if he didn't get the money, if he were shot of stabbed to death in the process then he was simply rewinding the clock six hours. Nothing ventured, nothing gained. He wondered at his sang froid. It was a new feeling for him.

His phone rang just as he was turning up his collar against the miserable rain. It was Janine.

"Where are you Ty?" she pleaded.

"I'm coming" he said calmly. "How's Rachel?"

There was a pause and Janine collapsed into sobs.

"Janine?" He pressed the phone against his ear and covered the other with his palm. "What's happening?"

Janine's feeble voice was lost in sniffles. Someone bumped into his shoulder jerking his phone from his ear just as she answered. All he heard her say was '...away'.

"What?" Tyler shouted. "Janine, I can't hear you."

"... intensive care" she continued.

"Intensive care!"

Janine re-succumbed to tears and self-re-crimination.

"What did they say? What did the doctor say?"

"It all happened so fast" she howled. "She had a seizure in emergency and... I thought she was going to die Tyler." She choked up then continued "They said her brain was... overheating.

Tyler stopped in his tracks. He felt a pain in his chest and his breath came in short shallow bursts. He tried to rally his thoughts. "What's happening now?"

Through her sobs he understood they were attempting to stabilize her condition and the next half an hour would be critical. "I'm really worried Ty" she wept. "She looked so fragile, so far away. I'm afraid. What if she..."

"Don't say it Janine. Don't. She's going to be OK." He had a flash vision of his daughter stretched out on a hospital bed with a doctor raising the sheet over her lifeless face.

"What if she's brain damaged, or worse? I couldn't live with myself Ty. I couldn't."

Nor could I he thought. He suppressed his tears by biting down hard on the inside of his lower lip until he tasted blood. He assured Janine he was coming straight there and hung up. His head was spinning. Once again he was plagued by self-doubt. What was he doing here when he should be at the hospital? When he thought of Francis, the cause of Rachel's suffering, the anger welled up inside him and he felt dizzy with hate. It took at least a minute of confused reflection before his senses came back into focus. Even then he had to look around him to check where he was.

Inside Joe's Bar, Yolanda was seated at a window table with a group of girlfriends. There were five of them in all, old friends from the same Aylesbury Estate and Crampton Primary School who, despite their divergent lives, had never lost the desire to stay in touch. It was the only company in which she felt truly relaxed. They had nothing to hide from each other. Between them they had eight children, five divorces and one hundred and nineteen lovers (many of them shared). Mayflower Brown had done twenty-six months in Holloway for aggravated burglary and was now living with a full back for Crystal Palace. Men were never invited to their regular hook-ups but dominated their conversation nonetheless.

She hadn't mentioned him by name but Tyler had been on Yolanda's mind ever since they had parted on Friday night. Maybe it was the effect of six Americanos but she felt guilty. She knew, or could guess at, most of the problems in Tyler's life and had never offered much in the way of sympathy. It just wasn't in her nature and listening to the cruel way her and her friends dissected the world she could understand why. The problem was that he was the only man she knew with whom she could relax. He was neither threatening nor pretentious - which was probably why she didn't fancy him.

She was just thinking how wet he was when she saw him standing in the rain across the road. He seemed to be staring straight ahead at nothing in particular completely oblivious to the rain.

That's just like him she thought. In a world of his own.

She smiled unconsciously, forgot the 'girls only' rule and knocked on the window in a futile attempt to get his attention.

"Tyler. Tyler!"

"Who's that, girl?" asked Mayflower.

"He works with me" Yolanda chuckled. "He fancies me like hell."

"Where's his white stick?" laughed twice-divorced Julie and waved at him through the glass. "Yoohoo Tyler" she screeched "she's over here honey."

Despite Yolanda's protestations the other four girls started to wave and raucously chant 'Tyler! Tyler!'

Zinic wasn't the only person to look over at the five drunk black girls near the window but he was the only one who understood what they were shouting. He pushed hurriedly through the crowd towards them causing more than a few annoyed comments.

There was too much street noise for Tyler to hear but as he floated slowly out of his stupor he saw the group in the window, franticly waving. What caught his attention however was the swarthy looking man behind them. A break in the traffic and he saw the man drop his eyes to the hold all he was carrying in his left hand. In that moment they both knew.

Zinic pushed his way back through the crowded room towards the door. Drinks flew and several men grabbed at his clothing slowing his progress. One even attempted a punch that caught him just behind the ear. He ignored them all, pulled himself free and charged through the door. Tyler had seen him coming and started to run. He tucked the bag up under his arm and sped along the pavement dodging the strollers and drinkers like a rugby player. At the first opportunity he swerved left into an alleyway and sprinted hell-for-leather.

Zinic burst out of the double doors. He scanned the opposite pavement but Tyler had disappeared with no indication which direction he had taken except some annoyed faces to his right. He trotted down the road without crossing so as to give himself the maximum field of vision. Twenty yards ahead he saw a woman being picked off the pavement by her boyfriend. Someone was shouting angrily and he sprinted over.

"What happened?" he asked the woman.

"Some stupid bastard" said the shouting man.

"Police" Zinic announced. "Which way did he go?"

The two men pointed to an alley running between two restaurants. Zinic heard a crash from inside and plunged in. It ran back the length of the restaurants and ended in a brick wall twice the height of a man. In the poor light he could make out rubbish bins and at the far end a stack of crates. One of these had fallen and Tyler was now precariously balanced on top of the remaining pile clawing at the wall on top of which was poised the black hold all. Zinic saw the prize and surged forward.

Tyler had scrambled up the crates and managed to place the bag but as soon as he had attempted to jump over the wall the top crate had fallen off and he was left balancing on top of an unstable pile of five others. When he saw Zinic in the head of the alley every hair on his body spiked in alarm. The top of the wall was now three inches beyond his fingertips. The crates rocked and started to fall away from the wall. In a second they would have fallen too far even to attempt a jump. He launched himself up and just caught the top of the slippery bricks with the ends of his fingers. Zinic was an arm's reach away from his dangling legs when the crates toppled over. They exploded on the concrete and forced him back. With a strength he didn't know he possessed Tyler pulled himself up the wall. His shoes slid over the wet bricks but eventually his right found a gap in the mortar and he managed to get an elbow over the top. Zinic crunched through the broken glass and swiped for his trailing left leg but Tyler pulled it up just in time. He lifted his torso up onto the wall and bent over the top. His right leg followed then his left until he was finally flat on his stomach twelve feet off the ground.

Zinic spun round looking for something to climb on, or another way up but there was nothing. He glanced briefly at the crowd that had gathered in the entrance to the alley but realized they were not about to come any closer. He pulled the envelope out of his pocket and waved it at Tyler.

"I have the money Tyler. Give me the bag."

Tyler pivoted round into a sitting position and stared down at him thoughtfully. He had a brief recollection of that moment when Francis was laid out on Janine's floor. The same feeling of power returned to him now. While Zinic held the envelope high over his head Tyler thought of all the confrontations he had avoided with his father, with Janine, with Francis and Thatcher. He had always searched for the easy route, the line of least resistance that had ultimately led to Rachel's hospital bed. This, he decided, was the moment when it all changed.

He drew the bag close to him and it slid easily along the top of the damp brickwork. He picked it up by the handles in his right fist, raised it off the wall, turned and dropped it on the far side. It made a soft thud as it hit the grass of the garden below. Zinic's lip curled into a lupine snarl and he hurled the pack of newspapers bills at Tyler's face. He made no attempt to catch it. The deceitful envelope bounced harmlessly off the jacket Tyler had made his own and dropped back into the alley. He lifted up his right leg and turned until he was straddling the wall, then lay flat again and eased himself over until he was hanging over the other side by his fingertips. Zinic couldn't see him drop to the ground. He ran back out of the alley, through the gawping crowd and back into the Northcott Road. He sprinted through lazy pedestrians blocking his way desperately searching for another street that would take him round but at the end of five frantic minutes he knew it was too late. He had lost him. He stopped by a blue Nissan, placed his hands on the roof and drove the toe of his shoe into the driver's panel.

The little shit had outwitted him.

"Tyler, Tyler" he murmured ominously. "I'm going to find you and I'm going to kill you. I'm going to find you and I'm going to kill you." He repeated this several times before he finally worked out how to do it.

46.

The Railway Tavern stuck out from the waste ground like an old tooth. The Victorian relic had somehow escaped the Blitzkrieg, post-war and Big-Bang redevelopment and now bordered Coldharbour Lane, one of the main commuter arteries into central London. It had been built on the expectation of a station that never arrived. The railway itself ran over a bridge from the same epoch one hundred and fifty yards up the road. The sidings gave onto the empty rubbish strewn land that surrounded the pub and its car park.

Tyler recognized Francis' car immediately. The muscular slate-grey BMW Jeep stood out amongst the smaller, older more commonplace cars just as it was supposed to. Quite why Janine had chosen to work there was beyond Tyler's comprehension. It was a horrible place. But he knew that was where she had met Francis and it was where he spent every Saturday night.

He parked his Fiat over the road and turned off the ignition. He had never been in the pub but had once plucked up the courage to peek through the window. Inside was a time capsule to an era that he thought had ended with the Richardsons and Krays. There were wooden spindle chairs, two snooker tables, red velvet curtains, brown cigarette-scarred linoleum and a small wooden bar with low, shaded lights. Tyler's impression of the clientele was of stocky men with earrings, tattoos cropped hair and pale complexions.

It was half past twelve. With the new opening hours it was impossible to tell what time the Tavern would close. His vague idea of waiting for Francis to leave was put out of his mind by the sight of a police car hurtling towards him, blue lights twirling like a hurricane. It came to a sudden halt outside the front of Tavern. Seconds later it was met by a police van arriving from the opposite direction. It stopped so that it blocked the entrance to the car park. Three officers alighted from the car, followed by a total of six from the van. The first group waited outside the front entrance while the others unloaded into the car park. Of these, four hurried out of sight around the back and two walked over to Francis' car and checked the number plate. One of them spoke into a radio on his lapel and then, after a moment, nodded to the three hovering out front.

Tyler could guess what had happened. Janine had quite rightly told them where the Ecstasy came from. He could well imagine that a thug like Francis was already known to the local constabulary and that explained the number of officers piling onto the scene. As he watched them prepare to enter the pub he had a maddening sense of frustration. He had built himself up to this confrontation. He had come to hate Francis with a passion and intended to... what exactly? He wasn't sure. He was probably only going to scare him with the rifle but even that satisfaction was now to be denied. Francis' arrest brought him no pleasure. It was too abstract. A trial, conviction, fine or prison term was a blur in some alternative future.

He started the engine and angrily swung the car out into the road. In his rear view he saw three policemen enter through the front door and could imagine the turmoil it would cause inside. He drove under the bridge, turned immediately left into Aston Grove and parked. The street followed the curve of the railway into the distance. Despite being well lit and adjacent to a major road it had a lonely, menacing air. The few cars dotted along its length were the only signs of human life at this hour. On his right was a high-walled building like a warehouse. The grimy windows, covered in steel mesh and boarded up at the lowest level gave it an abandoned air. On his left a wire fence separated the pavement from the overgrown incline up to the railway.

Tyler opened the door and stepped out. It had stopped raining but the moist night air settled on his skin like a cold sweat. He opened the boot and extracted the roll-up rifle sack from the black bag. There was still a steady flow of cars along Coldharbour Lane and they made a hollow sound and as they passed under the ancient bridge. The single iron span, sixteen feet above the tarmac was supported at both ends by granite walls that sloped down and away from the main road on each side at an angle or forty five degrees. He closed the boot and walked over to the base of the buttress where it met the pavement. The wire fence ran up it to the bridge leaving a narrow stone ledge on the outside.

He unzipped his jacket half way and forced the roll-up inside. It was bulky but it held, leaving him his two hands free. He grabbed the wire fence, put a foot on the damp slope and pulled himself up. It wasn't as easy as it looked. The stone was slippery and he found he had to drag himself up most of the way with his arms. The ledge stopped at the solid iron balustrade that ran parallel to the rail. Here the fence was only some three feet high and he was able to raise one foot onto the top and climb over.

The street lamps were below the level of the parapet and once on top of the bridge he found himself in a pool of blackness surrounded by light. It was a strange sensation looking down on the world. It reminded him of being in Thatcher's office and, now that he came to think of it, the moment Francis had been laid out on the floor in Janine's flat and, more recently, staring down at Greg from the top of the wall. Events all connected, he reflected, by the common theme of power.

To either side of him, the parallel iron rails faded away into the darkness. He felt for the edge of the rail line with his toe, then stepped gingerly across it to the far side. He looked down over the fence onto the empty waste ground. He had a perfect view over the Railway Tavern. The dimly illuminated car park was on the far side, and the front of the building was bathed in the glow of two strong up lighters on either side of the door. From this position it seemed more isolated than ever. He could see the droplets of mist sparkling inside the beams of light.

He placed the rifle pack on a patch of gravel and unrolled it. Unpacking and assembling the rifle, even in the dark, was beginning to feel like second nature. He screwed the two stocks together, clipped in the optical site and the second magazine. He charged the breech and flipped up the protective covers on the scope.

He went down on one knee in the four feet that separated the edge of the railway sleepers from the wire netting and threaded the barrel through the fence. The Tavern was perhaps fifty yards further than the target he had used to boresight the rifle on Rombalds Ridge but he couldn't believe that the vertical drop would be greatly increased over such a short distance. Since the elevation had already been adjusted for the humidity on the moor he wondered if he would need to do any more for the heavier precipitation. On the other hand, he was shooting down which, he assumed, may counteract some of the gravitational pull. In the end he decided to leave it as it was.

When he adjusted the focus, the scene outside the Tavern sprung into view. The police from the car park were beginning to file back into the van. Tyler couldn't immediately see the other police car and he wondered if he was too late. He swung back onto the front of the pub and followed two other officers inside. There was a hiatus and it wasn't at all clear where in the action he had arrived. Another police car arrived and two other men got out. There must have been a noise or disturbance that Tyler couldn't hear because they suddenly ran in. The van emptied again and they were approaching the door when two policemen burst out carrying a struggling body.

Tyler felt a strange rumbling in his knee. He supposed it was the awkward position he was in. It certainly wasn't fear. He felt perfectly calm and even completely detached from the events below him. He had the impression of looking down a microscope. The species under observation could have been ants or a strain of bacteria. He was a God looking down on a miniature world. He could name the species under observation but was no more involved in their proceedings than they were aware of his presence. He didn't hear the train until it was almost on top of him. When it hit the far side of the bridge there was an iron gurgling. He looked to his left to see the massive square bulk bearing down on him like a mailed fist. The headlights illuminated the track ahead and for a moment he could clearly see the face of driver in the window. He was too late to move so he flattened himself against the netting. Because of the slope away from the rails and the height of the carriages there was no danger and they trundled past above him with room to spare. It was a slow moving goods train and after the first carriage had passed he maneuvered back into a position.

By now, a crowd of men had gathered outside to confront the police. They gesticulated violently but their shouts were lost in the gargantuan growling of the train only a few feet behind him. On the pavement there was a squirming body face down on the ground. One policeman was kneeling on the back of his knees while the other struggled to trap his flailing arms in handcuffs. The prone man's bald head twisted and turned. His face contorted with rage and Tyler could see his mouth silently working. But the perspective and the lack of sound made him seem even more distant than he actually was. Once the handcuffs were fastened, the policemen stood up and pulled at the chain link to raise him to his feet. Tyler saw him clearly for the first time: it was Francis.

As they led him forward towards the second police car Tyler tried to center the glowing cross hairs on his chest. But before he had time to steady his aim the squad car reversed and Francis was swiveled round so that he was side on. A policeman blocked Tyler's line of sight. The car door opened and a hand pushed Francis' head down and into the car. Tyler's chance had gone and he wasn't sure if he was relieved or not. The possibility that he might have shot him seemed suddenly unreal.

He pulled his face back slightly from the scope and the effect was like watching a tiny television. At the same time the rattling, screeching and clanking of the passing train filled his skull as if he were wearing headphones at full volume. The two events, Francis and the train, seemed perfectly synchronized in terms of angry, percussive energy. On the small round screen, Francis continued to resist the policemen's efforts. The harder they tried to push him down and forward into the car the harder he fought back and up until he suddenly broke free. His head and shoulders shot up like a whale breaking for air. He launched himself backwards and his body hung momentarily in Tyler's scope. A sharp squeak from the train pierced his brain like a hatpin. Tyler tensed and bared his teeth at the noise in an ugly grimace. Francis was shunted back to earth as if punched in the chest by an invisible hand and disappeared under a scrum of blue uniforms. The tide of men from the pub surged forward and broke over them. Tyler stood up and looked down at the scene. The change in perspective was unexpected. The brawl outside the pub was no longer made of individual faces and they looked more like swarming ants than ever. The last carriage of the train swept mercifully away into the night and the soft sounds of traffic faded back in.

He shook the last of the brutal noise out of his head then unclenched and worked his jaw. His shoulders were tensed up round his neck and the muscles in his crooked arms were unnaturally stiff. He took his left hand off the rifle stock, stretched and splayed the fingers then slowly straightened his elbow. When it came to his right arm he realized his hand was still balled into fist round the trigger guard. He turned the rifle into the light. Starting with his little finger he unbent each one in turn. The last one was the index finger. He gently unhinged it and the trigger clicked back into place.

47.

Volya was in the middle of a two-day fishing expedition when he heard the screams.

Volya meant 'will' and he liked to live up to it. His father, 'Traktor' had received his name during the period of Red Baptisms that had swept the Soviet Union of the 1920s and he had passed this tradition on to his first-born son. But after losing a leg fighting on the Western Front, Traktor had returned home disillusioned and insisted on being called Ivan. He had also reverted to his father's family name, that is to say the name derived from the first name of his grandfather born in 1861, the year serfdom was abolished. So at sixty-nine years old Volya Pytorvich carried a history of Russia in those two words.

He had been born on his family's smallholding in the Remlev region and had never left it. His wife, Sonia, had died longer ago that he cared to remember. He had a daughter who lived in Moscow and was married with children. His only memory of them was a faded postcard that had been pinned to the kitchen wall for the last ten years. He had a son who had become addicted to vodka as a teenager. After lunch on the fourth of March 1983 he walked out of the house to by a bottle and never returned. The police never found him dead or alive. They probably never tried. Volya didn't even have a postcard to remember him by. He had never reflected on the purpose of life nor his reason to continue but to an outside observer Volya embodied the very meaning of his name. For twenty-five years he had managed the small farm alone, selling the surplus in the Saturday market at Pyortnan. He was tougher and stronger than most men half his age and, at five foot ten, was taller than most his own age. And unlike so many of the drunks, degenerates and lunatics this rural backwater seemed to breed he remained unbroken and unbowed. His face was lean, lined and the color of tanned leather. The muscles on his lithe body stood out like rope beneath wind-dried skin. Once every six months he treated himself to a haircut. So, depending on the time of year his full white hair was either cropped like a soldier or hung down to his eyebrows. At the moment, it was short. He preferred it that way.

He had set off immediately after the market on Saturday morning and worked his way up the stream that had no official name but was known locally as Laughing Beck. At dusk he chose a slight rise on the ground beneath a gnarled and lightening scarred pine under which he secured a tarpaulin. The fishing had been indifferent. He had caught nineteen brown trout of varying sizes and expected to do the same tomorrow. When he got home he would smoke them in his chimney in preparation for the winter. Tonight he would roast one on a wooden spit.

It was while he was away from the stream searching for dry tinder that he heard the noises from the abandoned Tevlevski dacha. At first he thought it was an owl. He cocked his ear, moved closer and waited. The second and third screeches were shorter but he could tell they were human. They were muffled in a way that made him think they were coming from inside a building. As he crept forward he thought how sorry he was not to have brought his hunting rifle. He had left it at home because it was incumbent to carry while fishing. Now he regretted it.

He skirted the bog and was crawling up the embankment to the level of the buildings when another scream split the night, more terrifying than all the others put together. It made him wince and brought back a sharp reminder of his father's nightmares. As the intense cry of pain continued, Volya's eyes widened with fear and amazement. When he poked his head over the top of the rise he thought he could hear thumping on the walls or floor. He was surprised to find no lights in the widows. The front door was closed but he could just make out a car parked behind the main building. Suddenly the screaming stopped and was replaced by an eerie silence. Volya waited. He was eager to peek through the windows but as a hunter of long years knew the value of patience.

The front door flew open and a naked woman leapt out carrying a bundle. She hesitated for a moment then ran behind the two-storied outhouse facing the main house. Volya waited a moment then dropped back down the slope and walked round to where he could see her. His curiosity made him careless and he broke a twig with his foot. By the time he could see the back of the outhouse the woman was dressed. She backed away cautiously then literally dropped out of sight. There was a slight cry and he heard, rather than saw, her running through the woods in the direction of the dirt road that fed the few lost properties strung out along Laughing Beck.

He counted to one hundred then climbed up to the back of the outhouse where the woman had left a bundle of clothing. He stepped over

it and moved on towards the main building. He decided to circle first, looking through
the windows. There was a dying fire in the
stove of the living room but otherwise the
house looked empty. He knew it wasn't. The
last scream had been a man's and no man had
emerged. A hollow feeling of fear swelled inside his stomach. When he had done the full
round he stepped cautiously through the open
front door. The filtered moonlight outside
gave a steady if subdued glow but inside was
dark and it took a moment for his eyes to adjust. The tiny entrance hall gave directly into
the kitchen. A body lay in the middle.

There was a warm sickly stench like a gut-
ted animal in the room and he soon noticed
why. From the amount of blood and offal on
the floor it was clear the man was dead. The
bloody knife close by indicated how he had
died and it didn't take a detective to work out
what had happened or even why. Every week
one heard of terrible goings on in Moscow
and even in Pyortnan - so why not here? He
sometimes felt his country had been better off
under Stalin. At least the violence was organized.

He had no feelings for the dead man. He
thought of the frightened naked woman and
imagined he probably deserved what he got.
He wondered about trying to find her but decided she would soon be back in town and

move on. What interested him was the car.

He made a cursory check that no one else was hiding in the house then returned outside. He took a deep breath and coughed the acrid smell of death out of his lungs. The car was unlocked and the keys hung in the ignition. He opened the driver's door and sat inside. By the soft gleam of the cabin light he could see a badly folded local map on the passenger seat and what looked like dried blood on the upholstery and the dashboard in front. There was an empty hamburger box in the foot-well and turning round he could see more such boxes, wrappers and paper cups strewn around the back. He turned the key and the engine purred into life. He grunted with satisfaction, noticed the petrol tank was three quarters full and cut the engine. The glove box was locked but opened with the ignition key. The plastic door dropped down and inside he found more litter, a grubby plastic folder containing the car documents and a dog-eared magazine that turned out to be the Russian version of Hustler. On the cover, a slim brunette was crouched inside a plastic tube wearing a yellow string vest cut off just below the nipples. Apart from the moonlit killer ten minutes ago, he couldn't remember the last time he had seen a naked woman. It must have been some time because he was more interested in her platform shoes with their twelve-inch high heels. He found himself wondering how she could possibly do any housework in such things and then chuckled at how old he had become. The contorted positions of the girls inside did nothing for him either and he threw the magazine on the seat with the rest of the junk. At the very bottom of the glove box he found a handgun.

He hesitated before touching it. His father had brought back a Tokarev TT-33 from the war. The grey metal had been battered and greasy and it had wooden grip panels one of which was split. It had no safety and he had blown off the small toe on his right foot when he had picked it up for the first time. Despite the inauspicious debut, he had maintained and fired it for fun over the decades until his son sold it to buy vodka just before he had disappeared. The pistol in the glove box was a double action 9mm Makarov PM, the gun that had eventually replaced the Tokarev as the standard military sidearm. He picked it out and looked for a safety catch that he found on the left side of the slide. The pistol was matt black with a brown plastic grip inlaid with the same star motif as the Tokarev. The date of manufacture, 1979, was stamped just below the safety. He pressed the magazine release at the base of the grip. It dropped out and he noted it was full. He pulled back the slide to find the chamber was empty then replaced the magazine. It was slightly smaller and quite a bit lighter than his father's but smoother to operate. The most important thing was that it had a safety which he made sure was firmly 'on' before sliding it into his jacket pocket. Keeping the cars keys in his hand, he got back out of the car. He shut the door and stood there for a minute admiring his new acquisition. For a moment he fantasized about getting rid of his battered old Zaporozhets and driving around in this fancy foreign vehicle. But he knew he would have to sell it. The money would be more than welcome and he didn't want to be mistaken for gangster.

He made up his mind what to do: he would go back to his camp, pack up and return immediately. What he had seen convinced him it would be best if he left tonight with what he had rather than wait until tomorrow and search the house for more. Who knows what may happen before then. After all, a titmouse in the hand is better than a crane in the sky, as the expression went.

48.

D r. Littlefield placed a small pink pill on the desk and sat down heavily. Tyler thought she looked tired and angry. He wouldn't have given her more than thirty five years but her hair was pearly white. It was gathered into a loose ponytail that she tidied by dividing it in two and tugging at the ends. He noticed her hands were tanned. If she had just returned from holiday the effects were wearing off fast. The whites of her eyes were misty and floated above red rims. Despite this her movements were brisk and alert. Taken together with her sharp nose and fine lips she reminded him of a small bird. She crossed her forearms, perched them on the desk and leaned forward.

"One of the paramedics brought this back from your house" she said sharply.

Tyler could see where this was heading. "It's not my house" he countered. "We're divorced."

She pursed her lips and drummed her short unvarnished talons on the top. The assured reply caused her to reassess her attack but the scolding tone remained.

"Do you know what it is?"

"Ecstasy?" He knew the inflection sounded flippant, but he really wasn't at all sure.

"Ecstasy, Adam, E, Cloud 9, Biscuit - whatever" she snapped. "It's a synthetic drug called methylenedioxy-methylamphetamine or MDMA. And it's illegal."

"Look doctor, I don't need a lecture in morality."

"Do you know how many O.D.s we get in here a day?"

He held up his palm. "Let me finish. I don't like this any more than you. I just want to know what's happening to my daughter."

She stood up sharply and stalked over the one end of the book shelves that lined the wall behind her. She flicked through an untidy pile of magazines, pulled one out and returned to her chair. When she had found the right page she placed it on the desk top and turned it round to Tyler.

The magazine was the British Medical Journal and the article spread across two pages was entitled Seratonin Syndrome.

"This will give you some idea" she said tapping on a picture.

Tyler looked down at two brightly colored

brain scans. The one on the left was mostly scarlet and the one on the right was mostly dark.

He pointed to the one on the left and said "this one looks overheated."

"That's a normal scan showing blood flow to all areas. The one on the right shows the damage after an overdose."

She fell silent and allowed Tyler to absorb the information. He stared blindly at the two scans for half a minute. His breath was shallow and he blinked rapidly as he struggled to formulate the question to which he did not want an answer.

"Is this what has happen to Rachel?"

"We don't know yet Mr Primovelli. The good news is that your wife was very quick off the mark. She gave Rachel a salt-water drink and made her vomit. Amphetamine absorption is very fast but it's likely she saved her life. We don't know how many she took but the paramedics pumped her stomach and found nothing. That could be good news, or it could be bad. On the bad side however, her blood pressure was unusually high. This is dangerous because it can result in organ failure."

"Organ failure?" The phrase terrified him.

"Normally the kidneys or liver. The paramedics administered a benzodiazepine and brought it down, but we have no way of knowing how long she was like that."

Tyler was stunned. "When... when will you know?"

"We'll get the results of the blood tests tomorrow. For the moment we're keeping her stable in intensive care."

"What do you think?" he asked slowly.

"I think we are doing everything we can."

Tyler was still too much in shock to cry. "What's Seratonin?" he asked

Dr. Littlefield sat back for the first time. She had intended to jolt what she took to be an irresponsible father, but if he really wasn't to blame then maybe she was being too hard. It was easy to judge too hastily. She often did it and kicked herself afterwards. This young man didn't look like a hardened drug user even if he looked (and smelled) as though he needed a wash.

"Seratonin is a chemical released in the brain" she answered in a softer tone. "It controls things like your emotions, sleep and appetite. MDMA causes massive releases of the stuff. That's what gives a high. But brain cells only manufacture so much and an overdose makes them... well, put simply it destroys them."

"You mean she could be brain damaged?"

"It's too early to say. I wish there was an easy diagnosis but it's only been a few hours. We have to wait and see." She knew that she would be up all night with this one, but she didn't see the point in going into the complications that could arise in the next twelve hours: hyperthermia, disseminated intravascular coagulation, rhabdomyolysis, arrhythmias, seizures, renal failure, hypotension etc etc... all the way through to thrombocytopenia and cerebral edema.

Instead she rose from her seat and said "I'm sorry if I've been snappy."

Tyler nodded his acceptance of the truce. "You must be tired."

"No, you get used to that." She tidied away the magazine. "This kind of thing is so..." she searched for the word... "unnecessary." It wasn't the word she wanted. She wanted something stronger, a word that encapsulated all the suffering and death she had seen caused by drugs but it didn't come. No single word would ever be enough. She shook her head and said, "let's go and see how she's doing."

Tyler trailed the doctor through a labyrinth of stairs, doors and blue-Lino corridors up to the fifth floor. Everywhere was the sour smell of disinfectant. Finally she pushed through a pair of glass swing doors under a blue sign marked Intensive Care Unit - Nursing Development Unit. She pressed a silver button on the wall and a nurse appeared. While they talked, Tyler looked out of a triple window over the dark terraces and illuminated canyons of Chelsea by night. In the middle distance there was a church tower and beyond that a tall stationary crane whose gravity defying extremities were indicated by bright red lights.

The elevation brought back the memory of the railway bridge.

He had shot Francis.

He was sure of that now. But try as he may he could not find within him one ounce of compassion or regret. Quite the contrary, he was still angry. If he was there now he would do the same again. Intellectually, he was proud to have settled the account. So why couldn't he shake off this profound feeling of dissatisfaction? Of something unfinished? His thoughts were broken by Dr. Littlefield.

"Mr Primovelli?"

He spun round with a sinister look in his eye.

"Are you alright?" she asked with real concern.

"Yes" he said. "I was thinking."

She nodded sympathetically. "Rachel's through here? So far, no complications."

She led him along another short corridor. Here they passed two notice boards (one red, one blue) covered in dozens of neatly organized headshots. She caught him looking at them.

"That's the staff roster for the Unit" she said. "They'll be caring for Rachel while she's here." She pointed to a photo of a pretty girl with dark hair. "That's me. I wish they'd change it, I look like a teenager."

They approached another set of swing doors on which was written in huge multi-colored letters PLEASE WASH YOUR HANDS. An arrow pointed to what looked like a soap dispenser on one side.

"Alcohol gel" said the doctor. She pressed the lever and a dollop dropped into her palm that she then rubbed over both hands. "Eighty percent of germs are transmitted by the hands. It evaporates. See?"

She held up her dry hands to Tyler and indicated for him to do the same. Careful not to touch the doors, she leaned into them with her back and they entered the ward.

It was a spacious, well-lit room with windows on two sides. During the day they must have given an even greater impression of space and light but for now they were black and covered in vertical louver blinds. Eight intensive care beds were arranged around three sides of the room. Each bed was separated from its neighbor by a dark blue pleated curtain that could be pulled round to screen off the unit completely from the rest of the room. The duty nurse guided the visitors over to one that was closed and pulled it partially back.

Tyler stopped at the foot of the bed. Rachel lay flat on her back with her eyes closed and a blanket half way up her chest. Three electrodes were attached to her bare chest with wires that linked to three screens that hovered on adjustable arms over her head. A thick plastic pipe was strapped into her mouth and ran into a machine the size of a suitcase to the right side of her head. Another thinner pipe ran from her nose into a smaller machine to her right. Yet another pipe wound in from behind her head and disappeared under a plaster on her neck.

"It's looks worse than it is" said Dr. Littlefield flatly. "We use everything for the first few hours whether we need it or not."

She stopped level with Rachel's waist and pointed to the wires. "These monitor her vital signs: heart beat, breathing etc. An alarm goes off if there's a problem. As you can see, she's perfectly stable. This is the respirator," she said pointing to the tube emerging from her mouth.

"She can't breath?" Tyler said with a note of panic.

"Yes but she's very young. It helps keep her airways clear."

Indicating the tube in her nose she continued, "This nasty looking thing is a nasogastric tube. That allows us to drain the stomach contents and generally keep an eye on things down there. And finally" pointing to the tube running into her neck "medicine, fluids and nutrition are inserted directly into the blood from the infusion bag via a pump." She pointed to the clear plastic udder suspended to the right above a briefcase-sized box of dials and lights.

She turned away to examine the monitors. Half way up the bed under the blanket, Tyler noticed the two small mounds. They were Rachel's feet. When Littlefield turned back he was in tears. It was the moment he had been dreading. He now realized that the meeting with Greg and the shooting of Francis had all been ways of putting it off. The reality had been manageable while it was still abstract. Up close the raw truth was more frightening than he had expected. She was alone and helplessness, just like him. He cried for them both. Large tears rolled down his cheeks. The last twelve hours had flayed his emotions bare. He had experienced some terrible things but Rachel's tiny, motionless feet were the worst of all. He dropped to his knees and rested his forehead on the edge of the bed. He covered his face and sobbed into his hands. He was exhausted. The self-pity was returning. He fought it down but it seemed to well up from the center of the earth.

Dr. Littlefield left him alone and made a tour of the other patients. She understood. There was barely a week that passed without the loss of a patient in her care. Each one was a horrible struggle that hacked another piece from her heart. After five minutes Tyler emerged. Littlefield didn't have to be a doctor to see the change in his physiognomy. His face sagged under the weight of fear. The brash young man who faced her off barely ten minutes ago had gone; beaten down by the fragility of life. She had seen it many times before.

"I'm sorry," he said.

"There's no need. Let's see how your wife is doing."

Janine had been sedated and given a guest room on the same floor as the ICU. When Tyler entered, it was dark and she was curled up in a ball on top of the bed. He took a blanket from the chair and threw it over her but she didn't stir. He stood over her for a moment examining his feelings. He looked for love and compassion and found neither. He should have stopped loving her long ago but he had had nothing to replace her with. He observed the strong line of her jaw and the way her hair feathered over her forehead. These were things he would have died for not so long ago but now they left him cold. Just the thought of touching her made him shiver. She must have known Francis was a dealer, he decided, even if she was unaware the drugs were actually in the house. She was always fascinated by money and its power. Why else would she have put up with such an obnoxious brute? She was equally responsible for Rachel's overdose and he hated her for it. The sound of her breathing and her smell in the room repulsed him.

49.

Tyler crossed Chelsea Bridge at quarter to three. He was exhausted and his eyes fluttered spasmodically. He was more than physically tired, he was mentally, emotionally and psychologically drained. So much had happened in the last twelve hours he couldn't keep his mind on any one single train of thought. They turned round incessantly in his head without beginning or end, each one linked and locked to all the others; indivisible and insoluble. All he wanted to do was close his eyes and sleep. He would have slept on the floor next to Rachel but Dr Littlefield had insisted he go home and rest. In no uncertain terms she had said he looked like 'shit' and Rachel would drop into a coma if she woke up and saw him like that. She had added that the results would be in by about ten. He would get five or six hours kip, take a shower and go back to the hospital.

Somewhere along Queenstown Road his front tire hit the pavement curb and he was jolted awake. He rolled down both front windows and forced his eyes wide open for the next ten minutes. When he reached Marley Road there was no space outside his apartment building. He would have been surprised if there had been. It was one of the reasons he rarely drove to work. Between the hours of six and seven at night the whole area hosted an impromptu game of musical parking spaces. By the end of it cars were double parked in the middle of the road or backed up onto the pavements. The weekend was even worse. He circled and circled until he found an empty corner that took half the length of his car. It would have to do. Tomorrow was Sunday anyway and he would be up early.

He staggered the three blocks back to his apartment. The main entrance door was ajar and when he closed it behind him it didn't lock. He fiddled with the latch but couldn't fix it. He was too tired to try harder and made a note to look at it on his way out in the morning. Six flights further up he unlocked his front door, entered and clicked it shut quietly behind him. He threw his keys on the kitchen worktop and sat down on the edge of the bed. His eyelids were drooping. As he kicked off his shoes he glanced round the room through narrow slits. The place was a mess - as usual. He wondered why he had left the sofa cushions on the floor and the kitchen cupboard doors open, but was too tired to give it any real effort. He fumbled uselessly with the zip on his jacket, gave it up and collapsed onto the rumpled sheets.

In his dream he returned to Badger Stone. He had the rifle with him, only that it resembled an expensive Mont Blanc fountain pen Thatcher used to sign contracts. The surrounding moor was full of people he knew but looked like strangers. His mother was there and Janine and others, though he would not have recognized them by their faces, clothes or even their sex. They were asking him questions he couldn't understand. He was inside the labyrinth carved on the stone except that it was a tunnel spiraling deep into the rock and he was being swept through it like a leaf in a stream. He fired the rifle at the baying crowd and as he did so the bullet cracked the Badger Stone in half. He felt terrible. The stone was a part of him and part of the people watching. He tried desperately to restore it and when he found he could not, he experienced a rising sense of panic. His heart pumped loudly. His breathing was labored and became more and more difficult until it stopped altogether. He tried to inhale but couldn't. He opened his mouth wide to suck in air but something blocked it. His lungs were emptied, his chest grew tighter and his heart was ready to burst. The wings of death folded in around him.

He woke up suddenly, gasping for air. His eyes were wide but he couldn't see. He opened his mouth to inhale but instead of air something solid filled the space and blocked his breath. He was awake now, he was sure of it but the terrifying sensation of death remained. It was surreal. He clawed at his mouth and face and found his skin was thick and damp and... no, it wasn't his skin at all. The pressure on his chest was immense, like a car had parked on him or the ceiling had collapsed. He got a grip of the thing on his face, pulled it off and gasped in a huge lungful of precious oxygen. His ribcage expanded gratefully and he lay there wheezing like a blacksmith's bellows for a good thirty seconds before he saw the man move.

50.

When Roman heard the engine of the car he assumed Ilya was on his way. When it cut out almost immediately he wondered what the stupid old goat was playing at. He lifted Marta out of his arms onto her feet and slapped her hard across the face. Marta gasped and came round in a flash. She automatically raised her hand to her face where it stung and gave a delayed cry of surprise. Before she knew what was happening, Roman was pushing her back along the road, picking out the way ahead with his flashlight.

After only a few minutes he found the two tree stumps that marked the entrance to the overgrown drive down to the dacha. When Marta realized she was being lead back to her prison cell and to Ilya's disemboweled corpse she broke suddenly to her left in blind desperation. Roman's sinuous arm snapped out, grabbed her collar and dragged her back. His right hand swung round and the base of the torch cracked against the side of her skull. Marta staggered and fell to her knees. She swayed unsteadily for no more than a few seconds before Roman yanked her to her feet again and threatened to do it again if she didn't do exactly as she was told.

Once they reached the Daewoo, he opened the door and shoved her into the passenger seat. There was no need to tell her not to move because as soon as she sat down her head dropped back and her eyes roll to the ceiling and closed. She wasn't going anywhere. The glove box was still open. He knew Ilya kept an old pistol in there and guessed he had taken it out to hunt Marta. Considering he was mad as hell and half blind to boot Roman called out to make sure he wasn't shot at by accident.

"Ilya. It's me. I've got the medicine." He pulled the paper bag out of a pocket. "Don't shoot."

When there was no reply he cautiously approached the house. The front door was wide open and as soon as he entered the kitchen he recognized a powerful and obscene odor. He screwed up his nose in disgust and wondered if Ilya hadn't gone to the toilet there. He noticed the dark lump right in front of him only when he stepped in the body fluids that had leaked over the floor. He couldn't see his face but knew what had happened as soon as he saw

Ilya's naked white bottom and his pants round his ankles. He kicked the body over and half Ilya's stomach stayed on the floor next to him, still steaming. The stench was overwhelming. He ran back outside and vomited on the wall.

"You stupid bastard" he said aloud when he had emptied himself.

The story clicked into place all too easily. He had taken the gun, tried to rape the girl... she had escaped... tried to take the car... No. She had been with him when the car was started so it must have been Ilya after all. No wait, that didn't make sense either. He returned to the car and noticed the keys were missing.

"Shit!"

Back in the kitchen he held his nose and prodded at Ilya's slimy remains with his foot for evidence of the keys or pistol. There was none. He stalked into the living room and searched with the flashlight without result. The more he searched the more he became convinced someone else had been here. Someone who had helped Marta escape then killed Ilya. Panic overcame him and he lashed out at the furniture. He tore a tapestry off the wall, kicked over the table and snapped off a leg with his foot. Holding it in both hands like a baseball bat he went back to the kitchen, ready to knock the living daylights out of whosoever he encountered.

Volya broke down his fishing rod and

packed it into his old waxed denim and leather knapsack along with the tarpaulin and
the fish. Within twenty minutes of leaving the
dacha he was on his way back. En route he
started to calculate how much the car might
fetch. Last summer Teo Popolev, who had a
garage on the main road just north of Portnyan, had had a Ford Primera for sale of about
the same size and condition. He seemed to remember the price had been around nine or ten
thousand Roubles. He wondered how old it had
been and made a mental note to check the age
of the Daewoo on the driver documents. His
thoughts were interrupted by more shouting
and banging from the direction of the dacha.
Once again he crawled up the embankment
and when he poked his head over the edge he
saw a thin young man with a wispy beard furiously smashing what looked like a table leg
against the trunk of a silver birch. What new
kind of madness was this? He instinctively felt
for the pistol in his hip pocket and thanked
God he had taken it when he had the chance.

Roman beat the tree until his hands were
numb and his arms were stunned with the vi-
brations. Then he dropped it and rubbed his
face in anguish. He ran to the car and jerked
open the passenger door. Marta awoke with a
start.

"Who was it?" he shouted in her face. "Who
helped you?"

Marta was too stunned to reply and Roman lashed out with his left fist. She flinched and the blow aimed at her face caught her on the ear. She cried out and fell sideways onto the driver's seat. Roman threw himself on top of her screaming at the top of his voice and raining blows on her head and neck with the knuckles of his right hand. Marta had no opportunity to reply and cowered as best she could.

From his entrenched position Volya saw the cabin light come on in the car when Roman opened the door. From her profile he was convinced the girl there was the same he had seen run out of the house. When Roman started to beat her he felt for the pistol in his hip pocket but checked his impulse to run forward. He was surprised to discover that he was frightened. Much as he was used to hardship in his life, casual human violence had more or less passed him by. Instead of rushing forward to her aid like he knew he should, he was frozen to the spot. The butterflies of fear swirled inside his stomach. He couldn't leave her like that and yet he was afraid to even stand up and be seen. The madman probably had a gun and even if he didn't, would he really be able to shoot him? He had been brought up in a strictly agnostic household yet instinctively recognized that killing an animal was not the same as killing a person. His father had known it and it was what had driven him mad.

The first thing to do, Volya decided, was get closer. He slipped back down the ridge and made a crouched run round to his right so he could come up again behind the cover of out-house.

Roman's fit subsided. He slid off Marta's body and back out of the car. He ran a trembling hand through his thin, matted hair and tried to think. Whoever had helped Marta was either hiding, or gone. Whatever the case, the hideout had been discovered. He could no longer stay put as Bruno Olevsky had instructed. The damage had been done and he had to concentrate on how to escape without leaving any trace of his presence for the police.

The first thing he did was pull open the back door of the car. He took the flashlight out of his pocket and searched through the litter on the floor until he found what he was looking for. He had seen Ilya drop the Korshun knife there when he had flopped onto the back seat following Marta's attack. It had been roughly wiped clean though the handle was still tacky with the blood of the first girl. Roman lifted up his jacket and wedged the blade between the belt and his trousers on his right hip.

He returned to the house and in a cupboard under the stairs found a large tin of lamp paraffin. He poured half of it over an old bed base-come-sofa in the living room that he then dragged over against the dividing wall to the kitchen. He took a mildewed old cushion, doused the end with paraffin and opened the stove door. The corner caught light from the embers and he touched it to the sofa. The paraffin on the sofa flared up and he piled on the rest of the cushions, the torn tapestry, the chairs and the broken table. Soon it was roaring dangerously. He waited to see that the wall itself was alight then when the flames were licking at the rafters he took the paraffin tin and a half burned cushion and ran out.

Marta was lying immobile across the two front seats with her feet hanging out of the open passenger door. He ignored her and emptied the rest of the paraffin over the back seat then hastily threw in the cushion that was on the point of burning his fingers. The explosion was terrifyingly sudden.

Volya had just made it to the back of the outhouse when he heard the sound like a rush of wind from the direction of the car. He hadn't seen what Roman had been up to inside the house but he could see the result. Bright and urgent fire danced inside the living room window and he could already smell the smoke. Its glow lit up the ground and trees directly outside as well as the facade of the outhouse forcing him to shrink further back into its shadow.

The fire inside the car was even more intense. It fanned out as it touched the roof and spluttered up through the open back door sending acrid black smoke billowing into the night sky. On the far side he saw the young man stumble away with his arms across his face to protect himself from the heat. But where was the girl?

51.

The man stooped and picked up the damp tea towel Tyler had thrown to the floor. He wore black driving gloves, a black bomber jacket zipped up to the neck and the kind of tweed flat cap Tyler associated with Yorkshire farmers. It seemed incongruous. When he stood up the dull streetlight caught the side of his horribly scarred face. It looked as though the skin had melted and been stretched into a macabre imitation of a spider web.

Tyler lay rigid in the faint hope it was a nightmare. Had it not been for the lingering pain in his chest he might have persuaded himself he was still asleep, closed his eyes and tried to wake up again.

Flatcap held up Tyler's car keys and rattled them suggestively.

"What d you wa...?"

He had hardly finished the phrase when,

with astonishing speed, Flatcap whipped the towel at his face. There was the sound of an almightily slap as it cut across his left cheek and ear. Tyler screeched and threw himself at the man without thinking. He hit him at waist level with his shoulder and sent him scudding back into the arm of the sofa. Flatcap was twice Tyler's weight but the momentum forced him back and he tumbled over. Tyler fell on top but having gained the advantage he had no idea how to follow up. Flatcap had no such problem. He brought up his knee between Tyler's legs then rolled him off the sofa onto the floor. Before he knew what was happening, Flatcap was sitting astride him stretching the damp cloth over his face. He felt the clammy material pulled tight over his nose and chin. When he opened his mouth it concaved inside. The blind panic returned. He clawed at the towel, at the gloved hands and the bomber jacket. His hands flailed blindly in the direction of Flatcap's face but were blocked by his elbows. Every effort required more air and each shallow breath pulled the cloth tighter over his mouth and nose. Once again Tyler felt his lungs compressing and his chest implode. He sucked desperately for air but none came. Suffocation was a terrible way to die. His brain started to spin from the lack oxygen. The pain in his chest was unbearable but the feeling of sheer helplessness in the face of death was even worse. Concentric circles appeared before his eyes and faded to a point of light somewhere in infinity. He could feel his spirit slipping away. The longer it went on the weaker he became until his hands collapsed by his side and he stopped struggling altogether.

Flatcap pulled off the towel and stood up. For the second time in as many minutes Tyler inhaled furiously. He filled his chest like a sail, exhaled then heaved in a fresh lungful. The rims of his eyes hurt from where they had almost popped out of their sockets and he was sure his ribcage was cracked. It took him a full three minutes to recover enough to realize he was still alive.

Flatcap picked up the keys from where they had fallen on the floor and kicked Tyler in the shoulder. When he didn't move he kicked him harder in the ribs.

"Poi'dem!" he said in a flat breathy voice.

Tyler reluctantly rolled onto one side. His vision filled with tiny dots of oscillating light and he felt dizzy. Flatcap grabbed him by the arm and pulled him to his feet.

52.

Zinic had recognized Flatcap immediately. He watched him leave Tyler's apartment block swinging a bunch of keys and strut down the street searching for a car. His presence confirmed Bruno's treachery. Somehow he had traced the rifle to Tyler and sent his thug to recover it. With the rifle out of the way Zinic couldn't possibly shoot O'Hagan.

He had had plenty of time to work out the scenario. The trial would go ahead as planned and Alexandr's dealing's would be exposed. He would either be deported or someone would be sent to execute him. Either way, his position at the head of an international company would be untenable and Bruno would replace him. Bruno's risk was minimal because, win or lose, he would blame the failure on Zinic. Bruno could claim he had hired the best assassin money could buy to kill O'Hagan and even abducted his girlfriend to make sure of it.

When the assassination failed, Bruno would be beyond reproach. Zinic would be to blame. He was the one who allowed the police to catch him and he was the one who lost his rifle. The retribution from either or both of the Olevsky brother's didn't bear thinking about. Their combined reach was very long indeed and there would be no escaping it. He tried to put Marta out of his mind. It was too painful to think of what would happen to her if he failed or even what she was going through now.

He watched Flatcap reach the end of the street then turn around and come back. Zinic receded into the shadow thrown by a plane tree in the front garden of a block facing Tyler's apartment. Flatcap's walk was brisker now. He passed Zinic and continued on to the far end of the street. He peered down the road that cut across it, hesitated then returned. He clearly knew what he was looking for - but hadn't found it. Zinic could feel the anger in his stiff trot. He had time to observe him. He was a large man, powerfully built. He tried to imagine his face without the burn scar. He looked no more than thirty. His nose was broad and his eyes widely spaced. He watched him re-enter Tyler's building and idly wondered if the young man was already dead.

There was nothing to be gained by following him. He stayed where he was and fixed his eyes on the illuminated entrance hall until the automatic switch cut out. The drizzle was getting heavier again and he was wet, cold and irritable. He stamped his feet in an attempt to bring some feeling back to his toes. It was hopeless. The moisture had soaked right through the seams of his Campers and infiltrated every fiber of his socks. He didn't mind the cold so much - he'd been used to that - but England was so damp. He clenched and unclenched his aching fingers fearful that he was suffering from rheumatism.

In the darkness he thought how Yolanda would take the news of Tyler's death. She was exactly the type of woman he would have gone for when he was younger. He thought of the few black girls he had fucked in the past. They had all been prostitutes. Yolanda wasn't like them although she did posses the same kind of mercenary charm as those willowy call girls that cluttered up the lobbies of the Hotel Ukraine. When he had returned to Joe's Bar he had managed to convince her he was a cousin of Tyler on a business trip to London. She told him Tyler had just left and offered to drop him off by taxi at his apartment. She was a little drunk but seemed genuinely pleased to meet someone that knew him. She chattered like a bird, mostly about him and he formed the impression they had been lovers.

Zinic turned his attention back to the decrepit apartment block opposite and the sound of footsteps on the unlit stairs. The door opened and Tyler was pushed out. He looked sallow and tired. Flatcap threw him the keys and Tyler hesitated as if unsure what he was being asked. Flatcap's hand dipped into his jacket pocket and flashed out again with a steel object twirling round his fingers, clacking angrily. Zinic recognized it immediately as a butterfly knife or Balisong.

He'd never understood the fascination for these showy weapons. They were supposed to have originated in the Philippines and become popular with US soldiers stationed there during the Second World War. In essence it was no more than a folding pocketknife. The difference was that the handle was divided into two vertical halves separately hinged to the bottom of the double-edged blade. They could be held together just like the handle of a conventional knife or folded up on either side to hide the blade completely. An aficionado could twirl these three arms in a frightening (and noisy) display that, in Zinic's opinion, was nothing more than showing off.

Tyler, however, was impressed. He wasn't exactly sure where he had parked but after the blurring swish of steel ended with the point digging into his throat he was prepared to make an effort. Zinic watched them to the end of the road then sprinted after. Tyler trudged up and down the streets in what he hoped was a methodical fashion. The only thing he could remember was that he had parked on a corner. Flatcap got more and more irritable, but there was little he could do apart from swear in a tongue so guttural it could have been invented for the purpose. Finally Tyler spied his Fiat Uno next to a post-box.

He was so relieved he picked up speed and Flatcap had to grab him by the collar. When they reached the car the Balisong clacked out another warning. Tyler unlocked the boot, put the keys in his pocket and popped the lid. The streetlights threw deep shadows over the black leather bag and the scattered detritus inside. He was about to reach in when Flatcap stepped forward menacingly.

"That's what you want isn't it?" Tyler protested tetchily.

With a flick of his chin Flatcap gestured for him to continue. Tyler pulled open the neck of the bag. There was another angry snapping twirl from the knife that sounded like an alligator licking its lips. Tyler had a bad feeling about where this was heading. It made him realize how easy it had been to shoot Francis from a distance - almost like a computer game. Up close, things were very different. Flatcap was a good four inches taller and thirty pounds heavier - all muscle. He reached into the hold-all. The shock of what he found there brought on a sudden cold sweat.

Zinic watched the scene through the windows of a VW Golf parked only ten yards away on the far side of the road. He could tell by Flatcap's intense concentration that his rifle was near. Zinic's search was over. It wasn't yet in his possession but he felt a strong sense of relief that he had tracked it down. Bruno would never defy his brother and kill Marta if he had the rifle and finished the job. Every time he thought of her now he had a vision of her tied naked to the rack. He couldn't shake it off. He swore it would not be his last image of her.

Without taking his eyes off Flatcap's back he pulled his right arm out of his jacket. Leaving his left arm in the sleeve up to elbow, he wrapped the entire jacket tightly around his left forearm and held it in place by grasping the end of the right sleeve in his left hand. With his right hand he quietly undid his belt buckle and slipped it out of the rings. The belt was a good weapon. He would like to have used the buckle as a mace but one clink from it would give him away and he would lose the element of surprise. Reluctantly he closed the buckle inside his fist and wrapped the belt once round his knuckles. The remainder gave him a thick leather whip a yard long.

Tyler's hand flapped at the interior of the empty holdall. What had he done with the rifle? Had he packed it? Had he left it at the bridge? Everything between shooting Francis and seeing Rachel in the ICU was more or less a blur. He screwed his eyes tight trying to re-member but it wouldn't come. He took his hands out again. Flatcap grunted suspiciously and gave an impatient twirl of the Balisong. Fi-nally he leaned in and opened the bag to see for himself.

"Chyort voz'mi!"

"I don't..."

Flatcap's gloved left hand shot up to Tyler's throat and squeezed hard. His right was poised at hip level ready to plunge the knife wherever his rage dictated.

Tyler saw him first. The flicker in his eye gave Zinic away. Flatcap turned his head just in time to catch a blur descend onto his left shoulder. He released his hold on Tyler and dodged down to his right. Zinic came crashing over. His momentum sent him spilling onto Tyler who dropped to the pavement. With no solid point of contact, Zinic lost balance but contrived to dive over him and into a shoulder roll on the pavement

Flatcap's timely spin had saved him from the full blow but it was still hard enough to knock him against the boot of Tyler's car. The back of his knees buckled at the level of the bumper and he sat down in the open boot. Zinic was up again in a flash. From his position beside the car all he could see were two legs hanging out over the back bumper. The chance for a quick finish was too good to miss. He flung himself onto the lid of boot and heard a deep groan from inside.

Flatcap was folded in two with the lid pressing down on his back. The initial impact would have broken the back of most men but he managed to resist the pressure and even push back up. To his right he could see the end of Zinic's legs where they projected out over the side of the lid. He lashed out with the knife and slashed across one of his shins.

Zinic grimaced and retracted his legs. When he was fully on top of the boot he turned so that his back was wedged against the window and his feet against the lid. He pushed down in an effort to crush his victim but the surfaces were greasy with rain and he couldn't get a grip. Flatcap closed and pocketed his knife. He put the palms of his hands against the underside of the boot and pushed up. Zinic's shoes slipped on the wet metal. It was a losing battle - but not lost. He slid his feet away from the point of maximum leverage down the lid towards the window. Flatcap felt the pressure decrease and pushed up. Zinic braced himself. The lid acted as a springboard and he used the final shove to launch himself back over the top of the car.

Zinic skidded along the roof and tumbled down the windscreen and bonnet onto the road. The force was more powerful than he had anticipated. He hit the tarmac on his back keeping his head tucked in to avoid concussion. He rolled away from the car to give himself more time from the imminent attack and uncoiled the belt as he went. When he stood up he was holding it with the buckle hanging out.

Flatcap climbed quickly out of the boot and slammed it shut. But rather than pressing the attack immediately he took off his jacket and cracked the compression out of spine by working his neck and shoulders. His cap had disappeared revealing a closely cropped, bony skull. He pulled off his black T-shirt exposing a heavily muscled torso adorned with tattoos. It was a show designed to intimidate and as if to complete the performance he strutted into the road twirling the Balisong like a gunfighter.

Zinic wasn't a specialist on gang markings but he knew they were not idle decoration. They had very specific meanings and misuse more often than not lead to them being cut out or worse. Consequentially the Ace of Clubs on his left breast certainly indicated a military background - probably served with distinction. Zinic wondered if the face wound was the result of some explosion that had ended in a medical discharge. Whatever the reason, a spell in prison had followed. The blurred rose on his right breast was a typical prison tattoo made with ink distilled from shaved shoe heels and urine. The ornate dagger on his right bicep with blood dripping to his elbow signified a killer and the double string of skulls round his wrist the number of victims. The dagger could, in certain circumstances, also mean a sexual predator. Here, however it was combined with a heart which, to the best of Zinic's knowledge indicated a homosexual (normally a badge of shame). To display it so openly was either extremely stupid or extremely brave. Tattooed on the front of each shoulder looking straight at Zinic was a pair of eyes.

Zinic wasn't impressed. He was programmed to look for weak spots. No amount of muscle could protect the eyes, ears, nose, throat, sternum and groin - and that was just the front axis. There were a total of thirty seven vital points on an opponent's body, a blow to any one of which could end the fight. All he needed was one. Zinic stepped into the road. His jacket was still tightly wrapped around his left arm and his right was poised high, ready to strike with the belt. Both men stood side on with their weaker (left) side leading and edged forward. Flatcap raised the knife in a handshake hold to the level of his ear ready to slash down, round and return to the same position like the tail of a scorpion. He would do his best to get in close where the knife and his strength would be to his advantage. Zinic would use the jacket to absorb the blows and the belt to beat him at a distance. Zinic flipped the belt once round his hand to protect his knuckles then started to swing it in a figure of eight. The heavy buckle tore through the air and the belt made a noise like a bullroarer.

Zinic advanced rapidly. The belt formed a square meter wall of of deadly turning metal. But rather than back away, Flatcap stepped into the vicious arc. The buckle caught above his left ear but he seemed unfazed. Once inside the range of the buckle he stabbed down at Zinic's neck. Zinic deflected the blow with his jacket but the stab was merely a feint. With the weight on his left foot, Flatcap spun into a roundhouse kick. Zinic anticipated, shifted his weight back and the sole of Flatcap's boot passed unbelievably high, only an inch in front of his nose. Blood cascaded down the side of Flatcap's neck from the buckle wound but he didn't seem to notice. Zinic added to it with another swing to the back of his skull as Flatcap turned with the kick. He landed on his right foot and at the moment he took the blow to the head he kicked back with his left foot and caught Zinic square in the chest. Zinic staggered back with the wind knocked out of him. He heard the click-clack of the knife and looked up to see the blade stabbing at his face. Zinic parried and stepped back. There followed three more stabs in quick succession, each one circling down and in to his neck and chest forcing Zinic to parry and retreat. His jacket was shredding and the knife cut his fore-arm.

The third stab took Flatcap too far. After an inside parry Zinic changed his weight un-expectedly, crunched his left elbow into Flat-cap's cheek and followed it with a reverse strike with the back of his fist to his nose. Zinic felt the cartilage crunch but even this had lit-tle effect. Flatcap ignored the beatings and continued to push forward. At close range he had a five-inch blade that would finish the fight wherever it landed. This was his advantage and he was playing it to the full. All he had to do was weather the blows.

Flatcap crashed into Zinic with his right shoulder, pinning him against the side of Tyler's car and trapping his left arm. He brought the knife up from the level of his waist aiming for the underside of Zinic's chin. Zinic moved his head to the right and the blade sliced up across the cheek bone under his left eye. Zinic released the belt that was of no use to him now. He brought his right hand across his face and belatedly drove his open palm into Flatcap's extended right elbow, shunting him back. He followed this almost simultaneously with a straight-fingered left-handed jab to his Trachea.

Flatcap choked and staggered back for the

first time. Zinic quickly unwound the shredded jacket from his arm and pushed away from
the car. The cut on his shin hurt like hell but
the one on his face hadn't kicked in yet. He
would like to have made a simple snap kick to
Flatcap's thigh but the man was half his age and
twice his strength. He would only parry and
come in again. It was the first time he had felt
too old for close combat. They had only been
fighting for about twenty seconds, but already
he was breathing heavily. He simply couldn't
outlast the younger man. He had to find a way
to end it quickly.

He snatched up the belt. This time he would
use it differently. It was pointless trying to
batter him from a distance. He would allow
him to come close and hope for the best. It was
risky, but what choice did he have?

Zinic grasped the belt at both ends and held
it in front of him like a staff. Flatcap recovered
quickly but once again bided his time, circling slowly, assessing Zinic's new defense. Zinic
crabbed round with him until they were both
straddling the broken white line down the
center of the empty road.

Tyler's father was standing on the wedding
car screaming at him. 'Why don't you do something?' he kept repeating. 'Why don't you do
something?' The noise gave him a headache. As
Tyler regained consciousness the sound faded
away. He felt queasy. He rolled over onto his

side, grimaced and rubbed a bump on his head. It hurt. For a moment, he had no idea where he was. The vision of his father's open mouth blaring like a trumpet hung doggedly in his mind. He had the vague idea that he missed his father but he couldn't recall why. Somewhere in the background he could hear scuffling. The floor under him was cold and wet. Why? It slowly dawned on him that it was a pavement.

He looked around him and blinked like a man emerging from a dark hole. There was a car in front of him. His car! He was lying on the pavement next to his car. Two bodies thumped into the far side. He could only see their heads from his angle but they were fighting. It was very fast. Two seconds later they were gone. Tyler stood up. In the middle of the road the two men were squaring off. One was half naked, covered in tattoos and brandishing a knife. The other was holding what looked like a belt. The tattooed man twirled his knife and the clacking sound brought the memories thumping back. He recognised the web-like scarring on the semi-naked man. He was the one who had almost killed him in the flat. The other was Greg, the man who had tried to kill him in the alley. Even in his semi-concussed state he knew he had to get away fast. He got up and cried out when he put weight on his left foot. His ankle was badly twisted.

Flatcap got in close and stabbed half-heartedly. Zinic brought the belt across to parry. Flatcap had known he would, but saw that the old man was slowing down. He made several more thrusting movements and Zinic retreated each time, parrying as he went. Flatcap could tell he was tiring. He feigned a kick but was wary of having his leg trapped by the belt. It was a good defense, he decided, even for an old man. But now he should end it. He punched with his left, deliberately over-extending. As he anticipated, Zinic trapped the forearm with the belt and he sliced up with the blade and cut it in two.

Zinic dropped the two ends to the ground and saw a cruel grin spread across Flatcap's face. He knew it was over. How many hours had he trained in unarmed combat against a knife? How many times had he had to use it in the field? The answers were little more than memories now. In a strange way he felt more confident without the jacket and the belt, as if they had been excuses. Flatcap was good, he told himself, even very good. He was younger and fitter and bigger, but he, Zinic was an officer with the Vympel. It may have been a long time ago but he was better than good - he was the best.

In combat, as in all things, success was a matter of character.

Zinic stopped moving.

He dropped his combat stance. His arms fell

to his side and his shoulders relaxed. It looked as though he was giving up but Flatcap had no intention of allowing him to walk away.

Tyler kept his head down and hobbled over to the car. He slipped the key in the driver's door and winced at the noise made by the central locking as it opened. As the two Russians rejoined the fight he opened the door and slid inside.

Flatcap led with a combination that had never failed. With his right leg he snapped out a side kick at Zinic's thigh. Rather than stepping back Zinic raised his knee and kick fell short. Flatcap shifted the weight onto his right foot. When it landed he followed through with a left-footed roundhouse to the outside of Zinic's right knee. Zinic stood firm and allowed him to advance. Flatcap shifted his weight onto his left. They were within touching distance and the knife gave Flatcap an additional hand's length. All he had to do was find the target. As he jabbed forward with his right hand he dropped the knife. His hand carried on towards Zinic's face where it was easily deflected. It wasn't important. With his left he caught the knife in mid air. The momentum carried him forward and he thrust at Zinic's sternum. Zinic didn't see the blow but his instinct didn't desert him. His right hand met the knife halfway and closed around the blade. It cut deep into his palm but the momentary snag caught Flatcap off balance. Zinic shifted his weight and brought his right knee up into Flatcap's extended left elbow. The forearm was trapped by his grip on the blade and there was a loud snap.

Flatcap howled. His left elbow was shattered and his arm hung limply at his side. The Balisong clattered to the floor and Zinic picked it up. It was over. Flatcap jogged backwards until he was sure Zinic was not about to follow then turned and ran.

The fight lasted less than a minute but Zinic was exhausted. He felt old. He closed his eyes and swayed. Blood poured from the numerous wounds on his leg, face and forearm and now a deep gash across his right hand that immobilized it. The life was draining out of him and he felt faint.

The faulty ignition was the bane of Tyler's life; and never been more baneful than at that moment. The motor coughed then died. Knowing it was the cold and damp did nothing to steady his nerves. He turned the key again and pumped the gas. With a roar it revved into life on the second attempt. A miracle at this hour of the night. He slipped into reverse and backed up. He changed back into first and the passenger door swung open. Zinic slipped inside and sat down.

Tyler froze with fear and looked across. There was a livid cut on his left cheek. Blood ran down his neck and his face was creased with pain. Before Tyler could reach the door handle Zinic raised the Balisong to his neck.

"Where is it?" he said coldly.

"Here. It's here." Tyler jerked round nervously and picked the assembled rifle up out of the back seat well where had thrown it after shooting Francis.

"Take it" Tyler implored. "And the car."

Zinic held up his right hand. It was bright red and clamped into the shape of a claw. Across the palm, from the heel to the base of his index finger was a deep laceration oozing blood. Zinic pinched the wrist with his left hand and the flow abated somewhat.

"You owe me" Zinic said then made a sucking sound through his teeth.

"But it's here" Tyler insisted. The knife prevented him from bring the rifle forward so he let it go. "I didn't mean to take it. It's my daughter. Someone... my ex-wife's boyfriend... he gave her some drugs... she's in hospital. She's only three. I had to do something. That's why I took the gun. You can have it now. I don't want the money."

Zinic looked across at Tyler and squinted in disbelief.

"Drive" he said.

"Where? A hospital?" he said hopefully.

Zinic pressed the point of the knife into his skin. "You shot somebody?" he asked.

Tyler nodded. "I had to."

Zinic smiled. "Then we're in this together. If they find me, they find you - and believe me, they'll be looking."

"You mean the police?"

"They're the least of your worries."

Zinic dropped the knife into his lap. "I'll protect you" he said. "But we have to do something about this." He indicated his hand. "I need stitches and painkillers."

"I'm not a doctor. What can I do?"

Zinic winced in pain. He dropped his head back against the headrest and screwed his eyes shut.

"You'll think of something."

53.

ob Grant pulled up outside the Railway Tavern just as the ambulance was leaving. D.I. Wicks' message had been brief but clear and Grant had ordered two Armed Response Units, one of which was already on the scene. He had lost no time. Ever since Commander Buckhurst's call on Friday night to say that he was personally reviewing his application for promotion, his blood had been up. He had a sense of vigor he hadn't felt in years.

Nanette felt it too. She had been just as pleased as him - even more so, if that were possible. They had made love like teenagers and Grant had discovered something he didn't know: it wasn't about the money. He had imagined she was drifting away because he didn't earn enough. All the signs had pointed to it: she wanted a proper holiday, they couldn't afford Michael's university fees, she couldn't afford to dress everyone etc. etc. The list was long and, as it turned out, existed only in his mind. They had sat in the kitchen and chatted their way through two bottles of Chardonnay without raised voices until three o'clock in the morning. They discussed moving home, Marion's Gothic wardrobe, Nanette's mother's Alzheimer's and Billy's fluctuating ambitions, lazy school work and obsession with playing the drums, amongst many, many other things. What struck them both was the way in which they kicked the subjects around as a team rather than two opposing sides. Grant felt they were both relieved by the change of atmosphere.

She had said she admired what he did and she was proud of him, but only when he was proud of himself. His work was such an important part of their life that it affected everything else. Sadly, over the past few years he had become frustrated and irritable and this had rubbed off on her. She had no other point of reference for him and as his opinion of himself had plummeted, so had hers. She told him quite frankly that after Buckhurst had called, he had been a different man. In the space of a few minutes his confidence and energy had revived. It was contagious.

Before getting out of the car, Grant reflected on the strange sequence of events that had pulled his marriage back together. An anonymous tip off about a Russian on the roof of a housing estate, the chance questioning of a young man nearby and the unexpected involvement of rich and seedy lawyer. He found it hard to think kindly of Julius Kriegmann. He hated his waxy skin, his greasy dandruff-ridden hair and familiarity with his superiors. It was this latter that made him think it would do no harm to invite him for lunch or even dinner at home. Now Grant had a taste of what life could be like, he was keen to follow through. A certain amount of 'grafting', for want of a better term, was par for the course. He had always known it but never had the chance to profit. Nanette wouldn't like Kriegmann at all, but she would make the effort once she understood how the new game was played.

Grant stepped out of the car. D.I. Wicks broke from a conference with another officer and walked over to meet him. He was a gruff, heavy set man with a square head and emerald green eyes. Rumor had it he had been extremely handsome (and slim) when young but thirty years of Players' unfiltered and late-night pizzas had taken their toll.

"I have no fucking idea Bob," he said in answer to Grant's question. "I didn't even know he was shot 'til I saw the wound."

"How bad is it?"

"Still breathing." Wicks dropped a cigarette and stubbed it out on the pavement. "Hit in the stomach. I thought it was pretty tasty but the medics said he'd pull through."

Grant adjusted his cap and surveyed the scene. Everything seemed under control but the crowd of men hanging around the entrance to the pub looked surly. There must have been about twenty of them. Too many to interview immediately.

"We knew there might be a bit of bother" Wicks added in his old-school London mockney that reminded Grant of The Sweeney." This Francis Matlock is a local face and the Railway Tavern... well, you know its rep. There was a bit of argy-bargy. Matlock was a right fucking monkey but we were on top of it. Then he drops to the floor. I thought it was a heart attack."

"Did you see who shot him or where it came from?"

"At the moment he was hit, he was standing here like this." Wicks stood perpendicular to the pavement with his arms out. "The shot must have come from that direction." He closed his arms into a ninety degree angle that indicted an area that encompassed the pavement, the road and a patch of waste ground. "But where exactly or how far, we haven't a fucking clue."

"Was there any one there?"

"In all honesty Bob no one was paying any attention. Matlock was kicking like a fucking mule and the mob from the Tavern were playing merry hell. When he dropped they went ape. It was a good thing we had the back-up because it was touch and go. The worst have already been booked and wagoned but I doubt we'll get anything from them."

"Could it be one of them?"

Wicks shook his head. "No" he said with conviction. "They were all over there, near the entrance, behind him and I'm sure we'll find the bullet entered from the front." He indicated his stomach.

Grant turned his attention back to the supposed angle of attack. Cars were stacking up along the road as an officer reduced the flow outside the Tavern to a single lane. A thin crowd of half a dozen onlookers had gathered at the edge of the police tape and were talking to an officer there. Beyond the crowd the road continued on under a railway bridge. Wicks saw him examine it.

"I thought of that but it must be a hundred and fifty yards to the bridge. Matlock isn't a big time player. If he pissed someone off enough to merit a contract it would be a bullet to the back of the head and a fast motorbike. To be sure of a shot from that distance, you're talking about a real pro. That's expensive and complicated and Matlock - well, you know - he just isn't worth it."

Grant nodded his head in agreement. Wicks gave orders to the officers standing warily by to take names and check the identities of the witnesses and let them go. They would be contacted and interviewed later. Grant added that they should also note down the registration numbers in the car park and along the road but Wicks had already done it. The forensic team arrived and the pub goers drifted angrily away. The second ARU had been called to a brawl in a Chinese restaurant and had never arrived. Grant thanked them all and caught up with Wicks.

"What was reason for the arrest?"

"Drugs" Wicks mumbled while lighting another cigarette. "Three year old girl OD-ed on Adam and the mother fingered Matlock as the perp."

"Do you think it's related to the shooting?"

Wicks made a face. "I doubt it. Only happened a few hours ago. Looks like an accident. Kid found a bottle of E under the sink. I'll write it up tomorrow and you can have a butchers."

"Leave it on my desk."

Grant nodded at Harold Foreman the chief forensic investigator and an old friend and started to walk over to greet him.

"Primovelli" Wicks added as he left.

"What?"

"The case file. The girl who took the overdose. Her name is Primovelli. I'll leave it on your desk. "

Grant stopped in his tracks.

"Ring a bell?" asked Wicks.

Grant hesitated. "Unusual name. Italian is it?"

54.

Flames from the burning car leaped up into the night sky and licked at the extremities of an overhanging pine. The sap inside heated, releasing gasses that exploded through the skin of the branches and needles with a crackling roar. Tiny showers of embers were either caught in the updraft or shot out and down towards the forest floor.

Roman staggered back. The heat was fearsome and he protected his face with his crossed forearms.

From his position behind the outhouse, Volya could only see the driver's side of the car. The fire that raged from the back seat and out through the open door on the far side hid Roman from his view. The girl he had last seen sitting upright in the front passenger seat had disappeared from sight. He searched amongst the trees in the circle of light that now surrounded the vehicle, but in vain. He had the horrifying idea that she had not left the car at all but was still somewhere inside. He moved to his right and up onto a small rise so he could look down through the driver's window. Sure enough, he caught a glimpse of her red coat and dark blond hair stretched along the two front seats.

Roman had no intention of letting Marta burn to death. She would certainly die soon enough but while she lived she was his ticket into the world of Bruno Olevsky. He wasn't about to allow that to go up in flames. But he had been taken by surprise. He hadn't expected the paraffin to explode with such severity and now he had recovered from the initial shock he ran back to the car. At a meter away the heat was almost unbearable. As he got close enough to grab Marta's ankles, it seemed hot enough to melt his skin off.

He kicked into the ground with his heels and dragged her limp body out of the open passenger door with such speed that her head cleared the chassis round the door and dropped straight onto the ground. Roman continued to pull her back and back until he, at least, was far enough away to feel the cool night air on his face and hands. Marta's coat rode up around her waist and her naked thighs and bottom scraped along the ground causing her to cry out again and roll onto her side. Her hair was alight but beside the bonfire blazing in the background the slow fizzle seemed wholly insignificant. Roman was mesmerized and sat watching it burn its way down towards her scalp like a dynamite fuse.

Volya appeared from out of nowhere. He ran in from behind the inferno and stamped on Marta's hair until it was out. Roman was so surprised he didn't move until Volya raised his clear blue eyes to his then shook his head with a look of bewildered contempt. If it hadn't been for the backpack and faded dungarees, the lean and lined old man could have been a wood spirit or possibly a figment of Roman's imagination. He closed his jaw with a snap, rose to his feet and had already pulled the knife out of his belt before he noticed Ilya's pistol. Volya leveled it between Roman's eyes.

"What are you doing?" Roman shouted against the roaring backdrop of the car and the now flaming house. "I just saved her. Didn't you see?"

Volya had seen quite enough to know where the truth lay. This evil young man had set fire to the house with the dead body inside (presumably to hide the evidence of their crimes). He had beaten the girl senseless then set fire to the car with her in it.

"Why are you pointing the gun at me? What did I do?" Roman continued to mewl. "I just saved this woman's life. Put the gun down for Christ's sake. Put it down and talk to me. This isn't what you think it is. Whatever you think, this isn't it."

Volya was a good shot. His father's service revolver had given him hundreds of hours of practice over half a decade. At twenty paces he could shoot the core out of an apple. Roman's jug-handle ears at three feet presented no obstacle at all. The bullet passed the opening of the ear at near sonic speed sending a sudden pressure wave down the canal and bursting the drum. The young man screeched and threw himself to one side. He pressed his hand to the side of his head in agony but it was almost a minute before he realized the bullet had also blown away the top of his auricle leaving a ragged and bloody edge. The pain was excruciating.

While Roman thrashed around on the ground, Volya pulled Marta to her feet. She was groggy but alive. When she was conscious enough to realize what had happened she panicked and attempted to push Volya away. He hung on to her jacket.

"It's OK" he repeated soothingly several times until she looked at him in the face. "It's OK. You're safe. You're safe. Look."

He pointed with the gun to where Roman was still writhing. "You see?"

Marta's eyes widened in horror at the sight of her former captor and, regardless of his injured state, the old fear filled her once again.

It was soon replaced, however, by stupefaction at the scene around her. Not so long ago she had been standing in the cold and dark, straining to hear the most intimate sounds of the forest. Now the silver stemmed trees were alive with a yellow and orange glow that filtered between them and penetrated deep into the gloom. The car she had fallen asleep in was an inferno. Tongues of fire also leapt up through the roof of the main cabin. The air was filled with a lively rushing sound like a hellish waterfall.

"Are there any more?" Volya asked.

When she didn't answer he shook her and repeated the question.

Marta looked at him without understanding. "More?"

"Yes. More like him." He waved the gun at Roman again." Or the one in the house."

"No!" she said as if he had threatened to conjure them up.

"Thank Christ" he said heavily. "We should go. I'll get the rest of your clothes." He set off in the direction of the outhouse by way of a wide detour round the car. Before he had gone three steps Marta hobbled up behind him.

"Wait" she called. She was terrified of being left anywhere near Roman.

"Are you alright?" asked Volya looking at the way she grimaced with every step. Marta felt her left hip. She had sustained a long cut down her buttock and the back of her leg to behind her knee. She could also feel a raw graze over her left hipbone. Quite apart from the psychological damage she was bruised all over her body. There had been Roman's first knock-out punch, the beating she had taken in the trunk, the rape, the escape through the woods, Roman's savage attack in the car and finally almost being roasted alive. She unconsciously smoothed down her hair and found that half of it was missing. She wondered why it felt so thick and frizzy but was too tired to pursue it.

She nodded in response to Volya's question and took his proffered left hand. When they found her bundle of clothes, Volya picked up her Ikea dress. It was thick with goo. He looked inquiringly at Marta who said nothing. She unzipped her jacket and when Volya saw her nakedness he turned his back.

"Don't go away" she pleaded, so he waited and watched the tiles at the apex of the roof explode with the heat.

Marta cried when she found her white knickers. They were some kind of symbol of innocence forever lost and they hurt when she slid them up over her wounded hips and the bruised outer-parts of her vagina. She couldn't find her bra. She put on her tights which made her feel both warmer and safer. Lastly, she held her breath and slipped her yellow and brown Ikea dress down over her head and zipped up the back. It was cold with the damp and she felt ill just thinking of what was on it but she had to keep warm. She put her coat and shoes back on and noticed Georgiy's headscarf lying in the shadows. She pressed it to her face with her two open palms and gave into her grief.

Volya left her to cry then said "we should go."

Marta screwed up her hidden face for a moment then emerged and wiped away the tears on the back of her hand. She quickly tidied what was left of her hair then secured it in place with the scarf knotted under her chin.

"Where to?" she asked.

"Back up to the road. The first farms are only a couple of miles away. We can phone from there." A thought stuck him. "Unless you have one of those portable phones."

Marta shook his head.

"Maybe the man...?" he nodded his head in the direction of Roman hidden from their view behind the blazing car.

"I don't know... " Then she recalled Roman taking a video of her on his phone. When was it? Last night? The night before? It seemed like years ago and she struggled to remember just how long this nightmare had been going on.

"Yes" she said. "He was... talking to someone about me." She didn't want to tell the old man that she had been videoed naked and tied to a bed base. It struck her that she would never be able to repeat some of those things anyone.

Not to her parents or to her lover. She would have to lock them away.

They took the same route back around the car but when they arrived on the far side, Roman was nowhere to be seen. Marta clung onto Volya's arm and they both scanned the dancing forest. Volya cursed his own weakness for not killing him when he had the chance or at least wounding him in the leg or tying him up. There was a loud creak from the main house followed by an even louder crack. They both looked over and the center of the roof collapsed. For a magical moment the fire inside the building could not be seen at all and lit up the night like a search beam. Then slowly the red tongues re-emerged, licking the sky with an even greater urgency.

"We should go" Volya said after a while.

"Why? We could stay here until light."

Volya nodded as if he had already considered it. "What if others come," he said. "The one you said he was talking to. Can you say for certain no one else will come?"

Marta chewed her lower lip. She preferred to stay here where it was warm and light. The blaze would surely last until morning when she would feel safer. The alternative was to plunge back into the cold, dark forest where there was no shelter.

"If the man has a phone" Volya prompted her, "he could be calling others for help." He took off his backpack, placed it on the ground and undid a side pocket.

The uncertainty of the forest was certainly preferable to what would happen if Roman did return with others like him.

"How long will it take to reach the farms?" she asked

"By day, maybe an hour." He pulled an old black rubber-coated flashlight out of his pack. "I have a torch, if the batteries still work. I never use it." He pressed a button with his thumb, knocked the reflector against his hand and it emitted a feeble yellow glow that was only visible when he held it six inches from his palm. He pouted with mild satisfaction and turned it off again to conserve the batteries.

"Well?" he said.

"What about him?" she said nodding to the patch of ground where Roman had been.

"I don't know. Maybe he's run off." He scanned the forest.

"Do you think he'll follow us?"

"I don't even know what you're all doing here." He snapped back testily. "Who is he? Who are you? What are you all doing here at the old Tevlevski Dacha? No one's been up here for years."

Marta closed her eyes for a moment. She was very tired. But not so far gone she forgot this old man had risked his life to save her. She nodded her acceptance.

"I'll tell you on the way."

55.

Zinic had been right about Flatcap. Viktor Landri had indeed been in the army where he had served with distinction; though not out of choice and not without consequences. His mother had been a prostitute in the Tvershaya district of Moscow and, after she attempted to beat him with an electric iron when he was five, he ran out and never returned. The capital city has over four thousand homeless children so Landri soon made those uneasy alliances that pass for friendship amongst the very desperate. By day he begged for money around the Kursky station and by night he would be strung out on butorphanol, an opiate analgesic costing only 50 Roubles an ampule. The first time he was captured and raped he thought he would die from the pain. But he survived and by the age of twelve he had turned the pain into a livelihood. He eventually found a permanent squat with a dozen other street kids in an attic near the Timiry-azevskaya metro station.

And so life would have continued for Landri until he contracted AIDS or met some other more violent end. Instead he was trapped by a military conscription team that were sweeping the metro platform when he was high on glue. Having no official papers or even birth certificate, he was a perfect candidate to fulfill their quota. All Russian boys are eligible for conscription but ninety percent buy their way out. This leaves only the poorest and the mentally unstable to actually fill the barracks. Of those, Landri was at the bottom of the ladder. He was homeless, penniless and family-less. He was scrawny, underweight and possibly under-age - although even he had no idea how old he was. He was also a drug addict and a homosexual prostitute. The first year was gruesome. All conscripts are subjected to 'hazing' when they arrive and he was no exception. In Russian it is called 'dedovshchina' or 'rule of the grand-fathers', a rite of passage in which the young-sters are ritually humiliated and tortured by their elders and supposed superiors. He would most likely have been one of the four thousand recruits that die every year from the practice had it not been for Captain Vladimir Vazmir-ski.

Once Vazmirski cottoned on to Landri's former profession he sent him back out to work.

Landri did exactly the same as he had done before only now he handed all his earnings to Vazmirski. The indentured slavery brought his superior officer a healthy new line of income he could add to the trafficking of food and clothes stolen from the new recruits.

Near the end of his first year he was the victim of a particularly bad hazing incident. His barracks was stormed by a drunken mob of second year recruits celebrating their imminent release from conscription. In the middle of the night, a barrel of sump oil was rolled inside with a lighted rag stuffed in the opening. No one ever found out what the revelers had expected to happen but the barrel exploded. Of the twenty recruits asleep in the beds only five survived. The rest were burned to death. The thick burning oil covered the ceiling walls, beds, clothes and of course people. Landri and the four others that escaped were all bunked at the very furthest end and managed to jump out of a broken window. During the explosion a flaming pat of oil had landed on the side of Landri's face and it was not until he got out of the building that he managed to put it out. For almost a minute it ate away at the skin and hair on the side of his face and left him with a permanent scar.

He spent six weeks in a military hospital answering the usual perfunctory questions of a military enquiry. But since everyone had been asleep at the moment of the attack there were no witnesses and the parents of the victims were told their own sons were the ones to blame for their misadventure. Landri was offered a medical discharge and surprised everyone by refusing it.

In his second year he reversed roles and became part of the system of vengeance whereby victims turn into perpetrators. He took up going to the gym. He started to hold back some of the money intended for Vazmirski and bought extra food. By the end of his second year he had begun to put on muscle. This in itself singled him out for respect. And the more respect he got the harder he pumped iron. At the end of his conscription he volunteered for a five-year term. Four years later he was Sergeant Viktor Landri, feared by new and old recruits alike as a sadistic homo.

At the age of twenty-two he was posted with his regiment to the Republic of Ingushetia to deal with Chechen and Ingush independence fighters. On the night of June 21, rebel guerrillas attacked fifteen government buildings across the republic killing almost a hundred officials including Russians. Instead of responding in force, the Russian Deputy Interior Minister, General Vyacheslav Tikhomirov, fell on his sword and resigned. Landri and others thought the sword should have been directed at the rebels and decided to take matters into his own hands. They received information that three trucks of weapons stolen during the raid were parked in a nearby barn. The pimping Colonel Vazmirski, who was still Landri's immediate superior, refused to act. He was making a healthy profit selling medical supplies to the guerrillas and had no intention of diminishing his client base.

So, three nights after the rebel attack, Landri and a dozen likeminded patriots stole out of their encampment and raided the barn. It was an overwhelming success. They not only recaptured the three trucks but stumbled upon an important Ingushetia smuggling ring. Nine guerrillas were killed outright and twenty more were captured. Not one Russian soldier was even wounded. Landri was feted like a hero until it came to the official report. Vazmirski wasn't the only one profiting from the illegal trade and Landri was returned to Moscow for a court marshal. The conclusion was preordained. He was dishonorably discharged and given a twenty-year prison sentence.

In the Butyrka, cells designed for twenty men often house four times as many and the inmates are forced to sleep in shifts. Almost all prisoners are drug users. The cells are damp and poorly aired and AIDS and TB are rampant. Their diet is porridge, porridge and more porridge. Not surprisingly prison life is dangerous and extremely violent. Landri fitted in well. He swiftly found his place at the top of the hierarchy and because of his army discipline he only traded, but did not take, drugs himself. If the Butyrka was hell then Landri was one of the tormenting devils. But even for him the desperate nature of the place took its toll. The endless turf wars, the stabbings, transferable diseases, the noise, the smell and most of all the thought of twenty years of incarceration almost drove him mad.

The reprieve was as unexpected as it was welcome. One of his cellmates Sergei Ratman worked for a Moscow crime syndicate affiliated to the Olevsky brothers. When he was released he recommended Landri as a possible enforcer. Landri wasn't to know about the homosexual connection until much later when he was entrusted with the 'procurement and dispatch' side of Bruno's affairs.

Landri gave Bruno Olevsky unconditional allegiance. He recognized Bruno was a brutal man but was so inured to violence and depravation that very little surprised him. Furthermore he was paid a good salary and lived like a king. He travelled everywhere with Bruno as his personal and most intimate bodyguard. They did not have a physical relationship of course but Landri knew his secrets - and catered to them. As a result he stayed in the same hotels as his boss, flew in their Gulfstream

G500 and was generally treated like royalty wherever they went. It was a long way from the attic over the Timiryazevskaya station. Bruno's attempt to usurp his brother didn't bother, or even surprise, him in the least. In prison he had seen throats cut for the right to squash a cockroach. He had done it himself. Ascension by violence was the natural order of things. Landri didn't ask questions and would back Bruno to the hilt. Over the years they had developed - if not exactly a friendship (Bruno had no friends) - then an understanding. It was borne out of the common ground of desensitization: Bruno by nature and Landri by experience.

When Landri reached the Aprilia MXV 450 motocross bike he had chained to the lamppost at the end of Tyler's road he realized he couldn't ride it. He sat down on a low wall nearby, cupped his broken elbow in his right hand and lifted it over so that his forearm rested across his lap rather than hung down at his side. Now that the adrenaline of war was subsiding, the pain kicked in. He leaned into his elbow to fully rest it on his left thigh and squeezed his eyes tight as an excruciating wave swept through his body. When it had leveled off to something slightly less than unbearable he reached into the side pocket of his trousers and pulled out a phone. Sweat dripped onto the keyboard from his head making it so slippery that he had to redial three times. Bruno answered immediately.

"You got it?"

Landri bit his lip hard to stop himself from groaning.

"Viktor!?" Bruno shouted.

"Zinic was waiting for me" he replied in a rush.

"Waiting...?"

"They're working together."

Bruno was puzzled. "Who? Zinic and this... Primovelli?"

"Yes." Landri suppressed a new surge of pain that this time brought tears to his eyes. Bruno heard him whimper but said nothing. "Primovelli hid the gun" Landri continued, "and they drove off together."

"So you didn't get it." Bruno made no effort to conceal his fractious tone.

"No."

"Where are they now?"

"I don't know. They just drove off."

Pause. "And they saw you."

Landri hesitated. "Yes. Of course they saw me."

"I mean either one of them could describe you to my brother" Bruno said ominously.

Landri fell silent. There was nothing more to say.

"Come back" Bruno said eventually.

"I can't. He broke my fucking arm."

"Where are you?"

Landri told him.

"Don't move. I'm coming." Bruno rang off abruptly.

Landri squeezed the dead phone in his hand for a moment then pressed it to his forehead. He was starting to feel sorry for himself and decided it wouldn't do. He had to get out of sight. He didn't doubt that a large semi-naked man covered in tattoos and nursing a broken arm would attract the attention of any neighbor that happened to peep through their curtains. He swung one leg over the wall, then the other. When he was facing away from the road he edged forward and slid down to the ground inside the garden wall.

He was sure his elbow was shattered into a thousand pieces. Every movement seemed to grate them against one another. Once he was in a stable position again he closed his eyes and attempted to take his mind off the pain by concentrating on something else. His usual trick was to relive the one moment of true happiness in his life. It was the return to barracks after the raid on the barn when the truck gates swung down revealing the Ingush prisoners and stolen arms. The soldiers he had terrorized and bullied for years lifted him up onto their shoulders cheering. He tried to recapture the sweet and unexpected bliss of that event which had touched him to his jaded heart but his mind kept wandering back to the telephone call.

He thought Bruno had taken the bad news rather well, all things considered. He didn't expect compassion from his boss but his voice had been unusually cold.

56.

Yolanda watched herself in the bathroom mirror while she combed out her hair. The jet-black mane that hung to her shoulders was her pride. Every two weeks she visited an expensive salon on Bond Street where a boy name Jason straightened it and cut out the split ends. The chemicals made the hair brittle. Jason had explained how blow-drying damaged it further and had taught her how to use a towel. She inclined her neck to one side then the other, dabbing her tresses with a towel and running them through with a wide-tooth comb. It generally took about ten to fifteen minutes. Jason would have applauded her technique and not given a thought to her naked body.

She was only twenty-seven years old but she was afraid her breasts were beginning to sag. It was natural after two children but she resented it all the same. Her nipples were the giveaway. She had insisted on suckling Michael and Athena as long as possible and the result was nipples like cherry stones. She often wore padded bras just to hide them. She also thought her shoulders were too round and disguised them with well-cut jackets. Other than that she was in fine form for a woman who never went to the gym. She stood back and admired her long, slender limbs and gently rounded stomach. It had taken five long years before it had come back into shape. She stood side on to see it in profile. She was glad she hadn't inherited her mother's large backside. From what little Petal had said it was clear she took after her father. He was supposed to have been Somalian. She guessed this was true because she was often compared to the model Iman. She tucked in her pelvis, retracted her buttocks and reminded herself to concentrate more on her posture when she was with clients.

Before her mother had left for the night shift they had talked while Yolanda took a shower. It was something they often did. Petal was a midwife at Queen Charlotte's. Mother and daughter both worked long hours and had developed a habit of conversing while one or other was in the shower. Neither of them were shy with their opinions but the barrier of the shower curtain allowed them to broach subjects they knew were delicate. Michael's dyslexia had been discussed through the plastic screen, as had Petal's tendency to dress Athena like a doll. Tonight it had been Yolanda's boyfriend - or lack thereof. Yolanda argued that she didn't have time, that she had had bad experiences and that the children came first.

'It's a waste' Petal had said. 'You're a beautiful woman but who knows it? All those rich men, all those parties you go to. There must be someone. It's not right to be stuck at home with two kids and a fat old woman.'

Petal was neither very old nor very fat but Yolanda took the point. It had been almost nine months. He was a famous Spanish tennis player and she had gone to bed with him just to get it out of her system. He had called again when Wimbledon came round but she had declined. There had been a lot of soul searching after that and she had put men (or at least sex) out of her mind. She touched a breast with her fingertips and tried to recall the memory of his large tanned hands caressing her polished brown skin, but it wouldn't come.

It isn't a 'waste', she convinced herself. That's an older generation talking. A woman's body isn't a gift for the purpose of pleasing a man. Even so, something was missing.

Once her hair was dry she left the bathroom and walked over to Michael's door. He had left it open as he always did. She didn't like him to see her naked anymore so just in case he was awake she merely poked her head inside. He was buried under his Spiderman duvet and she could hear him softly snoring. In the next room Athena lay completely uncovered. Yolanda pulled the duvet up and stroked back her hair. She wanted it straight like her mother's but Yolanda thought she was too young. It was a sore point on which Petal and her did not agree. She tidied up some of her toys from the floor and stole out again.

She was hungry. Petal was sure to have prepared something so she went downstairs. When she had bought the house on Clapham Common two years ago the kitchen was the only thing she could afford to redo. She had ripped out the faux-country pine cupboards and replaced them with a gleaming steel and red-lacquer installation and a floor of polished cement. It was the most impressive room in the house. The only thing she regretted were the metal seats on the stools which always felt cold on her bare skin. She checked the blinds were closed and opened the fridge. On the second shelf down she found a large bowl of salad prepared with anchovies and green olives. She placed it on the table and was in the process of removing the Clingfilm when she heard the distant ring of her mobile phone.

It was still in the handbag in her bedroom and she bounded up the stairs three at a time before it woke the children. She launched herself onto the bed and looked for the bag under her jacket on the far side. In the semi dark she couldn't see inside and by the time she had found it the ringing had stopped. She turned onto her back and searched for the missed calls. It was probably Petal. But it could also be one of her girlfriends or even a horny client. It wasn't unknown for them to call at this time of night after a few drinks.

"Tyler!" she exclaimed in disbelief. She had a rapid image of him standing in the rain on the far side of the road.

"Tyler" she repeated with a chuckle. "What the hell do you want babe?" Then she remembered the cousin whom she had dropped off at his apartment. Instinctively she felt that he was behind the call. He was just the right type to hit on a girl like her. She had been a little bit drunk and hadn't really paid attention but she remembered his poise and self-assurance. Yes, he was just the type.

She wondered if he would phone again. Maybe she was mistaken about the cousin but it was surely more than a coincidence. This was the first time she could remember Tyler had ever phoned her outside work hours. She held the phone up and wondered if he would dare to ring again. He didn't. Her amusement turned to intrigue, then consternation. Tyler had had a distracted air when she had seen him. Then he had disappeared and missed meeting his cousin. She thought it over again. Cousin? Was it really his cousin? He had seemed convincing enough, but it was Yolanda who had given Tyler's address to the taxi driver. He didn't look anything like Tyler either. In fact they were chalk and cheese in almost every way. The more she thought about it the more she convinced herself there was something rather sinister about the 'cousin'.

She thumbed redial and Tyler answered almost immediately.

"Ty?" she said tentatively.

"Hi Yolanda." He sounded tired.

"You called..."

"Yea" he paused then said, "I need your help."

She sat bolt upright. She had guessed right.

"What is it babe?"

"I can't tell you on the phone."

"Is it your cousin?"

"My what?"

"I knew it. What's happened?"

"I... I can't tell you over the phone. I need to see you."

"Where are you?

"Outside your front door."

"Wha..." she remembered her children and cut off her cry. "My front door? Now? What are you doing there?" She leapt off the bed and grabbed the white dressing gown off the back of her door. "Wait I'm coming down."

She threw the phone on the bed and ran

downstairs putting her dressing gown on as she went. At the door she tied it closed and pushed back her hair.

She barely recognized the man she opened to. Almost everything about him was different and she took a moment to absorb the changes. She only ever saw him at work so her image was defined by his cheap suit, neatly brushed hair and scraped chin. These were all gone. She recognized his expensive (though thoroughly wet) Belstaff jacket. His hair was greasy and flat to his skull except where he had pushed it up off his forehead. His shoes and jeans were scuffed and dirty. He drew one hand down over his face wiping off the worst of the water. He looked ten years older.

"Come in babe. What you doing here?"

Tyler hesitated and looked behind him into the road.

"What happened to you?" she grabbed his sleeve and pushed the door wider. "Come in, quick."

Tyler opened his mouth as if to say something then changed his mind and stepped inside. Yolanda shivered and shut the door. It was a miserable night outside. Tyler stood dripping onto the mat without saying a word.

"Stay there" she said, "I'll get you a towel."

"No."

His tone of voice stopped her at the bottom of the stairs. Exhaustion made it deeper and it didn't sound like his normal ingratiating tone at all.

"What is it Ty? What's happened? You can tell me babe. I'll help."

There were a lot of things he wanted to tell her but he didn't have time.

"Is you mother here?" he asked.

"My mother?"

Tyler didn't repeat himself and let the question hang in the air until Yolanda said "Why?"

"She's a nurse."

"A midwife" she corrected. "But she's at work."

Tyler leaned back against the door and closed his eyes.

"What is it Ty? Are you hurt?"

Tyler shook his head. "No. It doesn't matter." He turned to open the door and muttered something about the hospital.

"Who's going to hospital?"

He unlocked the door. "It doesn't matter I'll sort it out."

"Tyler!" she said sternly. I can't help you if you don't talk to me. Who's going to the hospital? Your cousin?"

Tyler frowned. "Who is this cousin?"

"Whoever" she said dismissively. "The old guy you were supposed to meet at Joe's Bar."

Tyler looked at her in astonishment. "How did you know?"

"Is that who it is? Has something happened?"

"But how did you..."

"It doesn't matter." She was exasperated. "You call me in the middle..." she lowered her voice remembering the children. "... of the night and ask me to help. I want to help Tyler. Just tell me what the fuck is going on."

"He's cut." Tyler touched his right hand as he spoke. "On his hand. It's bad."

"Then what are you doing here?"

Tyler looked awkward.

"Tyler?"

He was debating how many lies he could get away with when the door behind him was thrust open. It banged against Tyler's shoulder and Yolanda jumped up a couple of steps in fright.

"I told you to wait," said Tyler. He stepped back and Zinic stumbled in carrying the black hold all. He was even wetter than Tyler. Yolanda gasped when she noticed his injuries. He had a wide vertical gash on his left cheekbone. Where his face wasn't covered in blood it was haggard and pale. When he dropped the bag on the mat she could see his left forearm arm was crossed with cuts. His right hand was held up against his chest. It was curled into a talon and black with blood that ran down his arm and dripped off his elbow. He dropped the bag and clamped his left hand around the wrist to stem the flow.

"Hello again" he said with an attempted smile. Tyler wondered at this but said nothing. Yolanda's eyes were wide with horror.

Zinic turned to Tyler. "It can't wait" he said.

Yolanda recovered quickly. "Did you do this Ty?"

He almost laughed.

She came down the stairs. "I'll call an ambulance."

"No" said Tyler holding out a hand.

"I can fix it" Zinic said.

"You can..." Yolanda trailed off pensively. Clearly there was a lot more to this than met the eye.

Tyler watched her carefully. This was the defining moment. She might throw them out, call the police or shout for help. He didn't know what to expect. If it hadn't been for the shooting of Francis, he wouldn't have cared. But God knows what would happen now if they were arrested. Once the police made the connection between Tyler and Zinic it would take them long to link him to Francis' shooting.

A thousand questions passed through Yolanda's mind. It seemed that she didn't really have a handle on her timid work colleague after all. But she had a hidden history of her own and knew from experience there was only one important question: do I trust him?

The answer was easy.

"What do you want me to do?" she said finally.

Zinic stepped forward. "I need water and a kettle, iodine or some other antiseptic, plenty of bandages, a needle and thread and scissors."

Yolanda nodded slowly as she took in the implication and quickly gathered her thoughts.

"Go in the kitchen" she said indicating the open door at the end of the corridor. "And don't make a noise. The kids are asleep."

"Kids?" said Tyler, shocked, his fantasy image of her suddenly shattered.

"Kids" she affirmed. "You know, like humans but smaller." Yolanda leapt upstairs like a mountain gazelle.

At the tone of her voice Zinic gave Tyler a look.

"What?" Tyler snapped.

Zinic shrugged and entered the kitchen.

"Boil the kettle," he said. "And see if you can find some Whisky."

Tyler filled the kettle then Zinic ran the cold tap over his hand. It hurt. He closed his eyes and turned his face to the ceiling. His body shivered spasmodically but he forced himself to keep it under the water. It was the only way to cleanse the wound. Cold water stung more than warm, but was better against infection. It would also go some way toward anesthetizing the wound for what was about to come. The pain caused a film of sweat to form on his face and neck.

Tyler took off his jacket and hung it on a stool. He looked through a few cupboards then left the kitchen just as Yolanda returned.

"Do you have any Whisky?"

She shook her head. "There's a bottle of Vodka in the fridge."

While he went to find it she laid her medical bits on the high table unit in the center.

"I got you a towel and some painkillers" she said.

"Give me a few."

She put three in his left hand and he threw them into his mouth and chewed. He asked her to thread a good length of cotton through the needle. He up-righted a cereal bowl on the draining board and asked her to place the needle, thread and scissors inside. She did so then he instructed her to fill it with the boiling water.

Tyler returned with the bottle from the fridge. "Is Vodka OK?"

"Even better."

Yolanda handed Zinic the iodine. He turned off the tap and the blood flowed freely from the gaping wound into the steel sink. Yolanda could see the inside of his tendons and even a piece of white she took to be bone. She felt queasy. Zinic prepared himself then poured the iodine on his hand. Yolanda and Tyler looked on. He clamped his eyes and mouth shut. His body convulsed as though shot through with a thousand volts but he didn't make a sound.

After thirty seconds he stopped shaking, breathed heavily and opened his eyes. Tyler offered him the Vodka.

"It's for you" Zinic croaked. "Put your hands in the sink."

Tyler did as he was told and Zinic poured half the bottle over them.

"I can't do this alone. He said. I need two hands and I've only got one. Wait for the alcohol to dry and don't touch anything."

Tyler absorbed his designated role while Zinic put the bottle to his lips. He threw back his head, drained it as if it was water then put the empty bottle in the sink. He gently tipped over the cereal bowl until it was drained and handed it to Tyler.

"Have you ever done this before?" asked Zinic.

Tyler blinked with surprise. "I'm an estate agent," he said feeling slightly ridiculous at the statement.

Zinic placed his forearm on the table with his palm up.

"I think I'm going to be sick" said Yolanda and left the room. They heard her run upstairs.

Zinic looked at Tyler. "How are you feeling?"

He hesitated then nodded. Zinic explained what he was going to do. He spoke calmly and clearly in an effort to keep Tyler calm and concentrated himself. There would have to be about a dozen stitches a quarter of an inch apart. Since Tyler didn't have the skill to tie each one off he would have to make a running stitch. He showed Tyler how to wind the end of the thread around his index finger and then roll it to the end to make a large knot.

"Don't think about it" said Zinic when the moment of truth arrived. "Just do it. You can be sick later."

Tyler placed the point of the needle against the skin at one end of the cut and pushed. It wouldn't go in. He looked up.

"I'll tell you if it hurts" Zinic said grimly.

Tyler felt a frisson of awe at his sang froid then bowed his head and pressed harder. The needle punctured the skin and drew blood. He looked at Zinic apologetically.

Zinic closed his eyes for a moment then nodded encouragingly. "Carry on until it you see the point inside the wound."

Tyler felt faint. The bloody point of the needle appeared in the lacerated flesh on one side of the cut.

"Push it through to the other side and then up; like you were sowing a sock."

Tyler's mother had shown him how to darn socks as a child but this was quite different.

The needle seemed to snag on the underside of the skin and he was afraid he was going to tear the edge. Zinic prompted him to continue and the point eventually surfaced again on the far side. He carefully pulled the thread all the way through until it was stopped by the large knot.

"Now pull it shut," said Zinic.

Tyler tugged at the thread and pressed down the skin with his left hand until the corner of the wound was stitched tight. The bleeding reduced at the point where the skin came together. His eyes started to sting and he realised sweat was pouring down his face. Zinic picked up the towel and wiped it. Tyler looked back at what he had just done. He swallowed hard. He was exhausted.

"You're doing fine" said Zinic, with an unconscious touch of his native accent. "Only eleven more to go."

Yolanda wasn't sick but she was shaken. She returned to the bathroom and tidied up the mess she had made while raiding Petal's first aid cupboard. Then she checked herself in the mirror again. She was surprised to see she looked so normal. She went to her room and found a pink and grey tracksuit to put on. Then she tidied her room again. She wasn't exactly sure what she was doing. She felt disorientated. When finally she plucked up the courage to go back down Tyler was starting to stitch up Zinic's cheek. They needed to disinfect more thread so he instructed her to do what Zinic had shown them earlier. She took her courage and helped mop the wound and cut the gauze. When he was finished, Tyler bandaged Zinic's hand and put a large plaster over his face. The cuts to his forearm and shin, Zinic was content to wash with iodine and cover with plasters.

Yolanda watched Tyler intently through all this. She couldn't reconcile this Tyler with the frightened boy who sat opposite her five days a week. Had he changed or had she never really noticed him before? Even pale with horror and fatigue he seemed more focused and organized than she could ever remember. Zinic instructed him how to finish the stitching and how to prepare the bandages. He didn't have to be told twice. He quickly grasped what needed to be done and got Yolanda to help where it was needed. The entire operation took twenty minutes and he seemed to grow in confidence and assurance with each passing second. His movements became relaxed and fluent almost as though he were born to the task.

Zinic's eyes started to droop. The physical stress, the warmth of the kitchen, the painkillers and half a bottle of Vodka were taking their toll. He could feel himself going and didn't resist. He knew he would be safe with these two. He tried to think through what would happen the next day. He had to meet Bruno at the heliport and he had to take the rifle. Those were the minimum two requirements for postponing Marta's execution. But that was just the beginning. There was still the contract. Marta wouldn't be released until O'Hagan was dispatched and Zinic couldn't even hold the rifle, let alone fire it. He briefly toyed with the idea of getting Tyler to do it. After all he had just shot a man - if he were to be believed. But he rapidly dismissed it. A shot the length of a back garden was not the same as two miles even if he were there to hold his hand. There was only one other chance.

"Can I use your phone?" he asked Yolanda when they had finished wrapping him up.

"Sure."

She grabbed a phone off the wall but it was obvious he couldn't hold it and dial at the same time.

"I'll do it for you" she said.

He gave her the numbers. She recognized 007 as the code for Russia then punched in the ten digits that followed and handed him the phone. As he waited for a reply she tried to calculate what time it would be over there and why he was calling the other side of the world in the middle of the night. She still didn't know what had happened here on her doorstep. The mystery deepened when the phone was answered. Zinic's perfect English accent was transformed into fluent guttural Russian. She exchanged glances with Tyler but it was clear he was as uninformed as her. At least it answered one question: he wasn't a cousin.

Marta's parents had no more news. The manhunt had headed south. The case was reported in all the newspapers and had become something of a cause célèbre. Marta's photograph had been widely circulated and there had been spots on TV. Lots of people had called with information but so far the police had not confirmed anything. He could feel they were tired but hadn't lost hope. Raisa's tone had become insolent towards Zinic as though she felt he had not done enough or that she suspected him of something more sinister. The conversation was strained and made him depressed. He had hoped there might have been a development. He had already thought about contacting the Russian police himself but what could he really tell them that would advance the search? After a brief exchange he hung up. No one spoke for some time. Zinic's hangdog expression weighed them all down. Finally he turned to Yolanda.

"Can I sleep here?" he said.

Yolanda opened her mouth to say yes then felt a wave of indignation.

"You owe me an explanation. In fact loads of explanations. What..."

Yolanda's protest was cut off by the shrill tone of Tyler's mobile phone. He reached into his jacket.

'Number withheld.'

"It must be the hospital." He felt a knot in his stomach. If they were phoning now it could only be bad news.

"Yes."

A man's voice asked if he were Tyler Primovelli and he confirmed it.

"Inspector Robert Grant. Battersea Police."

57.

Tyler froze.

"I have some questions regarding your daughter's hospitalization." Grant said.

"Has something happened?"

"No. Don't worry. It's not about her health."

Tyler breathed out with relief. "What then?"

"We need to meet."

Tyler felt suspicious.

"Just a few routine questions" Grant added.

"OK" he said cautiously. "Tomorrow morning'

"Where are you now?"

The question threw him momentarily. "I'll come to you."

"No. Just tell me where you are" Grant insisted.

"I'll meet you at my apartment" he said then remembered the mess Flatcap had left and immediately regretted it.

"I'm there now. You're not at home."

"I'm at a friend's house."

"What's the address?"

"Can't it wait?"

"No" Grant said impatiently. "It's important and if necessary we'll track the signal off your mobile phone." Grant knew they didn't actually have the technology or the warrant to do that but the threat paid off.

"Alright." He gave Grant the address on Clapham Common and Grant said he would be there in ten minutes.

Yolanda couldn't believe what she had just heard. "What the fuck is going on Tyler? Who did you give my address to?"

"The police."

Yolanda went scarlet with indignation. Zinic asked what they wanted and Tyler told him what the Inspector had said. Both of them suspected it wasn't the real reason but said nothing.

"What's happened to Rachel?" Yolanda said with genuine concern.

Tyler told her that Rachel had found a bottle of Ecstasy in the Janine's house left there by Francis. He described the moment when he arrived and what had happened at the hospital. Yolanda was bowled over by the avalanche of events. Tyler wondered how she would react if she knew the whole of it. She had just asked where Zinic's injuries came into all this when the doorbell rang. Tyler looked at his watch. It had only been five minutes.

Zinic and Tyler exchanged glances.

"Can you put Greg somewhere?" he said "This has nothing to do with him."

"Tyler what are you getting me into?"

"I'll explain. I promise. But please hide him somewhere."

There was no time to take him upstairs so she led him out of the back of the kitchen through a larder area and into a laundry room.

"The bag" Zinic said urgently.

Tyler ran to the front door, crouching low to make sure he wouldn't be seen through the frosted glass and returned with it to the laundry room. There was a washing machine, a tumble dryer, a cupboard for the water heater and shelves of towels and other linen. In one corner was a pile of dirty washing. Zinic buried the bag underneath then collapsed on top. Tyler left and Yolanda turned off the light.

"Thank you" said Zinic.

The tone was genuine but Yolanda though she sensed something more. Something she didn't yet understand. By the time she returned, Tyler had tidied up the medications, scissors and bloody towel and stuffed them under the sink. Yolanda's face was finely balanced between sympathy and irritation. There had been a lot for her to take in and she didn't even know the half of it. He had a feeling he was going to have to tread very carefully.

Grant was wearing his uniform and the kind of dark blue gabardine raincoat Tyler associated with old films. Yolanda led them into the kitchen and offered him something to drink. To her surprise he accepted a glass of white wine. She considered leaving them alone but poured out three glasses and took a seat at the table. Grant had to remind himself that this was her house and Tyler was not being accused of any crime. He started by expressing his sympathy and best wishes for Rachel's recovery. He explained that he wasn't the investigating officer but as the station chief, he was assisting with the enquiry. Yolanda thought he was unnaturally hesitant. She had the impression he was beating around the bush but couldn't work out why. When he mentioned Francis she spoke for the first time.

"He's a first class shit," she said, repeating the opinion she had given to Tyler the night before.

"You knew him?"

"He made himself known. He's always turning up somewhere with his ugly mug and fancy..." She stopped because she realized she was talking about him in the present tense and the question had been in the past.

"'Knew'...?"

"He's dead," said Grant looking discretely at Tyler.

Tyler didn't react immediately. There was a prolonged silence. Yolanda broke it.

"When?"

"About forty minutes ago."

"What happened?"

"Internal haemorrhage. They couldn't stop the bleeding in time."

"What a night" she sighed.

"He was in the process of being arrested for possession of the drugs we found in Mrs Primovelli's house when he was shot."

"Shot?"

Tyler who felt he ought to react, tried to look astonished and repeated, "shot?"

Grant quietly monitored his reaction.

"Good for you" Yolanda said.

Grant suppressed a scowl. "It wasn't the police that shot him Ma'am."

"No? Then who?"

"That's what we're trying to establish."

"Someone shot Francis while you were arresting him" Tyler said.

"...and you didn't see who did it?" Yolanda added skeptically.

"I wasn't there personally you understand."

Yolanda shook her head. "Something doesn't make sense. You have no news on Rachel and you come round her at half past two in the morning to announce that someone Tyler barely knows has been shot. Forgive me if I'm missing something..."

"There's a suspicion that his killing may be connected to a rifle that went missing on Thursday night." He paused to look at their faces. Yolanda was puzzled. Tyler was unreadable. "In the course of the search for it, your car was stopped Mr. Primovelli."

Tyler thought carefully before giving his response. "Was I?"

This was the point beyond which Grant could not go. He could hardly admit to passing on information about a member of the public to a corrupt lawyer. Nonetheless Tyler's reactions up until now confirmed his instinct. He was involved, somehow, in the death of Francis Matlock. The bigger question was how this all related to Buckhurst and, most important of all, his promotion. He made a mental note to call Kriegmann.

"I thought you should know." He sipped his glass for the first time and got down from his stool. "Thank you for your time."

The ending to the meeting was so sudden and unexpected that neither Yolanda nor Tyler moved.

"I'll see myself out." Grant said.

Yolanda followed him to the door. But when he got to the entrance of the kitchen Grant's tenacity got the better of him and he turned round.

"Where were you at half past twelve tonight Mr Primovelli?"

Tyler was caught off guard.

"Half past twelve? I don't know. Everything has happened so fast."

"Let me help. Your daughter arrived at Chelsea and Westminster at eleven fifty three. Dr Littlefield says she saw you for the first time at around ten to one. If you weren't at the hospital where were you?"

"He was with me," said Yolanda quickly. "He picked me up at Joe's Bar at midnight as agreed and told me what had happened. We talked and I dropped him off in a taxi at the hospital. It would have been about that time."

Grant nodded and gave Tyler one last look. Her performance was so good he was almost tempted to believe it.

"Thank you for your help" he said. "We'll be in touch."

Yolanda walked Grant to the front door and dead-bolted it behind him. Tyler got up off his stool. He didn't want to face the firestorm sitting down. Yolanda walked studiously back into the kitchen, sat back down and toyed with her glass of wine without looking at him. Both of them followed their own train of thoughts leaving a curious silence in their wake.

"Thank you" Tyler said eventually.

Yolanda looked at him thoughtfully and said, "How much do you know about me Ty?"

He shrugged. "I didn't know you had kids."

"I was born on the Aylesbury Estate in Walworth. 'Hell's waiting room' they called it. Pushers on every walkway. Gangs on every block. Rape, murder, suicide. A daily fear that's hard to imagine if you haven't lived it. I went to a secondary school off the Old Kent Road and left when I was sixteen without a single grade except in woodwork - and only that because Ishtar Ramamurthy helped me in return for a handjob. My mum's a midwife - which is funny because she doesn't even know the father of her only child. I got pregnant when I was seventeen. The bastard dumped me then came back two years later and thought he could talk me back into bed. It worked and he dumped me again.

"One day - long before you arrived on the scene - I borrowed a smart suit from a friend and the highest heeled shoes I could find. I put my hair up like Audrey Hepburn and walked off the street straight into Thatcher's office. I lied about having worked at this and that agency. He offered me a desk on the spot. No questions, no check-ups just 'turn up Monday morning.'"

She paused and took a sip of wine.

"First day at work, someone from my old school walked in. He pretended he wanted to buy a house. I don't know what he was playing at; he couldn't afford a new pair of sneakers. He recognized me and started laughing. Said he couldn't believe me - Yolanda Wilson from 19 Taplow Block - with two kids and one GCSE working in a swanky place like that. I was humiliated. I pushed him out of the door faster than you can stuff a turkey with a bazooka. It was a different team at the agency then but they cottoned on fast and started ribbing me. They were all white and all middle class. I was an Untouchable and they let me know it. But I stayed on. I worked so fucking hard you wouldn't believe it. I promised myself I would build a wall so high the birds couldn't shit on it. Then I hid behind it. The team changed, agents came and went, but I stayed on. I stayed and I won. I earn more than anyone who ever sat at a desk, including Thatcher. I'm probably the only reason he's still there."

She fell silent and Tyler said, "he knows about you?"

"Knows what? By the time he bothered asking I was a homeowner in sunny Clapham, rubbing shoulders with advertising execs and partying with TV stars. No one knows about Yolanda from Taplow Block."

She stood up, wandered over to the sink and absent-mindedly rinsed her glass.

"Why are you telling me?" Tyler asked.

She put her damp hands on his cheeks and looked into his eyes.

"Did you kill Francis?"

Tyler dropped his gaze. It was all she needed

to know. She stepped forward until her body was pressed against his. Tyler looked up again in surprise. Her face moved closer and she sought out his lips. At first he thought it was another of her tricks, like the fake invitation outside his flat on Friday night. But the more he held back the more she nudged forward. She moaned. She parted his mouth with her own and ran her tongue over his lips. She tasted of sweet wine. Her arms snaked around his neck and her body relaxed into his until he was forced to hold her. Even then he wasn't sure. Yolanda had been much more than just a fantasy figure. She was a symbol of everything that was unattainable in his life: confidence, success, wealth, beauty and even happiness. How could he be a suitable mate for the Golden Woman - whatever her background? He could only ever disappoint her. Her mouth glided down over his stubble and kissed the small of his neck all the way round to his ear. He thought how foul he must smell after all he had been through. She didn't seem to notice. Her slender hands worked their way up the inside of his shirt caressing and exploring his skin like a cat preparing its bed. He wanted to resist but her smell, her taste, her allure were overwhelming. He was already embarrassingly aroused and soon she would notice. It was at this moment he saw the little girl standing in the doorway.

He pulled away.

Yolanda didn't understand at first and looked hurt.

"I thought I heard a noise," Athena said in a sleepy whine.

Yolanda spun round and extended her arms. With a big smile she picked up her daughter and lifted her onto her chest.

"It's nothing baby." Then she carried her over to where Tyler was trying to hide his excitement by pulling down his shirtfront. "Say hello to Tyler baby. He works with Mummy."

Tyler attempted a winning smile and Athena just stared at him blankly.

"Handsome isn't he" Yolanda said with a sly grin.

Athena made a face and buried her head in her mother's neck. "Come on" she said "let's get you back to bed."

She looked sternly at Tyler, licked her finger tip ran it down an imaginary line between them and said "Bookmark."

Yolanda carried Athena upstairs prepared for questions. She was aware that in all her daughter's eight years, she had never seen her with a man. Not a father, nor a grandfather, nor friend nor lover. She was anxious to know what she would make of it. She tucked her in and Athena stared at the ceiling with her eyes wide open.

"What are you thinking of baby?" she asked.

"God" said Athena.

"God? Why are you thinking of God?"

"Why did God make horses?"

She had no answer to that. "It's a good question. Maybe Tyler will know," she said fishing for a response. But none came and eventually Athena's eyes closed and she turned onto her side. Yolanda kissed her ear and pulled up the cover.

When she got back to the kitchen all that was left of Tyler were his shoes. She tracked the rest of him to the front room. In the darkness she could make out his form lying on the sofa. She knelt down beside him. He was on his back with his mouth wide open, fast asleep.

"Tyler" she whispered.

There was no reply and she tried again. She had an unbearable ache to lie next to him but there was no room. She tried to turn him but he was dead to the world. For some reason the loneliness of her existence struck her with full force. Large tears sprung out of her eyes and rolled down her cheeks.

This is ridiculous she thought, surprised at her own weakness.

She sniffed, wiped away the tears with the back of her hand and went upstairs. She pulled the duvet and cover from her bed, rolled them into a ball and carried them back down to the living room. She took a cushion from a chair and placed it under Tyler's head. His mouth closed but he stayed rigid. Then she laid the bed cover over the top of him. He made a noise and she thought he would wake at last but he didn't and she stood there for several minutes watching his face. She tried to imagine what he had gone through: finding his daughter in a coma and going out to shoot Francis. And there were so many other questions: who was the man in the laundry room? Who had attacked them? The reason they couldn't go to the police was at least clear, but there was so much else that she didn't know. It seemed strange to think of Tyler as an enigma but that is exactly what he had become.

She arranged her duvet on the floor next to him. It was queen sized so she lay down on one half and pulled the rest over her. Then she nestled her back into the edge of the sofa. It wasn't the same as being next to him but it was close. She rested her head on her outstretched arm with her eyes wide open. What was she doing? What was she thinking? She thought she would stay awake forever but fell asleep in seconds.

58.

The dim yellow light of the old torch gave Marta some comfort. It only illuminated a patch of ground the size of a tablecloth but she felt safer for its presence. Volya was indifferent. He was sure the batteries wouldn't last more than half an hour.

As they picked their way silently through the forest he tried to think which animals to his certain knowledge were afraid of the dark. He couldn't think of one. On the contrary, many, or even most of them hunted or fed at night. He went through a list in his head that included rabbits, cats, wolves, foxes and hedgehogs. He wasn't sure about birds or even bears but he was convinced they weren't afraid of the dark. At least not in the same abstract way as humans.

Marta tugged at his sleeve, stopped still and turned her head back the way they had come. Her eyes were wide and fearful.

"What?" he said softly.

"Shhh."

After another thirty seconds she turned to Volya and her chin was trembling.

"I heard something" she said. "I'm sure of it."

They had only been walking for five minutes and the noise of the fire was still audible despite the trees. As they listened there was a tumbling sound that made Volya think of a wall collapsing.

"It's just the house" he reassured her. "He'll not follow us. He's hurting bad and we have a gun. And if he got anywhere near us I'd hear him. He may be mad, but I'm sure he's not crazy. Come on."

They followed a gentle uphill gradient until they reached the overgrown track that passed for a road. As Volya climbed ahead up the embankment Marta thought of the last person she had encountered there and hesitated. She looked back down the way they had come and for a brief second she saw a light flicker between the trees. She held her breath and waited for it to reappear but it didn't.

"Hey" Volya called in a hoarse whisper.

Marta turned back to see him squatted down in the road above her extending one of his long, muscular arms.

"What's your name?" he said.

She paused to think. "Marta."

"Marta, give me your hand and let's go. I'm

getting cold."

Marta allowed herself to be hauled up the small ridge. When she was at the top, he introduced himself and told her not to worry. He smiled and she noticed a mouth full of missing teeth. The ones that remained were jagged and yellow with age. His kind eyes reassured her. At least she was no longer alone. They walked on in silence in the same direction she had taken only an hour before. Volya lead the way with his fading torch and she couldn't resist turning round to see if she could catch sight of the other light she had seen. She tried to persuade herself it was just a freak view of the fire and decided to say nothing unless she saw it again.

59.

Kriegmann had one suitcase open on the bed. It was small enough to take as hand luggage on a plane and he was now trying to decide which were the most essential items. Most of what he would need was already at his beach house on the aptly named Crooked Island. The problem was the flights. There was nothing direct to Nassau on Sunday afternoon. He had been tempted to take the Virgin Atlantic flight at one o'clock but that would mean missing the fatal meeting with O'Hagan all together. He came out in a cold sweat every time he thought of Bruno's threat.

The police would go mad when they found out he had skipped the country but they could hardly accuse him of assassinating O'Hagan himself. Besides, the Bahamas was only a category two extradition country and they would have no grounds to recall him. He had dropped into a travel agent near Leicester

Square and booked a flight to Orlando leaving at ten past seven in the evening. It was with Aer Lingus and meant an overnight stay in Shannon but he didn't care. He wanted to get out of harm's way as quickly as possible. Once he was in Florida he would catch a direct flight to Nassau. That meant two overnight stays.

He took a large swig of Talisker and looked at the pile of clothes he had accumulated next to the travel bag. It was twice as large. He would have to discard half of it. The problem was he couldn't concentrate. He pinched his eyebrows and tried to decide between the beige or white linen suit.

His mobile rang and for the briefest moment he thought it was O'Hagan who unscrupulously called him at any time of day or night from anywhere in the world. It took him a moment to remember Her Majesty's pleasure didn't include mobile phones. Then the fear cramped up his stomach again. There was only one other person who would call at this time. He wondered if the lead on Primovelli had worked out. Did he have the rifle? Was the assassination still on or not? He had to assume the answers to both these questions were 'yes' though he had reached the point where he almost didn't care. This time tomorrow he'd be out of the country - never to return. He pulled his phone out of the jacket lying across a chair. It was a number he didn't recognise but Bruno had a tendency to crop up in expected places.

"Yes" he answered warily.

"Mr. Kriegmann?"

It wasn't Bruno but he was sure he recognized the voice.

"Inspector Robert Grant."

"Grant." He paused and looked at his watch. "Yes Inspector. What can I do for you at quarter to two in the morning?"

"I'm sorry if I woke you."

"I'm sure you didn't do it for the fun."

Grant ignored the tone and said, "first of all you may like to know Commander Buckhurst called me yesterday to say he was personally reviewing my promotion."

Kriegmann was glad Grant could not see his broad smile. It was always a delight to be thanked for things one hadn't done. It gave a very strong feeling of omnipotence.

"I'm delighted" he said. "I'm sure it's merited."

"Merit doesn't come into it anymore I'm afraid."

Kriegmann didn't reply. If that wasn't the reason for the call at this hour then what was. Grant continued.

"How did that lead work out?"

"Work out?"

"Yes."

"Are you reopening the case?"

"I'm not sure."

Kriegmann had few hairs on his body, but those he did have stood up as if an ice-cold wind had blown through the room.

"I thought Buckhurst had closed it."

"There's been a development."

"What kind?"

"A shooting."

"Who's been shot?"

"A drug pusher."

"Who did it?"

"We don't know yet."

"Then I don't see..."

"There may be a link to the missing rifle."

"May be?"

"It's tenuous."

"Does Buckhurst know?"

"Not yet."

Kriegmann mulled this over. He's afraid his promotion is in jeopardy he thought. That's why he's calling me first.

"How can I help you further?" he said eventually with an ever so slight emphasis on the final word.

"You can tell me what the fuck is going on. Some ex-special forces Russian killer is found on top of a high rise flat and despite suspicions of terrorist activity he is released without consultation by your friend Commander Buckhurst..."

"I told you he's not really..."

"Let me finish. His rifle vanishes into thin

air and you turn up out of the blue looking for it because you're afraid your client is about to be assassinated. You get Primovelli's name as a possible collaborator with the Russian and all of a sudden he's implicated in shooting his ex-wife's boyfriend."

"You've arrested him then."

"Not yet. His girlfriend is covering for him."

"I still don't see..."

"What's the connection? That's all I want to know, what is the connection between you, Commander Buckhurst, Tyler Primovelli and Yolanda Wilson?"

"That's the girlfriend?"

"Yes."

Kriegmann took a sip of whisky while he absorbed this last information. "How much do you want to know?"

"All of it."

The lawyer was struck by an idea.

"Maybe we can help each other out Inspector, or can I now say Chief Inspector?"

Grant didn't answer.

"We can't discuss it over the phone and I have a long week ahead of me. My client's trial starts on Monday and I have a lot of preparation" he said lifting the beige linen suit into his travel case. "Why don't I come in and see you first thing Monday morning. Say five o'clock" he added with a mental chuckle. The thought of Grant struggling to wake up while he was fast asleep in an Orlando hotel, tickled him.

"Can't we do it tonight?"

"Absolutely impossible my dear fellow."

"I could just bring you in for questioning."

"Not without 'reasonable grounds' that I have committed an offence Inspector. Do you have 'reasonable grounds'?"

Grant had almost forgotten he was a lawyer. He was reluctant to wait but could hardly force Kriegmann to talk to him about something he himself should never have started. The strings attached to his promotion were beginning to feel more like a web. Grant said he would think about it and hung up.

Kriegmann didn't like this new turn of events. Not at all. He decided to clear out even faster than planned. He would stay at a hotel tonight and slip away early in the morning. He packed his toilet bag along with the last of his clothing, two pairs of cotton boxers and zipped up the bag. Anything else he needed, he could buy on the way. He looked around his room for things he might have missed. No, that was it. He didn't need the two Queen Anne chairs standing either side of the window. He didn't need the Chagall sketch hanging over his night table.

He put his blazer on and slipped the passport and tickets into his inside pocket. He checked his wallet was in the back pocket of his grey cotton slacks and pulled the travel bag off the bed. As he walked down the stairs, passed the expensive objets d'art he had collected over the years he didn't feel in the least bit sentimental. They were tools of his trade; only there to impress his most snobbish clients.

He would put the whole lot up at auction once he was safely out of the way. The house alone would fetch well over four million. He would almost certainly confer the job on the person who had arranged its purchase two years ago. It was one of life's splendid little ironies that Yolanda Wilson should now turn out to be the girlfriend of the man everyone was hunting. She was a remarkable woman and if his tendencies had not lain where they did he would certainly have made a pass at her. He had spent several wonderful dinners and parties in her company and she was as ruthlessly charming as she was professional. He wondered what kind of man Primovelli was. It sounded Mafia. He was sure he had once picked up a very silly crime book written by a man with a similar name.

He reached the bottom of the stairs, checked the front door was bolted then turned and walked back through the house in the direction of the garage trundling his case behind him. He thought about turning off the lights, but couldn't be bothered. The cleaner would be in Monday morning and she would tidy after him.

Before entering the garage he punched in the code for the alarm and it started its electronic countdown. The garage was situated in the mews running down behind the terraces of houses. He was proud that his was one of the few houses in London where the old stables had not been sold off and converted into a yuppie cottage. It was a large garage, capable of taking three cars even though he only had one, a burgundy 1998 Bentley Arnage. Twice a week a man called Peter Yearning came to service and clean it. Peter was a jack-of-all-trades. He did whatever little jobs needed doing around the house and kept the pocket-sized garden under control. Peter was impeccably tidy and his tools were hung neatly along the left hand side wall above the work bench.

Kriegmann turned on the two strip lights in the ceiling and reached for the car keys on a hook inside the door. For four weeks Peter had also been occupied building a new cabinet to stow odds and ends and Kriegmann noticed he had uncharacteristically left the door wide open.

He pointed the keyfob at the car and pressed. Clunk. He shut the self-locking door to the house and heard the alarm warning on the far side reach its climax and stop. He opened the boot of the Bentley, placed his travel bag inside and closed it again. He walked round to the driver's door, trailing a finger along the spotless roof. He would miss his Bentley, he decided. He wondered about the practicality of having it shipped over to the Bahamas. He was planning out the logistics in his mind as he sat down and slid the key into the ignition. He automatically reached up to adjust the rear view mirror and there, reflected in it, was an object that looked just like Peter's garden axe. He spun round. It was indeed the axe, buried in the face of a man he immediately recognized as Bruno's scar-faced thug.

Landri was slumped upright in the center of the backseat. His head dropped forward onto his chest under the weight of the four pounds of forged steel.

Kriegmann gasped, fumbled for the door handle behind him and stumbled out of the car. He backed away and stood in shock, staring at the bloody corpse with his mouth wide open. There was a squeak behind him. He spun round. The cupboard door swung shut revealing the ghoulish form of Bruno Olevsky.

"Going somewhere?" he said.

Kriegmann felt dizzy with fear. He backed away right up to the locked door to the house. Bruno picked a hammer off the wall and followed. There was nowhere to escape and, in the event, the lawyer didn't even try. He sunk to his knees and cried. Bruno hated people who cried. Landri, for instance, had maintained a stoic, almost apologetic silence to the end.

"I did everything you asked" Kriegmann blubbered. "Everything. It isn't fair."

"Where's my gun?" Bruno said.

"I don't know!" he pleaded. "I gave you the information that's all."

"Where are they now?"

"I don't know anything," the lawyer screamed hysterically.

Bruno slammed the hammer head down angrily on the roof of the Bentley. Kriegmann jumped.

"If you don't know anything then you're fucking useless to me." The garage reverberated as he shouted. He slammed the hammer repeatedly into the metal chassis and the noise filled the room causing Kriegmann to cover his ears.

When Bruno stopped and turned to him his face was flushed and his eyes were pinched with fury. Kriegmann was paralyzed with fear. He cowered on the floor against the door, moaning like a lunatic with eyes and nose streaming. His hands were cupped over the top of his head in anticipation of what was to come.

Bruno held the hammer lazily out to one side and advanced. Panic caused Kriegmann to lose his breath. His throat was dry and when he tried to talk no sound came out. He held up his hand to stave off the blow and eventually managed to croak out a single word.

"Wait!"

Bruno waited.

"Please..." he stammered. "I know someone. A girl. She knows where he is."

"Zinic?"

"Primovelli."

Bruno nodded appreciatively. "Who is she?"

Kriegmann swallowed hard. "His girlfriend."

Bruno relaxed his arm. This was sounding positive. "Where is she?"

"I don't know... but I have her phone number" he added hastily.

Bruno found the hook on the tool wall for the hammer and replaced it.

"See what you can do when you try Julius?"

60.

It wasn't long before Marta saw the light again; a small patch of white in the black of the forest to their left. She formed a quick impression that the way it oscillated on and off was caused by passing behind the trees - and therefore it was moving.

"Volya" she whispered urgently and pointed.

He stopped and turned but it was gone.

"It's him." She was almost in tears again. "He's following us."

They stood for a while peering into the blackness until Volya saw it.

"There!"

It was much further forward than before and appeared to be moving diagonally from their left to in front. Then it disappeared again. They watched for another half a minute but it didn't return.

Volya turned off his torch. Although the

batteries were fading the difference without it was startling. They were plunged into a darkness made even more acute by the passage of the moon behind a thick cloud.

"What are you doing?" Marta cried anxiously.

"He's following our light."

"But he's passed us. He's over there now."

"He's going to cut us off on the road ahead."

His voice was troubled. It was the first time Marta had noted anything other than absolute confidence.

"But you've got a gun."

He peered resolutely ahead without moving. "Yes, I've got a gun" he said, "but it's dark and I'm old."

"You said he wasn't crazy."

"I'm the one that's crazy getting into this mess" he snapped angrily.

"You're not going to leave me..." Marta said with horror.

Volya shifted from one foot to another, casting his nervous gaze between the Marta and the road ahead.

"I've no idea what's going on" he said throwing his arms out in a gesture of impotence.

"Nor have I." Marta found a reserve of strength at last. "Do you think I chose to be here in the middle of the night? They tied me up! That man... the dead one..." she fought through the choke in her voice "... he forced himself on me."

"What are you anyway: a prostitute?"

Marta swung without thinking and slapped Volya hard across his left cheek. There was a loud smack. He staggered back with his hand on his face. He ran his tongue round the inside of his mouth then probed his cheek with his fingers as if searching for a missing tooth.

"That's another one gone," he said matter-of-factly.

"I'm sorry" Marta said.

He spat out on the ground and drew air in over his gums with a loud sucking sound.

"I should have killed him when I had the chance" he mumbled. "I couldn't do it. It's my fault." He turned to face her. "I'm just as frightened as you."

Marta saw something over his shoulder. Her eyes widened and she gasped. Volya spun round to follow her stare. The light was straight ahead of them now no more than thirty yards away. It was growing larger and shaking as though Roman were running towards them. Then it turned off.

Volya grabbed Marta's wrist and pulled her off the road into the trees to their right. They ran as fast as they could but their progress was slowed by the uneven surface of the forest floor. The tangle of sticks and roots and small plants made for such noisy progress that Volya thought even a person with only one ear couldn't fail to follow them. After only two minutes both of them were breathing heavily.

"Why are you stopping" Marta hissed.

Volya put his hands on his knees and bent forward to catch his breath. "It's no good" he said between puffs. "You go on."

"What?"

Volya straightened up, took the Makarov out of his jacket pocket, pulled back and released the slide. A bullet lodged in the chamber with a loud click.

"We're never going to lose him. He can hear us a mile away" he said

"What are you going to do?"

"Shoot the other ear off."

"I'll stay with you."

"No. Keep going." He pulled the torch out of the pocket where he had stashed it and proffered it to her. "He'll follow you and I'll be waiting."

They both looked round when they heard the loud snap of a branch indicating he had left the road. The light came on for a second then flicked off again.

Volya waved her away with his left hand. "Go. Don't wait for me. Just go and keep running."

Marta drew her hands down over her face in a gesture of indecision and despair then clenched her lips. Volya turned on the torch and thrust it at her.

"Hurry!"

She hated to leave him on his own and she hated to be on her own but he was right. Roman was young and would certainly catch up with them sooner rather than later. She grabbed the torch, turned and crashed on through the undergrowth uncaring now how much noise she made. She thought of Volya waiting alone in the dark for sounds of Roman. She reassured herself that he was a woodsman, probably a hunter of long experience, and that he would certainly be able to trap and kill Roman.

After several minutes of interminable forest she reached a partial clearing where the forest was thinner with only younger trees and saplings. On entering, she noticed that it extended away in both directions as if there had once been a road. She stumbled over something she thought was a root but the torch revealed to be a heavy iron rod embedded in the ground and partially covered in moss. It ran through the center of the clearing as far as she could see. It was part of an old railway line. She could see the second parallel rail two steps to her left and just make out the rotted and overgrown wooden sleepers between them studded with spikes of silver birch.

Even this ancient sign of civilization was comforting. It was built by people and must lead to and from somewhere. Her thoughts returned to Volya. Should she wait for him? What if it went wrong? What if Roman surprised him? She couldn't shake the thought that she hadn't said goodbye. He had saved her life and she hadn't even thanked him. Suppose she escaped and he were left lying in the woods. How would she ever find him? A feeling of profound sorrow for an old man she hardly knew was shattered by the sound of a muted gunshot.

She held her breath to hear better. There was a second shot, a screech, then another shot followed by a guttural cry, then silence. She stood stock-still. Her mouth hung wide open. The blood rushed through her ears like a hurricane. She stayed like that for five minutes, straining every nerve until she heard the crackle of breaking twigs. Someone was approaching and she suddenly realized that she was holding the lighted torch in their direction, advertising her presence like a neon sign. As if in shamed recognition, the faded light guttered and finally gave out. She turned it off to make sure. In the clearing she was more exposed than ever, but dared not move for fear of making a noise that would give her away. She wondered where the courage she had found to fight and kill a man had gone. There was simply none left. Apprehension paralyzed her and she was rooted to the spot as surely as the iron rails.

The noise of the person approaching grew louder and she could now make out a form lumbering through the darkness. Suddenly a torch beam shot out and scanned the trees in her direction. Marta's heart skipped a beat and she dropped to her knees. A cold wind of terror swept over her, perversely bringing with it her lost valor. She scrambled around in the dark ground with her fingers looking for a weapon. She found a lump of rusty iron the size of a small fist lying in a patch of lichen. When she picked it up she discovered it was the head of a foot long rail spike. She brushed off the dirt and flakes of rust. It was heavy and she wasn't sure she would be able to throw it more than a few meters.

She stayed crouched on the ground. If she didn't move, there was a strong chance he would not see her and pass by. But as bad luck would have it the beam of light was heading straight for her. Was it possible he was following her track? Still she could not move. She adjusted her grip so she was holding the spike in the middle ready throw or stab. No more than ten yards away the figure came to a halt and tuned off the light.

This was Marta's chance. She rose and felt her way silently along the edge of the rail. When she had gotten as close as she could, she stole forward as stealthily as possible. She was only three meters away when he suddenly pointed the torch beam in her face. Marta was blinded. She flung the spike at the man who was now completely hidden from her view by the light.

"Marta, it's me." Volya cried out.

He let the torch drop to the ground and Marta ran forward. "Thank God!"

Volya was now rolling on his back clutching his right knee and groaning.

"What happened?"

"You almost killed me."

"I'm sorry. I didn't know it was you."

Volya released some choice swear words. She touched the wounded knee and he cried out.

"Is it broken?"

"I hope not." He grimaced and tried to flex it. "What the hell was that?"

"I don't know. A big nail or something."

Volya grumbled something about the reason he never remarried then rolled onto his left side and found the offending object. "Where the devil did you get it?"

"Over there. There's an old rail line."

Volya waved for her to come closer and put his right arm round her shoulder. She put her left arm round his waist and helped him to his feet. He put his right foot on the ground, tried to put weight on it then snatched it back up in pain. Marta apologized repeatedly and Volya dismissed it.

"Show me the line," he said.

As they hobbled together towards it Marta said she had heard shots and asked what had happened to Roman.

"I was wrong" Volya grunted without further explanation.

"Did you...you know. Is he's still alive."

He nodded. "I couldn't do it. Not kill a man. He's still alive, for now" he added cryptically.

They stopped at the railway line. Volya shone the torch along the rails and grunted his recognition.

"I rode this once as a youngster. Over fifty years ago."

"Where does it lead?"

"Back that way to a small village called Karak. Up ahead, an old sawmill." He thought back to when Karak had buzzed with activity. A hotel and five bars had welcomed the loggers and their weekly pay checks. He had a cousin whom he was sure had been a prostitute in one of them though she had always denied it. She would be an old woman now - or dead. It seemed that fifty years had passed in the blink of an eye.

Marta jogged him out of his reverie by circling round so they were facing towards the village.

"No no" he said. "You go. I'll never make it. The sawmill's only ten minutes from here. I need to rest. You go ahead and send someone back for me."

Marta refused point blank to go off on her own. She was also exhausted and was still uneasy about Roman.

"What happened back there?"

"I'll tell you on the way" he said and he hopped back round with his arm still over her shoulder. He gave her the torch and she lit the way. As they staggered along the old track he wondered how much he should tell her and if he had done the right thing. He could always tell her the truth, but she would have to have a strong stomach.

61.

Z inic dreamed of metal rain.

He was working in the fields at Marta's farm. The sun was shining and the wheat sprouted all around them like golden haired children. Then, from out of a clear blue sky fell a rain of bullets that cut it all down. Zinic himself remained untouched but the crops and buildings, even the earth itself was pounded into oblivion.

He knew there was a tap inside the house where he could turn the rain off. He ran into the building but it was unfamiliar. He knew the tap was in the basement and he found himself running down a stone staircase. But the basement had endless corridors and other staircases. He kept on descending and all the while the rain fell. It destroyed the house and the ground above him no matter how far down he went. Then Marta was with him. She wanted to guide him to the tap. She gave him one end of the yellow scarf he had given her. He took it and used it to follow her. But the scarf grew longer and longer and she got further and further ahead of him until she was completely out of sight. The scarf hung uselessly in his hand. The choice of corridors was infinite and he was lost. His panic mounted and the metal rain continued to pound down around him.

He woke up in a sweat.

The dream stayed vividly in his mind for several seconds. He associated holding the scarf with the cut in his hand. He also had the feeling he was responsible for the metal rain but he couldn't find any meaning to it. He tried to remember the beginning of the story but it started to fade. Very quickly the rest of it followed like the ashes of a photograph floating up a chimney.

He sat in the dark for several more seconds, disorientated by the dream, attempting to work out where he was. There was a smell of fresh laundry that reminded him of Marta and he wondered if he were in her bedroom. But the shapes were unfamiliar. A ghostly light fell through a single high window catching the outlines of boxlike objects he eventually recognized as washing and drying machines. Slowly, the events that had led him to Yolanda's laundry room came back to his mind.

He examined his hand. It was very painful and even in the dim light, he could see the fingers that poked out of the edge of the bandage were dark blue and greatly swollen. He hoped it would not turn septic. He sat still for a while longer reviewing his situation. Uppermost in his mind was the thought that he could not hope to fulfill his contract. He could not handle the rifle with his right hand and, by some anomaly of nature, he could not shoot straight with his left.

Bruno had well and truly screwed him. His thug may not have retrieved the rifle but he had certainly ensured he couldn't use it. He wondered if he could get that fact through to Alexandr. But how? He had no idea where he was. He didn't even know the location of that gruesome museum he had been taken to. It was now 6:43. He had just over five hours before meeting Bruno. He dismissed the Alexandr option from his mind as pointless. Even if by some miracle he managed to contact him would it change anything? He doubted it would save Marta's life. Alexandr may wear a Kiton suit but he was every bit as ruthless as his psychotic brother. He would be just as keen to see such compromising evidence well and truly buried.

Marta.

The guilt weighed heavily on him. Despite all his precautions he was responsible for her abduction. Despite all his training he couldn't save her. He turned the possibilities over and over in his head looking for new ways of approaching the problem but found nothing. There was no getting around the fact that she was two thousand miles away. If he had had any idea where she was or who was holding her he would have passed it on to the police. The only clue he possessed was the blurred footage of her tied to the bed, stored in his mobile phone. There was no clue as to its origin and it would only finger him as the suspect, were it to be found.

The frustration pushed him to his feet. He refused to believe there wasn't something he could do. He needed to think. When he moved, the pain in his hand grew stronger. The painkillers were never going to be enough but he ought to take some more.

He opened the door and cautiously made his way back through the pantry into the kitchen. After a brief search he found the packet of Nurofen stuffed under the sink with the bandages. He swallowed four with a mouthful of water from the tap.

He lifted the blind above the sink and looked outside. The sky was grey with pre-dawn light. He caught a glimpse of himself in the dark mirror of the window and thought he looked terrible. His left cheek was swollen and discolored and patched up with a large bandage. The worst of the blood had already been sponged off his face but the left side of his polo shirt was black with the stuff. The damage to his left arm and right shin was equally obvious.

He walked over to the open kitchen door leading to the entrance hall, front door and stairs and listened to the house. All was quiet. The hallway was indirectly lit from a low wattage bulb somewhere upstairs. The only signs of disorder from the previous night were Tyler's mud encrusted shoes by the kitchen table and his own leather jacket hung over the back of a metal stool.

He went back into the laundry room, turned on the light and pulled his holdall out from the pile of laundry. In the process he spotted a black T-shirt. It had what he took to be the name of a group on the front: GunzDown. It seemed appropriate. He pulled off his polo shirt with one hand and slipped it on. It was nice to wear something dry even if it smelt slightly rancid. He found a pair of tracksuit trousers but the waist was half his size. He thought that would be all until he noticed a pair of blue football socks. His own were still soaking wet so he kicked off his shoes and replaced them. Warm dry feet made him feel a hundred times better.

He packed the old socks and bloody shirt into the hold all then added the mobile phone and the pack of Nurofen. He scanned the shelves of neatly stacked linen and spotted what he wanted on the wall next to the boiler.

He took out two tea towels, tied them end-to-end then threaded the loop over his right shoulder and under his left armpit. Carefully, he rested his right forearm in the improvised sling with the bandaged palm facing upwards.

His jacket was still damp but the lining was dry. He draped it over his shoulders then slipped his left arm into the sleeve. With some difficulty, he fastened the bottom of the zip then closed it up over his slung arm. He was glad to have it back. He had paid a fortune for it in a Moscow fashion store two years ago and had worn it virtually non-stop ever since. It was part of his uniform. It took him a moment to realize what was missing: the icon.

He picked up the bag and returned to the hall entrance. Habit forced him to turn round and ask himself if he had left anything important behind. He thought of trying to clean up the fingerprints and traces of blood but decided it was a waste of time. As he passed the living room he sensed the presence of someone inside and stole a look through the gap in the door. To his surprise, Tyler was lying flat out on the sofa softly snoring and Yolanda was curled up on the floor below him like a faithful pet.

It had been a bizarre encounter with Tyler all round. Despite everything he had grown to like him. The conversation he had overheard with the policeman convinced him Tyler's

story was true. He had shot and killed someone. That wasn't an easy thing to do - even at
a distance. On the other hand maybe it wasn't
such a large step from suicide. He thought of all
those lunatics in America and elsewhere who
shot up their schools or neighborhoods before
turning the guns on themselves.

He left the split-level lovers, pulled back
the two heavy bolts on the front door and let
himself out. The air outside was deliciously
sharp. The door clicked softly behind him. The
small, elevated brick porch looked out over
the Common. The now clearly visible high
cloud indicated they were in for a dry day and
the pale glow above the horizon to his left
told him he was facing South West. He closed
his eyes and located Clapham Common in his
mental map of London. In his mind he traced
the route across Queenstown Road, passed
Clapham Railway Station and on down to the
Heliport on the south side of the Thames. No
more than three quarters of an hour away on
foot. He still had time. What he lacked, was a
plan.

62.

By the time Tyler awoke, Yolanda had gone.

The duvet had been tidied away and he had no idea how close she had been for most of the night. He stretched noisily and turned his head to look around him. Heavy curtains were drawn across a sizable bay window. The light that bled in round the edges illuminated a room that was tidy and tastefully furnished. At one end was a super size TV with a stack of children's DVDs and a games consol. There was something about the easy sense of order and unpretentious comfort that reminded him of Garth House. He couldn't help but compare it with the meager existence he provided for Rachel.

As soon as his daughter came into his mind he looked at his wristwatch. Half past nine. The hospital results were expected by ten. It would only take fifteen minutes to drive there.

He gave himself a moment to think over the extraordinary events of the night before. Not least, Yolanda's kiss. He closed his eyes and relived the moment. He conjured up her arms entwined around him and her fingers kneading his skin. He could still taste her mouth and feel her soft lips playing against his mouth and neck. If he breathed carefully through his nose he could even smell her. The feeling transported him. He luxuriated in the dream a while longer then opened his eyes.

In the cold light of morning he was convinced Yolanda didn't really feel anything for him. She had been stressed and probably drunk. He just happened to be there. He tried to picture scenarios in which he would try to kiss her but they all seemed awkward. Yolanda and Tyler. Tyler and Yolanda. The very thought of them together was just... well, ludicrous. The idea of her hanging off his arm in public or at work was downright shameful. What would Piers or Mark say?

He realized that Yolanda and Zinic must be somewhere in the house together and was seized by an irrational pang of jealousy. He pulled back the cover and swung his feet to the floor. He was still dressed. Was this the second or third night in a row he had slept in his clothes? The damp of his trousers had left a patch on the sofa and a chill in the small of his back. His stomach gurgled out a reminder that he hadn't eaten for at least twenty-four hours.

He opened the door to the corridor, stopped and listened. Nothing. His shoes had been cleaned and left on the front door mat. He turned right and headed towards the kitchen. Empty. He could hear a noise from the back room where Zinic had slept. He walked through the larder and opened the door to the laundry room. Zinic had gone and the pile of laundry was now gently rocking in the drum of the washing machine. He looked for the black holdall but Zinic had taken it.

When he returned to the kitchen he realized his leather jacket had disappeared from the stool. The thought that Zinic was repossessing these things was surprisingly depressing. He went back into the corridor to see if it had been hung up near the shoes but it hadn't.

"Hello" he called up the stairs.

There was no answer. He mounted them and searched through the upstairs rooms one by one. They were all empty. When he got to the one he assumed was Yolanda's he stood on the threshold looking in. An unaccountable wave of sadness swept over him. He had developed a surprising feeling of tenderness for Yolanda. He knew it could never be reciprocated and the empty room in an empty house seemed the perfect metaphor.

He was coming downstairs feeling lost and alone when a shadow fell across the frosted glass of the front door and he heard a key in the lock. A middle aged black woman in a blue and white uniform entered. She had a pleasant face and a large bottom. When she saw Tyler sitting there she gave a gasp of shock then placed her palm over her heart and laughed at herself.

"You must be Tyler" she said. "I'm Petal, Yolanda's mum." She had an accent he couldn't quite place. Yolanda's cultured accent, he now realized, was an attempt to disguising her origins. Petal had no such pretentions. Her long South London vowels were mixed in with something earthier that he associated with tropical climes. Her voice, however, was high pitched and plosive.

"Did you take a shower yet?"

"Er, no. Thank you but I don't have time."

She put down a plastic bag filled with magazines and took off the grey cardigan that he hadn't noticed hanging off her shoulders.

"She told me about your daughter. It's a terrible thing."

She hung the cardigan on a coat hook.

Tyler stood up. "Where is everybody?" he couldn't find the courage to ask after Yolanda alone.

"Michael plays football on Sunday mornings. Yolanda had a call to visit a client in Holland Park and she dropped Athena off at a friend on the way."

"Holland Park?"

Petal looked at him and he was sure she could read his green-eyed thoughts. "Why don't you give her a ring? She'd be please to know you're up."

"No battery. I'll call her later, from home" he lied. He reached down for his shoes. "I must get to the hospital."

"Have a cup of tea honey" she insisted. "I already called the hospital. My friend Millie works in the ICU and she says Rachel's doing fine. I'll put the kettle on and you can tell me what you think of my daughter. You're the first man she ever brought home."

Tyler felt flattered by the implication but faked a dismissive laugh.

"We just work together" he said.

"If you say so honey."

Tyler found himself intrigued by the possibility of what Yolanda may have said to her mother about him. Petal picked up her plastic bag and waddled into the kitchen. Tyler sat back down and laced up his shoes. He could hear the sounds of a kettle being filled and turned on. He was eager to know more but frightened to expose his interest by asking.

"Come on in" she said when she noticed him in the limbo of the doorframe.

"No I've really got to go" he said neither moving forward nor back.

Petal took out two mugs and dropped a tea-bag in each one.

"So?" she said. "What do you think?"

"Of Yolanda?"

"No" she said with a chuckle. "... the color of the kitchen. Not very sure of yourself are you Tyler. Nothing like her ex. Not that they were married. I mean the father of Mikey and Athena."

"No I don't suppose I am."

Petal looked at him discriminatingly. "He was taller. By about six inches."

"That's tall."

"He went to the gym a lot."

Tyler made a little gesture to indicate he could do with a little more exercise.

"And he was one of those Yardies" she said with strong distaste.

Tyler's mouth opened like a fish. Even he had heard of the violent Jamaican gangs that controlled much of London's drug scene. He had a strong urge to back straight out of the front door. Instead he nodded sagely and said: "Does he have much contact with the children?"

Petal filled the mugs with boiling water. "A letter now and then. I don't think he writes them himself."

"There's no chance of him turning up unexpectedly is there?"

"No honey" she laughed. "Not unless he's released on parole twenty years early. Milk?"

He thought back to a conversation they

had in a taxicab where they had talked about the sort of men that asked Yolanda out. This unseen gangster sounded remarkably like the image he had formed at the time. More than ever he was certain that her brief moment of weakness the night before had been just that - a brief moment of weakness. It was ridiculous of him to foster his fantasy about her any longer. He was fooling himself. He shook his head.

"No milk?" Petal asked with the pint bottle poised in her hand.

"No tea thank you" he said. "I'm sorry but I really have to go."

Petal seemed genuinely disappointed. "Can I give Yolanda a message?" she called after him. "She'll be back in an hour."

"You can say... er. No nothing. I'll call later."

He closed the door softly behind him and stood on the doorstep looking over the russet colored trees in the park. He only realized how warm the house had been when he stepped outside. His damp and rumpled shirt was no protection against the fresh autumn day. He flapped his arms and ran over to his car on the far side of the road pulling his keys out of his trouser pocket. It started on the third attempt. He took a last lingering look at Yolanda's front door and slipped into first.

63.

At the hospital he left his name at the reception desk for Dr. Littlefield. Janine appeared from nowhere dabbing at her red ringed eyes with toilet paper. Her face was blotchy and bloated. She was wearing the same jeans and T shirt from the night before underneath a flimsy white hospital gown. She looked awful and Tyler wondered if he didn't look just as bad. He guided her to a table in the nearby cafeteria and asked her if she wanted anything. She didn't. He went to order two teas and took his time choosing a croissant and a piece of orange and carrot cake.

"I'm so sorry" she said when he finally sat down. She made a fumbled attempt to grasp his hand.

He passed her the tea and placed the pastries on the table between them. She didn't touch either.

"It's not your fault" he said in a conciliatory

tone.

She sniffed and nodded her head. "It is." I should have known. I knew what he did. I just never asked."

He had suspected as much. Her confession made little difference now. He sipped his tea and broke off a piece of cake. It was five to ten.

"I've been a bad mother" she whined.

"You've been a good mother. Francis was a mistake."

"My mistake was leaving you" she said suddenly.

Tyler could hardly believe his ears. He waited for more but it didn't come. Janine picked the horns off the croissant. He didn't know what to say and wasn't at all sure he wanted her to say any more. So it was with some relief that he saw the birdlike Dr. Littlefield cross the reception hall to the desk.

"That's her" he said to Janine and got up immediately.

The doctor looked even more exhausted than the last time he had seen her. She had obviously been up all night. She greeted the two of them as energetically as she could and invited them to sit down with her in reception.

"You're lucky to have caught me" she said "I'm just going home. You daughter's dossier is up in the ICU but I've just looked in on her. I can tell you what I know then you'll have to see who's on duty, probably Dr. Amoh. The good news is there have been no major traumas overnight. Everything seems to be functioning normally. The blood test show a high level of MDMA as we suspected but also amphetamine and even caffeine."

"Caffeine?" said Janine

"It means the tablets weren't very pure." She resisted a discourse on the dishonesty of drug dealers and continued. "The crisis period is normally the first three hours. It's been over eight hours now and the toxin levels in the blood have halved. The relatively low levels of MDMA maybe also be the result of your quick action Mrs. Primovelli. I imagine she'll be moved out of intensive care sometime today and she could be ready to go home in about four days."

"Thank God" said Janine pressing the toilet paper to her leaking eyes.

"What about long term effects?" Tyler asked. "Brain damage, organ failure..."

"Her heart, liver, kidney etc all seem to have survived. As for the rest... we'll know more when she wakes up. There will be further tests."

Dr. Littlefield stood up.

"Can we see her?" Tyler asked.

She told them they could go straight up then bid them goodbye and good luck with a cheery wave. Tyler wondered how she was still standing after all-night on the job. No wonder she was prematurely grey.

Dr Amoh was with a patient but one of the nurses who recognized Janine led them into the ICU. The blinds had been opened and the room was light and airy. Several of the beds had been filled overnight. One of them next to the door was curtained off and Tyler could hear talking inside.

Janine gripped Tyler's hand as they entered and approached Rachel's bed. The curtains had been pulled right back but the only other discernable difference was that the ventilator mask had been removed from her face. Otherwise all the wires and tubes were in the same place as he remembered them.

Her eyes were closed and her pale eyelids were streaked with blue veins. Janine unconsciously squeezed his hand and he thought she was going to cry again. She sat down on the bed and touched one of the tiny feet that had been the catalyst for his own breakdown the night before. Tyler brushed a hair back from her forehead and planted a kiss. To his surprise, her eyes began to flicker. He could see the eyeball jerk erratically underneath the skin and he became alarmed.

"What's happening?" Janine said nervously.

Rachel opened her eyes. She looked at Tyler, her breathing came faster then she closed them again.

"Rachel?" he said.

Janine stood up and gripped him tightly around the waist. Ten seconds later she looked at them again then noiselessly opened and closed her dry lips. Tears welled in both parents' eyes as they caressed her face and head.

"Oh my baby" Janine repeated over and over. "I'm so sorry."

It was only the tubes that stopped Janine climbing on the bed and lying down next to her. Tyler walked around to the other side.

"I'm thirsty" Rachel croaked eventually.

"I'll get some water" Tyler said, happy to have a break from Janine's intensity. He kissed the back of his daughter's hand and left the bed. As he approached the door, two men slipped out of the screen surrounding the bed there. They both wore dark suits and no ties. One of them was in his fifties and heavy set with bright green eyes. The other was younger. They looked more like policemen that doctors he thought. Instead of heading for the door the older man indicated a bed further into the ward to his colleague.

"That's the girl with her mother now" he said.

The younger man looked over, nodded and they left together.

Tyler froze. He hardly dared think what he was thinking. He hesitated then stepped over to where they had just emerged. The curtain opening was overlapped and he had to pull it back to look inside. The bed was rigged up much like Rachel's. But in this case the patient was sitting up, wide awake. When he saw Tyler, Francis gave him a lupine grin.

"Come to finish the job have you Ty?"

He looked drawn and battered. He had a plaster over half his forehead and several bruises and scrapes visible on his bare shoulders and large arms. There was a box underneath the bedcover protecting the area around his stomach. (Where he'd been hit?) Somehow he seemed more angular and bony than normal as if he had lost several pounds over night.

"I thought you were dead" said Tyler.

"That's exactly what the doc said. Looks like you can't keep a good man down."

Tyler was incensed. He parted the curtains and walked inside. "You fucking bastard" he spat 'you almost killed my daughter."

"So she's better then."

"Did you hear me?"

"Do I look they shot me in the ears?"

"What the hell are you're doing leaving Ecstasy lying around..."

"It's not mine" Francis interrupted.

"Don't talk shit."

"My my Ty. Aren't you coming on the hard man all of a sudden. Janine been training you up has she?"

Tyler bristled with anger.

"You gonna have a go at me are you Ty? Here

in the hospital? You gonna throw a tantrum and pull me wires out?"

There was a pause.

"No. I didn't think so. You're just as much a tosser as you ever were."

Again he waited for a reaction but Tyler was too stunned. Francis had abused Rachel, taken his wife, stashed drugs in her house, persuaded Janine to stop his access to his daughter whom he had almost killed and now he had the balls to insult him. His lack of remorse, guilt and common humanity was breathtaking.

How do you get through to someone like that?

He knew the answer and bitterly regretted having failed.

"If you'll let me finish" Francis continued arrogantly "the police have just informed me the only fingerprints on the bottle of drugs Rachel found in that house were her own."

Tyler felt sick.

"So I think you owe me an apology." He finished with a supercilious tilt of the head.

Tyler blinked rapidly as though he were about to faint. The implications of what Francis had told him were too awful to be swallowed in one go. If there was nothing to link him to the drugs then he would be set free. Janine may even be suspected of hiding them there herself. At the very least the social services would come down hard on her. What would happen to Rachel? Would she be taken away? How could he look after her in a bed-sit? And while they were scrambling to pull their lives together Francis would be there in the background, laughing.

Tyler fumbled for the gap in the curtain and made his way back out.

"See ya tough guy" Francis taunted as he staggered out.

Rachel's bed was surrounded by the kind of activity that reminded him of that moment in her bedroom. There were three nurses and a short Malaysian looking man in a white coat that Janine introduced as Dr. Amoh.

"Don't worry" he said off Tyler's stunned look. "We're taking her out of intensive care and moving her to a ward."

The nurses had already started to unplug the various electrodes and tubes. Tyler found it hard to take in this one single piece of good news. Janine grabbed his arm warmly and rubbed herself against it.

"Thank God" she said.

"She's still very weak" Dr. Amoh continued. "I'm going to administer a mild sedative to help her sleep. If you'd like to wait outside we'll be ready in a moment and you can accompany her."

Tyler didn't move and Janine had to nudge him away. The strong light from the windows caused the curtains around Francis' bed to cast a shadow across the entrance to the room. It sent a chill through Tyler's heart just to know he was there. Janine stopped at the threshold and turned around to look at Rachel.

"I'm sorry" she said again though with a stronger undercurrent of meaning.

"I know" Tyler replied, eager to push on through the doors.

"I'll make it up to you. I promise."

"It's Rachel that matters" he said, "not me."

"I know what she wants."

"What?"

"She wants us to be together."

Tyler was dumbstruck.

"I've been really stupid Tyler" she continued. "I did and said things to you I never should of. I almost ruined her life - and mine. Can you forgive me?"

Tyler wasn't sure he wanted to understand what she was driving at. "Let's talk about it later."

"I've already thought it through Tyler. I want you come back. I want to make things right for you. I made a dreadful mistake leaving you. I was being selfish and thoughtless. The truth is I still..." She dropped her head and looked at the hands she was nervously wringing. "I love you."

64.

Fifty years ago the abandoned sawmill had been a large bungalow in the center of a wide forest clearing. There had been pyramids of lumber stacked all about and men scurrying over and round them like ants. Volya could recall the smell of freshly cut wood and the incessant noise of machinery. There had been large trucks and tractors shifting and stacking the timber, loading it onto the rail wagons pulled by (what seemed then) a huge steam powered engine. There had been a large generator behind the wood mill that belched black smoke and clattered like it was full of stones. Inside the mill itself the various band and buzz saws had sung out their own tunes accompanied by the turning cogs, rolling pins and other contraptions that processed the silver sided trunks into pale yellow planks.

Now only the mill itself remained, smaller than he remembered it, battered and broken.

At one end the roof had entirely collapsed and the silver birch had repossessed the clearing right up to the old slaughterhouse. All that remained of the bustle and industry were a few pieces of ironwork poking out of the undergrowth: the skeleton of a tractor and what looked like once to have been a lathe. Both stripped down to the raw, red rust. The railway led right up to one end of the mill where large iron doors lay fallen on the ground and pierced with weeds.

Volya and Marta had taken refuge inside. Dawn had revealed large metal-framed windows running down both sides. The glass was long since knocked out but he was surprised how well much of the machinery had survived. Marta had found herself a corner on the filthy concrete floor next a machine the size of a fridge covered in old-fashioned dials and gages. She had had a restless night. She was now fast asleep and shivering feverishly.

She was awoken by the smell of grilled fish. Volya had built a fire below a conveyer bench of metal rollers raised three feet off the ground. He had speared two trout on thin sticks and balanced them between two rungs to cook. Her eyes flickered wearily open. She felt dreadful. Every muscle in her body ached. She could feel the bruises on her face and back where she had been beaten and her legs were on fire with all the scratches they had taken. Furthermore she felt inwardly soiled. She could still feel Ilya's hands on her breasts and his penis moving inside her. When she breathed out her breath felt hot and acrid. She touched her forehead.

"You've got a temperature," Volya said.

He stooped over her with a battered steel cup full of fresh water from a nearby brook. She pushed herself up against the corner and winced when she sat on the large gash on her left buttock.

"How do you feel?" he asked.

"Not so bad" she replied. "How's your leg?"

"Not so bad."

"I'm sorry" she whispered. He grunted and she watched him limp back to the fire. The cold liquid filtered into her chest but failed to reduce the burning sensation in her throat and head. Volya returned with a transpierced and charred looking fish.

"I don't think I can" she said.

"When was the last time you ate?"

She thought back to when Roman had fed her something meaty as she was tied to the bed. It hadn't stayed down. "I can't remember."

"Try it anyway."

She put the cup on the floor, painfully adjusted her position and took the stick with both hands.

"Best to eat it like that" he said. "Careful of the bones."

Marta hesitantly pulled off the burned skin with her teeth. Inside, the sweet pink flesh came away easily from the white skeleton and dissolved like honey on her tongue. Her mouth flushed with saliva and she thought it was the best food she had ever tasted.

Volya nodded contentedly. He sat on a small metal box with his fish and they ate in silence. When he was finished he wiped his mouth on the back of his hand.

"If you're cold" he said, "you should sit by the fire. I've left enough wood to keep it going until the end of the day."

"Where are you going?" Marta said in a panic.

Volya got up, pulled a revolver out of his pocket, grasped it by the barrel and offered it to her. Marta's eyes widened.

"No. I'm coming with you." She struggled to her feet but as soon as she was up her head turned and she began to sway. Volya grasped her by the shoulders to stop her from falling. She sat back down feeling sorry for herself and utterly helpless.

He placed the gun on the ground beside her.

"I don't know how to use it."

"You won't need to" he said, "but you'll feel better. There's no way he can have tracked us out here even if he were fit - which he isn't."

"You didn't tell me what happened."

"Later. When you're better - maybe. All you

need to know is that he won't be back. I promise."

He swung his rucksack over to the floor next to her. "There's more fish inside if you get hungry. And a bag of peanuts. Planters. American. My favorite."

"How long will you be?"

He looked down the track and pursed his lips. "About four hours to reach Karak" he said. "Then I've got to find the police or ambulance or whatever. They'll be quicker than me on the way back. Before dark." He paused for thought then added, "I'll bring some more wood."

"No" she said pushing herself unsteadily to her feet. "I'll do it. Please go. I don't want to be here alone at dark."

He nodded his head and looked at the floor. She reached out and took his hand. "Thank you" she said and kissed his stubbled cheek.

He couldn't remember the last time anyone had felt the urge to kiss him. He made an embarrassed smile, turned and walked back along the track. Marta watched him negotiate the uneven path until he was swallowed up by the silver and yellow forest.

65.

Tyler was surprised to find a parking space right outside his own front door. He had left the hospital as soon as Rachel had fallen asleep. Francis' presence there spooked him and he did not want to get sucked into a heart-to-heart with Janine. He needed to be alone to think.

He sat in his car and reflected on his situation. It seemed Rachel would make a full recovery - thank God. He should also be jubilant about Janine's overture to reconciliation. Instead it made him ill at ease. All the way back from the hospital he had been trying to work out why that should be and he still had no answer.

It's what I always wanted. So why does it feel wrong?

His thoughts were broken by his mobile phone ringing. It was Yolanda. He couldn't deal with her rejection at that moment. He doubted she would let him down gently. He would be prepared for it when the time came, but not yet. He found the courage to let it ring out, though not without an audible sigh.

He got out of the car. That morning's low cloud had dispersed and the Indian summer, so long predicted, had finally arrived. He didn't notice. The lock on the front door of his building was still broken and yesterday's firm decision to fix it was now no more than a...(one of his father's obscure words came to mind)... a 'velleity'. He tramped up the five floors and stopped in front of his apartment with his key in his hand.

A minute later he was still staring at the badly painted fake paneling on his door. He couldn't go in. After all that had happened to him he had no desire to return to his poor and empty flat, to his old humiliating job or even to his once-adored wife. But he knew he had no choice. The key hovered reluctantly in front of the lock. Where else could he go?

Before he had a chance to regret his decision, the door swung open. Zinic stood there in 'his' leather jacket with the empty right sleeve hanging loose. In his left hand he held a glass containing a pale fluid that he raised in salute.

"Budem zdorovy Tyler" he said and drained the glass.

Zinic stepped back and theatrically ushered him inside. Tyler had the impression he was unsteady.

His work computer was open on the kitchen bar next to a ravaged packet of Nurofen and a bottle of brandy. He recognized it as a wedding present from his father that he had vowed only to share with the person who had given it to him. It didn't seem to matter any more. Zinic refilled his glass and Tyler could see the bottle was almost empty.

"I guess there's no point in asking how you got in here" said Tyler, closing the door behind him. "How's your hand?"

"It hurts." Zinic reached into a kitchen cupboard for a glass. "Have a drink my friend."

Tyler was in no mood to resist. "What are you doing here?"

Zinic poured out three fingers of brandy and handed it over. "You had something of mine." He picked up the wooden icon that had been hidden behind the computer. Tyler remembered finding it in the bag.

Zinic saluted with his glass. "To evil hearts."

"Evil hearts?"

Zinic drained his glass and, not for the first time, Tyler marveled at his capacity to absorb sudden and large quantities of alcohol.

"This" he held up the icon "is the Softener of Evil Hearts. It's a bible story. When Mary brought the infant Jesus to the temple in Jerusalem, Symeon prophesized great things for him. Naturally. But when he had finished he turned to Mary and said... 'a sword shall pierce thine own soul too, so that the thoughts of many hearts may be revealed.' But being Russian we take things to extreme. So there isn't just one sword in the picture there are seven. Seven is the number of completeness. So the seven swords pointed at her heart represent her complete suffering. She suffers for our evil hearts and we weep for her."

His narration ground to a maudlin halt.

"I wouldn't have thought you were a religious man" Tyler said eventually.

"I'm not I bought it in a flea market in St Petersburg because it looked like Marta."

Tyler blinked. "I'm sorry Greg but I have no idea what you're talking about."

Zinic turned the computer screen towards him. It was open at an English language page on www.pravda.ru. The title read 'Search continues for abducted Ikea girl'. A picture of a smiling round-faced woman was prominently displayed and underneath was her name, Marta Rozhdestvensky.

Zinic held up the icon next to it. "Do you see?"

It was true. There was a certain similarity in the cup-shaped jaw and fine long nose.

Tyler frowned. "What's this about?"

"Read it" Zinic said. He looked at his watch. "She still has another hour."

Zinic poured himself drink. Tyler felt he

was determined to get drunk. By the look of him it wasn't going to work. He vaguely recalled reading in a magazine that Russians had special enzymes that allowed them to process alcohol better than normal humans. Pravda explained how the girl in the photo had been taken from the car park outside an Ikea center on the outskirts of Nizhniy Novgorod where she worked on Thursday night. Her friend had been brutally murdered and Marta had disappeared. The car that had taken her had been traced heading south on Friday morning with two men. Despite a huge manhunt nothing had been seen or heard of her since.

"You know her?"

Zinic was about to speak when Tyler's phone rang. It was Yolanda again. He studied it for a moment, thinking, then turned it off. Zinic tapped a few words into the Google title bar and up popped another article.

"Marta was taken to ensure I shot this man before he goes to trial tomorrow morning."

Tyler took this in. He had to admit it he wasn't surprised by it. He wondered if he would ever be surprised by anything ever again. He shook his head in wonder then concentrated on the computer screen. It was a leading article in The Times entitled 'Rotten to the Core' about a man called Desmond O'Hagan.

"Someone betrayed me to the police..."

"Wait!" Tyler shouted. "Olevsky." He pointed to the name in the article. That's who you said was trying to kill me. It says he's an associate of O'Hagan."

Zinic found photos of Bruno and Alexandr Olevsky on Google Images and explained how it was that Tyler - a mild mannered estate agent from Clapham - had got wound up in a murder plot that had almost cost him his life. When he got to the bit about Marta being tied up somewhere two thousand miles away awaiting execution he thought Zinic had entered the realms of fantasy.

The mobile phone put that straight. Zinic found the video Bruno had left him of Marta and handed it over without a word. At first Tyler could barely make out what he was watching. There was no sound and the bad lighting made it look like a webcam in a shoebox. There wasn't much movement and what little there was, was blurred and indistinct. Gradually he thought he could make out a human form but viewed from a low angle. Were they naked? It was too dark to see between the legs but he thought he could make out breasts. She seemed to be struggling. He was so absorbed in trying to make sense of the shifting shapes that when she suddenly sat up, opened her mouth and released a long and silent scream he almost dropped the phone.

The video cut out and Tyler stood for a long

moment tying to get passed the horror.

"Have you been to the police?" he asked.

"I have nothing to say. I don't know where she is or who has taken her. And if I don't meet Bruno Olevsky at the London Heliport in fifty five minutes he will have her executed."

"Then what are you waiting for?"

Zinic patted the bandaged hand inside his jacket. "As soon as he sees this, he will know for sure that I can't do the job."

"And?"

"He will execute her." Zinic drank down another glass. "He likes to win."

"Would he really kill her?"

Zinic snorted with amusement. "Olevsky is betraying his own brother to get control of a multi billion dollar company. You and I and Marta are small players."

"Can't you just - you know - kill him? That's what you do isn't it?"

"Then how would I find Marta?"

"Who is she to you?"

"My fiancé." It was a technical lie because she had never answered his SMS but he thought of her that way.

Tyler walked over to the window thinking carefully over everything that he had been told. He couldn't let go of the vision of that face rising at him form out of the screen.

"Why are you telling me all this?"

Zinic walked over to him and clinked his

glass against Tyler's. "Because, my friend, you can save her."

66.

The foundations of the Chelsea Harbour development go back to the beginning of the nineteen century. The then riverside marshland of Fan Mead was sold for the princely sum of fifty pounds to create the entrance to the Kensington Canal. For over a hundred years, it was a point of access to the vital canal network that supplied coal and other goods to the ever-expanding Victorian London. In the 1960s, the Clean Air Act sounded the death knell to its principle cargo and canals fell out of fashion. For thirty years Chelsea Basin (as it was then called) lay neglected except as a dumping ground for old fridges and cars. Mallards, herons, black headed gulls and wagtails came back in force and were, for decades, the only residents. Then Ray Moxley drove by.

Ray had huge vision and even greater drive. Planning permission was signed at 11pm on

15 April 1986 and work started at 8am the next morning. Within two years the eighteen acre site contained residential and business buildings, a gym and indoor tennis center, a two hundred suite luxury hotel and a two hundred foot tower. All gathered around the refurbished 'basin', now a marina for pleasure boats and yachts. It had taken twenty years for the canal developers of Fan Mead to make their money back. Ray Moxley did it in as many months.

They turned around at the security boom and since it was a Sunday, they found a parking space in Upcerne Road. Time was short. It was already eleven thirty five. The jog back to Chelsea Harbour took them three minutes. They strolled into the complex and Zinic guided them around and under the various security cameras he could see positioned on high posts and building corners.

The Wyndham Grand is a semi-circular, eight story building that curves around the north side of the marina. Zinic had telephoned in advance and asked if there was a room available as high and as easterly as possible. As luck would have it, room 712 was free. He established it was already cleaned and asked them to hold it for him until one o'clock under the name of John Hillman.

At eleven forty, Tyler and Zinic joined with a group of IT consultants arriving for a conference. Halfway across the marble lobby they peeled off and took the elevator. On the way up Zinic took off his shoes and socks and put only his shoes back on. He made Tyler do the same.

At the seventh floor they exited the lift and turned left. The long, red-carpeted corridor curved around to the right. They didn't meet anyone on the way and within two minutes were standing outside the dark wood door marked 712. Zinic put his socks over his hands and Tyler copied.

Zinic held out his socked hand and Tyler gave him his American Express card. The lock was operated with a swipe card mechanism installed in the door itself just above the handle. Zinic pushed his weight against the door with his shoulder until a gap appeared between the door and the frame. He then fed the card into the space next to the handle until it touched the inner side of the frame. By jerking it this way and that he managed to bend the card around between the door and the frame. There was a click, Zinic pushed the handle down and the door sprung open.

Tyler's jaw dropped. He had a vision of living in hotels free for the rest of his life. Zinic bundled him inside and shut the door behind them.

"Keep the socks on your hands" he said returning his Amex. "Don't touch anything unless you have to. Don't piss in the toilet, don't spit, don't bleed. Don't drink from the mini-bar. Don't scratch your head and leave hair lying around. In short don't do anything that could leave a single trace of DNA. Got it."

Tyler nodded his understanding of the rules and Zinic crossed the main room to the terrace window where he deposited the hold all. He opened the sliding glass door and stepped outside. The terrace was no more than four feet across, just wide enough for a small breakfast table and two chairs.

When he came back in he unzipped the holdall and rolled the rifle sack out on the floor. As he pulled out the rifle parts Tyler went to the window. The room offered a hundred and eighty degree view over South London. The sky was pale blue with high thin lines of broken Cirrostratus in the west. The air was clear and he tried to pick out the landmarks he recognized. To the east, the Thames curved under Battersea then Albert Bridge. On the far bank, beyond Battersea Park he could make out the distinctive cooling towers of the long defunct Battersea Power Station and next to it the huge metal drum that was a dry gasholder. Looking to the west, the river swung round behind the Chelsea Harbour development and the Belvedere Tower. On the south side of the river was a depressing vista over the grey suburbs that sprawled to the horizon in every direction.

His attention was caught by the batting sound of a helicopter following the river in from the east. It passed the hotel at the level of the room and was close enough for Tyler to make out two figures in the back. After flying over the Battersea rail bridge it started to descend. For a moment it looked as if it would land on the river. Then it turned perpendicular to the bank and faced south. That's when Tyler noticed the T shaped pier jutting out into the Thames. The helicopter advanced until it was directly over the yellow circle in the center of the crossbar of the T. At some unseen signal it taxied down the pier still airborne until it was over a tarmac piste the size of a small football pitch. It turned right and touched ground beside a bright red helicopter to the far side.

Zinc stood up with the fully assembled rifle.

"I can't hit that" said Tyler with dismay. "It must be half a mile away."

"Seven hundred and seventy six yards" Zinic said. He could have added *thanks to Google Earth*. He indicated for Tyler to come back into the room and Zinic lay down with the rifle on the floor just inside the terrace door. Knowing the exact distance of the target meant he could adjust the vertical elevation blindfolded. The air was still and he zeroed the windage.

When he was satisfied, he looked at his watch and jumped to his feet. It was ten to twelve.

"Give me the car keys."

Tyler handed them over.

"You know what to do?" Zinic said.

"Wait for him to give you the phone."

"Its the only way the police can track the kidnappers' signal. I must get Bruno's phone first. Then I'll turn to face you. OK?"

Tyler hesitated.

"What?" said Zinic. "I don't have time for this. What?"

Tyler gnawed his lip, knowing his request was going to sound childish.

"I want the jacket."

Zinic took it off and handed it over without question. "Looking the part is half the battle" he said. "Anything else?"

Tyler shrugged. "Words of advice?"

"Don't fuck up" Zinic said grimly. He picked up the hold all and disappeared into the corridor. He turned just inside the door. "Take the emergency stairs when you leave, not the lift."

67.

Volya found a stout stick and used it to support his weight as he walked. His knee wasn't broken after all but it still hurt like hell. He stayed in the middle of the railway because there was less growth and the ground was more even. From time to time he made wide diversions because of thick copses of saplings. He always came back to the track, however, so he didn't get lost.

He adored the autumn. The trees wore their most beautiful red and golden livery, the air was fresh but not yet freezing and he loved blueberries. He picked them from the low bushes if they were close by and his fingers and tongue were already purple with their juice.

He thought of the young woman he had left behind him. Her presence, if only for a short time, had brought something to his life he wasn't aware had been missing: responsibility. No one had been dependent on him since the disappearance of his son. He had plenty of friends, of course, and people that traded with him in the market or sold him goods for the smallholding, but it wasn't the same. Responsibility made him feel worthwhile. Someone's life depended on him and it was a commission he was determined to see through.

As he walked he sung a lament known to every Russian schoolboy.

Steppe, endless steppe,
the way lies far before us.
And in that dense steppe
a coachman lay dying.
He summoned up all his strength,
as he felt death approaching,
and he gave an order
to his comrade:
"My dear friend,
do not think of the bad times,
but bury me here
in this dense steppe.
Give to my wife
a word of farewell;
and give back to her
this wedding ring.
Tell her that I died here,
in the freezing steppe,
and that I have taken her love
away with me.

The spear hit him in the back, piercing the Latissimus Dorsi between his fourth and fifth rib. He bent his arms round to his back and grabbed the shaft. He could feel the rough bark and realised it was no more than a sharpened stick. In that cramped position his arms were not strong enough to pull it out and very soon the pain started. Volya strained his neck round to see Roman holding the other end. He couldn't understand how he had not heard him approach. He had been too far in his thoughts. He was pale and feeble looking but his eyes betrayed an evil determination. Roman let go of the stake and staggered back as if the effort had drained him. Volya swung completely round and tried to shake the stick out.

Even in his frenzy he noticed Roman's crutch was black with blood from where he had shot him. The trousers were shredded from where the young man must have torn at the material to get to the wound. It was a mess of fabric, flesh and gore.

Not for the first time, Volya thought this was all madness. He had fired two warning shots but the crazed idiot had kept on coming with his knife held high. He had almost been on him by the time he had fired wild. In truth he had aimed low, even at the last moment hoping not to kill him. His compassion had been misplaced.

Roman watched the old man stumble

about, swinging his torso back and forth hoping to dislodge the stake. But it was hopeless. The point had pierced his heart and soon he dropped to his knees. The life force drained away and he fell backwards so that the stick propped him up. Volya twitched and moaned. He had a brief vision of his father returning from the war with one leg and a can of chewing tobacco. In forty seconds he was dead.

68.

Vienna. 1950. Black and white. Orson Wells and Joseph Cotten are high up in the cabin of a giant Ferris wheel looking out over the war torn city. Wells plays a trafficker in toxic penicillin and Cotten has just tracked him down. Cotten doesn't understand how he can justify killing innocent people. Wells doesn't try. He points to the figures in the fairground far below: 'Would you really feel any pity if one of those dots stopped moving forever?' he asks. 'If I offered you twenty thousand pounds for every dot that stopped would you really tell me to keep my money old man?'

The scene from The Third Man came back to Tyler as he lay on his stomach sighting targets at the heliport. Tyler asked himself how much he would really care if one of the ten millions dots in London stopped moving because of him? Or to put it another way, how many of those ten million would care if he stopped moving. Not many, he guessed. Especially for twenty thousand pounds - even at today's rates. He had once read that for every fifteen pounds a high street bank pays out in interest, someone in Africa or Asia dies from malnutrition, disease and war; the direct result of inequitable investment. Yet he had never, ever heard of anyone telling the bank to stop paying them interest and keep their money - 'old man'.

Wells was right, he decided: there was a moral theory of relativity. Tyler was sure he couldn't kill someone close up like Zinic, but half a mile across the Thames stretched the guilt very thin.

Another helicopter approached along the river from the east. It was larger than the first. He judged it to be at least fifty feet long. With its sharp snout, aerodynamic body and tapered tail it looked like a great white shark floating in the blue sky. He wondered if the similarity was deliberate. There were two large front windows for eyes and a row of passenger windows for gills. Too dark to see inside.

He wondered if Zinic would get there in time. There was no mistaking his attachment to the girl in the video. When Zinic had proposed shooting Olevsky, he had thought of it more as a game. The fifty thousand pounds he had offered was enticing, but not the principal reason he had accepted. The truth was he was bored; bored with himself and his life. He was bored with always being the victim. He wanted to regain the power he had felt after shooting Francis and assuage the frustration of discovering he was still alive. Moreover, he wanted to succeed. This was a new sensation.

When he thought of success, he thought of Yolanda. The doubts he had felt earlier seemed to vanish now that he was holding the rifle again. He wanted to kiss her passionately and possess her completely. His success would be shared with her, and measured against her. He would dedicate it to her.

The helicopter drew level with the heliport and hovered to a halt over the river. He decided he had time to call her. He pulled his phone out of his trouser pocket and turned it on. In 'missed calls' he discovered Yolanda had tried to get him five times that morning. He redialed the last attempt and the phone was almost immediately answered.

The helicopter turned, tilted forward and advanced towards the pier. The change in position or perhaps a change in the wind brought the beating sound of the rotors to his ears. Yolanda didn't speak at first and by some curious effect the noise of the helicopter echoed in the background of the open phone line. Having reached the pier, it started a vertical descent and a man with ear protectors and a fluorescent waistcoat beckoned it forward.

"Yolanda?" he called. He could hear what sounded like a stifled cry.

"Ty" she said plaintively "Why didn't you call?"

"I didn't have time. Listen" he continued quickly. He had decided what he was going to say and he wanted to get it out. "I've been thinking about you, about last night. It was good, you know - being with you. I think we can be friends. Good friends. And I owe you an explanation for what happened. I want to see you again and tell you the truth."

"I already know." She was shouting as if over a noise. She sounded stressed and distressed.

"I mean everything: about me, about us."

"Oh Ty" she sobbed "why didn't you call earlier?"

69.

Z inic's name had been registered with security. He passed through without further question and the guard indicated a blue squat building twenty yards ahead on his right, a single story prefabricated structure that ran along the side of the taxiing piste. The drop into the river was twenty yards beyond that.

The white Sikorsky Spirit was just touching down when he arrived. A man in a yellow jacket flagged it into a large yellow circle on the far side of the cement apron. The wheels touched the ground and the blades slowed until they reached a point where they seemed to be rotating backwards.

The 'executive customer lounges' resembled garage waiting rooms. Zinic noticed two heavily built men in shirts and sports jackets staring out at him through the windows. Zinic ignored them. From where he was standing he couldn't see the end of the Wyndham Grand Hotel where Tyler was. That meant he had to meet Bruno out in the open, on the helipad itself.

The Sikorsky's steps unfolded onto the tarmac. As Bruno's long legs appeared in the opening, Zinic ran across. A couple of the ground staff raised their heads, but he was soon on the far side of the piste and they went back to their work. Zinic looked to his right over the river and could now see the far end of the hotel.

Bruno met him at the bottom of the steps. The engine continued to run and the blades whirled noisily six feet over head. He took one look at Zinic's empty right sleeve and his mouth crinkled with pleasure.

"Looks like you've had an accident," he shouted.

70.

Smoke rose through a hole in the roof of the abandoned sawmill. Roman looked at his watch. The dial swum in his hazy vision but it looked like just before three o'clock, the time Olevsky said he would call. He was light-headed from loss of blood. This was good and bad. Good, because he was completely detached from his pain and any emotion associated with killing the old man. Bad, because he could barely think straight. He was, nonetheless, perfectly aware of his injury and what it meant. If he was not hospitalized soon he would likely die from loss of blood.

It was pure luck he had stumbled upon Volya. He had been blundering around aimlessly looking for the road until he heard him singing. On reflection, killing him was a mistake. He should have got him to lead him out of the forest. On the other hand, he needed to find the girl and complete his mission. The only person who could help him now was Bruno Olevsky, and he wouldn't lift a finger until his instructions had been followed to the letter.

The old man didn't have the gun on him so he assumed Marta had it. From where he stood, he could see through the open portal, right the way into the guts of the mill but the girl wasn't visible. If the phone rang now it would give him away. He had to move fast. By circling round to his right he was able to keep the large opening in view but reduce his exposure to it. It was hard going. The old clearing had attracted a large amount of ground ivy. His injury prevented him from moving fluidly and his feet caught in the thick covering. Finally he worked his way back towards the angle of the mill.

His knife was stashed in his belt and he carried the yard long stake he had cut from a birch sapling out in front of him like a blind man. When he had drawn it out of the old man's body it had been followed by an unbelievable amount of blood. The viscous red fluid pumped out of the unseen hole and flooded the back of his green jacket creating a spreading black stain. Within seconds his back was covered and the body lay face down in a pool of living scarlet.

Once he reached the concrete wall he felt safer but had to lean against it for support. He shook his head to dispel another spell of dizziness. They were getting increasingly frequent and prolonged. He stared up at the treetops gently swaying in the breeze and breathed deeply. He closed his eyes for a moment and his head drooped. When his chin touched his chest he woke with a start and it sprung back up. He was more tired than he had realized.

He edged along wall, treading carefully over the fallen metal door. When he reached the opening he could see more of the interior but not Marta. She could be hidden anywhere amongst the machinery or just the other side of the wall. She could be standing only a foot away with a loaded gun waiting for him to come charging in. He pulled out his phone and held it out in front of him so that the black screen formed an angle that reflected the area behind the wall.

Marta came into view. She was lying where Volya had left her slumped in a corner with her eyes closed and the pistol lying on the ground beside her. Roman fought back another bout of fatigue and stepped through the opening. His boots crunched on the solid floor. Marta's eyed flicked opened and she felt for the gun. It was just out of reach and before she could move Roman had the bloody stick rested in the V of her throat. The point pressed into her windpipe and since her head was rested in a corner she couldn't move in any direction without impaling herself. She grabbed the stick with her hands but Roman pressed it forward till she could feel it was on the brink of rupturing her pipe.

"Let go," he said "or I'll do it. Let go!"

She tentatively relaxed her grip and he eased off the pressure. When she was sure he was not going to push she dropped her hands into her lap. Roman kicked the gun so that he could pick it up, but it went too far for him to get it without releasing Marta. So he painfully bent his knees and, without releasing the pressure on the stick, dropped exhausted against the wall just beyond her feet.

71.

"It was no accident" Zinic replied. "Maybe your brother would like to know how I got it."

"You're right. Let's go tell him" Bruno replied indicating the helicopter.

Zinic hesitated. His bluff had been called. Bruno would certainly need to prove to his brother that Zinic was to blame. But he didn't have to be alive to do it. A dead bandaged hand was as good as live one. Better, in fact. The invitation was a one-way ticket.

"I'll come with you," he said, "if you let Marta go."

"Sure" Bruno said. "Let's talk about it inside."

Zinic shook his head. "I want proof she's still alive."

Bruno looked at a man in a blue uniform and tie approaching from the control tower.

"We don't have time," he said irascibly.

"Then I stay here."

This was the gamble he had to take. How badly did Bruno need him? He could easily turn around and say goodbye. No phone, no shot. Marta dismembered in a shallow grave.

The man in the uniform arrived at a trot. "You have two minutes to turn around sir. Or you lose your slot."

"Yes yes. I know," snapped Bruno. "Go away."

The uniformed man was taken aback by the rudeness of the reply. Under Bruno's glare, he withdrew to a spot a few yards away and made his presence felt.

"Alright" Bruno said. He pulled a phone from inside his jacket pocket, scrolled to menu and hit redial.

Roman sat up to attention and turned the phone on.

"Hand me the girl" Bruno growled.

"You've got to send someone to get me," Roman breathed heavily. "I'm hurt bad."

"Have you got the girl?"

"Send someone please" Roman pleaded.

"Yes yes" Bruno said irritably. "As soon as we're done. Now pass me the girl."

Zinic gritted his teeth at the crude reminder of Marta's fate. He knew Bruno had no intention of letting her live whatever he promised. Tyler was her only chance now.

Roman threw the phone onto Marta's lap. "The boss wants to talk to you," he said.

Marta didn't budge. For the past three days

she hadn't ceased to ask herself what this was all about. At first the kidnapping had seemed like a botched rape. But when they had tied her to the bed and taken a picture, she began to wonder. She had caught snippets of conversations that suggested they were working for someone else. In her fevered imagination she had considered prostitution or some other kind of human trafficking. In the end she had largely discounted it because of her age and, frankly, unsexiness. She had also discounted ransom, since her parents were poor and had no access to her own meager savings. With those ideas aside her mind had tuned to even more horrible possibilities such as snuff movies or organ theft. Now that the 'boss' wanted to speak to her, she was terrified to find out.

"Answer it you fat cow" Roman shouted hoarsely. The effort made him cough and the stick jabbed into her skin drawing blood.

"O wow ow" she cried, grasping it with her right hand to alleviate the pressure. "Stop it. Stop!"

"Marta! Marta!"

Georgiy's voice came like a call from a dream.

"Marta it's me, Gosha. Marta. Answer me are you there?" Tears streamed down his face. "Marta for God's sake. Talk to me. Please."

With her free hand she searched blindly for

the bloody phone in the folds of her coat then raised it to her face.

"Georgiy?" she choked.

Zinic had no hand to wipe away the tears. He had momentarily forgotten Tyler, but unthinkingly turned towards him to hide his face from Bruno's smug smirk.

At that very moment there was a commotion from the direction of the helicopter. In his peripheral vision, he caught sight of a figure running down the steps. He turned at the same time as Bruno to see Yolanda fight away clinging hands from inside the cabin and run towards him.

It was so unexpected that he stepped to one side to avoid her. That was when he felt a hard object hit him in the back. He was shunted abruptly forward into her. She was as equally surprised. She checked herself to avoid him but not soon enough. Zinic crumpled awkwardly. The next few seconds lasted an eternity. He had been shot often enough in the past to realize what had happened and had plenty of time to curse Tyler before he hit the tarmac. With his left arm bandaged he failed to control his fall and the side of his head cracked solidly against the ground. Yolanda screeched and fell on her backside. The last thing Zinic saw was the phone slip from his grasp, skitter across the smooth black surface and come to rest at Bruno's feet.

72.

I t was a mystery that made the newspaper headlines for almost a week. It took that long for Detective Chief Inspector Peter Granger of the Serious Organised Crime Agency to pull together the various strands of the assassination. They already had a file open on Bruno Olevsky drawn from Interpol and their own intelligence. No one was sorry to see him dead apart from his brother who used the occasion to denounce 'dark forces with the Kremlin'.

Granger's initial instincts were confirmed by a detailed ballistics report. It revealed the two bullets to be .338 Match Hybrid BoreRiders, very-low-drag used only by hunters and professional marksmen. Computer modeling showed that the shot had been fired from high up in the eastern block of the Wyndham Grand Hotel across the river. Upon inquiry, they discovered the terrace door to number 712 had been found open that particular evening. A man called Hillman had called to see if the room was available but never arrived. The call was impossible to trace and Granger had no doubt the name was false. There were no signs of forced entry and for a while suspicion fell on an assistant floor manager whose uncle was a suspected member of the Albanian mafia. He was eliminated from enquiries when it was discovered he was robbing a warehouse in Chatham at the time.

Fingerprint and DNA analysis of the room took much longer. There was a lot of information. Previous guests to the room were contacted for hair or print samples. They was laboriously matched up against the samples from the room and excluded until there were none left. Close examination of CCTV footage from around Chelsea Harbour and the hotel itself seemed to suggest one or possibly two men carefully avoiding being filmed. Only one image of any use was found. It showed two men of average height with their backs to the camera waiting to get in the lift. One was wearing a leather jacket and carrying a dark hold all. It was typical low quality security camera black and white and nothing other than their proximity at the lift suggested they were actually together. It caused some initial excitement when the police realized the hold all resembled the one carried by the injured Georgiy

Zinic at the heliport. There was also some re-semblance between the figures. But Zinic's bag contained nothing but his laundry and since he wasn't wearing a leather jacket when he was shot, the theory seemed thin. It vanished altogether when it was pointed out that he would hardly stage his own shooting. Even more surprising, they could find no footage of the two mean leaving. It was as if they had van-ished.

The investigation took a surprising twist when it was discovered that a small-time south London drug pusher had been shot two days earlier using exactly the same bullets and weapon. Francis Matlock had no fathomable connection to either of the two Russians and the SOCA spent a lot of time scratching their heads. Zinic's previous arrest on the rooftop of a nearby housing estate caused a lot of raised eyebrows. There was little or no co-operation from the Russian police or authorities, espe-cially when it came to a background check on an ex-Vympel officer.

Zinic was badly injured. He spent five days on life support during which time surgeons re-stitched his hand and saved it from infec-tion and almost certain amputation. When they eventually interviewed him in hospital he stuck to his story that he had been on the roof to look at the stars and - no, he never had any gun. He explained his presence at the heliport by saying he had met Olevsky, a fellow Russian, in a bar. No, he couldn't remember where exactly, but Olevsky had invited him to spend a few days at his house in the country. He even boasted about his private collection of modern art. This was the reason Zinic had checked out of his hotel and was carrying a bag with his clothing. His hand injuries were the result of an unprovoked attack in the street that, now he came to think of it, may have been connected to Olevsky. When Granger explained Olevsky was a serious gangster, Zinic was (quite naturally) horrified and speculated he may have been the victim of a politically inspired attack. He admitted breaking into a house to stitch his hand up because he didn't trust English hospitals. But since he couldn't remember where it was and since no one reported a corresponding crime there was really nothing to book him on despite Granger's multitude of suspicions.

No information was forthcoming on the telephone call Olevsky had placed to a Russian mobile phone just before he and Zinic were shot. The lack of co-operation from all sections of the Russian police was annoying but Granger decided it was most likely a dead end anyway.

The presence of Yolanda Wilson in the helicopter of Olevsky was both confusing and fruitful. It had started with a phone call from a lawyer called Julius Kriegmann on Sunday morning. The call was verified by Ms. Wilson's phone records. Kriegmann was a lawyer working for a man called Desmond O'Hagan currently on trial at the Old Bailey in a massive fraud case. O'Hagan counted the Olevsky brothers as some of his best clients. There was some suggestion he was to have denounced them during the trial as sponsoring terrorism in Russia, but that never happened. Kriegmann was believed to be a bagman for O'Hagan and certainly knew the Russian twins.

Ms. Wilson had been called to Kriegmann's house to handle its urgent sale. According to her testimony, he was extremely nervous and (so it turned out) disappeared to the Bahamas that very afternoon. Bruno Olevsky was also present at Kriegmann's house and invited Ms. Wilson to evaluate a property of his. The two of them drove to Halwich Palace near Farnham where, once done, they boarded a helicopter back into London. Ms. Wilson admitted to being very unsettled by the experience and called her boyfriend five times during the course of the morning - without success - until they were about to touch down in Battersea.

In the back of Kriegmann's Bentley in his garage, police found a semi-naked, heavily muscled and tattooed man with a broken elbow and an axe though his forehead. The man had no identification but his tattoos suggested he was yet another Russian gangster. Suspicion for his death initially fell on Kriegmann, but traces of blood and tissue were discovered on Bruno Olevsky's hands and clothing. His fingerprints were also found on the weapon itself. Medical tests placed the time of death at around three o'clock on Sunday morning, long before Ms. Wilson arrived on the scene. Kriegmann would need to be questioned and the Home Office made an extradition request to the Bahamian government. But since he was not actually accused of any crime they were in for a long wait. It was assumed he had fled England in fear of his life.

DCI Ganger and the SOCA chased all these leads around like a dozen dogs after their tails. There were many possible connections, but no cohesive story seemed to tie them all together. The crucial element, the key that would unlock the mystery was the assassin. They could find no trace of him except by the bullet holes left in the bodies. The entire team agreed they were looking for a seasoned professional who was simply unlucky his first two targets hadn't died. Exactly who had hired them to murder three such diverse men was part of the mystery. They accepted, however, that such a person had more than likely already left the country.

The hidden player in the drama was known only to the newly promoted Chief Inspector

Bob Grant. Grant was troubled by his conscience. He had 'sold' Primovelli to Kriegmann for promotion and, though he did not understand all the twists and turns, he suspected that his self-serving act had somehow lit the fuse.

It was while on holiday with his wife in the Maldives that he made a crucial decision. To be more specific, it was while they were making love in their thatched cabin overlooking the pearl white sand and sapphire blue sea. Nanette was bouncing on top of him, her still magnificent breasts, golden with moisture. A gentle breeze through the open window carried with it the soft lapping of the ocean on the sand. Grant's mind drifted back to his first days on the beat and meeting John Thaw on the set of the TV series.

What would Thaw's alter ego, his hero, Inspector Jack Regan of the Sweeney have done his place? The thought was almost ridiculous. He knew exactly what Regan would have said.

Nannette paused for breath and leaned forward to kiss her husband. "Why are you smiling Chief Inspector?" she teased.

"Fuck 'em." he said.

"Excuse me?"

"And fuck you."

She chuckled. "That's what I've been waiting for."

Grant kissed her breasts then rolled her

onto her back.

73.

For weeks after the assassination, Tyler struggled with his conscience. But to no avail, his conscience refused to fight back. He expected a crisis of guilt much the same as he expected a midnight knock at the door. Neither came to pass. To be sure, he had several further encounters with the police and social workers but they concerned the drugs in Janine's house and questions about her stability and comportment.

For a week, Tyler slept with the loaded rifle in his bed. It made him feel safe. He returned to work on Monday morning and pleased Thatcher immeasurably by selling a loft conversion to a young woman who had simply walked in off the street.

Though he often thought of the events of the weekend, he found they stimulated rather than troubled him.

I'm a killer.

He repeated the phrase to himself several times a day and felt neither shame nor guilt. In fact he was rather pleased with himself. He no longer felt that cramping fear in the presence of clients, however rich or powerful they seemed. It wasn't that he visualized shooting them; that would have been too crude. It was more that the feeling of ultimate power had settled into his unconscious forming bedrock of confidence. As a result everything in his life began to change. The most dramatic was his performance at work. His public school colleagues noticed the change in his character. It was variously defined as maturity, confidence, self-assurance etc. These newly acquired qualities inspired similar feelings in his clients and work mates and, as a result his position in the official balance sheets and unofficial hierarchy improved.

After her week-long break following the shooting, Yolanda phoned Thatcher and resigned. This left Tyler as the agent of longest standing in Morton & Brown, a position that he crystallized as his sales improved and he began to enjoy the job. His colleagues stopped poking fun and started asking for leads. He breezed in and out of Thatcher's office as if he owned it, little caring what this one time Olympian thought of him.

Thatcher took the credit for the transformation himself. The thought that his peptalk had been so rewarding pleased him immensely. One day Tyler told him plainly he had broken completely with his father. Thatcher surprised him by saying that he (and everyone else at school) had hated the 'little shit'. It was the first time Tyler had felt any real affection for his boss.

74.

*L*e coeur a ses raisons que la raison ne con-
nait pas.

For reasons even she could not explain Yolanda had fallen in love with Tyler.
When she resigned, Tyler plucked up the courage to go round to her house and apologize. She
had avoided his calls and messages and he was
certain he was responsible for her leaving the
job she loved. It was Sunday morning, exactly
a week after that fateful morning. He regretted
his decision as soon as Petal opened the door.

She was livid. She swore at him using words
he had never heard before. Her face was scarlet
and he thought she was going to hit him with
the kettle she was holding. He retreated halfway down the entrance steps and was edging
towards the road when she screamed 'where
the hell do you think you're going. She's waiting for you inside. She's been waiting all week
you stupid man.'

Yolanda and Tyler slept together for the first time that night. When they had finished making love she said he needed to do some exercise and he said she was perfect. Not long after, Thatcher saw them together in a restaurant where he was eating with his wife. He invited them to join them and they spent a very pleasant evening during which Tyler discovered his boss was an ordinary mortal after all. Olivia Thatcher said Tyler and Yolanda made a lovely couple. Her husband agreed. Now their relationship was public he begged her to return but she said she didn't want to have to compete with Tyler. What she didn't say was that Tyler brought her a level of confidence only Petal had been aware she lacked. The difference was clear - if not easy to define - in her tone of voice and body language. She was still loud and abrasive, but those who knew her would have said she cast a thinner shadow.

A greatly relived Janine took Rachel back home but suffered repeated bouts of depression. Francis had disappeared all together. From her friends at the Railway Tavern, she heard he thought there was a contract on his head and had packed up and fled.

For several months Tyler came to see her almost every day. They both felt individually responsible for what had happened to Rachel. She found it hard to pull her life and sanity back together but she did her best. It took endless amounts of pills and she would burst into tears at the most banal things. Through it all, Tyler remained stoic and dependable - just as he had with his mother. He passed by most evenings to put Rachel to bed. He took them both out at the weekends and sat up long into the night listening to Janine's interminable confessional. It was almost like being a family again.

The test came as Christmas approached. Janine wanted to spend it with her parents who had recently moved from Camberwell to a small town on the Essex coast. Her uncle's family lived nearby and it promised to be a large and lively few days. Her parents had always liked Tyler and extended him an invitation. Tyler was delighted but he hadn't foreseen the undercurrent. After dinner the following evening, Tyler put Rachel to bed and they watched a movie on TV. It was a perfectly natural sequence of events and it seemed perfectly natural when Janine kissed him and asked if he wanted to stay the night. He said he didn't. Janine went alone with Rachel to Essex and Tyler joined them for lunch on Christmas day. He had reserved the evening for Yolanda, Petal, Michael and Athena.

Dr Littlefield received the largest bunch of flowers she had ever seen. She never knew where they came from. It was the day she decided to update her photo. She was proud of every one of her white hairs and when her husband took the photo, she made sure she was holding a white rose from the bunch. The portrait (with rose) now hangs in its proper place on the wall in the ICU at Chelsea and Westminster.

The knock Tyler had so feared came at eight thirty on the evening of nineteenth of December. Yolanda was in the shower washing off the early evening exercise and intoning a tuneless piece of hip-hop. The rifle lying fully charged under his bed had long passed from being an emergency tool to a kind of symbol.

Tyler opened the door in his T-shirt and boxer shorts.

Zinic watched his face carefully. He had learned to read people from their first reaction and was never disappointed. Tyler was frightened. He backed into the room and sat down on the bed without saying a word. Zinic entered and closed the door behind him.

There was a livid scar on his left cheek. The skin around it still had greeny-yellow traces of bruising and the red dots from Tyler's crude attempt to stitch it were still visible. His right arm was in a sling and his hand was wrapped in fresh bandage. Otherwise, five weeks in hospital had done nothing to diminish his powerful health. He paced into the room and looked around. Half a dozen cardboard boxes lay scattered about, some empty and some half filled with books, papers and household objects. Zinic put down the black holdall.

"Going back to your wife?" he asked casually.

Tyler took a deep breath. "No. Just moving."

Zinic registered the sound of the shower and the singing from the bathroom but didn't enquire further. He peered out of the window. In the street below a gang of half a dozen young kids played football with a squashed Tango can. They jostled and shouted and competed, not for the ball, but against each other.

"I have an apartment like this in St Petersburg" he said quietly, "overlooking the back of the Mayakovskaya station. About the same size."

He heard Tyler scuffle for the rifle under the bed but continued to look at the kids.

"I've had it for twenty six years."

He heard the click of the safety and turned slowly round.

Tyler had moved to the kitchen and was standing behind the waist-high divide pointing the rifle at the Russian's chest. Zinic raised his left hand slowly, fed it inside his new tweed jacket and pulled out a manila envelope. He tossed it on the bar next to Tyler.

"Fifty thousand" he said. "As agreed."

"Tyler?" Yolanda called from the shower. "You want me to wash you again?" She laughed at her own brazen humor and carried on with her rap poem.

Tyler regained his composure. "I saw they found Marta."

Zinic nodded. "The man who was supposed to kill her waited for an order that never came and bled to death. Marta made it home."

"You don't look so pleased."

Zinic shrugged. He wasn't going to tell Tyler he wouldn't see her again. He didn't have the courage to face her. He was too ashamed.

"I'm sorry about shooting you. I didn't mean to."

Zinic shrugged.

"I would have come to the hospital but under the circumstances..."

Zinic waved away the suggestion and nodded at the rifle. "You should pack that up now."

Tyler hesitated and glanced at the envelope on the bar top. It looked as if he were trying to decide between the two. Zinic smiled for the first time.

"Up close it's very different" he said. "You wouldn't like it."

He picked up his holdall and placed it on the bed. He pulled the rifle wrap out from under the bed and unrolled it onto the sheets. Then he reached over and took hold of the rifle barrel. Tyler released it slowly. Zinic clicked on the safety and held it up to the light. As he turned and examined it, Tyler experienced an unreasonable twinge of jealousy.

When he was satisfied, Zinic tucked the stock under his crooked right arm. With his left hand, he pulled back the bolt, the breach opened and the bullet sprung out. It flew straight at Tyler who reflexively caught it in mid air.

The shower turned off. Tyler watched Zinic disassemble the rifle one handed in less than thirty seconds. He slid the pieces carefully into the sleeve, rolled it up and placed it back into the bag.

Zinic nodded his farewell and walked over to the door with the bag. Tyler stopped him on the threshold.

"How do you do it?" he asked.

Zinic raised his eyebrows in surprise. "I think you should know by now."

"No." Tyler paused. He looked troubled. "I mean how do you stop?"

Zinic nodded his understanding. He stepped out into the hallway and pulled the door behind him until it clicked shut.

Yolanda opened the door to the shower room and let the steam out. Tyler crossed to the window and watched Zinic emerge from the front door. The kids ignored him completely. He walked passed them and continued on until he turned the corner and was out of sight.

If you have enjoyed this book, please add your review to Amazon. It makes a real difference.

If you have comments or if you would like advanced information about my next book, please write to me at

HansBaernhoft@gmail.com.

Thanks for reading.

38389267R00331

Printed in Poland
by Amazon Fulfillment
Poland Sp. z o.o., Wrocław